Michael E. Fawcett had been earning a good living writing brochures, which tried to make a very dull software sound exciting. One day, after something called the credit crunch had taken his job, Michael found that he had the opportunity to stop writing about dull software and start telling all of those stories that had been rattling around in his head for so many years.

Michael lives in Yorkshire with his wife Gillian, his two boys Richard and Sam and the dogs, Pippa and Maisie.

TO SARAH

The Mayor of Rheinhagen

BEST WISHES

To my wonderful wife, Gillian, and in memory of my wonderful Mother.

I have been truly blessed.

Michael E. Fawcett

The Mayor of Rheinhagen

Vanguard Press

A CIP catalogue record for this title is
available from the British Library.

ISBN 978 184386 697 8

*Vanguard Press is an imprint of
Pegasus Elliot MacKenzie Publishers Ltd.*
www.pegasuspublishers.com

First Published in 2011

**Vanguard Press
Sheraton House Castle Park
Cambridge England**

Printed & Bound in Great Britain

Contents

Chapter 1 – Solitary Sunset   13

Chapter 2 – The Den   17

Chapter 3 – Granddad   29

Chapter 4 – An Arrival and a Departure   37

Chapter 5 – The Face of God   49

Chapter 6 – Granddad's Story   63

Chapter 7 – Packing Up and Setting Off   73

Chapter 8 - Lawrence   83

Chapter 9 – Abroad   99

Chapter 10 – A Long Day   114

Chapter 11 – A Long Way From Home   125

Chapter 12 – Rheinhagen   131

Chapter 13 – An Appointment with the Bürgermeister   141

Chapter 14 – Taking the Tour   156

Chapter 15 – Plan B   164

Chapter 16 – Stakeout   179

Chapter 17 – Saving Private Hargreaves   188

Chapter 18 – Rescue Mission   205

Chapter 19 – In the Waiting Room   219

Chapter 20 – On the Run   227

Chapter 21 – The Mayor of Rheinhagen   234

Chapter 22 – Pandora's Box   245

Chapter 23 – Josef's Story   258

Chapter 24 – Packing Up   274

Chapter 25 – Heading Home   282

Chapter 1

Solitary Sunset

Beautiful was not a word that Jake was in the habit of using. The word just didn't fit into the vocabulary of a 14 year old. Whilst among his friends, Jake would perhaps occasionally use the word to describe a goal scored by his favourite football team or perhaps the curves of a passing sports car and even then he would pronounce the word as Bee-you-dee-full as if enunciating the "T" made it somehow soft and foppish. If he was with his friends, Jake would never have described the scene that lay before him now as beautiful and yet he could not help but recognise that it was.

For some hours the early summer sun had been announcing its intention to give a spectacular ending to the day. The sky had remained cloudless from dawn and, as it gradually inched its way towards the horizon, the sun had become bigger and redder until this moment when, just before it dipped behind the far hills, it bathed the land around Jake in a light like molten gold. Sitting astride his mountain bike, Jake became conscious of just how quiet the countryside around him had become. Birds still sang, but, it seemed to be a sleepier chattering than the businesslike squawking and cheeping of the daytime. Apart from the distant swish of traffic on the main road far away on the other side of the valley, all was quiet. Nature was settling down for the night.

He let his eyes take in the landscape around him. Between the silver birch trees that grew either side of the pathway he caught glimpses of fields, their grasses turned into fireworks in the sunset. Sheep, normally the dullest of animals, still stumped and grazed lazily, but in this light, they glowed with truly golden fleeces. Millions of silken threads, the tiny webs of even tinier spiders, usually invisible, but now changed by the sunset into a spectacular carpet, billowed gently in the slightest breath of wind. Everywhere floated the fluffy seeds of dandelions, transformed into glowing motes of light, which glided across Jake's vision like stray stars that had aimlessly wandered down from the heavens on a whim. The stillness pressed in upon Jake like a blanket.

Riding further along the path, the trees gave way to a low wall and the track rose gradually upwards along the side of the valley. Stopping again and looking west, back the way he came, Jake could now see the sprawl of Churnthorpe, the town where he lived. The rooftops were etched with the same golden light that surrounded him, turning a small, uninteresting market town into a glowing city of magic. Shielding his eyes from the shimmering ball of the sun, Jake could just about see the clump of white houses, one of which was his. Try as he might he could not pick out the one where his mum and dad were, no doubt, still finishing their tea, talking the way that long-married people do, where conversation would start suddenly and then seemed to fizzle out into another lingering silence built of long familiarity. A sick, swooping, addictive surge of resentment and indignation welled up inside him at the thought of them and their cosy, safe, orderly lifestyles, seemingly uncaring in the face of the huge injustice they had put upon Jake.

Beyond the church spires and office buildings of the town centre, a hill loomed upwards. The hillside was now completely in shadow as the sun set behind it. Somewhere, in its mottled, grey-green shadows there was the familiar row of stone terraced houses where granddad lived, but in the fading light Jake couldn't make it out.

Jake's eyes began to smart due to looking into the setting sun, so he turned his eyes away. Once the floating, bursting, rainbow-coloured retinal images faded, he saw that the distant hills to the east were reflecting the sunset. He was suddenly aware of an acute longing to simply set off on his bike and see what lay beyond those hills, leaving behind mum, dad, granddad – leaving it all behind. The feelings of resentment came upon him again. 'That would teach them,' Jake thought, as the idea of simply checking out of his well-ordered existence to roam the world took hold. A delicious, malicious thought occurred to Jake, a vision of his parents appearing on the TV news tearful and ashamed, haltingly asking for information on their 'dear, dear son's whereabouts'. They would plead through the camera lens for Jake to return to them, they would beg for forgiveness. Then the report would interview his headteacher. She would tell the world what a wonderful student Jake was, how clever and witty and popular he had become and how they all wanted him back. Perhaps they might even interview Katie Johnson who would choke back the tears as she implored Jake to return. Jake would be hunted. The police and interfering do-gooders who recognised him, would try to track him down. He would be a fugitive, travelling by night, hiding by day and living on his wits. Then, years later, he would return, a grown man suntanned, bearded, tattooed perhaps? He would walk through town, conscious of the stares and twitching curtains that would follow him. Small children would trail behind this mysterious stranger, then he would turn up his drive, knock on the door and, as his parents' astonished faces looked once more upon their long lost son, he would say… What would he say? Suddenly the vision faded and Jake laughed out loud at the melodrama of his own thoughts.

A faint rumbling noise gradually intruded into Jake's consciousness. High above, a jet plane traced a distant chalk mark across the perfect blue of the evening sky. A soaring, searing yearning to be on that plane hit Jake so forcefully that, for a moment, he almost forgot to breathe. Where was the plane going? He longed to know. Who was on it? Bored businesspeople? Families heading to a new life in a new country? Holidaymakers excitedly chattering about the two weeks or so that lay ahead? All Jake knew was that he was not amongst them and his mood changed again. Turning once more he saw that the sun had now sunk behind the far hill and the light had gone. Churnthorpe had lost its glow of magic and was once more the dark, grey, slightly shabby town, settled down for the night in the gathering dusk. The sheep carried on munching, their ethereal haloes gone, doomed once more to their dull, grey existence.

With a sigh, Jake checked his watch, turned his bike around and headed back down the path towards home. Gradually, as the dusk descended, the familiarity of his surroundings thickened and deepened around him like he was pulling on an old, familiar coat. High above, the plane carried on upon its way towards the horizon, where the dying sunlight caught on it and turned it into a flaring star until it vanished from view.

Chapter 2

The Den

By the time Jake turned his bike onto the neat gravel of his driveway with a crunch, the light of day had almost given way to the night. A tiny bat flickered across Jake's vision against the backdrop of the deepening blue of the sky as he emerged out of the shadows of the oak trees which lined the street.

Clayfields Avenue had been built some years ago as a broad, tree-lined crescent of high quality houses. It was constructed as a testament to post war prosperity, long before developers started to squeeze in as many buildings as they could on the smallest possible space. Each of the white painted dwellings had reassuringly large gardens all around them and the trees and bushes in them were sizeable, orderly, mature specimens. Here, nature was controlled, snipped, trimmed, tidied, pruned, refined, nurtured and adapted to life in the suburbs.

As usual, the curtain in the front room window was open. Inside, he knew his mum and dad would be watching TV, but they would also have half an eye out for their son's return. Normally Jake would look in and wave as he passed, making sure they knew he'd got back safely from wherever he'd been, but tonight, he almost wanted them to think that he was still missing. He wanted them to suffer and worry and blame themselves for what they had done to him, his anger returned with renewed heat. These feelings nearly made Jake duck down under the window so they couldn't see him return; they would worry that something might have happened to him if he didn't show, but he checked himself and simply walked past quickly without waving or glancing in to see if his parents had spotted him. 'It's not my fault if they're not looking,' Jake thought and he wheeled his bike to the shed at the side of the house.

Jake was confident that he could describe the scene in the front room without having to look. After all, they seemed to have developed a routine over the years that they stuck to almost without fail. His dad, almost always returned from work around six o'clock. He would remove his black, highly polished shoes, his suit jacket and his tie before they would all sit at the kitchen table for dinner. Dinner seemed to appear at almost exactly the same time as his dad sat down, as if it was part of a carefully co-ordinated and rehearsed exercise.

Once they had eaten, mum would make mugs of tea for everyone and take hers into the front room to watch soap operas. This was the unspoken signal for his dad to roll up the sleeves of his white shirt to tackle the washing up.

After Jake's dad had finished tidying the kitchen, he would go through to the front room to join his wife. She would always be sitting on the left hand side of the sofa and, as Jake's dad sat down on the right, she would invariably change position so she was reclining on him, insisting that he put an arm around her. This was how they always seemed to pass their evenings and Jake could picture them in this familiar scene as clearly as if he were there.

Their predictability and routine stung Jake. Where was the excitement in this existence? Where was the impetuousness? Would the world end if they ate at seven thirty maybe, instead of six on the dot? Or, what if they went out to eat? Or popped some popcorn and watched a movie, instead of those soaps that were full of anguished storylines being acted out badly.

Jake struggled with the impulse to do something to try and shake them out of their everyday routine. Surely they wanted more from life than this? Jake knew that his dad didn't even like soaps, so why did he sit through them night after night? Why did they never even think about doing something different? Even the clothes they wore were safely unexciting. They were so unremarkable as to make themselves almost invisible.

Deep down, Jake knew that he probably wasn't going to be able to change them now. It was all far too late, but he did want exciting things in his life. He did want to do impetuous stuff, but whenever he suggested something that didn't fit in with his parents blueprint of what life should be all about, he encountered their disapproval and mistrust. It seemed to Jake that it wasn't so much that the things he wanted to do were dangerous, or illegal, but they took his parents outside of their comfort zone and, as such, were judged to be simply wrong. Even now, even as Jake seemed to be approaching adulthood at breakneck speed, his parents still seemed to consider him a child. His mum especially seemed to make it her life's mission to eliminate any risk from Jake's life. He sometimes wondered if he wasn't actually living at all, but could only be said to be existing, a never ending round of school – home – school – home etc. Every time he tried to take another step towards independence, or just try something new, she would be there to try and organise, sanitise and sterilise things until most of the fun and sense of challenge had gone out of it. Jake often wondered bitterly how he was supposed to learn from his own mistakes if he was never going to be allowed to make them. Only his older brother Chris seemed immune to his mum's ways. Several years older than Jake, Chris now toured the world setting up new hotels for a large chain. Chris casually dismissed his mum's worries as if they were of no regard to him whatsoever. Flying to exotic locations, taking part in "dangerous" activities like snowboarding, surfing and bungee jumping and generally living life to the full, gave Jake's mum more than enough to cluck and fuss about on the occasions when Chris arrived home for a few days, but Chris would simply refuse to even acknowledge his mum's concerns or would put on his best charming smile across his handsome, tanned face until the tide of protestations had dried up. Jake sighed with suppressed irritation, shoved his bike into the shed and snapped shut the padlock on the door.

The light in the den was on. This usually meant that one of his friends would be waiting for him inside. These days, visitors for Jake would bypass the front door and let themselves straight into the den through the door at the side of the house, before making themselves at home. Jake got the idea that his mum preferred it that way; it meant that she didn't have to try and engage teenage boys in conversation (though why she thought that they might want to talk to her in the first place was beyond Jake) and it meant that there wasn't a pile of scruffy trainers left in the "oh-so-tidy hall".

At the far end of the house, there had once been a garage, with an "up and over" door. The previous owner had decided to extend the house by adding a bedroom over the top of this garage and it was this room that was Jake's. It was a long slim room with windows at either end that made it bright, welcoming and spacious. It seems, however, that the owner had even more ambitious plans. The garage below was then targeted for a makeover. Jake's dad seemed to recall that the owner had wanted to turn it into a home office from which the he could run a small business. A large window had replaced the garage door, making it a "proper" room and part of the house. Apparently ill health meant that the work stalled and eventually forced the sale of the house. Even now, propped against the breezeblock wall, were sheets of plasterboard and old, dusty, unopened tins of magnolia-coloured paint, patiently waiting to be used.

The den was divided into three areas. The main part, at the front of the house, contained an old sofa and a TV. An upturned tea chest that had been used to move their stuff in years ago and had never made it back to the removal firm, acted as a make-do table. Further back, kitchen units jutted out of the wall to halfway across the width of the room, forming an effective division. The doors for the units were yet to be fitted and were piled up inside one of the cupboards. In the worktop there was a steel sink with ugly, basic-looking taps. Jake and his friends kept some squash and some plastic beakers so they could make their own drinks (his mum hadn't allowed real glasses in case they got broken). Unfortunately, the task of washing up was never really kept up to. If you needed a drink, you had to pick out the cleanest looking beaker from the pile in the sink and rinse it out. Occasionally Jake's mum would brave the den to tidy up and the newly cleaned beakers would be discovered in neat rows on the draining board. His mum would always moan at the state of the place and Jake would always have to promise to keep things tidier under the rather vague threat of having the den taken from him. Unfortunately, despite some genuine effort on Jake's part, things would eventually slip back to their previous state.

The kitchen area contained a spare fridge that hardly ever held any food, but did usually have a few cans of fizzy drink in it. Next to the sink, a small gas hob waited forlornly to be connected. Jake's Uncle Bernie was a qualified gas fitter and he had promised to sort it out, but it seemed that he was always busy and Jake's mum didn't like to pester him. Behind the kitchen area there was the door that connected the den to the rest of the house. Beyond this, a short passage led past a tiny toilet and shower room, through to a space that would serve as a small office or bedroom. The door was still propped loosely in the corner, another of Uncle Bernie's "little jobs". Down the side of this room were two large rolls of carpet, still wrapped in plastic, destined at some point, to cover the den's concrete floor.

The den always smelled of dust and stale pizza and yet it was Jake's favourite part of the house, because it was his.

Jake remembered clearly the day that they had moved in. He had been seven years old and spent most of the day exploring and playing in the garden. It had been a good job that the day had been bright and warm and he could keep out of the way. His mum had been more than usually stressed out that day, trying to remember what box needed to go where, whilst trying to keep an eye on how well the removal men were taking care of her ornaments. Most of the boxes ended up in the den. It was just too hard to find homes for everything and the den was a convenient space on the ground floor in which to dump anything that could not be given an immediate home.

Over time, most of the boxes were emptied of their contents and moved to where they belonged. Some remained where they were, because they contained stuff that was hardly ever needed, battered suitcases, photo albums, old board games and the like, so no one got around to emptying them. Not long after moving in, they took delivery of a new sofa and the old one had been put into the den until they got round to organising a trailer to take it to a charity furniture store. The addition of this sofa seemed to change the room. Suddenly, Jake realised that this might be a useable space that he could lay claim to. This dusty, unfinished room could be somewhere where he and his friends could sit and watch TV or play computer games and with its kitchen and loo, it was almost like having his own flat.

Gradually, almost by stealth, Jake took possession. He had sneaked his portable TV in, along with his games console. His mum had realised what was going on a week or so later. In vain she had shouted up the stairs for Jake to come for his tea and, when he had emerged surprisingly into the kitchen from the side door, she discovered his new hideout. 'Well, I suppose you can use it as a den for a couple of weeks until we get the rest of the boxes sorted out,' she had pronounced, but that day was yet to arrive. The name stuck and Jake, his friends and their associated clutter, had taken over.

As Jake opened the door into the den, he found his friend Howard standing near the TV set, bending the loop aerial this way and that, in order to improve a rather fuzzy picture of a young presenter interviewing the latest rock band whilst trying to "out cool" them with a series of well-rehearsed ad-lib lines.

Although they had been firm friends since infant school, Jake and Howard Atkinson were very different in just about every respect. Physically, Jake had grown up seemingly overnight and now he could almost claim to be taller than his mum, but he had, for the moment, stopped agonisingly short. Howard, had also gone through a growth spurt, one that was yet to stop and he towered even over Jake's dad. Unlike Jake, who had broadened as he grew, Howard seemed to have stretched and his frame was bordering on the skinny. He seemed to react to this newfound height with the clumsiness and gawkiness of a young giraffe, as if his brain was still catching up to the fact that it was much further away from the ground than it had been before.

Howard's hair was fair and straight and flopped stylishly forward over an angular, but open and friendly face, Jake's dark hair was neither straight nor curly. Jake had tried to grow his hair longer in the style of a movie star he admired, but instead of looking stylish and interesting, it merely seemed to bush out in a wavy thatch. Having given up on that look, Jake's hair was now back to a shorter style and yet, despite all encouragement to behave, it always seemed to need taming with a brush every morning.

These dissimilarities were not the only thing that set them apart. Howard was contemplative, thoughtful and quietly witty, where Jake see-sawed from shyness to over-enthusiasm. Jake became tongue-tied and self-conscious when talking to teachers, girls or people he did not know very well, but Howard had no reservations about engaging anyone in conversation in his trademark measured, thoughtful manner. He had a gift for hovering on the edges of a conversation and then delivering an immaculately timed, droll comment or punch line to set everyone laughing. This laid back, withdrawn style had, within his circle of friends, been termed "doing a Howard". At odds with Howard's coolness Jake could alternate between being withdrawn one minute and then the next, doing or saying something impetuous, hot-headed or rash. Jake always knew the right thing to say after the event, but he often found himself cringing at some of the things he'd come out with when he was trying to be funny and wondered how Howard always made it look so easy.

"Alright?" Howard rumbled; Jake could swear that Howard's voice was getting deeper by the hour.

Jake looked down and exhaled noisily. 'Not bad I guess,' he replied and he wandered to the fridge to retrieve two cans of Coke. He offered Howard one with a tilt of his head and a raised eyebrow.

'Cheers,' said Howard as Jake tossed it to him.

'No change on the holiday front then?' asked Howard.

'Nah,' Jake replied. 'Mum's still going to do her Florence Nightingale bit and so it's "au revoir" to the south of France.' Jake was surprised at how talking about the great injustice had so quickly reawakened his anger. His voice had quavered slightly with emotion and he hoped that Howard hadn't noticed. The hint of tears prickled the backs of his eyes and he looked away as he plucked absently at the tab on his coke can.

'Bummer,' Howard responded without taking his eyes off the TV and nothing else was said for a while as the rock band played on.

It had all seemed too good to be true. Jake had been delighted and surprised in equal measure when his parents announced that they would be holidaying in the south of France. Suddenly, Jake's dreams of foreign travel seemed to be within his grasp. Every family holiday they ever had was a trip to Cornwall or Wales or the Lake District or being eaten alive by midges in the Scottish Highlands. To be fair, Jake had enjoyed all of these holidays, but his desire to broaden his horizons and travel abroad like his older brother had become more and more insistent. There was a great big world out there and Jake wanted to see it all. For the last few years Jake's suggestions of far off holiday destinations had been quickly dismissed, firstly by his dad – "too expensive son" then his mum who simply claimed to be too scared of flying.

'But Mum, statistically it's the safest form of transport!' Jake would protest to no avail.

However, things had looked different this year. This year, Chris had invited them all out to Cannes. He was setting up a hotel there and had been given a large apartment to live in. 'Come on over, I have enough rooms for all of you!' Chris had shouted over a crackly telephone line. 'You can get flights out here for next to nothing, so I won't take no for an answer.' And he didn't. Jake was going abroad. Heck! He was going on a plane for the first time in his life and he couldn't wait.

However, Jake's joy was to be short lived. A week ago he'd been told that they wouldn't be going away to stay with Chris after all. In fact, it looked like they might not have a holiday of any description. Jake thought bitterly of that evening when his mum had broken the news that the holiday to France was not going ahead. She had asked Jake to stay at the table after tea because 'There's something we need to talk about'. Jake's heart sank. The first thing he thought (most likely prompted by a guilty conscience) was that he must be in trouble at school. Jake wasn't the best in his class, but usually did pretty well in tests and his school reports, although not full of praise, were mostly positive.

Jake had found that, by using his wit, ingenuity and occasionally bare-faced cheek, he was able to get by in school without ever really having to work too hard. The key was to try and remain as anonymous as possible, in order to stay off the teacher's radar. That meant doing enough to keep the heat off, but without putting yourself forward. Jake believed that answering questions in class was something to avoid at all costs. Shoving your hand in the air was as good as waving a banner to the teacher saying, 'Look at me! I'm really dumb and need help!' if you got the answer wrong, or, if you had the right answer, 'Hey! I'm really bright and should put my hand up more in class!' Jake prided himself on his ability to fade into the background like a chameleon. Sometimes he would read his school report and wonder how the teacher could ever form an opinion of his work, when Jake was certain that they would be hard pressed to remember his name.

Of course, this way of life had its drawbacks. Jake was always wary of the time when he'd be found out and his life of cruising at the back of class would be over. Also, some teachers were easier to dodge than others. His languages teacher, Mr Brown, seemed to think that Jake wasn't putting the effort into his work that he could be and had insisted that Jake do a piece of German homework during the holidays that he had firstly "forgotten" to do two weeks previously and then "conveniently" neglected to bring into school for marking on the last day of term. Jake knew Mr Brown was the kind of teacher that would not forget about this and had no doubt that, come September, he'd look around the class, blinking like a pedantic owl over his half-moon spectacles and, in his measured, baritone voice that dripped with sarcasm say, 'Jake Hargreaves? Can I assume that at some point during the last six weeks you have taken enough time from your hectic social life to complete that piece of homework? And, having done so, could it also be possible that you have had the presence of mind this morning to bring it in for marking?'

At this point his classmates, scenting trouble, would start to snigger as Mr Brown would continue. 'Or, as I suspect, shall we be having that little chat at the end of class about the detention we talked about?'

Detentions were bad news for Jake. They were marked indelibly on his weekly planner, which meant of course, that his mum would get to know about it. Jake had found that his life was much less fraught when his mum was kept uninformed about parts of Jake's life. A detention was not a big deal really, but by the time his mum had done with "talking it through", it would feel like his career prospects were in ruins and his life was at an end and that all of this could have been avoided if he would just "make a little more effort". This was usually rounded off by a hugely embarrassing "I do love you, you know" speech that made Jake squirm and feel, not only hugely guilty, but that he was being patronised at the same time. It was no use trying to put over his point of view, because his mum was always right, end of conversation. No, it was far simpler just to keep her out of the loop and this had resulted in Jake becoming adept at letting his mum know enough to keep her satisfied, but still keep her in the dark about the things of which she might not approve. He was skilled at not actually lying. He'd been caught lying once before when he'd been much younger and had been made to feel so bad, that now it was instinctive to merely "bend the truth".

And now, sat at the table expecting the worst, his mum had completely thrown Jake with a half smile that looked deeply apologetic. 'I'm afraid there's been some bad news.' Jake's heart seemed to do a double back flip. Bad news didn't sound like he was in trouble at school, but the realisation that it suddenly sounded much more serious, left Jake with a sudden sick feeling in his stomach. His mum tilted her head on one side slightly which made Jake feel that she was talking to him in the same way she would talk to a young child. 'It seems that Auntie June has taken a turn for the worse.'

Relief flooded through Jake guiltily. At least he wasn't in trouble! Auntie June was not his favourite relation and they didn't see much of her, these occasions usually being an afternoon spent in her front room where it was always kept far too hot, being served milky tea in tiny cups, whilst the dull conversation murmured on and on, usually about the illnesses of people that Jake didn't even know.

'Someone needs to look after her. She's been really ill and she's got a lot to come to terms with, what with the move into a home as well. And then someone has got to empty her house and sort out her belongings. Anyway, there'll always be another time, maybe next year?' Jake's vision of palm trees and perfect blue skies and the smell of coffee from street cafés crumbled into a dull grey lump of what might have been.

'Someone has got to do it,' thought Jake. Someone. But why does it always have to be you and dad? Why is it that whenever there's a family crisis, you have to go and organise things and sort things out and smooth things over? Why can't you get someone else to do it? You're not the only person in this family. Or is it just that you like controlling other people's lives? The anger rushed over him again like a hot tide and a prickling sensation in the corner of his eyes betrayed Jake's deep resentment.

After a moment, Jake looked up. He noticed with relief that Howard was now sitting with his back to him watching the band mime along to their latest single and so he would not spot the wetness in Jake's eyes. Exhaling deeply, Jake gathered himself together, cracked open his can, walked round to the sofa and flopped down on it to watch TV.

Chapter 3

Granddad

The next day, Jake's mum and dad were disappearing off to Norfolk for a fortnight to help Auntie June move out and get her house cleared. Of course, this left the problem of what to do with Jake. His mum was firmly of the opinion that Jake was too young to be left on his own. Jake complained hotly that he could manage very well by himself, but despite his protestations to the contrary, the only course of action was to get granddad to move in.

Jake was very fond of his granddad; one of his earliest memories was riding piggy-back on the shoulders of his rough tweed jacket, holding onto handfuls of his Brylcreemed, grey hair and the musky, heady fragrance of pipe smoke. Granddad had not smoked for a long time. He had given up shortly after granny had died when Jake had been five years old but every time Jake caught the smell of pipe smoke, he was taken back to a time where everything seemed to be simple, loving and wonderful. A period of his life when there was always time to play and there was always a toffee for Jake in his granddad's jacket pocket.

Granddad had always been able to make Jake laugh out loud with just a raised eyebrow and a roguish glance from his impish, glittering eyes. His wicked teasing of Jake's mum seemed to be something that they could share in and sometimes it seemed to be an almost psychic link between them as they told her more and more ridiculous stories about what had happened to them at the park or on the bus. Jake would almost feel sorry for his mum, who could not seem to tell when they were being truthful or winding her up, but it was just too much fun to stop.

Jake's memories of his granny were faded and blurry. When he tried to recall her face, he found that he struggled to build a clear image in his head, but looking at the photograph of his granny on his dad's bedside table would bring back the memories of teatimes, picnics, sandy beach holidays and a host of smells and textures that presumably had been lying around in the back of Jake's mind the whole time, just waiting for the right trigger to set them off. For some reason, when he thought of granny, Jake mostly remembered her funeral. He vaguely remembered the family gathering afterwards, a mosaic of tuna and meat paste sandwiches, cakes and cup after cup of tea being passed around. The conversation above Jake's head seemed to mould itself into a comforting murmur that gave him a curiously drowsy feeling behind the eyes. Jake had remembered a lot of white-haired elderly men and women paying him lots of attention, making a fuss of him and smiling. Jake wondered at the time why would people smile at a funeral.

The loss of grandma seemed to make granddad quieter, more serious. For a while at least, the teasing stopped and there were no more toffees. From time to time, Jake saw another side to granddad. The happy-go-lucky cheeky old man seemed to disappear. He would be more abrupt and the endless patience and kindness he displayed before was replaced with a certain sharpness and detachment. However, after a few months had passed, he seemed to relax a bit more and, although he tried to be cheeky and mischievous like before, it was never quite the same and Jake sometimes felt that he was trying just a little too hard.

Granddad would still wear the tweed jacket, and his hair, now white and thinning, was still neatly groomed in place, but he seemed to have shrunk as Jake had grown up. This wasn't a physical shrinking, but it seemed to Jake as if the person that granddad was, had somehow retreated and diminished.

The only time where Jake would see flashes of the "old" granddad was when he would tell Jake of his experiences of what he did during World War II. He was a wonderful storyteller and would excitedly regale Jake with tales about being dropped behind enemy lines in France and living with the French Resistance. As soon as he'd begun telling the story, the old glint in granddad's eye returned, he became more animated and he would draw himself forward in his chair to engage with his audience.

As Jake heard the words of the familiar stories, he would try and regain those feelings of childhood once more. These times made Jake feel like he was a little kid again sat wide-eyed. It was a comforting feeling and one that Jake found increasingly rare. However, the process of growing up had lent a certain cynicism to Jake's character and now when he heard granddad's war stories over again, he realised that sometimes the accounts would vary in certain details. Some aspects would be exaggerated, or left out altogether and it was this that made Jake start to wonder how much of the truth was in the stories after all. He still enjoyed hearing them, but it seemed now to be more like a work of fiction than historical fact.

So much in his life seemed to be changing right now. He was constantly being told to take responsibility, to grow up, to act his age. Jake felt that his grip on his childhood was being prised from him. He seemed to be experiencing a slow and remorseless push into adulthood that some parts of him did not want to accept just yet. He missed the simple laughter, messing about and daftness that a child could get away with. This relentless push seemed to be all around him. At school he had been made to think hard about his future career when the time came to take his options. Long conversations over the tea table about what Jake would do when he left school, left him with the feeling that he actually didn't have a clue what he wanted to do with his life. Anxious thoughts crowded round him. Did everyone else at his age have a firm career plan? One or two of his classmates seemed to have very definite ideas about what qualifications they were going for and even which university they wanted to get into. Was he just not motivated or ambitious enough? Had he been so busy trying to coast through school that he had somehow failed to map out his future? Was it too late?

Jake didn't often talk about this sort of thing with his friends, but these worries had prompted him to ask Howard what his plans were. Howard had inclined his head thoughtfully and after a pause said, 'I dunno what I want to do. Nobody knows what might happen to us. We could do great things, be really rich or famous or something.' Then he grinned broadly at Jake. 'Don't stress yourself! We're only 14 years old! Do you really think our choices we make now are going to be that big a deal by the time we're 20 or 30? I reckon that you should just choose the subjects you want to do and make the best of what you get.' This had momentarily made Jake feel a whole lot better, but then Howard had continued, 'That's what my dad thinks anyway.'

Howard's dad was the town's general handyman. He seemed to do a lot of different jobs like bits of plumbing, bricklaying, gardening or joinery. He wasn't a qualified master craftsman, so he didn't take on big jobs, he just made a living driving his battered, rusty white van around, picking up small pieces of work here and there. He didn't seem to have a proper business as such, he didn't advertise at all, he was just known in the town and everyone seemed to have his number. Jake couldn't help but think that career advice from Howard's dad might not be something on which to base his own profession.

The next morning was Saturday and Jake woke to a beam of sunlight streaming though a gap in his curtains and falling across his floor that was strewn with his school uniform, casually discarded the night before and gloriously not required for another six wonderful weeks of leisure. Jake savoured the moment, his sleepiness enfolding him like his warm quilt. Tiny, invisible specks of dust would suddenly glint as they drifted through the ray of sunlight only to pass on, unseen once more. The quietness of a suburban Saturday morning seemed to lie on the house like a mantle. Gradually, as the shaft of light tracked across Jake's bed, things slowly woke and stirred. Mr Grimshaw from over the road could be heard shepherding his three Jack Russell terriers down the road towards the path that lead into the woods. Occasionally a car would swish past and the noisier clattering of a bus's engine could be heard pulling up at the bus stop at the junction where Clayfields Avenue met Churnthorpe Road. Gradually the house woke up too. Jake's dad could be heard stumbling downstairs in his striped dressing gown and his aging blue slippers. The hiss and grumble of the kettle announced that a pot of tea was being made and a little later, his dad, not wanting to spill the contents of either of the cups he held, carefully made his way up the stairs and back to bed. Peace descended once more, but the stillness was not quite the same. It had been fractured and now Clayfields Avenue was awake and preparing to tackle the day.

Now fully awake, Jake's thoughts turned to the summer holidays that lay in front of him and, with a sickening lurching sensation, realised that granddad would be coming over to stay later on that morning. It was actually going to happen and this situation with Auntie June was not just a bad dream after all. This realisation made Jake feel restless and his bed no longer seemed to be the cocoon of warmth and cosiness that it had been before. With a heavy sigh, Jake threw back the quilt and sat down on the end of his bed. He dressed quickly in some khaki cargo shorts and a black T-shirt with a skull logo on it that he'd just spotted under his bed. It was creased and possibly needed a wash, but Jake just couldn't be bothered to get a fresh shirt from the drawer.

Going downstairs, Jake entered the kitchen, poured himself a cup of tea from the pot that was still warm, shuffled into the lounge, switched on the TV in the front room and watched an over-energetic children's TV presenter introducing the latest "hilarious" cartoon. Despite the disappointment about his holiday, Jake still felt a sudden fluttering of joy at the prospect of six weeks off school, 'After all, who knows what might happen?' he thought to himself and he chuckled out loud, curled up and settled back into the floral printed cushions of the sofa.

At around 10 o'clock his mum arrived downstairs fluttering and fussing that she'd fallen back to sleep and they'd never get off to Auntie June's at the allotted time of 1 o'clock now as they had so much to sort out. Jake's dad followed her around looking like a sleepy, yet loyal and obedient dog, nodding in agreement when reassurance was required and occasionally making suggestions with a kind of wariness, as if his thoughts might be dismissed out of hand or, given the highly strung state of his wife, trigger a wave of scorn. Going away on holiday always seemed to stress his mum out. Even a weekend away somewhere caused a lot of checking and rechecking that everything was in order. Was the TV unplugged? Were the plants watered? Was the newspaper delivery cancelled? Everything seemed to be a big deal. Once a time for leaving the house had been agreed, even if they didn't have to be at their destination for a certain time, that target seemed to be set in stone and must be met, otherwise disaster would surely follow.

Jake's mum at once set about making lists. List-making seemed to be her way of dealing with the stress of getting out of the house on time. There was a list of things they needed to pack, a list of things to do before they went, a list of things to remember for granddad when he arrived and, much to Jake's disgust, a list of tasks for him to complete whilst they were away. 'But I'm on holiday!' exclaimed Jake causing his clearly stressed mum to look up at him so fiercely Jake nearly stammered an apology immediately.

'I'm sorry that we're not going away this year Jake, I really am,' his mum said rapidly in a dangerously quiet voice. 'But while you are going to be here, it's up to you to take some responsibility around the place. Granddad can't do everything himself these days,' she said whilst rhythmically jabbing her finger at Jake to emphasise her point. 'So no arguments, no discussions and no telling me how dreadfully unfair things are, OK?'

Jake's temper flared within him and he fought the impulse to tell his mum exactly where she could put her list. He felt his cheeks redden and was horrified to feel tears of anger forming; he didn't want his mum to think she'd made him cry. Jake struggled inwardly to think of a crushing reply. Some response to make his mum see just how unfair and unreasonable she was, but, like on so many other occasions the right words would not come to him. Instead, Jake rose from the sofa and walked from the room. He didn't know where he was going. He just wanted to get away.

His mum called after him. 'Where are you going now?'

Jake carried on walking and called out in a voice that he thought still quavered a little with the anger he felt. 'Howard's.' He quickly passed through the kitchen where his dad was ticking off items on his "things to do" list and muttering to himself.

His mum's voice called after him. 'We're going at one, so be back for lunch at twelve when granddad's coming round.' It was clearly not a request. For a moment Jake considered the merits of staying at Howard's for the rest of the day and letting them leave without saying goodbye, but they would only phone up and make a fuss, so he decided to return a few minutes after twelve, leaving it just long enough for them to worry about where he'd got to.

Walking through the den and emerging into the sunlit garden, Jake's mood remained volatile. Crossing to the shed, he reached in to bring his bike out, but the pedal caught on a folded garden seat and wouldn't release itself. Thwarted, Jake's temper suddenly broke like a dam and he was suddenly wrenching and pulling his bike, cursing and swearing all the time. Finally the bike was pulled clear, but the chairs and a garden rake all fell in a tumbled heap on the floor. Past caring, Jake jammed his helmet on and stamped hard on the pedals, the gravel of the driveway popping and spitting from beneath his tyres as he sped away.

Chapter 4

An Arrival and a Departure

By the time Jake reached Howard's house, his fierce temper had subsided a little; the heat of his anger had made him ride his bike hard through the middle of Churnthorpe. He had taken the shortcut through the park. He'd ignored the "no cycling" signs and the angry glares of the young mothers who were sitting on benches watching their children on the swings. Jake hopped over pavements, dodged pedestrians and weaved through traffic. It seemed that his fury had given him a surge of energy which he used to race along at top speed. However, turning into Howard's driveway after attacking the sharp climb out of town, Jake felt spent. His T-shirt was sticking damply to his back, his lungs were burning and his legs were feeling decidedly wobbly as he dismounted.

Jake had been so wrapped up in his own holiday problems, that he had forgotten Howard's mum and dad would be busy preparing to go away. Their usual cottage in Cornwall which they had booked for the last six years awaited them and they were planning to set off very early the next day. Jake had once asked Howard if he minded going to the same place year after year; Howard had simply said, 'I guess it just feels like we're on holiday when we get there.'

'But don't you want to see different parts of the world? Or even different parts of Britain?' Jake considered himself fortunate that his family holidays were at least in different places each year. 'Aren't there places you'd rather go to?

37

Things you want to do?' Jake pressed on. 'When we were doing Geography in school this term and we did that project on China, didn't it make you want to walk on the Great Wall, or look round the Forbidden City? Didn't you want to taste the food and meet the people?'

After a pause, Howard shrugged noncommittally. 'Yeah. S'pose I did and I s'pose I will someday, but that's not a proper family holiday is it?'

Jake had given up trying to broaden Howard's horizons after that. Clearly a family holiday was one spent in Cornwall and that seemed to be good enough for Howard for the time being. Of course, Jake knew that over the last few years, most of Howard's enthusiasm for going back was spurred on by the fact that their cottage was a short walk away from a wonderful surfing beach. Howard had taken lessons a few years ago and apparently, he was now pretty good at it. In fact, Howard seemed to spend a large part of each day in the sea and was heavily into the surf culture. Jake had noticed that each time Howard returned from Cornwall, his hair had been bleached by the sun, his face tanned through exposure to the sun, wind and salt and he usually had some new baggy shorts and cool branded T-shirts bought from the surf boutiques.

Howard's house was a white, pebble-dashed semi-detached. Down the side of the house, a driveway led to a rather rickety old garage with doors covered in flaking black paint. As he rode into the driveway, Jake could hear the whistling of Mr Atkinson accompanying the radio coming from inside the garage.

Along the side of the driveway and in parts of the back garden, were various piles of sand, bricks, paving stones and other building materials stacked untidily in no particular order. These were leftovers from various jobs that Howard's dad had worked on and were kept around in case he needed them. However, the stacks never seemed to diminish and it was one of the few things that made Howard's mum, who always seemed fairly calm and generally relaxed, get rather frustrated with.

Howard emerged from the house with the surfboard he'd bought last year zipped up in its bright red and white cover. He lifted it onto the roof bars of their estate car ready to strap it down for the journey. Propping his bike against one of the neater stacks of breezeblocks, Jake greeted his friend. Howard was definitely in the holiday mood and was wearing some faded three quarter length, navy blue cargo shorts, flip flops, a white O'Neill rash vest that clung to his skinny torso, over which he wore a pale blue Hawaiian shirt with a large white floral design across it. Jake's instinct was to make a disparaging comment about his sense of style, it did look rather out of place in this driveway that looked like a builder's yard. However, Jake couldn't help but notice that Howard's height and generally confident, chilled and relaxed manner seemed somehow to fit perfectly with his clothes.

Howard asked if Jake wanted a drink, and Jake readily accepted. The day had already started to lose its early morning freshness and the sun was starting to feel much warmer, promising to be scorching hot by midday. Jake admitted that after his ride over he was very thirsty and he followed Howard inside.

The inside of the Atkinson house was very different to the extreme tidiness of Jake's mum's domain. Although everything was clean enough, it seemed that any surface where things could be stacked, or propped or wedged, held its own pile of papers, envelopes, CD cases, folders, headphones, cricket and tennis balls, scissors and other items the function of which Jake really couldn't guess. It always made Jake smile when he thought about how his mum would react if she were confronted with this clutter. At home, she would complain to Jake if he didn't put his shoes on the rack immediately and yet, here at Howard's, the function of the shoe rack in the hall seemed to be to act as a backdrop for the large pile of shoes that was congregating in front of it.

Howard led Jake into the kitchen where Mrs Atkinson was sweeping the floor around their large, fat Labrador called Monty who had curled up in the middle of the kitchen. Despite increasingly vigorous prodding with the broom, Monty seemed indisposed to move. 'Daft dog!' Mrs Atkinson exclaimed with a shake of her head. 'Move why don't you?' Monty did not move. He did, however, lift his head to acknowledge Jake's appearance and thump his tail twice on the floor in welcome.

Exhausted by this effort, Monty returned to his slumber. 'I give up!' Mrs Atkinson said with a half exasperated – half amused shake of her head. 'Anyway, how are you dear?' she said, turning to Jake with her usual welcoming smile. 'Did your mum and dad get off OK?'

As usual, she seemed to know everything that was going on in the town, but not in the same way a nosy, gossipy neighbour would, she was just one of those people who was concerned about the well-being of others.

'They're going after lunch,' Jake returned, thinking that it couldn't be soon enough.

'Such a shame, them having to go and look after June and spoil their holiday. They must have been devastated.' Jake did not know what to say, so he simply nodded.

'Never mind his mum and dad!' chimed in Howard, 'what about Jake having to spend the summer with his granddad?'

'Oh, he'll be fine!' Mrs Atkinson ruffled Jake's hair affectionately. 'Two young men together for a few days? There's no telling what sort of fun and games lie in store, eh Jake?'

Jake remained silent. He certainly didn't regard granddad as a young man, especially one who was fond of "fun and games", but Mrs Atkinson seemed to be being positive for Jake's benefit and it was difficult not to go along with it, so Jake simply nodded again and smiled weakly.

Thanking Mrs Atkinson for the large glass of chilled fruit juice that she handed him, Jake followed Howard through to the cool of the lounge, leaving her to continue to plead with Monty to move himself. Howard plugged in his games console and they spent an hour or so, blowing away ever more dangerous zombies in more and more imaginative ways.

Glancing at his watch Jake realised that he'd better set off back home. He said goodbye to Mrs Atkinson and was surprised to be enveloped in a warm hug and a kiss on the cheek. Somewhat startled, Jake stood stiffly as Mrs Atkinson smiled. 'It's such a shame that we couldn't fit you in down at Tregennan Cottage, or we'd have had you along like a shot. But you'll have fun with Walter. Your granddad won't let you mope around for long.' Then, after another quick peck on the cheek, she turned and disappeared back into the kitchen.

Jake walked down the drive with Howard to where he'd left his bike, waving to the overall-clad figure of Mr Atkinson who was still whistling tunelessly in the garage. 'I'll see you when I get back then,' Howard said with what sounded like reluctant finality.

'Yep,' returned Jake with a wry smile. 'Have a good time dude! Hang ten, or whatever it is you do on that thing!' Howard laughed and returned to strapping his board to the roof rack. Envious, but resigned to his situation, Jake pushed off and pedalled away.

The ride back across town was much slower, as Jake didn't want to get back too soon, but despite taking his time through town, it was five minutes before twelve when he pulled into the driveway. Jake's dad was doing the final check to see if they had packed everything. His mum's voice could be heard from within the house where, no doubt, she was doing her last minute tidying and organising.

'Did you pack my toiletries bag?'

'Yes.' Jake's dad managed to make his voice sound both uninterested and slightly mocking at the same time. As usual, his mum was making going away a major operation, checking and re-checking everything. She made it so very different from the chilled out holiday atmosphere at Howard's. 'And your spare shoes?'

'Yes.'

'And the plant we're taking her?'

'Yes.'

'And have you put it somewhere where it's not going to get squashed?'

'Yes.' His dad winked at Jake. Jake gave him a half-smile in return and wheeled his bike over to the shed.

Back in the den, the dark, cool atmosphere contrasted with the almost unbearably bright sunshine outdoors and suited Jake's mood. He listened to the noises of his parents getting things packed into the back of his dad's estate car and fussing around trying to find this and that, until they were officially ten minutes late and his mum's clucking had become more strident. Suddenly she bustled into the den.

'Ah there you are Jake, did you have a good time at Howard's?' Jake got the impression that she wasn't really all that interested if he had or not and this was confirmed when she continued without waiting for Jake's response. 'I need you through here now, we're about to set off and your granddad hasn't shown up yet.'

Jake slowly got up and followed his mum through into the kitchen as she rattled off an unrelenting stream of instructions and information at him. He wanted to give her the impression that he really wasn't interested and would forget everything she had said as soon as she had gone. He did take in most of what his mum was saying though, he just wanted her to worry that he hadn't.

'So, here's your list with everything you will need to do.' His mum directed Jake's attention to a sheet of A4 paper covered with her small, neat writing. Each entry was numbered and to Jake's horror he realised that it ran up to number twenty-three. 'Here's the milk money ready in this envelope for when the milkman calls on Tuesday teatime, I've done you a casserole for tonight and there's a load of ready meals for you and granddad in the freezer, so I'm sure you won't go hungry, but just in case, I've put some cash in the best china teapot for emergencies.' Jake nodded absently. 'Your dad will have his mobile with him and we'll give you a call later on today to let you know we've got there OK.'

'Don't bother,' thought Jake meanly. His mum's instructions droned on and this time Jake really did tune out. He just wanted them to go now. At least with them out of his hair he could relax on the sofa in the lounge, watching the big TV and, just to demonstrate his independence, he would sit with his feet up, something that was never allowed when his mum was around.

'I said are you listening Jake!' his mum's voice cut across Jake's wanderings sharply and he started. 'I said, you will have to look after granddad, he's not getting any younger you know and he gets very forgetful and vague. I mean, he was supposed to be here ten minutes ago so I can give him his list, but he's late. You would think he'd at least try and be more considerate.'

She suddenly seemed to think better of complaining about granddad and switched into "concerned relative" mode. 'I do hope he's alright, those steps down the side of his house are treacherous for somebody his age.'

43

Granddad's house was built on the side of a steep hill above Churnthorpe. To get to his door you had to climb 14 concrete steps that were starting to crumble in one or two places and really needed replacing. 'He's going to fall and break his neck someday. We've tried to talk to him about him selling up and going into Meadowlands, but he simply won't discuss it.'

Jake was staggered by this casual pronouncement from his mum. Meadowlands was the old people's home near the park, but granddad wasn't that old, how could she think that granddad was at the stage of going into a home? Jake knew that granddad was very independent and would hate the idea of not having his own space and needing to be looked after. But before he could comment on it, his mum glanced out of the window and tutted. 'Oh bother! I told him not to come in his car. He's too old to be on the road. I asked him to get the bus over here!' A shiny red Rover was pulling slowly into the drive. Jake and his mum walked out to meet him.

Granddad levered himself out of his car slowly. He was wearing a neatly pressed, light blue, short sleeved shirt with some fawn slacks and brown, open-toed sandals with dark blue socks. On his normal glasses he had clipped on some dark lenses, which he could flip up and down. As he emerged, he flipped them up so they were sticking out in front. 'Hello all! Sorry I'm late Louise, the bus didn't show up, so I just ran back for my keys and came straight over.' Granddad winked at Jake and fumbled with the keys to the boot. Jake smiled a small smile at the thought of granddad running anywhere, let alone sprinting up and down those steps.

'You should have given us a call Granddad,' said Jake's mum slightly mollified at his explanation. 'We could have popped over for you.'

'Oh I didn't want to delay you any more than was necessary, I know that you like to get away on time.' He flashed Jake's dad a knowing smile. 'Alright son?'

Jake's mum seemed to realise that there was something in granddad's tone that was gently mocking her, but she couldn't be sure, so she gave him the benefit of the doubt and fell to organising things again. 'Jake will take that for you Granddad,' she said, ushering Jake forward to relieve him of his blue and red holdall. 'Take it up to the spare bedroom please Jake and then your dad and I will have to get going.'

By the time Jake had come back downstairs, granddad was sitting at the kitchen table, his glasses pushed up onto his forehead and nodding at the list that his mum was discussing with him. '...and here's our mobile number and the address and number of Auntie June's house where we'll probably be busy most of the time sorting out her things. Ah Jake, we're just about ready to go now.'

'Thank God for that!' thought Jake, he realised that a tension in the house had been gradually building up all morning. Jake didn't really know how he was going to react when his mum and dad would set off. He wasn't going to miss them, but he knew that his mum would say something peace-making about how sorry she was that things had worked out this way and Jake wasn't certain if he could keep a lid on all the hurt feelings he had boiling around inside him. The last thing he wanted to do was to make them think he was crying like a little kid, just because he wasn't going with them. No, he was determined to be cool. Cool and in control, as if he wasn't bothered if they were around at all.

'Right then...!' Jake's dad breezed in. 'All done here?' looking expectantly at Jake's mum.

'Alright then Granddad?' she said as if trying to think of anything they might have forgotten, 'I told Jake earlier that we'd call when we get there to see how you're getting on.'

She hesitantly moved towards Jake. He flinched away and walked rapidly down the hall after his dad and into the heat of the midday sunshine. The pale grey gravel on the driveway seemed to be a dazzling white in the sun and made Jake screw his eyes up.

His dad turned and gave Jake a quick hug. 'Be good son, I'm sure you will be.' Jake's dad was not one of nature's natural huggers. Jake couldn't make up his mind if it was because he was just someone who was uncomfortable doing it, or simply too "British" and just not brought up in a world that hugged each other. Probably the latter Jake thought, as his dad turned to granddad and shook hands rather formally.

With a sinking feeling, Jake realised it was time to say goodbye to his mum. 'Please don't let her go on about how sorry she is!' Jake prayed as he felt his mum's arms flung around him. She squeezed him much harder and for a lot longer than she usually did. Jake found that the tension he had felt building all morning had, now the moment had arrived, frozen his arms at his sides. He didn't want to speak in case his voice cracked with emotion.

His mum emerged from the hug, held his shoulders and looked long and hard at Jake. Jake's insides seemed to lurch as he noticed tears in his mum's eyes. 'Oh please don't let her get all emotional! Please!' Jake pleaded. His arms were still stiff and straight and he couldn't bring himself to move them at all. He knew instinctively that if he tried to say something to comfort her, he would lose his cool completely.

'I'm so sorry Jake…' his mum began.

'Don't!' Jake's words cut across his mum's apology sharply like a large, red, verbal stop sign and his mum looked hurt.

Jake cursed himself for sounding angry. So much for being cool! He searched for the words that would let his mum know that he didn't mean to sound so abrupt. He smiled a somewhat lop-sided smile and managed to stammer, 'It's fine... we'll be fine... say hello to Auntie June for me... I'll speak to you tonight.' The words tumbled out of Jake in a torrent and he twitched away from his mum's hands and her watery, concerned stare and turned back towards the house, momentarily at a loss as to what to do with himself.

He was cross with himself for not handling the situation like he wanted to and was tempted simply to run away indoors, but knew he couldn't. Instead, he sat down on the doorstep, a hand shading his eyes, conscious that the burning sensation on his face was not due to the sun beating down on him from the clear, blue sky.

His mum hesitated for just a second, as if part of her wanted to go to Jake and make things right with him, when his dad, who was already settled in the driving seat, leaned across to the open passenger door and said, 'Come on then Louise, we need to get going. You said that June will be expecting us around 4 o'clock.'

This reminder of her duty seemed to make Jake's mum reconsider and she turned and got into the car. Jake caught a glance from his dad and he wondered if he had deliberately manoeuvred his mum away from Jake. Although Jake's dad was not the type to get into conversations about feelings, it seemed to Jake that there were times when he displayed an instinct about these sort of things and sometimes he acted as sort of interpreter between him and his mum when there was conflict. On one such occasion his mum had asked his dad, 'How come you seem to know so much about the way Jake's mind works?'

His dad had replied with a shrug, 'Well, I guess I have an advantage over you, in that, I was a teenage boy once and you weren't.'

Finally, and to Jake's enormous relief, the car started and his dad drove slowly out of the driveway. The windows were wound down and hands were waving energetically out of them. Granddad stood on the curiously empty-looking gravel and waved back. He turned to look at Jake to see him still sat on the doorstep shading his eyes with his hands. 'Wave then!' granddad instructed tersely and Jake, still sitting, raised one hand in a motionless salute just before the car disappeared behind Mr Nicholson's large privet hedge. The engine noise gradually faded away as they turned down Churnthorpe Road and quiet descended once more over Clayfields Avenue.

Chapter 5

The Face of God

For a while they both remained where they were, the silence punctuated by the sporadic twittering of birdsong. The distant rumble of a jet could be heard, but it was so high and the sun so bright that Jake couldn't make it out in the sweep of unbroken hazy blue, no matter how hard he screwed his eyes up against the blinding sunlight.

'Cup of tea?' Granddad's voice seemed to come from a detached reality. Jake blinked hard, echoes of the brightness of the sky still dancing across his vision and saw that granddad was looking at him with a half smile and a eyebrow raised questioningly. 'Cup of tea?' he repeated.

'I'll make you one,' said Jake. Now his parents had finally gone Jake felt the rising excitement at the prospect of being in charge of his own house. A bubbling giddiness, maybe it was partly relief that his parents had gone at last, seemed to want to force its way out as a chuckle, but Jake fought it down. He didn't want granddad to know that he might possibly be starting to enjoy himself.

One of his school friends, Will Beadnall nicknamed "The Weasel", had offered Jake some advice when he'd heard that Jake would be spending some of his holidays with his granddad. 'I got sent to my grandma's one Easter, 'cos my eldest sister was havin' a kid.' The Weasel seemed to be a somehow fitting name for Will; he had a sharp, pointy face and eyes that seemed to dart around busily all the time. 'I had a great time, I was spoilt rotten. Days out, shopping trips, special treats for being such a good boy!' The Weasel had eased back in his plastic school chair as they waited for their form tutor to arrive and take registration. 'Yeah, it was great!' he continued, seemingly lost in his happy memories.

'Dunno if this'll be quite the same,' Jake said. 'My granddad can't afford shopping trips and he's not the type for special treats.'

'Nah, my gran was great!' The Weasel said. 'First day, she took me straight down to Paxton's toy shop and said I could choose anything I wanted!'

'Hang on!' interrupted Jake. 'Just how old were you when this happened?'

'Errm...' The Weasel thought. He was one of those people who found that their brain would work better if they screwed up their face. '...So, if my nephew Harry is six years old now, that would have made me...' His brain tried to process this data, but found that, despite creasing his face up to the point where his eyes completely disappeared, it wasn't any use. His face un-crinkled itself and he turned again to Jake. 'Seven or eight,' he pronounced.

'Seven or eight?' Jake laughed, 'I'm fourteen! I don't think my granddad will be taking me down to Paxton's somehow!'

'No,' The Weasel was adamant. 'It don't matter! You're what them lawyers on TV call the "injured party" and it's up to your granddad to make you happy again. So just give him a hard time over the first day or so and he'll do anything to make things right.'

The arrival of the form tutor stopped any further discussion on the subject. Jake had thought about what The Weasel had said. The idea of days out at theme parks, or an expensive present like the latest games console, or even a new PC had flitted appealingly around Jake's head over the last few days. However, despite his feelings of injustice, Jake didn't think that he could exploit his granddad as The Weasel had suggested. On the other hand, he reasoned to himself, he didn't want granddad reporting back to his parents that everything was hunky-dory and Jake was having a wonderful time. No, he would play the part of the "injured party" for a little while longer.

The kitchen seemed cool, dark and strangely quiet. Their shoes squeaked and clattered noisily across the tiled flooring as they entered. It was as if the house was breathing a sigh of relief now the departure of Jake's parents had dissipated the tension.

Without a word, Jake filled the kettle and switched it on. He took two mugs and two teabags out of the cupboard as the kettle began to sputter and hiss into life. Granddad pulled up a chair at the breakfast table. He unfolded the newspaper that had been delivered that morning and began to read it, as he always did, by starting at the back with sports pages. The headline announced that a football team in Manchester had bought a young, nineteen-year-old Brazilian striker for a record fee. Granddad tutted and shook his head. 'It's ridiculous,' he stated. Jake didn't know if granddad was expecting a response to this, or if it was just a pronouncement on the huge amounts of money that was in the game of modern football.

He determined that, as the injured party, he would not make conversation easy and would maintain the air of withdrawn, hurt dignity. 'Have you seen this?' granddad continued, not looking up from the paper. 'Fifteen million pounds! Nobody's worth 15 million pounds! Ridiculous.' As it came to the boil, the noise coming from the kettle became quieter. It started bubbling and steam leaped from the spout. Jake waited for it to switch itself off and poured the boiling water carefully onto the teabags that were waiting in the pot. 'It's daft these days. Teams have more foreigners on them than they have British players. It's no wonder that England hasn't won anything for years, they can't get a game in the top leagues in their own country!'

Jake had heard this conversation so many times before, he knew it almost off by heart. 'When I was a lad…' Jake muttered under his breath, predicting what would come next.

'When I was a youngster…' granddad continued and Jake smiled to himself, he'd been so close, '…you played for the team in the town where you came from.' Jake let the familiar argument wash over him without taking it in. He stirred the contents of the teapot, took the milk from the fridge, poured a small amount into the bottom of the mugs and finally poured out the steaming amber-coloured tea. All the while, the familiar argument was being voiced to an uncaring kitchen and an inattentive grandson. Jake handed a mug to granddad. '…Fall over as soon as you look at them and act on like they've been half killed. In my day, a player nearly had to have his leg broken before the ref would blow for a foul. Oh thanks Jake.' Granddad took his mug and blew on the hot tea.

Out of nowhere, an impulse to argue violently with his granddad hit Jake so suddenly, that he nearly shouted at him angrily. Jake desperately wanted to silence him, with his old-fashioned, stunningly predictable waffling about nothing important at all. Jake wanted to roar 'Shut up! Shut up! SHUT UP!' over and over again. He knew in his heart that none of these angry feelings were his granddad's fault. He'd not ruined Jake's holiday plans, but Jake wanted to lash out at someone and there was only granddad around. Stiffly, he turned away to stare, unseeing out of the window, exhaling slowly as he struggled to regain his composure.

Silence fell as they sipped their tea. Jake leaned against the kitchen units and granddad leafed absently through the paper, gradually getting ever closer to the front page. Jake finished his tea first, gulping the scalding liquid down as quickly as he could. He put his cup into the sink for washing up at some other time and headed towards the door to the hallway. 'So, Jake, is there anything you want to do?'

Granddad's question halted Jake's progress just as he'd reached the doorway and he turned to see him staring at Jake with a half smile, his head slightly tilted to one side and questioning, watery eyes as if he'd noticed Jake's unseen, internal raging. The thought made Jake angry and embarrassed and he wished that granddad had not chosen to have this conversation right now. All he wanted to do was to go and watch some television, or shoot a few aliens on his PC, anything to just give him some time to cool down, but granddad persisted. 'It's a shame to be inside on such a lovely day. We could pop down to the park and watch the cricket, or have a walk on the canal towpath to the tearooms at the lock?'

Both suggestions would normally have appealed to Jake. Indeed, he would often meet up with granddad at the cricket ground in the park during the summer, Jake with some money for ice creams jingling in his jeans pocket and granddad with a thermos of coffee. Jake always enjoyed the time they spent there, discussing the merits or highlighting the obvious weaknesses of the players. Jake would also take along his ageing, weather-stained bat and his rather faded and badly scuffed ball to play in the practice nets afterwards. Granddad would bowl very slow, looping deliveries until he declared himself too tired and hot to continue. The lock tearoom served some spectacular cakes and ice cream sundaes and was another favourite haunt of theirs. Granddad always took Jake there at the end of the summer holidays as a rare "special treat" before school recommenced. The fact that granddad was offering to take Jake there at the beginning of the holidays made him feel curiously unsettled and he wondered if this enforced period of being together had somehow made what had been an easy-going and relaxed friendship into something strained and awkward, as if they were suddenly strangers.

Still wanting to make his escape, Jake struggled to find something to say. He realised that he didn't want to do anything that he might find enjoyable right now. Watching cricket, or eating cakes did sound good and Jake wondered if he went along with granddad's suggestions, that he might have a good time despite feeling sorry for himself. But Jake just couldn't bring himself to submit and his hurt feelings seemed to wag their fingers at him their righteous voices proclaiming: 'You can't have fun! You're the injured party!'

'Why can't granddad just back off and leave me alone?' Jake thought. 'He's only being nice so that you won't give him a hard time!' The feelings chimed in again and there was granddad, still watching Jake with his watery stare and enquiring eyebrow. Jake didn't know what to say to turn granddad down. After all, there was no good reason to do so and he desperately tried to think of something that would mean he couldn't go out with him, but in the end, he could only mumble something about maybe seeing a friend later on.

Granddad's eyebrow fell and gathered with the other one into a concerned frown. 'Is everything alright Jake?' The question fell into the pool of silence that lay between them. Jake realised that he could tell granddad exactly what was wrong, but he knew that he would sound like a spoilt little kid having a whinge, something that made Jake feel cross and humiliated, why couldn't he just drop it?

And then, inspiration struck him and he silently thanked Mr Brown for insisting that he complete his German homework. 'I can't go out this afternoon anyway, I've got some homework to do.'

Granddad's eyebrow shot up again. 'Homework? But you've got six weeks to get that done Jake!'

Oh just leave it Granddad please! Jake pleaded silently 'I... I always like to get it out of the way as soon as I can. I don't want it hanging over me all holiday.' What a joke! Jake thought, I'm always doing homework at the last minute and here I am saying exactly what my mum's been nagging me to do for years! Jake could scarcely suppress a smile.

'Well... I suppose that's the best way really.' Granddad's tone let Jake know that he knew something wasn't quite as it should be, but at least the admission gave Jake the chance to make a break for it and he turned and walked quickly away, trying to avoid the impulse to run.

Once in his room, Jake switched on his PC and flopped on the bed listening to the rhythmic clicking, whooshing and whirring that it made as it started up. Shortly, the familiar musical chords chimed out to let him know it was ready to be used and yet Jake didn't move. The noise of a neighbour's garden mower seemed to waft in through the open window carrying with it the tantalising smells of new mown grass. A small fly, confused at being confronted with a pane of glass, flew into it over and over again before landing, dazed on the windowsill, collecting itself and taking off to start all over again. Jake wondered why the fly simply didn't try the window a few inches away to the left, which was the one that was opened, but no. The determined insect seemed to believe that if it bashed into its window long enough, it would give way and the fly would have its freedom.

Someone, a few gardens away, was lighting up a barbeque and the chatter of their guests seemed to merge into a happy bubbling soundtrack of background noise. 'They seem to be enjoying themselves,' Jake thought bitterly. All he had to look forward to was actually getting on with his homework. After what he'd said to granddad, there was no way he could dodge it now. With a long sigh, Jake prepared to get up and make a start, when a musical bleep from his PC announced that an email had just landed in his inbox. Curious, Jake sat up quickly, crossed the room to the computer and slid into the swivel chair. The email, standing out in bold type at the top of his inbox was from his brother. It read:

From: chris.hargreaves@forbes.hotels.com

To: hargreavesfamily211@egateway.net

Subject: chin up!

Hi Bro, guess the folks have gone by now. It's tough on you, but you'll be busy keeping granddad in order! ☺

There'll be other times, promise!

Speak soon

Chris

Jake wondered where Chris was right now. In a modern, air conditioned office overlooking the marina? Or perhaps he was sitting at a cool beachfront café with his laptop on his knee sipping an ice-cold coke? Envy burned within him for a moment and then Jake realised that he was tired of being angry and envious, tired of being the injured party. What was the point anyway if he was only going to spoil things for himself? He'd go back down to be with granddad in a bit and maybe they could catch the last few overs of the cricket, but right now, he needed to get his German homework out of the way.

Jake retrieved his schoolbag from underneath his bed where he'd slung it in end of term high spirits when he'd got home the day before. He fished out his homework planner, textbook and English/German dictionary. He leafed through the homework planner just to check what the task was and found where his scrawled writing said: German homework – find a web page with a news story written in German, print it out and translate it into English. Beneath it there was Mr Brown's red biro that read: To be completed. No Excuses! The last bit was underlined three times. 'OK then,' Jake murmured to himself and he set to work.

Twenty minutes later Jake thought he'd finally found a news story that suited his needs. He'd discounted many already, even the exciting looking ones that were about armed robberies, or sports stars, because they were simply too long. The one he'd selected seemed to be from the website of a small, regional newspaper and wasn't particularly interesting, but it was fairly short. At the top, it showed a large photo of an old man dressed in a smart brown suit, white shirt and a forgettable brown tie with a diamond pattern on it. He was shaking hands with an enormous lady who was also dressed smartly in a floral print dress and blue blazer. The headline said that the man in the photo was receiving a special award for 50 years of work in a town called Rheinhagen, serving on the Gemeinderat which Jake assumed was something like the local council.

Jake was starting to get hungry. His normal lunchtime was long past, but he didn't want to give up just yet, as he'd built up some momentum and, as he'd made the effort to get it started, he wanted to get it finished and out of the way. Just then, there was a soft knock on the door. 'Jake? Can I come in?' Jake had almost forgotten about his granddad and his resolution to make things right with him. Jake rushed to open the door to see granddad holding a tray with a steaming mug of tea and a large cheese sandwich on it. 'I won't disturb you, just thought you might be getting hungry,' granddad said without meeting Jake's eyes.

He stepped inside, put the tea and sandwiches down on Jake's desk and turned to go. Jake felt a keen pang of guilt. After all, Jake was supposed to look after granddad and here he was serving food and drink to Jake as if he was the hired help. Jake knew he had to say something now before he went back downstairs or things would just get more and more awkward. 'Thanks Granddad.' He didn't stop. 'Sorry. I should have made lunch for you. You're the guest.'

Granddad halted and turned, smiling warmly at Jake. 'That's alright. I mustn't stop the workers working!' Jake grinned back. The tension had gone and it was good to be back on friendly terms again.

Granddad glanced at Jake's computer screen. 'So what are you working on?' he asked and Jake explained what he had to do. 'So this is a German newspaper?' Jake immediately detected the tone of disapproval in his voice. Granddad had never really got over the war, nor had he forgiven the Germans for "winning the peace" by being so successful in businesses like engineering and car manufacturing afterwards. Whenever he saw two or three BMWs, Audi's or Mercedes parked together he'd huff and say, 'I sometimes wonder who actually won the war.' There was a deep distrust there that Jake knew he could never fully understand and wondered if it could ever be erased. Granddad looked closer at the photo. 'And this bloke is the one getting the award eh?' He lifted his glasses (still with the dark shades clipped up) on to his forehead, leaned forward and peered at the screen, 'What's the award for?'

Jake hurriedly turned back to the screen and started to trace his finger along the text 'Dunno what that bit says… oh, it says here that he's from the town of Rheinhagen, (wherever that is) it says Josef Enkmann – has – been – Bürgermeister, (I think that's like a town mayor) with – the – Gemeinderat? (I haven't a clue what that could be, maybe like the council or something?) Anyway, it says something about fünfzig Jahre and that means fifty years, so it looks like he's getting a long service award.'

Granddad said nothing. He had been staring ever more intently at the photo of the old man on the screen. Something in the way granddad was standing shocked Jake and he turned to him to ask if he was feeling alright. His shoulders had become hunched and tense. His gnarled, liver-spotted hands had been transformed into trembling fists, bunched so tightly that his knuckles stood out white. With a panicky swoop of fear, Jake thought granddad was having a stroke or heart attack. He grabbed one of the fists and asked, 'Granddad! What's wrong?'

With a great effort, granddad seemed to come round. He blinked his watery eyes and shuffled backwards a pace, still with his eyes fixed on the screen. 'Don't lose that picture whatever you do, I've got to get something from home. I'll be right back.' And with that he turned and strode off. Jake was so stunned by granddad's strange behaviour, that for a moment he couldn't move. What on earth was that all about?

The sound of the front door being opened and closed again galvanised Jake into action. He leaped from the chair and took the stairs three at a time. But by the time he'd emerged on to the drive, granddad was behind the wheel of his car and starting the engine, his mouth drawn in a thin, grim, straight line and with a determined set to his jaw. 'Where are you going?' Jake spluttered. 'What's wrong Granddad?'

The window of the Rover wound itself smoothly down and granddad smiled weakly at Jake. 'Don't worry Jake I just have to go home for something, something I need. It'll only take about half an hour. Bung the kettle on and we'll have another cuppa when I get back.'

'But...' Jake began, but the window was already winding itself back up and the car pulled smoothly out of the drive leaving behind a very confused young man.

After a few moments of just standing on the drive letting the warmth of the sun soak into his back and neck whilst he tried to take in what had just happened, Jake turned and slowly made his way back inside. Walking up the stairs, Jake felt drained somehow, as if granddad's sudden departure had taken all his energy. Nothing felt quite normal, not even the familiar décor of the hall, the landing, the sticker on his door saying "Keep Out! Genius at Work!" His bedroom carpet, his desk, everything felt changed and different and it was something to do with this smiling old man from Rheinhagen.

Jake realised that there might be a clue as to granddad's disappearance in the news story and he set about translating the remaining paragraphs.

However, twenty minutes later, with the story now written down in English, there didn't seem to be anything particularly notable about the smiling old man. Enkmann had been the Mayor of Rheinhagen for years, for much longer than was usual for mayors in rural politics, but it seemed that the people of Rheinhagen would not let him stand down because they had so much faith in him. This faith had been returned by Enkmann over the years and the townspeople had prospered under his leadership. That was it. That was all there was. 'How unremarkable,' Jake muttered to himself as he munched absently on the nearly forgotten cheese sandwich which had started to go dry and curl up at the edges. He couldn't wait for granddad to get back and to discover what this was all about, so Jake headed outside and sat in the sun on the garden bench, gazing down the Clayfields Avenue for sign of the familiar red Rover. Time passed slowly. A bumblebee swooped jerkily past Jake's nose. He checked his watch. Granddad had been gone well over an hour now. What could he be up to?

Jake decided that he was getting too hot in the sun, so he sauntered inside, switched on the TV in the lounge and pulled the curtains to make the room darker. He slipped off his trainers and put his feet up on the comfy cushions of the sofa, smiling to think of what his mum would have said if she'd seen him.

Just as he was getting comfortable, the noise of a car pulling up and a door being opened and closed again had Jake jumping up to see what granddad had dashed off so suddenly for. In the hall, granddad was removing his sandals and putting on his slippers. He had an old, rather dog-eared green folder under his arm. 'Is that it?' Jake thought to himself, 'a manky old folder? What's so exciting about that?'

When granddad caught Jake's querying glance, Jake noticed that there was a definite gleam of excitement in his eyes and a certain thrilled giddiness in his manner. 'Sorry I took longer than I'd thought,' granddad said. 'It took me ages to find what I went back for, thought I'd lost it and then found it in the loft nowhere near where I thought it was!'

Jake noticed that granddad's previously smart trousers now had grubby knees and there was a strand of old cobweb caught in his hair. 'What's in the folder?' Jake asked.

'All in good time m'boy! All in good time!' Granddad seemed to be relishing the moment, like he was an Agatha Christie detective about to reveal the murderer to the family gathered in the drawing room of an old mansion house. 'So, have you still got his picture on your computer?' granddad asked.

'Sure, come on.' It was clear that granddad would not be revealing anything here in the hall. Jake went up the stairs two at a time and waited impatiently by his PC for granddad to join him. A screensaver of multicoloured patterns danced and swirled across the monitor screen, so Jake moved the mouse to switch it off. The patterns froze momentarily and then disappeared to reveal Josef Enkmann's smiling face once more.

'So what's this all about Granddad?' Jake's curiosity was beginning to get the better of his patience.

'Well.' Granddad's gaze was no longer watery and vague, but direct, purposeful, almost angry. 'What does he call himself these days? Mr Enkmann is it? Well I couldn't help thinking that I'd seen him before somewhere. I couldn't help thinking that he'd been someone of meaning, someone important in my life. Of course that was ridiculous. The last time I was in Germany it was 1946 and I spent most of my time there in an office, so where would I have seen this bloke then? And then I realised something. This chap in the photo is missing three fingers on his right hand.'

There was a pause. Jake seemed to think that granddad was trying to give him a hint about the mysterious Enkmann. Pointing him to some key fact that Jake should know, but try as he might, Jake couldn't bring to mind any German guy with some missing fingers that granddad had mentioned in the past, so he waited patiently for him to continue. 'And then I realised that I knew this Enkmann bloke. At one time, long ago, I knew him very well indeed. I even had a photograph that I'd taken of him back then and here it is.'

Granddad's hands with their parchment-like skin and liver spots trembled slightly as he opened the folder and removed an old black and white photograph. The young man in the photo had the same square jaw, the same straight nose, the same thin-lipped smile. Jake could even see the right hand with the missing fingers. The photo of the young man showed this clearly as he had thrust his maimed right hand forward and upward. The man in the photos was clearly one and the same person, but there was a very important difference between the two images. Where the old Josef Enkmann was wearing a smart business suit, the young Josef Enkmann in granddad's photo was wearing the black and silver uniform of a Nazi SS officer. 'You know what that is Jake?' Granddad's voice was hushed; almost reverent. 'That, my lad, is the face of God.'

Chapter 6

Granddad's Story

Ten minutes later, they were sat at the kitchen table each sipping a steaming mug of tea. The sunlit world outside seemed to Jake to be strangely detached from his and granddad's reality. As if time was now something that happened to other people.

A freshly printed image of the old Enkmann lay on the table alongside the photo of the young Nazi officer. Jake realised that they were both just staring at the two images and neither of them had said a word for two minutes or more. The likeness could not be denied. Time had softened the features of the young man, but they were still present. Heavy lids now framed the piercing, slightly mocking eyes and there were deep creases at their corners. His closely cropped hair, or at least the little that could be seen from beneath the black peaked cap with the silver skull on the front of it, had been replaced by neatly cut grey hair, smoothed into place by oil that plastered it to the skull.

Granddad sipped his tea and gulped noisily. He looked at Jake with an excited glint in his eyes and said, 'So, Jake, what do you think we're going to do about this here chappy then?' Jake always wondered if granddad was looking for an answer when he asked this sort of question, or was he just leading up to telling Jake exactly what they were going to do.

After a pause where granddad's grin got wider and wider and in an effort to make him come to the point, Jake asked, 'Why have you got a photo of this bloke anyway?'

'Oh, that's right, you wouldn't know the significance would you?' granddad said. 'Well, I'm going to have to tell you one of my war stories again I'm afraid.' He smiled. 'Try and stay awake for this one won't you? I've never told you it before.' They both grinned. Granddad always had to go through a few little rituals before starting a story. It helped to build a sense of expectation, although there was little need to create an air of excitement this time as Jake was already leaning forward, eager to hear about the Enkmann connection. Not to be hurried, granddad settled himself back into his chair. Gathering his thoughts, he stared into his teacup for a few moments as if expecting something to pop out of it and then, after a deep breath and a noisy exhale, he started to tell his story.

'I've already told you some of the things that I got up to when I was in France, but your mum didn't want me to tell you about the detention camp. Probably thought that you were too young to hear about what happened then. Might have given you nightmares, I know it did me. You see I was attached to a Special Forces unit as a translator. You'll remember that I was brought up in Calais where my dad, your great granddad, had his export business? Well I had been fluent in French since I was just a kid and so, although I was very young, they needed someone with my skills to help a unit that was operating in north-east France. I was parachuted in just as the Allied forces were about to start the big push from the French coast. Our job was to disrupt supply lines and sabotage rail links, but in April 1944, after a few weeks of living rough in the forest, I was given new orders. An officer called Lawrence Nabb and I were told to find out what was going on near a town called St Gille sur Vallone. The bods at Whitehall had been receiving worrying reports about the scale of what was going on at the big death camps like the one in Auschwitz. Apparently, initial reports of the scale of the slaughter were so horrific, that they simply didn't believe it at first. However, it became clear that there was murder happening on an industrial scale and they wanted to know how big it was, how bad it was and who was in charge. The war had turned the corner for us, D-day was being planned and the end of the war was being cautiously anticipated, so when it was all over they wanted evidence to prosecute those who were responsible.'

Granddad took another drink of tea, glanced at Jake to check he was still listening and continued. 'Intelligence had reported that there was a large detention camp at St Gille which was expanding, with new structures being built. They wanted to check that the camp was still being used just as a holding centre and not being upgraded into a death camp. Lawrence and I made our way cross-country after dark until, after a couple of days, we came across the camp. From our observation point we could see the rows and rows of long wooden huts with people just wandering aimlessly round, or they'd be sitting in small groups as the guards patrolled with their dogs, endlessly circling outside the high barbed wire fence.

'Our mission was just to observe and photograph what was going on. The forest came down the hill and ended not far away from the front gates. There was plenty of cover within it, but we had to move into position at night to avoid detection. Once we were in place, we were so close to the gates that movement during daylight was very dangerous. Imagine having to lie still for hours and hours. Not daring to move for a drink or food or even to go to the toilet until it got really dark. We weren't too pleasant to be around I can tell you.'

Granddad paused, took off his glasses, rubbed his eyes and steepled his fingers in front of his lips. 'It didn't take us long to figure out that this fellow was running the show.' Granddad's stubby finger prodded the photo of the young Enkmann. 'At least, if he wasn't actually in charge, he behaved like he was. He was only about my age and I was just a youngster, but everyone seemed to be afraid of him and I'm not just talking about the detainees, but everyone, even the Wehrmacht, the German infantry who guarded the camp, most of whom were much older men, even they seemed scared of him. These days they'd call him a psycho, you never knew what was going on in his mind. Mostly he walked around the camp smiling and laughing with people, and you could see that the detainees were kind of laughing along, just to humour him like, keep him sweet you know? 'Cos when he went off on one, he was an unholy terror and I mean really evil.'

Granddad paused again and seemed to be gathering his thoughts. Jake noticed that his eyes were staring unfocused and unseeing on the kitchen wallpaper opposite. Jake got the feeling that granddad was travelling back in his mind to a time that he'd nearly forgotten, a time he had spent a large part of his life trying to forget. 'Maybe I'm getting ahead of myself. Have you learned about the holocaust in your history lessons?'

Jake nodded. 'Yeah, we did it last year. That's where the Jews were rounded up wasn't it?'

'Aye, the Jews, and just about everyone else who didn't fit in with Hitler's vision for a perfect German master race, they were all rounded up and imprisoned. You have got to understand, it wasn't like today when prisoners have three meals a day, a TV in their cell and get to study for new qualifications. Once you were detained, all these "human rights" they bang on about today went right out of the window. It was as if you were no longer human at all, but cattle. No, you were less than cattle, 'cos cattle are looked after better than those poor souls were in the camps back then. I saw some awful things. Things that I sometimes struggle to believe actually happened today.

'The war showed me the very lowest level that a man could stoop to and Enkmann was the person who showed it to me most clearly of all. The detainees had had everything taken from them, their homes, their jobs, their belongings and they were herded into the camp from special trains that stopped in the railway goods yard half a mile or so away on the edge of St Gille. And there, waiting to welcome them was Enkmann, or Günter Meyer as I knew him then. He would stand at the gates to welcome any new detainees. He'd be all smiles, ruffling the hair of the children, talking charmingly to the ladies and shaking hands with the men as they trooped in through the gates. Some of the detainees seemed to be heartened by his cheerful greeting and smiled and laughed with him. Once inside however, everything changed and the full horror of the nightmare became clear. Painfully thin, starved and starving people sat around fading and dying right before your eyes. The beatings, the abuse I saw handed out was vicious and brutal, the struggle to survive was rewarded by one more day in hell. No wonder so many simply gave up. And then there was the shipments.'

As he had recounted these memories, granddad's voice had lost its usual soft, soporific quality that characterised Jake's memories of hours spent listening to his war stories. Now it had taken on a harder edge, as if just talking about Enkmann, or rather, Günter had reawakened all the silent fury which granddad had stored up since that time. His face had a strangely ruthless, determined look about it and his jaw was thrust forward as if he was grinding his teeth, fighting back a murderous rage that the years could never erode away.

After a moment, granddad blinked, shot a quick, wan smile at Jake and continued. 'At this time of the war, the death camps at places like Auschwitz were at full capacity. The Nazis had perfected the means of processing the detainees and if that sounds a bit like I'm describing a factory, that's because that's the way it worked. Nice and efficient.' A shudder ran involuntarily up Jake's spine as granddad had spat these words out. The horrors that he'd read about with a passing morbidity in his school's history textbooks, seemed somehow to be much more "real" now granddad was describing them.

'So, places like St Gille started to send off shipments of detainees for processing. It was about now that we really started to notice Günter. The war was going badly for the Nazi's, Allied forces were starting to make inroads across Italy and an Allied invasion in France was expected at any point. Some of the camp guards became even more inhuman, taking out their frustration, anger and fear on the helpless. Günter reacted differently; he swanned about the camp like he was on a Sunday stroll around the park. Against the backdrop of the sick, the starving and the scared, he looked young and fit and invincible. When a shipment was due to be sent, Günter took charge.

'Now I'd seen some bad stuff during those weeks we were lying up in the woods, but I'd never seen Günter get his hands dirty. Other people would carry out beatings, and steal the prisoner's stuff, but not Günter. He was always polite and charming to the detainees, finding out about the different families that were in the camp, whose kids belonged to which parents, that kind of thing. We had a spy inside the camp, a French girl who cleaned the officers' quarters and helped serve their meals. She reported to the resistance that some of the detainees thought that Günter was the best of the Nazi officers. He was certainly friendlier than the others and they simply thought that he was asking about their different families out of human interest.

'And then the day of the first shipment arrived and it became clear why Günter had been so interested. He lined everyone up in their family groups and then walked through the lines of people, choosing just two or three members of each family to go in the shipment. I remember seeing him do this time and again. I was lying in my filthy stinking foxhole in the woods and I couldn't do a thing about it. These desperate, half dead people who had already suffered so much, were going on a journey that was probably going to end with their death in a gas chamber and Günter denied them the small comfort of having their families with them.'

Granddad's chin creased and trembled slightly as the long buried images emerged clearly once again. 'Children were torn away from their parents, husbands from wives, mothers from daughters. It was so...' he struggled for the words. '...so cruel for these humiliated and broken people. I remember one mother, screaming and screaming as her son was dragged from her. Günter sauntered over to see what was going on, he leaned in closely and said something to her, smiling that taunting, mocking smile. She flew at him like a wild, fierce animal. The soldiers grabbed her and held her fast. Günter stared coolly right in her face as she screamed, "Why are you doing this to us? You're just a young boy! Who do think you are?" That must have stung him because Günter's smile left in an instant, his face changed. It sort of stretched and creased into a grimace of pure fury. It was then that I realised why people were scared of him. In a second, all the charm and all the smiles and all the laughing disappeared and was replaced by a... a demon. He put his face right up to hers and roared. "Who am I? Who am I? In this place I am life, in this place I am death! In this place, I – AM – GOD!"'

Jake was only dimly aware of the normal life carrying on outside the kitchen. Cars passed on the way to somewhere, birds sang, a neighbour's lawnmower droned rhythmically through the summer air, but for Jake, at this moment, he had been transported to a time of cruelty and brutality and death. He could almost hear the screams.

After a pause, granddad continued in a quieter voice that seemed to convey a kind of long repressed, helpless fury. 'All those weeks we'd spent hiding out in the forest, there never was another moment when I was more tempted just to rush out of cover and get at him. If I could have got close enough to Günter then, I would have choked the life out of him with my bare hands.' The ageing cracked and spotted skin of granddad's hands stretched and flexed over his whitened knuckles. His face seemed like a grim, grey mask, as he wrestled with painful memories and the white-heat of the hatred he still held for the young man in the silver and black uniform.

'Those he'd selected were dragged out of the gates and formed into lines. And then they were marched off to the goods yard and, from there, they were packed on to the trains to the death camps. And there at the gates was our Günter, waving them off and saluting them as they marched past. That's where I took this photo.' He picked up the photo of Günter and stared at it. The silence deepened.

'What happened to the woman?' Jake asked. Granddad looked up at him as if considering what to tell him and then simply shook his head. Jake thought better of trying to get more details from him and inclined his head to indicate that he understood.

'After a month or so of keeping watch over the camp, we got involved in a few "projects" with the resistance and, months later, when we returned, we found confusion and panic amongst the guards. Things elsewhere were going badly for the Nazis. Not only were Allied troops rolling across France and Italy and the Russian front was a nightmare, but troops were starting to run away like rats jumping off a sinking ship.

'A week or so before we got there, Günter had deserted his post. Just upped and off he went. No one knew where he'd gone. There was no sign of him, not even after it had all finished and the trials for war crimes had begun. There was an investigation about what had happened at St Gille, I even had to go over and give evidence. Günter was wanted to stand trial. It seemed that he'd been instrumental in all sorts of terrible things. Soldiers had confessed to some dreadful crimes, but they'd say that it was always on Günter's direct orders. All they could really achieve by the time the investigation was finished, was to put out an arrest warrant for him.

'I managed to keep hold of this photo, I didn't know why I wanted a copy at the time, I guess I just didn't want to forget his face and what he'd been responsible for. I remember walking out of the courthouse, I was literally shaking with anger, I was so furious that Günter had got clean away.' Granddad put down the photo of Günter and picked up the picture of Enkmann, a grim smile animated the mask of his face. 'Until now that is.'

Jake sat back in his chair, exhaled and tried to take everything in that granddad had been telling him. He now felt ashamed of the times when he'd treated granddad's war stories with cynicism. Try as he might, he simply couldn't picture granddad as a young lad, not much older than Jake was himself, dropping behind enemy lines, witnessing some of the worst atrocities of human history happening right before his eyes.

'So what do we do about him Granddad?' Jake asked. 'Do we call the police? Or the newspapers? Or is there an organisation that handles this sort of thing?'

Jake struggled to keep his increasing excitement out of his voice. It had started to build as he wondered what granddad's plan was. He imagined reporters and TV crews jostling them for an interview on how they had finally brought the greatest untried war criminal to justice. He saw himself standing outside a courthouse somewhere, holding up both photos for the cameras to a chorus of clicks and flashes from the press. He wondered if he could be cool, smiling at the shouted questions. Getting Günter. That would make it a summer holiday to be remembered after all.

Granddad thought for a moment, his face and voice more like it normally was. 'The problem we've got Jake is that there's no proof.'

'But the photo!' Jake protested.

'The photo isn't enough Jake. We can't just accuse people because of a likeness they have to an old photo.'

'So what's this been all about?' Jake's voice rose in anger as he indicated the photos with a sweep of his hand Surely, after everything he'd told Jake, surely he wasn't going to simply ignore it and walk away?

Granddad seemed to pick up on Jake's tone of voice. 'Calm down sunshine, don't worry! I'm not about to give up on this.' His friendly face crinkled into the familiar grin. 'I'm just saying that the photo alone is not enough evidence for me. Don't get me wrong. I want to get him just as badly now as I did back then. I want to string him up for what he did, I want to see him suffer, but we've got to be absolutely sure before we can go any further.'

Granddad stared at Jake thoughtfully for a moment. 'Now listen,' he began in a decisive tone. 'Here's what we're going to do.' Jake found that he was involuntarily holding his breath and had to inhale sharply. 'Since the investigation all them years ago, I've kept looking out for news of him and there's never a week gone by that I've not wondered where he'd ended up. I spent blooming months in that forest taking photos of Günter. I knew what time he got up, what time he went to bed, what he had eaten for dinner and the colour of his blooming socks! I knew the way he walked, the way he'd stand and the sound of his laugh, so I know for a fact, that if I got to see him again, in the flesh like, I'd be able to say if it was him or not for certain, without any doubt in my mind at all.'

A thrill of excitement passed through Jake's stomach. 'So do you mean we're going to go...?' Jake found that he couldn't bring himself to finish the question off.

'That's right Jake.' Granddad's face had changed again from the mask of anger it had been before, to the familiar, smiling, eager, mischievous face that Jake knew so well, lit up by the glow of anticipation and shared excitement. 'Pack your bags sunshine, we're off to Rheinhagen!'

Chapter 7

Packing Up and Setting Off

The next morning Jake woke late from a heavy slumber to find the sunlight had already crept over his bedroom floor and was pooling on his pillow in a dazzling, almost painfully bright strip of light. He blinked and screwed his eyes up before rolling over and trying to get back to sleep. A constant, muffled noise from downstairs intruded on Jake's slumber and prevented the warm, drowsy feeling from taking hold. Gradually, Jake woke up. All at once he recalled what had happened the previous evening in a rush of excitement. Had it been a dream? Or were they actually going to Germany to track down a war criminal and bring him to justice? Granddad already seemed to have a good idea of how they were going to go about it, although he wasn't sharing it with Jake just yet. When Jake had asked how they were going to get to Rheinhagen and what they'd do when they'd got there, granddad had touched the side of his nose with one of his stubby fingers and said, 'Don't worry Jakey, I've got it all under control!'

The excitement caused by their discovery and the prospect of a trip to Germany meant that the previous evening had been spent in an almost celebratory manner. Granddad had decided to ignore the chicken casserole that Jake's mum had left in the fridge for them and had asked Jake what he'd like to eat instead. 'Anything you want Jakey boy, just say the word,' he had said with bow of mock deference and a tea towel over his arm, as if Jake was a diner at a posh restaurant and granddad was the headwaiter.

Jake's mum had called to say they had arrived safely just as they were tucking in to the pizzas they'd had delivered. His mum's familiar voice informed Jake that they'd not had a very good journey, as the traffic had been terrible. 'I don't know why they have to do roadworks when people are going to be going away on holiday.' Her exasperated comments about lazy, disorganised council workers washed over Jake as he took another large bite of Pepperoni pizza. She continued to talk about how Auntie June was looking quite well considering, how her new accommodation at the home was lovely, how the staff were so friendly and welcoming and how much there was to sort out in the house that she was leaving behind.

Jake continued to munch on the pizza, the spicy sweetness of the pepperoni and the richness of the mozzarella cheese and tomato complemented perfectly by the salty tang of the anchovies that Jake loved. He realised from the silence on the other end of the line that his mum must have asked him a question. 'Sorry, what did you say?' Jake muttered through a mouthful of pizza.

'Honestly Jake! Aren't you listening to a word I'm saying?' Jake's mum scolded. 'I asked if you had eaten tea yet!'

'Right,' Jake mumbled. 'We're having tea now actually.'

'And how is it? Did you manage to reheat it OK?' The question flummoxed Jake for a second, until he realised that she was talking about the chicken casserole she had left in the fridge.

'Oh the casserole!' Jake stammered. 'Yeah, it's very nice!' Across the table granddad made a big show of holding up a slice of his cheese and tomato pizza, taking a bite and making theatrical hand signs to express how delicious it was. Jake almost guffawed and had to suppress his giggles.

'So, what have you boys been doing today? Have you been out anywhere?'

'No, actually we've just had a quiet day at home, pretty boring really!' Jake picked up the photo of Enkmann and looked at it with a comic expression of huge shock and surprise. Today had in fact turned out to be anything but boring! Now it was granddad's turn to fight back his laughter.

'Oh… right…' Jake's mum's tone of voice seemed to indicate that she was aware that there was something going on at the other end of the line that she wasn't being told about. After a short, thoughtful pause, she clearly decided that it was just another of those Jake-and-granddad moments and it wasn't worth pursuing. She reverted back to her familiar, business-like manner.

'Now Jake, I know that you and granddad will be going on trips out, but I really would feel much better if you tried to go by bus or train if possible. Don't say anything about this to him, but I think that he's getting too old to be driving any long distances, so just bear it in mind OK?'

His mum's concern seemed to rile Jake. Why did she think that she knew what was best for everyone? Is granddad getting a little old? – Stop him driving. Is granddad not as nimble as he used to be? – Put him in a home. It just seemed somehow disrespectful to Jake. Yes, granddad was not as young as he used to be, but that shouldn't mean that he should be shut away, or not to be allowed to do anything, or treated like a baby.

Jake realised that his attention had drifted again and his mum was saying something to him. 'I said can you put him on the phone please? Honestly Jake! What's got into you?'

Jake murmured an apology and passed the phone to granddad. "Louise! How was your journey?' Granddad's voice was cheerful and hearty and he winked at Jake. 'The casserole? Oh yes. Very tasty thank you!' After a short conversation that seemed mostly to revolve around the type and number of ready meals there were in the freezer and how to heat them through properly, Jake's mum said goodbye and granddad (after peering over his spectacles at the phone to find the right button to press) hung up.

'When do you think we should tell them about what we're going to do?' Jake asked.

Granddad looked thoughtful for a while as he pondered the question. 'Well, the way I see it Jake, it's best all round if we don't mention it for the moment. You mustn't tell them any lies, but if we're clever about what we say when they call, they don't have to know anything. We'll only be gone for four or five nights, we'll be back here before they're finished sorting out your Aunty June's stuff.

Jake frowned. 'My mum will go ballistic when she finds out.'

'Now listen!' granddad replied firmly. 'You won't get into any trouble, I'll take full responsibility, so don't you worry!'

Then he laughed. 'Imagine, ringing them up to say, "just to let you know that we're off out of the country to unmask a war criminal".' He barked a short laugh. 'At best they'll not believe us and just laugh, telling us not to be so daft, before coming home to stop us going anywhere. Or at worst, they'll come straight home and use it as a reason to chuck me into a home!' Jake didn't know what to say. He didn't want granddad to think he'd been party to his mum's conversations about getting him into a home, but he didn't want to lie to granddad either. In the end, he didn't have to say anything.

'Don't fret Jake, I've known for ages that your mum thinks I should move out of my little house. She makes it plain, always going on about how difficult it must be for me to manage those steps up to my door and how hard it must be to feed and clothe myself, like I've lost my bloomin' marbles! Well maybe they are going, but they've not all gone just yet!' Jake couldn't speak. He felt embarrassed that his mum had been so obvious and he wanted to say something to make granddad understand that he didn't think the way his mum did, but no words came.

'Don't worry yourself Jake!' Granddad's smile broadened. 'I've been a stubborn old codger for quite a while now and I think that I'm getting really quite good at it, so it'll take more than your mum's subtle hints on how lovely the tea dances are at the Meadowlands retirement home to get me to shift!' They both laughed, the awkwardness was dispelled and the mood was lifted. 'Now eat up your "casserole" young man, or you'll never grow up big and strong!' He raised his glass of beer in a toast. 'Here's to adventures at any age!'

From under his quilt, Jake heard the noise from downstairs become louder for a moment as the kitchen door was opened, the conversation on the radio became more defined, but he still couldn't make out the words. Jake remembered that granddad liked to listen to the radio in the morning. Footsteps now approached up the stairs and granddad's face appeared around Jake's door.

'Morning sleepyhead!' granddad chimed. 'I don't know! Lying in until all hours, anyone would think you're on holiday!' he grinned. 'There's a cup of tea going cold downstairs if you want it. I've got to nip back home this morning and probably won't be back until after lunchtime. Will you be OK without me?'

'Oh, I think I'll survive,' Jake mumbled, rubbing the sleep from his eyes and stretching before returning granddad's smile. 'What are you going to be doing?' Jake enquired, 'is it to do with Enkmann?'

Granddad chuckled. 'Aye, I've got to prepare for our mission behind enemy lines and I've got some calls to make as well. In the meantime, you can be packing up the stuff you'll need for the journey, have you still got your euros?'

Jake nodded, he had converted his holiday money into Euros two weeks before in preparation to go to France. At the time, handling the unfamiliar notes had given him butterflies of excited anticipation of his trip and he'd not yet got round to the depressing task of changing them back to sterling.

'Right then, get up, tidy up, be good and don't burn the place down whilst I'm gone OK?' Jake laughed, granddad's smiling face disappeared, his footsteps retreated and the sound of the radio was switched off.

Jake emerged from his bedroom a few minutes later, tying his dressing gown up over his pyjamas. He descended to the kitchen with the swimmy, detached feeling of someone who has woken too quickly from a deep sleep. The house seemed strangely quiet, so Jake switched on the TV in the kitchen to provide a bit of background noise. Having poured himself a bowl of cereal, he sat at the table munching absently. The Enkmann photo was still on the table and as he looked at it, Jake pondered how quickly things had changed as he sipped his steaming mug of tea. It seemed almost impossible that instead of spending his summer holidays watching cricket and going for walks by the river, he was going across Europe on a real adventure.

Granddad didn't return until nearly 3 o'clock. He looked tired, but triumphant as he flopped into a kitchen chair and put the carrier bag he'd been holding on the table. 'Right then! We've got some work to do Jake, the pieces are all falling into place!' he said, rubbing his hands together eagerly.

'Really?' Jake enquired, 'what have you been up to?'

'Well, I wanted to make sure that we weren't going on a wild goose chase. I needed to know that Günter hadn't already been found and arrested years ago and that Enkmann was just a completely innocent look alike. Now, I remembered last night that I still had the number of the bloke in the Foreign Office called Percy Henderson who had been involved in the investigation all those years ago. I'd kept it with the photo and some other letters that I'd had about Günter over the years.

'I'd kept in touch with Henderson every now and then, just so as I could see Günter strung up when they eventually caught him. I knew that he probably would have retired ages ago, but I rung it anyway and got straight through to a really nice young lady who pointed me in the right direction. Anyway, to cut a long story short, I got passed around a few people before this bloke could help me. I'd told them that I was writing my memoirs and I was doing some research to see if Günter had ever been found.'

Jake smiled as he imagined just how good granddad could play the role of a helpless old man. 'Anyway, this bloke, Andrew something his name was, he was ever so helpful. He had a big list of war criminals that had never been caught and it seems that Günter is still on it. They never caught up with him, so now we know that it's possible that Enkmann and Günter are one and the same.'

Renewed excitement flooded through Jake and he chuckled giddily. He'd not really doubted the proof of the photos, mostly because the resemblance was striking, but also, he knew that deep down he wanted to believe that this was going to be a big adventure. Granddad's discovery meant that there was some circumstantial evidence that Enkmann *could* be Günter. Jake knew that, in all likelihood, things might still turn out to be the wild goose chase that granddad mentioned. He knew that Enkmann could be exactly what he appeared to be, but for now the adventure was still on.

'So when do we leave Granddad?' Jake asked, struggling not to grin like a lunatic.

'I've been down the travel agents and booked the ferry for Tuesday night,' granddad said producing an envelope from the carrier bag. 'It's a late crossing, but it gives us a chance to visit an old friend tomorrow, someone that we really need to tag along with us if we can persuade him.'

'Ferry?' Jake blurted out in surprise, 'we're not flying then?' Jake had been so looking forward to going on a plane for the first time, that he could not keep the disappointment from his voice.

'Aye, we're going on the ferry. I couldn't afford the cost of flying and I've never been too keen on aeroplanes anyway, so a ferry it'll have to be.'

'Hang on.' Jake was struggling to realise the implications of what granddad was saying. 'So we're crossing to…?'

'Rotterdam,' granddad replied, unfolding what looked like tickets. 'And we're driving all the way to Germany?'

Jake could not keep the creeping worry from his voice. After all, his mum had expressly asked Jake to persuade granddad not to drive long distances and here he was, proposing a round trip of what must be thousands of miles! Part of him felt he should say something to try and change granddad's mind, but at the same time he didn't want to risk losing this chance for an adventure.

'I know what your mum would say about all that driving,' granddad said as if he'd read Jake's mind. 'But we'll be perfectly fine if we just take it steady and have plenty of breaks. Anyway we'll have a wonderful navigator who will make sure we won't get lost.'

'Who's that then?' Jake asked, assuming granddad was referring to the old friend he'd mentioned. Granddad reached into his carrier bag and pulled out a large book with a glossy cover and handed it to Jake. Jake took the book and read "Road Atlas of Europe".

'Well done for volunteering Jake, you'd better start planning our route!'

Jake shook his head. 'You're kidding! No way!' The thought of negotiating the tangle of motorways across Europe was downright scary. Jake had never had to do any navigating before. Normally his mum would calmly issue instructions to his dad whenever they had been on road trips before and, he now realised somewhat naively, he had assumed that he would be simply a passenger this time as well. Being the navigator meant being constantly alert to where they were, where they needed to turn off, which lane to be in or which road to take next. Jake was not at all convinced that he could do it. He was sure to get them completely lost, or heading down the wrong motorway or something like that. Surely there must be some other way?

'Now Jake!' granddad said firmly, looking Jake squarely in the eye over the top of his spectacles. 'Someone has to do it and I can't as I'll be the driver.'

'Yeah but...' Jake began, but granddad cut across him.

'No buts young man, you're our navigator and that's that!' The firm, businesslike tone of his voice indicated to Jake that granddad wasn't prepared to discuss it anymore and the silence between them deepened as Jake flicked randomly through the pages of the atlas.

After a few moments when no one spoke, granddad seemed to realise that Jake was unhappy about having this responsibility thrust upon him and with an altogether gentler voice he said, 'Look Jake, you're going to have to do this 'cos it's just you and me.' His voice seemed to have a plea in it and his eyes blinked seriously. 'But there's really no need to worry. I'll not be charging along at high speed, so you'll be able to manage easily and if you do make a mistake, well don't fret. We'll get there, you see if we don't.' The kindly reassurances didn't altogether dismiss Jake's uneasiness, but he managed a wan smile.

'Your first job is to plan the route between Rotterdam and St Gille; I've arranged to meet up with a friend there and stay over. After that, we'll be off to Rheinhagen.' Granddad smiled warmly at Jake. 'You're a smart kid Jake, you'll be fine.' Granddad paused, 'Of course, if Lawrence agrees to come along, you'll be off the hook. Lawrence was always good with maps!'

'Lawrence?' Jake enquired with a frown. 'Oh! Is he the old friend that you mentioned?'

'Second Lieutenant Lawrence Nabb!' granddad barked loudly. He sat up stiffly and gave a smart salute before dissolving into laughter. 'He was the fella I spent all that time in the woods with at St Gille,' granddad reminded Jake. 'We've always kept in touch, you know, Christmas cards and the like and we made a promise to each other after the investigation, that we'd both try our best to listen out for news on Günter and keep each other informed.'

Granddad's grin broadened. 'He's going to do cartwheels when we show him what we've got!' Jake grinned back at granddad. He could tell that the prospect of seeing his old friend again and maybe even working with him to track down their sworn enemy was making him feel as excited as if he was still the teenage soldier from 1944.

'So do you think that Lawrence will come with us?' Jake asked, fervently praying that he would and at the same time relieve Jake of navigating duties.

'He's bound to. In fact I'd go as far as saying that I'm practically certain that he will,' granddad replied with a knowing look.

'How come you're so sure?' Jake asked, a bemused smile spreading across his face.

'Oh he'll come,' granddad reaffirmed. 'Anything to get out of that old people's home he's stuck in!'

Chapter 8

Lawrence

Lawrence Nabb leant over the images of Enkmann and Günter once again, his forehead creased with a frown of intense concentration. 'I'm sorry Walter, I just don't see it,' he said, his voice sounded heavily apologetic. 'There is a similarity as I've said before, but that's all it is, I couldn't be as certain as you seem to be.' Lawrence sat back in his chair, his mouth tracing a rueful smile beneath his neatly trimmed moustache.

'Oh come on Lawrence!' granddad's voice seemed scornful and frustrated and at odds with the peaceful atmosphere of the Bluebell Woods Retirement Home. Across the other side of the lounge area, a brightly lit room with large windows and floral wallpaper, Jake noticed a white-haired lady sit up from one of the many high-backed chairs and gaze about for the reason why her nap had been interrupted, an expression of deep disapproval etched on her face.

'Just look at his missing fingers!' granddad continued, oblivious to the old lady's scowl. 'It's Günter, no doubt about it!'

'How can you be so sure?' Lawrence's challenge hung in the air between the two old soldiers. 'This photo, what's his name? Enkmann? Well, just look at it! You've got to admit that it isn't all that detailed, the fingers are indistinct, yes they could be missing, but he's shaking hands with this

83

fat old Fräulein and it might be that it's just the way the photo turned out, a trick of the light, that makes it look as if there's something wrong with his hand.'

The pause that followed seemed to add more and more cold water to the already sizeable amount that Lawrence had poured on their discovery. Jake realised that what Lawrence was saying could not be denied. The Enkmann photo was a bit blurry and, now he looked afresh, Jake wondered if the resemblance between the old man and the Nazi officer was quite as close as he'd previously thought. Could it be that they had seen a similarity because that's what they wanted to see? Granddad had been looking out for news of Günter for most of his life, could his desire to track him down be clouding his judgement? Jake had desperately wanted granddad to be right about Enkmann for other reasons entirely. He'd been faced with the prospect of a dull summer and the photo had offered the tantalizing prospect of mystery, excitement and travelling across Europe. Granddad said nothing, his face set and unreadable. Was he going to admit that Lawrence was right? Was this the end of the Enkmann mystery? Were they going to come all this way only to troop dejectedly back up the motorway?

The alarm had gone off early that morning, its insistent, infuriating bleeping rousing Jake from a deep sleep. He and granddad appeared downstairs at approximately the same time. Both looked bleary-eyed and still half asleep. They had gone about getting breakfast in the near silence of the not-fully-awake, trudging to and fro across the kitchen for toast, butter, juice, tea and cutlery in a quiet dance. By the time the red Rover's engine coughed into life and they slowly pulled out of the drive, it was still only 7.15am.

On the journey down, Jake had asked granddad what Lawrence was like. Granddad had laughed to himself at the memories that the question had prompted. 'Lawrence was what we used to call a toff,' granddad explained. 'The war mixed everyone up together, we were from all sorts of different backgrounds and Lawrence had come from an old family that used to have a country estate somewhere. Anyway, he was the second son, so instead of inheriting the house and grounds, he got to make his own way in life and went into the forces. He was an officer, obviously. Back then people like me weren't judged to be officer material, you had to have gone to the right schools, or know the right people.

'Anyway, when I first met him, I thought he was going to be just another stuck up sort, keeping his distance from the commoners like us. But he couldn't have been more different. He didn't make any secret of his privileged background, but somehow it wasn't a barrier with him. He was the first officer I met who didn't stand for calling him "Sir" and saluting, not in the field anyway. When I first met him, he was lounging around on a haystack in a barn not far from St Gille. I'd just been taken there by the resistance after dropping in and he looked at me, just a spotty kid, saluting and telling him I was reporting for duty and he said to me, "Now then Hargreaves, the likelihood is that we're all going to die tomorrow, so let's have no more of this "Sir" nonsense and if you salute me again, you'll be on K.P. for a week!" That meant Kitchen Patrol, peeling spuds and washing up, that sort of thing. I was taken right aback I can tell you. He was posh alright, but he was one of us.

'Anyway, we got to know each other pretty well after St Gille. Lying up in a wood with someone for a few weeks does that you know. He could make me laugh though, oh yes! He could have me in stitches. Even when we were observing the camp from the forest and there were guards only a dozen yards away he would deliberately whisper something to get me helpless with laughter and stuffing my fist in my mouth to stop making any noise. He was one of the bravest men I've ever known, to the point where you'd think he was being reckless, but he was clever with it. Dead smart he was. Yes he took risks, but he always had a Plan B and that's why we all got through it alive.'

Granddad paused as the memories replayed themselves over again in his mind. 'What did he do after the war?' Jake asked.

'He stayed on for a few years, but the top brass didn't like the way he went about things. They thought that officers should be called "Sir" no matter what and they didn't like his relaxed manner with the men. Truth was that they were jealous, that's what I think anyway. We didn't have to call him "Sir" to know that he was in charge. There was no doubt in our minds at all who our leader was and we'd have followed him anywhere, but there were other officers who didn't have Lawrence's leadership skills. They relied on their rank and a lot of shouting to keep us mere mortals in our place. Eventually it all became a bit much for him and he resigned his commission. I remember him saying that peacetime soldiering was a lot harder than being at war. Anyway, he made a small fortune as a security consultant for oil companies in the Middle East and retired back to England.'

A sort of wistful smile passed over granddad's face. 'He offered me a job out there as a matter of fact, working with him to help him set up his business, but your granny was expecting at the time and I had to turn him down.' For a while there was silence in the car apart from the steady thrum of the tyres as they sped over the tarmac. 'I wonder if he's changed at all? We don't meet up much, but whenever we used to get together it was just like we'd never been apart and he can still make me laugh.'

The trip had been the first real test of Jake's navigating skills. Granddad had known how to get to the motorway and, once they were safely on the inside lane, all they had to do was follow it for about an hour, with Jake counting down the junction numbers until their turn off appeared. Jake had a road map of Great Britain and the directions that he'd downloaded from the Bluebell Woods website. He read the staged instructions out clearly until, with a wave of relief, the retirement home's pleasant, honey-coloured stone façade came into view.

The house was set back from the tree-lined lane. It was on a low rise in the landscape, at the end of a curving driveway, which bisected an immaculate lawn. Bluebell Woods was a squarely built, Edwardian manor house. The glossy, bright-red front door was flanked by two large bay windows. The three windows on the second storey were distributed evenly underneath a triangular sloping tiled roof. The symmetry of the building made Jake think that the house looked like a child's drawing and only needed a looping crayon-line of smoke coming from the chimney to complete the impression.

Granddad had followed the signs for visitors' parking that directed him down the side of the building, where they saw for the first time the modern addition to the old square house. The stone was the same colour, but that was the only similarity as a large, curved, sweep of glass fronted the reception area.

Having parked the car, Jake and granddad got out and stretched. Sitting in one place for over an hour made the muscles in Jake's legs and back feel like they'd been fused into immoveable lumps. He noticed that granddad was suffering more and was still trying to ease his joints as he walked slowly and stiffly towards the glass doors.

Jake thought that the reception area looked like what you would find in a posh hotel. A high, curved reception desk with a polished granite top flowed sensuously from the wall near the door. At one end was a large glass bowl containing green, shiny apples that looked too perfect to be edible and at the other, a tall vase containing a flower display which seemed to be made up of two exotic blooms and a few twisted bamboo sticks.

Behind it sat a lady talking into a telephone headset. She had a rather business-like manner, which was reflected in her appearance. Her pinstripe trouser suit, stylish rectangular glasses and crisp white blouse, set off her expertly applied make-up and pinned up hair. Granddad made his way to the desk, leaned on it and asked, 'Excuse me Miss, we're here to see...'

A neatly manicured hand was raised in an unmistakeable gesture that demanded silence. 'Yes, that's right Mrs Jacobs, your mother's room will be available from the 24th... that's right... yes, the 24th, that's right...' The look of complete confusion that crossed granddad's face made Jake want to snort with laughter. Clearly he hadn't seen the receptionist's small phone headset and could not understand why this lady appeared to be carrying out a conversation with herself. '...OK then Mrs Jacobs we'll see you then.' The receptionist continued in a brighter voice. 'Bye for now then... goodbye!' and she pressed a button that beeped to signal that the call was at an end.

'Sorry about that.' The receptionist's welcoming smile looked about as phoney as her apology had sounded.

'Errm... yes...' granddad stammered, still getting back up to speed. 'Umm... yes, we're here to see Lawrence Nabb?' The receptionist's eyes took them in coolly and Jake became acutely aware of his un-brushed hair, crumpled Vans T-shirt and grass-stained cargo shorts.

After a short pause, she appeared to come to the conclusion that they weren't a security risk and opened her mouth to reply. Just then, a cheerful cry came from behind them. 'Walter Hargreaves! You old dog! What on earth do you think you're doing with that young lady?'

Jake spun round to see who the speaker was, granddad turned as well, but he had to do it in more of a shuffling motion, his legs still stiff from the journey. Jake saw a tall, elegant man entering the reception room through some double doors with a purposeful stride. He looked a little older than granddad, but moved with the ease of a younger man.

He wore a pale pink polo shirt and beige, pleat-fronted trousers that somehow made him seem even taller. His gleaming brown brogues shone almost as brightly as his smile. His thinning, grey and black hair had been neatly cropped and, as he shook hands warmly with granddad, a musky waft of aftershave enveloped them.

'Lawrence!' Granddad returned the handshake and smile heartily. Jake could see clearly that there was a great deal of unspoken affection between the two men. 'You're looking very dapper! The nurse that dressed you this morning clearly has an eye for fashion.' Lawrence nodded with mock seriousness at granddad's jibe, a smile slowly curling at the corner of his mouth.

'Well she made a special effort when she knew you were coming Walter. She even made me wear a bib when she spoon fed me my breakfast, so that I wouldn't dribble bran flakes down my shirt.' Both men seemed to pause on the brink, enjoying the moment, before dissolving into genial, noisy laughter and renewed handshaking. The receptionist, who had been looking at her computer screen, glanced up with a rather disdainful look at the sound, before returning her cold stare back below the desktop once more.

'And this young man must be Jake!' Lawrence's voice was cultured and clipped. Jake thought that it sounded almost like someone doing a caricature of the way the way actors would speak in old black and white movies. Lawrence's smooth, tanned hand was extended and Jake was surprised at the firmness of the grip. Lawrence brought his other hand firmly down on top of the handshake with a clapping noise and Jake became aware that Lawrence was looking at him intently.

'Very, very pleased to meet you young man.' His eyes were a piercing blue and hinted at a lively mind behind them.

'Walter has spoken of you often. A cricket fan I seem to recall?' Under Lawrence's unblinking gaze, Jake suddenly felt on edge as if he were being examined.

He stammered a reply, 'Errm, yes... yes I am... into cricket that is.' Jake winced inwardly and cursed himself for sounding like a complete idiot. Lawrence's eyes crinkled at the edges as his face beamed Jake a warm smile.

'Not having any children of my own, I couldn't comment from direct experience, but when my nephew was your age we couldn't fill him up, hollow legs I'm sure. Breakfast must seem ages ago now, so what do you say we round up some drinks and a few cakes perhaps?'

Relieved to be given a reason to get out of the spotlight, Jake nodded in agreement. 'Yes please.'

Just then a voice from behind Jake seemed to cut across the conversation sharply. 'Now then Mr Nabb! You know very well that you aren't to have high fat and high sugar foods like cake. Remember what the nutritionist said about your cholesterol?'

The receptionist had reappeared over her desktop and was looking sternly over the top of her glasses at Lawrence as if he was been a naughty child. He switched his smile from Jake on to her and beamed genially. It was the same smile, but somehow Jake sensed that there was now an intense annoyance behind it, directed at this young woman who thought she could tell him what he could and couldn't do.

There was a dangerous pause as Lawrence continued to smile at the receptionist and then he spoke. 'Firstly my dear, if you had been eavesdropping effectively, you would have heard that I was merely offering cake to my guests and not suggesting that I was going to partake in the forbidden delights of cook's rich Dundee or moist carrot and ginger.' The receptionist looked taken aback at Lawrence's accusation of eavesdropping, 'but she really had been,' Jake thought.

'Secondly, I realise that you're still fairly new here and that you're trying to make a good impression, but you need to understand that it's not the blessed nutritionist who is paying you enough to afford your smart suits. So, if I choose to eat cake at breakfast, dinner and tea that's what I'll jolly well do and you and the nutritionist… can go hang!'

There was a long pause. The shocked receptionist seemed to be struggling for words. Clearly she wasn't used to being spoken to by the residents in this way. Lawrence's smile still beamed at her as if they were sharing some pleasant chitchat about the weather. She squirmed. Just as she was about to stammer a response, Lawrence's upper class voice cut across her. 'I'm so glad we've had a chance to set things straight,' he said sunnily, 'I do think that it will make things much more pleasant around here now you understand the way it works.' He turned, still smiling, to Jake and granddad. 'Shall we?' and he swept off through the double doors leaving an outraged-looking receptionist in his wake.

Jake and granddad followed Lawrence as he passed through a number of tastefully decorated rooms, Lawrence nodding and greeting various different people as he passed by. Jake noticed that Lawrence always stopped to talk to the ladies, whom he set laughing with a joke, or left agape in pretend shock at his outrageous flirting and teasing. Granddad didn't seem at all surprised and whispered to Jake, 'Nothing changes, he was always one for the ladies.'

'Now never mind that young upstart back there,' Lawrence said, referring to the scene in reception for the first time. 'I want to introduce you to the person who is really in charge!' He had paused in front of a door marked "Private. Kitchen Staff Only". He knocked sharply on it before pushing it open and calling out, 'Ruby my darling. Can I have a quick word with you my precious angel?' Granddad snorted and shook his head grinning.

A loud voice with a distinct West Indian accent called back, 'If dat's Mr Nabb at my door, there ain't nobody at home!' and a large, round, black lady appeared at the door wearing an apron over the top of a pale blue work clothes and the widest, whitest smile Jake had ever seen.

'Ruby!' Lawrence exclaimed. 'Really! Trying to get rid of me like that! And after all that we've come to mean to each other my sweet!' He took one of Ruby's pudgy hands and kissed it tenderly.

Ruby pulled her hand away and swatted gently towards Lawrence. 'I hear you talk like dat to all der ladies, all der time!'

'My dearest flower!' Lawrence returned, a look of enormous shock and hurt on his face. 'There has never been anyone else but you!'

Jake was certain that Ruby's laugh would register on the Richter scale as a small earthquake. After it had subsided, she dabbed at her eyes and said, 'What is it you want Mr Nabb?' with pretend annoyance. "I am a very busy person you know!'

'Please! My dear! I have just had a small altercation with the ice queen and am in a state of post traumatic stress!'

Ruby's smile disappeared and one eyebrow raised itself in disapproval. 'Oh, have you now? What's she been up to dis time?' Clearly there was no love lost between Ruby and the receptionist.

'Oh I just set her straight on who was actually in charge around here,' explained Lawrence.

'Oh yes?'

'Absolutely old girl! I told her straight! I said listen here you, you're just a glorified "Hello Girl". Ruby's in charge around here, I said, and the sooner you learn that, the better it will be all round! And then I said, here's 50p, go out and buy yourself a personality next time you're shopping for suits!'

Enormous gales of Ruby's laughter echoed up and down the corridors. She sagged helplessly onto Lawrence's shoulder, tears streaming down her round cheeks. Eventually, she subsided, dabbing again at her eyes, still juddering with silent giggles.

'So to celebrate our famous victory and in honour of my distinguished guests, I wondered if we could have some coffee and cakes?' Lawrence's appeal prompted nods from Ruby as she still was struggling to talk through her chuckles. 'I'll be at my usual table my darling.' More nods and Ruby turned and disappeared back into the kitchen, shoulders still shaking. 'Absolute diamond that one,' said Lawrence after the door closed behind her. Jake and granddad nodded in mute agreement.

A few minutes later, Ruby wheeled a trolley into the room where Lawrence, Jake and granddad were sitting. Jake was impatient to break the news about Enkmann, but granddad seemed determined to wait for the right moment and the conversation had been restricted to news of old comrades.

'No, I didn't hear about Kitson until a few weeks after his funeral,' Lawrence was saying. 'Otherwise I'd have certainly gone down to pay my respects. Ah! Ruby! Aren't you a sight for sore eyes!' Ruby met Lawrence's compliment with another raised eyebrow and a sceptical look, but Jake noticed that she couldn't quite mask her smile that spoke of a great fondness for the old man.

Granddad and Jake were properly introduced and they both received Ruby's crushing handshake and a most dazzling smile that was, without doubt, absolutely genuine. She then proceeded to unload the trolley. It seemed that Ruby's dislike of the receptionist had spurred her on to bring the biggest tray of cakes and home made biscuits that she possibly could. Jakes eyes grew wider and wider at the delicious goodies that appeared in front of him, along with a large pot of coffee and he realised that breakfast had been a long time ago. Just then, Ruby produced three more plates and set them down on the table. The smell of the bacon rolls was heavenly.

'Now just remember Mr Nabb,' Ruby said in a stern voice. 'This is only for your guests now, don't let me catch you tucking in, think of your cholesterol now!' Her fat finger wagged sternly, but Jake could see that she was struggling hard not to laugh again.

'Ruby, you are a precious gem beyond price! I could kiss you! In fact, I think I will!' and Lawrence rose to his feet and kissed her on both cheeks. 'Bless you my love!' he said theatrically, holding her hands in his.

This demonstration of affection seemed to make Ruby all flustered and she blushed and swiped gently at Lawrence, 'Ah, go on now!' and she wheeled her trolley away.

For a while, the three of them munched in silence, occasionally making "Mmm" noises to indicate how delicious the food was. At one point, Lawrence caught sight of the receptionist walking past and made sure he was holding up a large slice of chocolate cake. Jake thought that she had been looking at them out of the corner of her eye, but she passed on, walking purposefully as if she hadn't noticed. As she exited down the corridor, they all chortled.

'So Walter, what's all this about then? Why did you call me to tell me to pack my bags and dig out my passport?' The coffee pot had been drained, the tray of food looked like it had been ravaged and the three of them were sat back in their high-backed seats contentedly full. Jake's heart was pounding. Lawrence was about to come face to face with Günter once again.

'Well...' Granddad replied, reaching down for the dog-eared folder with the photos in it. 'You'll remember this chap won't you?' He slid the photo of Günter across the table.

Lawrence picked it up, his smile and warmth suddenly gone. 'Of course I do. You're not telling me that he's been found after all this time are you?'

Granddad fished around in the folder again, retrieved the picture of Enkmann passed it to Lawrence and said, 'Well, in a way I suppose he has.'

Lawrence stared at the two pictures and said nothing whilst granddad told them the story of how they'd come across the photo of Enkmann. Jake was becoming increasingly worried about what Lawrence's reaction was going to be. He'd expected an outburst of surprise or shock. He'd expected a similar reaction to granddad when he had spotted the likeness, but as granddad talked, Lawrence's frown deepened. Eventually granddad's explanation ended and there was silence.

'You mean to tell me Walter,' Lawrence said slowly, 'that you've come all this way just to show me this?'

The discussion that followed became quite heated at times, but neither side would budge. Granddad was convinced that Enkmann was really Günter and Lawrence could not be persuaded that the resemblance was anything other but a passing likeness. Lawrence had scoffed at their plans to drive to Rheinhagen. 'We're far too old to be doing that sort of dangerous nonsense,' and that had only riled granddad further.

After a pause in the debate, which was clearly going round in circles, granddad had said, 'Lawrence, you know how much I respect you, but I believe that there's something in this.' His index finger tapped the photo of Enkmann rhythmically. 'And I'd hoped that you would remember the promise we made to each other about Günter all those years ago and want to see it through.' This accusation from his old friend stung Lawrence and he looked hurt. 'Now you may be right and we may be barking up the wrong tree completely,' Granddad continued, 'but I haven't got so comfortable with my surroundings as to forget what Günter did.'

Granddad's hand swept around indicating the plush furnishings and tasteful décor of Bluebell Woods. For a mad second, Jake thought Lawrence was going to hit granddad. A barely contained rage made his usually strong voice tremble slightly. 'I think Walter, if that's what you believe, I think that this conversation is at an end.'

All the laughter, banter and the bonhomie had disappeared. Jake wondered if the two old friends would ever speak to each other again as the silence between them stretched. He could understand granddad's frustration, but even now, glancing at the photos as they were being put away back into the folder, Jake found that a small seed of doubt had been placed in his mind.

Lawrence walked them back out towards the entrance. The conversation was the same sort of small talk they'd shared before, but things had changed between the two men now and it seemed somehow forced and uncomfortable.

Once back in reception, granddad headed for the toilets, leaving Jake and Lawrence standing in an awkward silence. Behind her desk, the receptionist kept her head firmly down over her computer screen and pointedly ignored them. 'I'm relying on you to look after the old goat.' Lawrence's voice carried the same conviction that Jake could see in his intense gaze. 'I know Walter of old and he's always been the type to see things through no matter what, but this trip of his, I think he might be biting off more than he can chew.'

Jake nodded, not because he agreed with him, but because he wanted to show Lawrence that he understood. Jake was feeling sorry for him. Granddad had practically called him lazy, spoilt and unadventurous for not coming along and Jake wanted to say something to make things better between the two men, but he didn't know where to begin.

Just then granddad returned. In the two short minutes that he'd been away, both of them seemed to have decided independently to ignore what had just happened and pretend that everything was fine again. 'Well, send me a postcard when you get there Walter!'

'Of course Lawrence! We'll be in touch to keep you informed don't worry.'

A thought creased Lawrence's forehead. 'I've just been thinking. I wonder if I can still be of some service to you Walter.' Jake's heart leaped, had he changed his mind? Was he coming along after all? 'I don't agree with your intention of not telling the boy's parents, but perhaps I could be some sort of liaison between you and Louise and your John if something happens whilst you're over there.' Jake's heart gave up leaping and went back to sinking. 'If you give me your parents' contact number Jake, you can call me if there's a problem and I'll pass the message to your mum and dad. They'll probably take the news of what you've been getting up to a little more calmly if they hear it from me rather than if you call them direct. I would be a sort of communications post.'

Granddad considered Lawrence's proposal and nodded in approval. 'Right you are Lawrence. Jake have you got your dad's mobile number?'

As it turned out, Jake had both his dad's number and the contact number at Aunty June's old house already entered into his mobile. After a bit of button pushing, Jake wrote down the numbers on a piece of notepaper that was lying on the top of the reception desk.

'And that's my number.' Lawrence picked up a Bluebell Woods business card from a neat pile next to the bowl of apples. Jake put it into his pocket.

'Well then Walter! All I can say is best of luck old chap and I look forward to hearing of your successful mission when you get back to Blighty!' Lawrence's tone was warm again and his handshake spoke of his genuine goodwill.

Granddad returned the handshake with his natural smile back in place. 'We'll be seeing you Lawrence!' and he turned and headed towards the door to the car park.

'Jake!' Lawrence's voice made Jake turn quickly. 'Something for the trip back young man!' And he picked up one of the shiny, green apples in the bowl on reception and threw to Jake who caught it cleanly.

"Howzat!' Lawrence cried and a broad grin spread across his face. Jake grinned back and waved a hand in farewell. As he turned again to go, he could have sworn he heard the receptionist tut softly to herself at the way Lawrence had spoilt her display.

The Rover pulled slowly out of the car park and headed back towards the road. Jake looked back one last time at the glass entrance to Bluebell Woods. Lawrence was stood in reception, a lonely looking figure of an old man. Was it Jake's imagination? Or was there a sorrowful look etched on Lawrence's face? He had his hand raised in a forlorn farewell, Jake waved back, then they rounded the corner and he was gone.

Chapter 9

Abroad

By the time they pulled back into Jake's driveway it was late afternoon. Jake's confidence in his ability as a map-reader had been dented when they had got lost shortly after leaving Bluebell Woods. The problem being that the sheet of directions that Jake had been following to get them there, were no use when trying to do the reverse route and get back to the motorway. After a short detour around a scruffy-looking industrial estate and pulling into a bus stop to check the map, they managed to find their way.

Granddad hadn't said much, but clearly Lawrence's decision not to come along had put a dampener on the whole idea. Jake had hoped that he would have been enthusiastic about their mission and jumped at the chance to unmask their old acquaintance. Jake admitted to himself that Lawrence's doubts had made him wonder if he should try to persuade granddad to think of a different plan, one that didn't include hundreds of miles of driving.

Jake had to admit that granddad was not a bad driver. However, he did get a little frustrated about how slowly granddad did things, even changing gear and indicating was done in a very deliberate, thoughtful manner without the instinctive, fluid driving of his dad that Jake was used to. However, it was clear that granddad wasn't used to driving long distances. On the journey back he had started shaking his head and blinking, as if he was straining to see something, his eyes watering behind his glasses. This happened more and more until he said, 'It's no use Jakey, I'm nodding off here, I'm going to have to pull off at the next services just to close my eyes for a while.'

Five minutes later, a sign for a service station came into view and they signalled, peeled off the motorway, drove down the slip road and into the car park. Granddad drove slowly past the bright red signs that flanked the glass entrance to the services, having to stop from time to time to let people cross to and from their cars. It was quieter on the far side of the car park, where there was a field with picnic tables dotted around. A large lady dressed in pink T-shirt and trousers was trying to persuade her overweight West Highland Terrier to have a drink of water from a bowl decorated with pink bones and the word "Dog" in bulging, cartoon lettering.

Parked overlooking the field, was an ageing Volkswagen camper van with a retired couple inside it, who were boiling a kettle for a cup of tea. Granddad parked two spaces away and switched off the engine. The sudden quiet made Jake realise how noisy the car had been, a buzzing continued in his ears as if it were still running. In the camper van, the kettle started to whistle with increasing volume as it came to the boil, only for the noise to fade rapidly away as if it had lost all enthusiasm when the gas was turned off.

Granddad sat back in his seat, shuffling around trying to get comfortable. He reached across to the back seat and retrieved his jacket. He took his wallet out of the inside pocket and pulled out a five pound note. 'Right then Jake, I need to rest my eyes for a bit, so take this and find something to do for half an hour or so. Then, come and wake me up and we'll get going again.'

Jake thanked granddad for the fiver, opened the door, got out and stretched his cramped muscles. 'See you in a bit then,' he called out behind him, before closing the car door with a clunk. Jake loved motorway service stations and a slow grin spread over his face as he walked across the oil-stained tarmac. The different people who called into these places had always fascinated him. There were families in holiday clothes, mums and dads trying to keep their young children from running off to the racing car amusement ride that would cost them 50p for two minutes of rocking gently backwards and forwards. Older children seemed to trail reluctantly after their parents looking bored, texting constantly or nodding silently along with their MP3 players. An overweight businessman wearing sweat-stained shirt with the sleeves rolled up and talking on his mobile phone, sipped gingerly on his hot take-out coffee. A van driver in a delivery company's uniform appeared as the automatic glass doors of the entrance swished open. He cracked open a can of coke with a sharp hiss and click whilst holding a large chocolate bar and a bag of crisps underneath his arm. Wherever he looked, he saw people on their way to, or from somewhere. It felt like anything could happen, or anybody could appear at any moment.

Passing through the entrance, Jake paused to look around the tiled interior. A delicious savoury smell from the burger bar opposite wafted over him. Had it not been for the fact that Jake was still feeling full after all the food he'd eaten at Bluebell Woods, he would have joined the queue straight away. As it was, Jake was determined to savour the moment. He had money in his pocket and half an hour to spend mooching around doing whatever he liked. After wandering up and down the aisles of the shop, looking at the overpriced CDs and books, Jake walked over to the coffee shop where there were some comfortable-looking brown leather sofas. Jake ordered a hot chocolate from the youth behind the counter. He didn't look that much older than Jake was and seemed determined to convey an expression of being cool. However, the spotty young man's efforts merely gave Jake the impression that he was indescribably bored.

Sitting on the leather sofa which was so soft it threatened to engulf him, Jake sipped his hot chocolate. It was delicious. Creamy, foamy and sweet with the slightest bitter aftertaste of cacao. He watched the people pass by and allowed himself to relax and start to feel excited about the trip once more. So what if Lawrence didn't want to come along? They'd be fine without him. They would just take their time driving over there. Jake eased back into the sofa, a sense of tingling giddiness at the prospect. Granddad could have regular snoozes on the way and Jake could hang out at the coffee bar. Motorway service stations abroad must be ten times more exciting than the ones at home Jake thought.

The sound of Jake opening the door and getting into the car woke granddad with a start. He blinked dumbly at Jake and stared around as if he was trying to figure out where he was. 'Alright Jakey boy?' He peered at his watch over the top of his glasses. 'I must have gone straight off there,' he said stretching. It took granddad another twenty minutes to wake up enough to continue their journey, long enough to make Jake wonder just how long he was going to take them to get to Rheinhagen.

Back home, as the clattering of the engine died and the familiar sounds of Clayfields Avenue surrounded them once more, granddad turned to Jake. 'I need to get one or two things from home Jake. You need to start packing your bags and find your passport.'

'So we're still definitely going then?' Jake asked, half of him still thinking of what Lawrence had said about dangerous nonsense.

Granddad smiled wearily. 'You don't have to worry Jake, it's just a little road trip we're going on. Yes, I would have liked Lawrence to come along as well, but if he feels that he's too old for this sort of adventure it's his choice. Now, get your stuff together and I'll be back for tea at six-ish.'

The house seemed strangely quiet, as if it had been deserted, as if it somehow knew that there would be no one home for the next few days. Jake stood in the kitchen for a full minute trying to think of what to do first, the echo of the Rover's engine still whooshing in his ears even though granddad had driven off some minutes previously. Finally, Jake's blank stare rested on the kitchen notepad and this sparked a thought that gradually rebooted his brain. The notepad was where his mum wrote down her lists and with any luck... Jake picked up the A4 pad. On the front sheet was Jake's list of things to do whilst they were away. Jake barked a short laugh at the neat rows of tasks which were now never going to be done.

He flicked over the sheet on the back of the pad to find the list she had worked through for her trip to Auntie June's and behind that was a sheet with a few scrawled telephone numbers and a message for his dad about a neighbourhood watch meeting. He turned over the next sheet: Bingo! In his mum's neat handwriting the title read "France Holiday Checklist" and beneath there was row after row of items of things to remember. Jake breathed a sigh of relief and said a silent thank you for his mum's organisational skills. The business of going abroad had been preying on Jake's mind. He'd never had to actually organise a trip before, what if he forgot anything important? But, now he had his mum's list, all he had to do was follow it and everything would be OK. She never forgot anything and he laughed to read: "Number seventeen. Check Jake packs his toothbrush". He had everything he needed now and so he made a start.

Two hours later, just as Jake was ticking off the item "Leave note for milkman", the phone rang. Jake's mum's voice crackled, 'Hello Jake darling! What have you been up to?' For a second or two, Jake didn't know what to say. Granddad said that they shouldn't lie about their plans and be clever about what they said. Unfortunately, Jake had been taken off guard and didn't feel very clever at all just at that moment. His mouth worked, but no words were forthcoming. 'Are you alright Jake?' His mum's voice was concerned. Bad move. If she gets worried, she asks questions. Jake knew this from years of dodging questions about his schoolwork.

'Hello?' Jake called down the line as if he couldn't hear the caller on the other end. 'Hello?'

'Hello Jake? Can you hear me love?'

Now he'd had a second or two to think, Jake was more confident 'Oh. Hi Mum! I couldn't hear you there for a sec.'

'I know love, we're at June's old house and the phone's been disconnected, so I'm on your dad's works mobile. So what's been going on there then?'

'Oh, not much really, we went to see an old friend of granddad's. You know the kind of thing, swapping war stories and stuff.'

His mum couldn't keep the surprise out of her voice, 'Oh! That doesn't sound like much fun for you.'

Jake chuckled. 'No, it was cool actually. We got fed and everything.'

'Oh... right then... that was nice of them. What else have you got planned?'

'Oh we're kind of just seeing what each day brings.' Jake tried to keep things deliberately vague. 'We're off to the coast tomorrow,' Jake said. 'I'm not actually lying,' he told himself.

'The coast?' his mum asked. 'Which part?'

In the kitchen Jake squirmed and pulled a face. 'Not quite sure whereabouts it is, granddad's got all the details.' Not quite the truth, not quite a lie. There was silence on the other end of the line.

Then, 'Oh well, you'll be able to tell me all about it tomorrow I suppose.' His mum had that tone again. The one that sounded like she knew that she wasn't being told everything and Jake prayed that she wouldn't want to get to the bottom of it just now. He could almost picture her, her forehead creased with concern.

'Yeah, will do. Speak to you then.' Jake hoped that the goodbye in his voice didn't sound too much like he was trying to get rid of her.

'I'll have a quick word with granddad before I go.' Jake swore inwardly and instinctively looked around the kitchen despite knowing granddad wasn't there.

'He's not around at the moment, he... realised he'd left something back at his place and went back to get it.'

'Oh... what was it he left?'

'Not more questions please!' Jake thought. 'I dunno, he didn't say.' A tense silence fell between them. Then Jake had an idea. 'I could ask him to call you once he gets back if you'd like?' He knew his mum was a bit obsessive about keeping the phone bill down and calls to a mobile could be quite pricey.

'No, that's alright Jake, I just wanted a quick chat, it can wait.' Jake sagged with relief. 'I'll speak to you again tomorrow then Jake, take care darling. Bye.'

A short while later Jake heard granddad's car pull into the drive. Granddad looked rather dishevelled with dust on the knees of his trousers and a grubby cobweb stuck on his shoulder. 'Where on earth have you been?' Jake asked, picking the cobweb off his shirt with a look of extreme distaste.

'Never mind that Jakey boy,' granddad said, tapping the side of his nose to indicate that it was a secret.

Jake was intrigued and was also a little taken aback that he was keeping things from him. 'After all, we are in this together!' he thought to himself.

Granddad must have picked up on Jake's shock because he quickly added, 'It's nothing really! Just getting a plan B in place, that's all!' The pause that followed indicated to Jake that granddad wasn't going to talk about it, so Jake changed the subject and told him about the call from his mum.

'Going to the coast! I like that. Good lad!' granddad had said. 'And by the time she calls tomorrow, we'll be well on our way to the ferry terminal! Now let's see what's in the freezer for tea tonight!'

Halfway through the following day Jake realised just how useful his mum's list was. There seemed to be such a lot to sort out and they had a deadline to meet, or risk missing their ferry. 'Don't pack too much stuff Jake,' granddad had said. 'We're only going to be away for five or six days, so let's try to travel light.' Jake had selected a large sports bag and stuffed everything he needed into it until it bulged dangerously and the zip had to be forced to close. By lunchtime, most of the items on the list had been scrawled through by Jake's green felt tip pen to indicate that they had been completed.

'If your bags are ready to go you might as well put them in the boot and then it's done,' granddad instructed Jake as they munched ham sandwiches on the bench in the garden. The day had started with a misty dawn, the lawn heavy with dew. The mist had been quickly banished by the sun and by breakfast, the sky was an unbroken blue. Jake had seen the dawn because he had woken very early, worrying that he would forget to pack something vital. The prospect of navigating all the way to Germany and granddad's ability to drive safely all that way resurfaced, as Jake's wide-awake brain imagined all the bad things that could happen to them. It seemed that he'd been awake for hours when he finally drifted off to sleep again, only to have his alarm bleep noisily to let him know it was time to get up.

Wearily, Jake stretched and tilted his head back, until the midday sunshine was falling squarely on to his face. His eyes were shut, but he could see the reddish glow of the sunlight on his eyelids. He felt tired, his lack of sleep catching up with him. With an effort he rose from the bench, stretched again and went back inside the cool dark of the house, retinal images blooming and dancing in front of his eyes.

Jake heaved his bag on to his shoulder and lugged it downstairs and out to the car. He fumbled with the key, fitted it into the boot's keyhole and turned it. He had expected it to be mostly empty, but instead, at the back, there was a large green canvas bag. It was so large that it barely fitted across the width of the boot and was tied up with a drawstring in a complicated-looking knot at one end. Jake called out over his shoulder to granddad, who was still munching thoughtfully on his sandwich. 'What's in this big old bag Granddad?'

Granddad took a few seconds to finish his mouthful and then said, 'That's plan B, Jakey boy, just leave it alone.' His voice sounded serious and his dark lenses were clipped back in place, so Jake couldn't tell if he was being teased or not. He decided that if granddad was waiting for Jake to ask more questions, he'd disappoint him, so he dropped his bag in the boot and shut it with a clunk.

All too soon the time for leaving was upon them. Jake checked through the list for the tenth time, but it didn't stop the nagging doubt that they hadn't got everything. Granddad also appeared to be tense and had been fussing around under the bonnet of the Rover, checking oil and water levels. He wiped his hands on a length of paper towel and closed the bonnet before fishing out a zipped up plastic folder from the passenger-side foot well. He held it up to Jake and said, 'You might want to put your passport in with mine so we've got everything we need in one place.'

107

An enormous sinking sensation lurched through Jake's insides. His passport! Why had he not thought of his passport before! It wasn't on the list! It can't have been! He yanked the crumpled paper out of his jeans. 'What's wrong Jake?' Granddad's concerned voice seemed to come from a long way off as Jake scanned down the list again. The word now leaped out at him "3 – Tickets and Passports". There it was! With a renewed sickening lurch, he realised that he'd only read the word "tickets" and thought that he would be safe crossing it off because granddad was looking after them.

'Passport!' Jake blurted out and he turned and ran back inside taking the stairs three at a time. Where would his mum keep his passport? 'Come on!' Jake implored himself as images of getting to the port only in time to see the ferry disappearing over the horizon.

They must be in the study somewhere! Jake dashed into the small, cluttered room. A desk in the corner held an overflowing in-tray, a monitor for his dad's computer, numerous pieces of opened and unopened mail and a basket of washing that had been mentioned on his list of things to do, but which Jake still had not folded neatly and put away. Where would they keep the passports? Jake spotted the filing cabinet on the floor beneath the desk and wrenched the top draw open in a frenzy, his eyes scanning the labels on each section.

'Home insurance. Car Insurance. Receipts and Guarantees,' Jake read. 'COME ON!' he shouted in frustration. Surely this whole adventure wasn't going to flounder before it had even begun, just because he couldn't find a bit of paper! Granddad called upstairs, Jake heard him, but paid him no attention. Having read all the labels in the top drawer, Jake slammed it shut and pulled open the drawer below. He saw it immediately. "Passports and Travel Documents". He snatched the file from its cradle and opened it. It was empty.

For a while Jake just stared at it, trying to think, trying to take it in. His passport wasn't there. It wasn't there! He couldn't go abroad if he didn't have his passport! All this planning and work to get ready was going to count for nothing! Gradually a realisation emerged from the fog of his panic. 'Hang on,' he spoke his thought out loud as if to try to explain it to himself. 'Nobody's passport is here, not mine or mum's or dad's. So where the heck are they?' From what seemed like a long way off, granddad could be heard coming up the stairs. Another idea reluctantly shuffled into Jake's consciousness. 'Mum had already packed a load of things to go to France, what if she'd packed the passports?' Jake shot back across the landing in a blur just as granddad reached the top step.

Jake's parents' bedroom had two wardrobes with double doors. He rarely came inside his parents' cream coloured room and since his childhood days of trying to find Christmas and birthday presents was behind him, he never had any reason to look inside their wardrobes, but he simply couldn't think where else his passport could be. Some weeks earlier, his mum had returned from a shopping trip looking very pleased with herself. She had shown Jake her new travel bag she'd bought for their holiday. 'It's got lots of security features so I can feel safe keeping the money and tickets and passports in it.' Passports! Jake was banking on his mum's liking for being well prepared. The first wardrobe he opened was clearly his dad's. Several suits and shirts hung neatly in rows and a rather complicated-looking rack held a colourful selection of ties.

Jake slammed the doors shut and moved to the other wardrobe. Granddad was speaking again, but Jake wasn't listening. This was more promising! Blouses and skirts and jackets were all hung in what seemed to be a regimented order. Jake looked wildly around for the bag. He remembered that it was navy blue, but he couldn't recall much more about it as he hadn't really been all that interested at the time. The bottom of the wardrobe was stacked with shoe boxes and a few handbags, but not the one he was looking for. Where could it be? Where? Despair was just about to take hold, when Jake spotted a wide nylon strap hanging over the edge of a shelf above the rails.

Jake tried to keep calm, as he reached up and pulled on the strap. The blue travel bag flopped off the shelf and into his gratefully waiting arms. It felt heavy. He opened the chunky zipper and reached in. Oh the relief! As he took the three red passports out of the bag, Jake let out a huge exhalation and threw a triumphant, yet slightly sheepish look at granddad. 'Shall we go then?' Jake enquired calmly, as if nothing had been amiss at all, as if they had all the time in the world, as if the adrenaline thundering round Jake's veins wasn't making him want to whoop with relieved delight.

The journey to the ferry port turned out to be straightforward. The motorway was quiet and they made good time. Jake had been concerned about getting them hopelessly lost with the time of departure rapidly approaching. However, the ferry port had been signed clearly, miles before their last junction and it was easy enough to just keep following them.

The town around the ferry port seemed to be nothing but a collection of scruffy industrial units surrounded by tall stacks of shipping containers. Heavily laden motorbikes and cars with families in, the windows blocked by all their luggage, manoeuvred around lines of huge articulated trucks which rumbled around the oil-stained tarmac of the numerous roundabouts. Cranes reared up behind the unhealthy-looking trees that lined the road, their rusting structure looking like enormous skeletal dinosaurs. Suddenly the sign for "Passenger Ferries – Embarkations" appeared and they turned right at the next roundabout. They swept past some office buildings and suddenly there was the ferry, a vast slab of white and navy blue. Jake hadn't really known what to expect, but he couldn't believe how big it was. It seemed like a cruise liner, except for the lines of cars and motorbikes that were slowly filing up a causeway leading through a door in its side.

'Wow!' was all that Jake could manage to say. Granddad chuckled at Jake's obvious excitement and slowed the car. There was a queue ahead where a lady in a glass booth was checking tickets. When they eventually rolled up to the booth, the lady smiled at Jake as she waited for some documents to print off. She handed them a couple of small pieces of card that had a dark magnetic strip down the back like a credit card.

'These are your room keys. You are in cabin 534. Hang this on your rear view mirror, follow the yellow line and the staff at the top of the ramp will direct you. Have a good journey.' She handed granddad a purple card with a hook shape on the top of it like a "Do Not Disturb" sign that you get in hotels. Granddad hooked it over the rear-view mirror and headed off towards the ship.

Once at the top of the ramp, a cross-looking man in an overall and a grubby day-glo high visibility vest waved them impatiently down a lane beside a row of caravans. Another man in a day-glo vest at the bottom of the lane gestured them forward with his walkie-talkie until they were parked snugly up against the car in front. He made a cutting motion with his hand to indicate they should switch off the engine and they were on board.

Having made their way up several flights of stairs they emerged opposite a brightly lit shop selling perfume. Lots of people were walking past. Some, like them, were trying to find their cabins, some already exploring. A young boy ran through the crowds shouting, 'Dave! DAVE! There's a sweet shop along here! Come and have a look!'

'Let's take stock Jakey boy,' granddad said consulting a colour-coded map of the different levels of the ship. 'Now then, where's cabin 534?'

A smartly uniformed young man, in white shirt and a blazer sporting the ferry companies logo on the pocket, looked round. '534 sir?' He pointed at the purple level on the map with the bendy aerial on his walkie-talkie. 'Just one level up from here, turn left and through the piano bar sir.' Granddad thanked the young officer and they set off up the stairs again.

Jake couldn't help but be a little disappointed at the cabin. He'd been expecting a round porthole, so they could look out on the green-grey waves as they crossed and wake to see the coast of Holland sliding past outside. However, there were no windows of any sort. 'These internal cabins were much better value,' granddad had explained. Jake looked around. Down one side of the room there was a bed which looked rather functional and Jake didn't think that it would be very comfy at all. Opposite, there was a sofa that obviously converted into the other bed. There was no TV, and the bathroom and shower was a tiny room which looked more like a cupboard.

'Well Jakey boy, we're on our way!' granddad said cheerfully as he dropped his bag on the floor and stretched out on the sofa. 'Go have a look around if you like, I'm just going to have forty winks.' Jake didn't need asking twice. He couldn't wait to explore. He took one of the key-cards, retrieved his wallet stuffed with euros and the spare money that his mum had left for emergencies and set off.

For a while, Jake just wandered around soaking in the sights and sounds. He gazed at the shops selling designer goods and was thick with the heady fragrance of expensive perfume. He wandered through the bar area where a group of leather-clad bikers had congregated, laughing and sipping on tall glasses of lager. The savoury aroma coming from the restaurant made Jake realise that he was hungry, but he was too excited to sit at a dining table just yet, so he made his way to the back of the ship where the map had indicated that there was a viewing deck. Feeling very grown up, Jake ordered a large coke and a packet of crisps at the bar and made his way through the glass doors out to the white rail where people were gathering to see the ship go to sea.

Finding a space at the rail, Jake sipped his coke and revelled in the feeling that this adventure had really begun. The ship trembled as if it were alive. He realised that he was smiling broadly to himself. 'People will think I'm a nutter!' he thought, which made him smile all the more.

The sun was starting to go down, turning the wispy high clouds a delicate pink. On the viewing deck, Jake recalled another spectacular sunset only a few days before when the summer was promising to be dull and boring and he had been full of anger. What a difference a chance discovery and few days had made! He munched his crisps and let his gaze roam over the activity on the dock. Thick ropes were unhooked from the dockside and were hauled, dripping on to the deck far below. Shouts and waves between the crew. A man in a hard hat and oil-stained orange overalls talked loudly into his walkie-talkie and the sea at the back of the ship roiled and hissed. They were on their way.

Gradually the crowds at the rail thinned as the ferry port retreated. The sun was almost down now and the wind had increased and cooled. Jake still remained at the rail, gazing back through the increasing gloom at the twinkling lights of the port in the distance. 'Thought I might find you here.' Jake turned to see granddad leaning up against the rail next to him with a wide smile across his face. Jake realised that granddad was as excited as he was. He grinned back and they both burst into laughter. They stood in silence for a while after the laughter faded, looking back along the fizzing, churning wake of the ship. Looking at the thin smudge that was the English coast. 'Well Jakey boy, we're off!' granddad said, still staring back to where they'd come from. Then he shivered and turned to Jake. 'Come on, I'm getting cold here. Let's go and see what's for dinner!'

Chapter 10

A Long Day

'BING BING BONG BONG!' The speaker in the ceiling of their darkened cabin had suddenly crackled into life and, as the musical chimes faded, a cultured lady's voice brought them to full wakefulness.

'Good morning Ladies and Gentlemen, the time now is six thirty.' Granddad groaned from beneath his quilt on the other side of the cabin. 'The Wavetop Buffet will be opening in fifteen minutes to serve you breakfast. Please ensure that you are assembled in your designated assembly points at nine o'clock ready to disembark. Coach parties should assemble in the Starlight Piano Bar...'

Jake turned over in bed and tried to block out the intrusive noise, but once the announcement had finished in English, the voice repeated it in Dutch, German and French, ensuring that the prospect of dropping back off to sleep was impossible.

By chance, they breakfasted at the same table that they'd used the previous evening at dinner. However, instead of looking out onto slate-grey waves as the darkness descended, a landscape of docks, cranes, ships and dirty, rusting warehouses glided slowly past their window. Granddad clucked and tutted at the cost of the food as he had done the previous evening, but told Jake to get a good meal as they had a long journey in front of them.

More announcements from the well-spoken, multi-lingual lady would periodically bing and bong, disturbing the still-drowsy diners who were shuffling around holding trays of food and trying to locate tables. As the time came to disembark, the announcements became more insistent that passengers should wake up, pack their stuff and get ready to leave the ship.

Jake and granddad were sat on a sofa near their assembly point in good time. The ferry had docked now and the industrial backdrop outside the window was stationary. The group of people which had gathered at the same point now seemed somehow impatient to be away. Stressed-looking dads scanned road maps. Mums tried to persuade their over-excited kids that they should not be running around. The group of bikers sprawled around in a group, either lying back with their eyes closed, or talking quietly about the amount of beer they had consumed the previous night, massaging their temples and exchanging rueful smiles.

When the announcement came for their deck to disembark, everyone headed down the stairs, shuffling in a single crowd, to emerge on the darkly exciting, diesel-smelling car deck. Sat back in the familiar surroundings of the Rover, Jake opened the atlas at the page he'd marked the day before. There was a sheet of lined notepaper with names of the roads and junction numbers along their route. He exhaled, feeling the tension all around as people wove their way through the parked cars to find their own. Suddenly the huge, steel doors up ahead swung open and daylight streamed into the car deck, making Jake blink and screw his eyes up. After a minute or two where nothing seemed to be happening, the row of traffic next to them started their engines and began to move off. Men in orange overalls gestured impatiently to get the cars moving. Soon that line had emptied and Jake waited for their line to be beckoned forward, but with a roar that echoed around the car deck, all the motorbikes rolled past them and headed out into the sunlight. Suddenly Jake was aware that engines were starting up all around them. Granddad followed suit and soon the cars in front set off.

A thrill ran through Jake as he got his first proper look at a foreign country. Amid the industrial and office buildings Jake could see that they were heading down a ramp towards another queue of traffic. The hold up was caused by a number of booths where cars were stopping to hand over documents. 'Passport control,' granddad said and Jake fumbled beneath his seat to retrieve the folder that contained theirs.

The pistol attached to the belt of the policeman standing outside the booths fascinated Jake. He'd never seen an armed policeman before and this one looked like an extra in a cop movie. They showed their passports to the unsmiling man in the booth, he checked the photos inside disinterestedly, handed them back and waved them through. Granddad found first gear after a crunch and they set off.

St Gille was a four and a half hour drive from the ferry terminal. Six hours after they had set off, sitting in yet another roadside café, Jake calculated that they still had a couple of hours to go. They had done well initially. Driving on the right seemed very weird at first, but they had found their way to the motorway without mishap, despite Jake panicking that they were on the wrong road on a couple of occasions. Driver and navigator concentrated quietly on their own responsibilities and conversation was short and businesslike.

They crossed into Belgium surprisingly quickly, but then the stops had begun. The first stop was midmorning for coffee. Their lunch break happened at twelve after they had crossed into France (granddad had a snooze afterwards). He had to have another quick nap about an hour after that, and now they were stopping for the second time in one afternoon with well over a hundred miles still to go. Granddad was becoming fatigued more quickly as the day wore on. He had told Jake that he hadn't slept much on the ferry, but Jake remembered hearing his snoring above the juddering of the engine long before he had dropped off to sleep.

After visiting so many motorway service stations, Jake was starting to wonder what it was that he had ever liked about them. Yes, the different food in the shops had been a novelty at first and listening to granddad speaking French at the checkout had sounded funny and made Jake chuckle, but now the journey seemed to be going on forever. The roadside café in which he was now sitting, was a rather small, shabby looking affair. Jake was seated on a bar stool at a narrow table that ran down the side of the large window overlooking the car park. The sun came out again from behind one of the many fluffy white clouds which were dotted across the sky. He could see the boot of the Rover sticking out at the end of a line of parked cars. Inside it, granddad would be asleep again. Jake was getting more and more frustrated at just how long this journey was taking. 'If only he'd drive a bit faster!' Jake thought, but it was always the same. Get onto the motorway, get up to about 50 miles an hour and just pootle along in the slow lane with the trucks and caravans. Jake itched to fly along at 70 or 80 like some of the cars which had flashed past them. 'We would have been at St Gille ages ago if he'd just get his foot down!'

Jake had been watching granddad's driving technique and, although he himself had never driven anything more than a motorised go-kart at the seaside, he was pretty confident that he could drive much more smoothly, more confidently and certainly far quicker than granddad's measured methodical, doddery driving style.

A girl's voice, talking in English made Jake sit up and take notice. He realised that he hadn't seen or heard another British person since the ferry that morning. 'I can't see any knives and forks Dad.' The voice whined and a young girl with a blonde ponytail sprouting out from under a sunhat came around the corner, flip flops slapping the cool, tiled floor. A rather podgy man followed her, concentrating hard on not spilling the food and drink that he carried on a tray.

'They must be here somewhere, the bloke at the checkout said they were.'

'Cutlery's behind you,' Jake pointed out.

'Oh!' The man seemed surprised to hear another English voice. 'Thanks son.' As the little girl went off to pick up what they needed, the man stood with his tray, the plates steaming. 'Going far?' he asked.

'A place called St Gille and then we're going to Germany,' Jake replied. The man nodded, as if that was what he'd suspected, but Jake was sure that the man had never heard of St Gille.

'We're heading to Switzerland eventually,' the man explained. 'It's my first time driving abroad, quite an experience! Funny how few British people you come across once you're on the road isn't it?' He looked down at the girl who had returned with handfuls of silver cutlery. 'Have you got them Abby? Well done. Best of luck then son, hope you have a good holiday!'

Jake realised that what the man had said was true, he'd not heard anybody talking English at any of the places they'd stopped before now. The realisation made Jake feel isolated and alone. He checked his watch. Granddad's twenty minutes was up and it always took him at least another ten to come round fully after a nap. Jake drained his can of coke, dismounted the barstool and headed back to the car to wake granddad up.

One hour and fifty-five minutes later, they saw the first sign that mentioned St Gille and fifteen minutes after that, they were taking the turn off the motorway on to a wide, straight, tree lined road that led off across a flat landscape into the distance. The afternoon sun flashed rhythmically as they passed under the shadows of the trees on their left, causing them to hold a hand up to shield their eyes.

The French countryside rolled past them. Jake hadn't really seen too much of the passing landscape from the motorway. It seemed to offer tantalising glimpses when they were not travelling between embankments, or when the road was not bordered by a seemingly endless forest. The fields and farms in the afternoon sunshine looked like something off a tourism brochure or a calendar. Every farm looked quaintly dishevelled and suitably rustic. Jake noticed that each farm was made up of a hotchpotch of different buildings of varying ages, each had signs for local bars or hotels painted on their barn walls and each seemed to have a battered old Citroen van abandoned in the weeds out in front.

Another road sign crept steadily nearer. "St Gille 5km" it read and up ahead they could see the small spike of a church spire rising above the grey jumble of what must be the small town they had been heading towards all day. Jake stretched in his seat. The muscles in his back were cramping again, but he consoled himself with the fact that they were, at last, nearly there.

'Veronique told me that we turn left straight after we cross the railway line and then right at a bar on the corner after about a kilometre and they are on Rue Du Vallone on the right.' Jake nodded. He hadn't asked granddad too much about the lady who was putting them up for the night. He knew that she was the daughter of someone that granddad knew from when he was working with the French resistance, but so long as she had food and a bed for him to sleep in, Jake frankly didn't care if she had two heads and a long white beard.

The outskirts of St Gille were uninspiring and dull. They drove past large furniture stores with big, dusty car parks at the front, none of which contained any cars whatsoever. Jake saw fresh fruit stalls, their colourful, striped tarpaulin covers and hand-chalked pricelists now forlornly bare and abandoned for the day.

Houses with large windows and green shutters started to appear and soon they drove slowly past the sign indicating they were entering St Gille. Now that the end of their day's journey was in sight, Jake felt more alert than he had been for a while. They crossed the bridge over the railway line and trundled around the next turning to the left and into a street lined at either side with houses with front doors that opened directly onto the pavement. They followed this road for a while. The traffic was light and there were no pedestrians. It felt to Jake as if it were a ghost town, abandoned by its people. The shabby-looking bar on the corner did show some sign of life, even if it was just two old men with craggy, deeply tanned faces smoking cigarettes and nursing small glasses of beer at a rusty metal table outside. As granddad turned right at the junction, the men just stared at them as if the red Rover and its occupants was the most interesting thing they had seen all day. 'Mind you, by the look of this place,' Jake thought with a smile. 'We probably are.'

Rue Du Vallone was a wide avenue with trees dotted at regular intervals along each side. The trees had an odd, mottled, whitish bark and broad, bright green leaves. The rows of houses were taller here and set back behind a broad pavement. The Rover made its way slowly along the road as it climbed gently up the slight hill towards the church spire which rose up above over the old town. They crept along the road, looking for number 42 where Veronique lived. 'That's it!' Jake called out, spotting the number on a small ceramic plate near a green door they were passing. Granddad pulled into the next available parking space a few cars down and switched the engine off. Jake sighed, happy that he would not have to listen to the engine anymore that day as the quiet of the sleepy town crowded round them.

For a while they just sat there, summoning up the will and the energy to open the door and get out of their seats.

'Well done Jake, you did a grand job as a navigator.' Granddad's voice was low and his eyes were sincere. Jake nodded thoughtfully as he tried to think of what to say.

'Thanks…Nice driving by the way.' Jake looked up, their eyes met and they both grinned.

'Come on then Jakey Boy.' They got out of the car stiffly into the warm dappled sunshine that fell on them through the leaves of the trees. A large pear-shaped lady with dark hair pinned back in a tight bun was shuffling down the dusty pavement towards them in tatty carpet slippers. She wore a dress with a small black and white check pattern on it under a blue and white striped apron. She was smiling broadly at them, arms outstretched in welcome.

'Ah! Veronique! Comment ca va?' Granddad greeted her warmly with outstretched arms. They exchanged a brief hug and then kissed on each cheek.

'Vault-air!' Veronique's French accent made Jake smile. She held granddad's arms and stood back a little, looking at him appraisingly.

They talked in animated and rapid French before granddad turned to indicate Jake.

'Et c'est Jake, mon petit-fils.'

'Ah! Jake!' Veronique hugged him and kissed him lightly, her sweet, floral perfume seemed to cling to him afterwards and he had to repress the urge to wipe his cheek with the back of his hand. Veronique was saying something to granddad whilst she was looking at Jake.

'She says you are a very handsome young Englishman and that it's a shame we aren't staying longer as she has a niece who would be very interested in meeting you!'

Jake's startled, embarrassed grin made granddad and Veronique laugh kindly. 'Vous devez être fatigué, venez à l'intérieur.' Veronique turned and linked arms with granddad, picked up his small overnight case in her free hand and gestured with a nod of her head that Jake should follow them inside.

Number 42, Rue Du Vallone was a tall, grey house with white windows and dusty, cobwebbed, green shutters which looked like they hadn't been closed for a long time. The front door led straight into the lounge where large, chunky leather chairs with oak arms were draped with lace edged sheets. The pale lemon coloured walls were covered in framed pictures. Some were paintings of rural scenes and some held photos. Jake scanned the various pictures, of friends and family, some portrait photos of boys and girls in school uniform, some of whole families seated at a table raising glasses in a frozen toast to the photographer.

Granddad and Veronique chattered away to each other as she led them through a dark, cool hallway and up the stairs. Jake glanced into the kitchen as he walked past. It was small and cluttered, with old-fashioned cupboards and an ancient range set into a chimneybreast at the back. The aroma that came from the large blackened pan which sat on top and steamed gently, was savoury and pungent. Jake was normally starving by this time in the day, but he found that he was feeling so tired from having to concentrate on navigating, his normal appetite had disappeared altogether. Instead, he felt a little sick, his head still buzzing with the thrumming echo of the car's engine.

Upstairs, Veronique had turned to Jake indicating the room at the far end of the landing was his. Jake wearily dragged his bag into the room and heaved it on to the single bed. 'This is the room her grandson stays in when he comes to visit,' Granddad interpreted. Jake smiled wryly. He had already worked that one out. Given the shelves bearing model dinosaurs, children's books and a bright border on the wall printed with Asterix the Gaul, it couldn't be anything but a young boy's room.

Veronique led granddad away to the room next to Jake's where he would be sleeping, leaving Jake alone. He sat heavily on the bed that creaked loudly in protest. The tall, sash window opposite the end of the bed looked out of the back of the house over gardens, tiled rooftops and trees. The window was wide open and, suddenly curious to see what St Gille looked like, Jake eased himself off the bed, crossed to the window and leaned out. Somewhere in the chaotic, untidy jumble of the town, the sound of a motor scooter fizzed like an annoyed hornet, its nasal whine deepening as it passed up the hill into town. A sleepy quietness descended once more. Fragments of a disembodied conversation floated up to Jake's window from a neighbouring garden. A pigeon cooed loudly from its perch on next door's guttering, Jake felt his whole body relaxing after the tensions of the day. He chuckled to himself. It seemed incredible that only a few days before, he had been resigned to a summer at home and now... now he was a long way from home, looking down on to the roofs and gardens of a strange foreign town from the window of a stranger's house... How did this happen?

The sun reappeared from behind one of the fluffy white clouds and a bird in Veronique's garden trilled its approval. 'What will mum say when granddad calls her?' At the thought of his parents, Jake's stomach gave a guilty lurch. He knew that if they were not at home tonight when she called, his mum would really start to worry. Jake resolved to tell granddad that he should call them tonight to let them know what was going on. They'd be shocked, but at least they'd know where they were.

'Jake?' Granddad's voice echoed up the staircase. 'Jake? Veronique is going to take us to where the camp used to be, come on!' He sounded excited, but Jake was feeling too drained and lethargic to go out again and the thought of getting back into the car after spending almost all day in it, filled him with dread.

'Can't we go tomorrow?' Jake called back down the stairs unenthusiastically.

In reply, granddad's steps could be heard coming up the stairs. As he came into Jake's room, he wore a smile that seemed to be a question. 'Feeling OK Jake?'

'Just tired,' Jake replied, 'I really don't want to get back into the Rover again today.'

'Don't worry Jake. Veronique is going to take us in her car. Come on! You'll feel fine once you get going.' Something in granddad's voice seemed to plead with Jake as if he was afraid of losing his support for the whole adventure. Jake sat thoughtfully for a second, then stretched and followed granddad down the stairs.

Chapter 11

A Long Way From Home

Veronique owned a tiny, red Renault which was parked outside her front door. It had bubbled, rusty bits on the side of the front wheel arches. One of the fog lamps below the scratched front bumper was missing, the other dangled uselessly on its wire.

Veronique opened the passenger door, and stale, hot air escaped from the interior. She gestured to Jake, inviting him to get in the back seat. Jake cleared a space to sit down. The seat had a shopping basket, a cardigan, several old newspapers and a pair of shoes scattered across it. Veronique lowered the passenger seat back on to his knees. The sweltering air inside the car increased his feeling of claustrophobia and Jake prayed that this trip wouldn't take too long. Granddad was still stiff from the day's driving as he lowered himself gingerly into the front seat which sagged even further on to Jake's knees. Veronique closed her door with a crash and the glass in her door window rattled. She smiled around at her passengers. 'Allez!' She turned the key in the ignition. Nothing happened. Veronique muttered some rapid French as she tried again without effect. Tutting and sighing Veronique took the key out of the ignition, rolled her eyes upward as if she was appealing to heaven and then, with an aggressive stab she rammed the key back in and turned it quickly, as if she was trying to take the little car by surprise. The engine gasped, coughed, whirred and eventually, a deafening, clattering rumble leaped from under the bonnet. A crunch of gears and they were away.

Jake was convinced that the Renault was going to shake itself to pieces as Veronique drove them at what seemed like breakneck speed through the small town of St Gille. Over the last couple of days, Jake had got used to granddad's slow, methodical, careful driving style. In contrast, Veronique's seemingly reckless disregard for speed limits, passenger comfort and other road users came as a great shock and made Jake feel like he was riding on a rocket.

Blurred images of restaurants, bars and the market square, all flashed past Jake's window. The car seemed to rattle from just about every part. Tyres skipped and whined on the dusty tarmac as they were flung into another corner. Jake couldn't see granddad's face, but his shoulders were hunched and tense and the knuckles on his hand were white as he clung on to the door handle. He grunted short responses to Veronique's cheerful chattering. She seemed oblivious to the fact that they were all about to die in a terrible car crash.

After a while, the roads started to widen as they came out of the other side of town. After flying round another bend, Jake saw that the road was running parallel to a railway goods yard where a number of rusty wagons stood, dotted seemingly at random across four or five tracks. Dry, dead-looking weeds had found space to grow between the tracks and down the side of the road, giving the whole place a neglected feel, as if it had been abandoned. Without any warning and without going to the trouble of indicating, Veronique swung the battered Renault to the right, across a narrow, concrete bridge which climbed steeply and crossed the tracks. There were fewer houses on the far side. It seemed to Jake as if the railway line had cut them off from the town and the place had a forgotten, backwater feel about it. Several buildings were half-finished and looked as if no one had done any work on them for years. Other houses seemed unkempt and uncared for, their front yards littered with abandoned children's toys, or cars rusting on blocks. A small, scruffy bar had its door open for business. Above the door a fading flag advertising Pepsi swung feebly to and fro in the light breeze. As they sped past, Jake glanced into the dark interior to see if there was any sign of life, but there was none.

Jake was wondering what sort of ghost town Veronique had taken them to, when she swept around a tight turn off to the right. Suddenly, the houses stopped and they were travelling down a narrow road which crossed between fields. They were in a wide, shallow valley. The rolling, tree-covered hills sprang up either side behind tilled fields. Over the course of the next half-mile, the road surface disintegrated from smooth tarmac into a rough, pitted, dusty farm track. 'At least Veronique has slowed down,' Jake thought, 'even she must think her car is falling to bits.' It was true that the increased bouncing around that the track's dips and lumps was making the brave little Renault emit the strangest squeaks, bangs and rattles. After one particularly savage bump the glass in granddad's window, which had been half rolled down, simply disappeared into the door with a swoosh and a clunk. Granddad glanced over his shoulder at Jake as if to check that he hadn't been bounced out of the car.

They passed a farm whose buildings straddled the track. It was another jumble of rusting vehicles and ivy-covered barns similar to the farms Jake had seen on the road into St Gille. However this farm was different somehow. It felt sad, like it had become trapped in the valley and was slowly decaying in this backwater, unloved and forgotten. As they passed by, Jake caught the dead stare of a dark-haired man leaning on a gate. His green overalls were stained and he was smoking a cigarette. He didn't register any emotion behind his stare; it was as if this forgotten valley had drained all the curiosity and human spark from him.

The car crossed a cattle-grid with a ringing clatter. They were passing fields which held clumps of long, dry grasses.

The saplings of birch trees rose up here and there. The valley seemed to be closing in on either side of them.

Without warning, Veronique brought the car to a halt with a swoosh of loose gravel and dust. Jake looked around wondering why they'd stopped. He couldn't see any evidence of a camp. He'd expected high fences and the remains of watchtowers and long sheds, but they were looking on to a broad, flat area covered with high tufts of the dead looking grass. Shrubs and small trees grew here and there across the valley floor until it reached the forest which rose up on either side.

They got out of the car; the air in the valley was as musty as the air in the car had been, seeming somehow thick and syrupy. There was no sound at all except the fizzing of crickets, chirruping constantly in the undergrowth. Jake could see that the track in front of them gradually gave way to the coarse grass and shrubs, until it couldn't be seen at all and nature took over.

'Ah yes!' granddad said, staring intently at the forest behind Jake. 'There's the crag, of course.' The sudden eager giddiness in his voice made Jake turn round, looking for the reason for granddad's excitement. 'You see Jake? Do you see it?' Jake couldn't see anything but trees, but granddad pointed impatiently. 'To the left of that big pine tree, that rock face do you see it now?' Jake could see a bulbous overhang of grey rock amongst the trees which grew on and around it, but he didn't understand why granddad was getting all excited.

'Just behind that crag there's a gap in the rock, that's where we had our bivouac. It was where we caught a few hours' sleep and kept our food and ammo.' Granddad's eyes shone. Being here again, where it all happened, was bringing the memories flooding back. 'And it was in there somewhere, somewhere at the base of the crag, where we spent all those weeks.' His hand waved vaguely towards the thickly forested hill. 'So, if we were over there…' Granddad looked around for a landmark, trying to measure out where things should be in relationship to the crag. '…Then the gates should be over here somewhere on this side of the track.' He walked down what was left of the track, the grass crackling beneath his feet, and crickets pinging away from his tread.

After a few yards of wading through the long grass, granddad shouted back to Veronique and Jake. 'It's here! The gate! You can see it! Veronique, regardez ici!'

Jake ran through the grass up to where granddad was standing. He turned to Jake, a gleam of triumph in his eyes. 'Look Jake! This is where the gate used to be!' Jake looked hard at the tangle of grass, thorn bushes and saplings which granddad was pointing at. A jagged, crumbling piece of rusting metal protruded from the top and now Jake could see the flaky remnants of wire fencing within the undergrowth beneath. Stepping back, Jake could now see that the clumps of grass, shrubs and thorn bushes hid what used to be fences and gates and buildings. It was like the camp itself had died and left behind only the bare, crumbling bones of what it used to be.

Jake waded through the grass and came across the brick foundations of what had once been a hut. Now they only supported a rectangular hedge of intertwined thorns and the remains of its wooden walls, reduced to mouldering stumps like rotten teeth in a skeletal jawbone. A small lizard scampered down the wall from where it had been basking in the sun. Apart from a sleepy warbling from a bird in the forest behind them, nothing stirred. The ghosts of St Gille whispered in the quiet on the edge of Jake's consciousness. As Jake's gaze revealed more and more of what used to be the camp, the voices of another time echoed around his head. The crying, the wailing, the harsh shouts, the fearful pleading and the screaming. The mournful spirit of this place made Jake feel like he was an intruder. Unwanted, unwelcome and a long way from home.

'Come on Jake.' Granddad's voice sounded flat and solemn. There was no longer any excitement in it. It had been eradicated by the newly recalled memories of which this place had once been a part.

The drive back was spent in a thoughtful silence. Veronique drove comparatively slowly. They were all thinking of the abandoned, derelict tangle of brick and steel, the scene of so much suffering and fear that now was slowly being eaten into dust by nature.

As they pulled back into the vacant parking space outside Veronique's front door, she turned to granddad and spoke earnestly in rapid French to him. Granddad nodded as she spoke saying softly, 'Oui, oui...d'accord.' As Veronique smiled weakly and opened the door, granddad turned in his seat to speak to Jake. Jake noticed that there was a serious, determined set to granddad's chin, as if he were fighting back an internal rage.

'Veronique lost a childhood friend to St Gille, she's asked me to promise that we will get Gunter and expose him for all the world to see.' His chin creased upwards, for a second, bending his mouth downwards into a bow. For an uncomfortable moment, Jake thought he was going to start crying, but his gaze was steady and his voice was firm and almost chilling in its grim determination. 'I promised her that we'll do it, even if it's the last bloomin' thing I ever do!'

Chapter 12

Rheinhagen

By the time they had followed Veronique into the house, the sombre mood was lifting and in its place came a peculiar, shared elation, an unspoken agreement between them all that they would, for this evening at least, put aside the memories of what had gone before and be thankful.

They ate on a shaky iron table in Veronique's garden. The savoury smell coming from the pot on her stove had jolted Jake's stomach into reminding him just how hungry he was. And Veronique's cooking was wonderful. Jake ate bowl after bowl of a heavenly, rich beef dish which had the heady aroma of red wine and garlic, served with buttery potatoes sprinkled with herbs. As she cut more of the delicious baguette into neat slices, Veronique smiled approvingly at how much Jake was appreciating her cooking. Granddad looked worn out. He sipped his glass of wine as the sun's shadow crept up the old mossy brick of the garden wall and their talk was of families and friends. The subject of their visit to the camp was not mentioned again. By the time they had cleared away, the sun had nearly disappeared and granddad declared himself too tired to stay awake any longer and he shambled off upstairs. Jake murmured 'bon nuit' to Veronique and followed him up.

As he lay in bed, his limbs aching with tiredness, Jake found that, frustratingly, sleep didn't come. A dog barked a few streets away, a van passed outside, its diesel engine clattering, Veronique could be heard tidying up downstairs and granddad's snores rumbled through the wall. Jake stared at the high ceiling of his bedroom, listening to these noises wondering what the next day would bring. 'This time two days ago, I was in Britain,' Jake thought. 'Now we're in France and tomorrow...?' Tomorrow they would be in Rheinhagen.

With a guilty lurch, Jake realised that they had not called his parents to tell them where they were and what they planned to do. He imagined his mum at Auntie June's, trying to call their home and his mobile over and over again wondering what had happened to them. He'd check his mobile in the morning and see how many messages she'd left. He winced inwardly at the prospect of breaking the news to them, but granddad had said he'd do that. He'd take responsibility, Jake was off the hook. However, he could not shake the feeling of foreboding that he'd catch blame for this anyway and, for a while, Jake rehearsed in his head how the conversation might go and what he would say to his mum. Sleep crept up on Jake stealthily and he slept deeply and dreamlessly while granddad's snores rumbled on.

'There's a sign for Rheinhagen! Look!' Jake referred back to his atlas once again, running his finger along the thick curving red line that was the motorway they were driving down, checking to see where they were. 'Another three junctions and that'll be our turning.' This day's travelling had been much better Jake thought. His confidence as a navigator had increased dramatically with practice and granddad had become more used to the driving; they had only stopped twice so far.

After a breakfast of pastries and cups of dark, strong, bitter coffee, Veronique had bade them farewell and 'bonne chance', with kisses on each cheek for them both and a short, earnest conversation with granddad. They settled themselves back into the Rover, wound down the windows and called,

'Au revoir! Merci beaucoup!' at the rather lonely-looking figure in apron and slippers waving from her doorstep.

They retraced their route from the day before, until they reached the motorway, stopping at the tollbooth for Jake to pluck a ticket from the machine, in what was now a well-rehearsed operation. The sky had only a few small clouds spoiling the expanse of hazy blue. It looked like it was going to be a hot day.

The sign said that there was still eight kilometres to Rheinhagen when they turned off the motorway. The area around the junction had been developed for industry and retail, the large, industrial, shed-like buildings clustered around. From the wide roundabout of the motorway junction, they turned down the Rheinhagen road, a broad, straight, dual carriageway that ran parallel to a river on their right. Furniture warehouses and fast food drive-ins were scattered at intervals on either side, before a sprawling, white, modern hospital appeared on their left. Behind a large car park and beyond a neat line of ambulances, Jake noticed that a big hotel with a familiar large green sign on the roof that read: "Forbes Hotel", the chain that Chris worked for. The familiarity of the branding brought to mind Chris's smiling face and prompted another guilty swoop in Jake's stomach as he thought of his family and the call they would have to make later.

Jake reached into the glove box in the dashboard and pulled out his mobile phone. He held down the on/off button until the keyboard and small screen lit up as the phone came to life. 'We'll have to call my mum and dad today,' Jake reminded granddad.

Granddad winced at the prospect of what would be a difficult call to make. 'Yes Jake, they'll be wondering where we've got to.' They travelled on in silence for a while, each wondering how the conversation would go. Then Jake's mobile trilled loudly, its sudden vibration startling him and he almost dropped it. He looked at the screen, it read:

4 Missed Calls

1 New Voice Message

1 New Text Message

He sighed. The calls were all from a landline with a code that he didn't recognise, with another guilty pang, he realised that it must be his mum calling from Auntie June's phone.

He opened the text message inbox. It was from Chris. Jake exhaled, somehow relieved that it wasn't from his mum, although he wasn't convinced that his mum would know how to send a text without Jake there to tell her what to do. The message read: "Where R U bruv? M&D trying to call U". That was that then. They would have to call them and own up, he didn't like to think that his mum and dad would be worrying, wondering where they had disappeared to.

The voicemail message made him feel even worse. He knew his mum hated leaving messages on answer phones and avoided it wherever possible, so Jake surmised that she must be really worried to do so now. Her recorded voice sounded tense, self-conscious and hesitant.

'Hello love, it's mum here. We had hoped to speak to you, but you're obviously off somewhere with granddad. Just give us a call back at June's or on your dad's mobile to let us know you're OK… we're still busy sorting June's stuff out, I never knew she had so many things… OK then… call us when you can, hope you're having fun… speak to you soon…' and the call ended, seeming to simply fizzle out.

Jake told granddad what she'd said in the message. He nodded gravely, but said nothing in return. Jake grimaced at the small red battery icon in the top corner that was flashing at him and he switched the phone off to conserve power.

The gently rolling fields and woods moved relentlessly across Jake's vision, when suddenly, after sweeping around a wide bend in the road, the town of Rheinhagen stood before them. Behind a foreground of modern houses which looked exactly like the new housing estate back in Churnthorpe, the old town rose up on a slight bump in the landscape. A large, salmon-pink church with a pointed spire was the highest point of the chaotic clutter of competing roofs, towers and spires that tumbled down on either side.

Jake realised that both he and granddad were smiling to themselves. They exchanged a look and laughed out loud. Just getting to Rheinhagen had seemed like a huge task a day or so before, but here they were. They didn't know where they were going to stay tonight, or if this whole adventure would prove to be a wild goose chase, but right now, they basked in the sense of achievement that, whatever happened after this point, they had at least arrived safely.

The wide road they were on crossed the river and skirted around the town, held at bay by the town's ancient defences, a huge grassy mound encircled the old town, protecting it from the invasion of the twenty-first century.

They followed signs for the town centre car park, leaving the wide road for narrow streets. The road looped around the hill, spiralling gradually upwards. It was lined with tall buildings, some were new, with wide windows and vertical blinds, but mostly they seemed old. There was a hotchpotch of styles. Rather grand looking white offices, with ornate scroll work around the roof and windows, stood next to older buildings which had crooked roofs and a criss-cross pattern of ancient wooden beams over their walls.

Eventually, after the road had turned into a cobbled avenue, a small car park appeared behind a grand-looking structure which stood next to the church they had seen from afar. They patrolled the leafy car park for a space, before diving into one that a rather serious-looking young mother had just vacated whilst talking over her shoulder at her child in the back seat. Once they had parked, granddad pulled on the handbrake in his usual studied, methodical fashion, eased the car out of gear and turned the engine off.

For a while they just sat there, windows down, the dappled sunshine moving over them rhythmically as the warm breeze moved the branches of the trees. Children scampered around the small play park nearby. Jake could not make out what they were saying and their chatterings merged into a one constant background sound, just like the noise that the children made in the park back home.

Flowers seemed to be everywhere. Every windowsill had a box from which trails of colourful blue, red and pink blooms hung. The privet hedges and gravel pathways that led past the play park and into the town square were neat and tidy and free of litter and weeds. The swings, slides and the climbing frame which the small children played on, were quite new and well cared for and Jake thought what a contrast it was to the graffiti daubed, rusty old swings and roundabout in Churnthorpe park.

They got out of the car with stretches and yawns and walked slowly and stiffly down the path which led to a gap between the church on their right and what they assumed was the town hall on the left. The path emerged into a large, cobbled square. At the top of a row of stone steps, the town hall took pride of place at the head of the square. Tall, medieval buildings with criss-cross beams lined the other three sides, the ground floor of most of them being bars and restaurants with colourful striped awnings and their shiny steel tables gleaming in the sunshine.

Some businessmen sat at a table near them, sipping their end-of-the-day beers, ties loosened, shirtsleeves rolled up and dark glasses on. Further down, three young mothers sat in the shade sipping their coffees and chatting whilst one of the babies was being spoon-fed and the other two slept in their pushchairs. Three young boys ran across the cobbles of the square, round and round in some complicated game of their own design. On the town hall steps, a small group of teenage girls squealed and laughed as one of their number, a pretty girl with striking blue eyes and dark hair which curled and cascaded across her shoulders, seemed to be reading aloud a text message that she had received.

The whole place had a relaxed, but busy air about it. There were no tourists, Rheinhagen didn't seem to be a tourism hot spot. It was just a normal town at the end of a normal day.

'So what do we do now Granddad?' Jake asked. He hadn't pressed for any more details about granddad's plan during the journey to Rheinhagen, but now they were here, Jake thought that he'd earned the right to know.

'First things first Jakey boy. We need a place to stay for the night. Tell you what, why don't you ask those girls where the tourist office is? They'll be able to help.'

Jake groaned internally. He'd noticed that the girls had been listening to granddad speaking English and were looking appraisingly at Jake, who started to feel, as he always seemed to do around girls his age, very self-conscious. He cringed inside and wished that granddad hadn't put him on the spot. Now he'd no choice but to try and get an answer from the giggling gaggle of girls.

With a deep breath, he wandered over to them feeling their eyes on him and hoping he didn't look too much of a mess after the journey. He certainly felt rather crumpled and sticky.

Jake decided not to address the whole group, as he wasn't sure he could translate half a dozen responses at once. Instead, he chose to talk with just one of them, so he spoke directly to the dark-haired girl. 'Entschuldigen, wo die Touristinformation ist?' He didn't know what to do with his accent. Back home he could do a convincing impersonation of a German speaking English, but now he was actually speaking German, he thought that he probably sounded very English indeed to the girl whose bright blue eyes were now fixed on his. A couple of her friends burst into mocking laughter, leading Jake to believe that his accent was as bad as he'd feared, but the dark-haired girl smiled back at him.

'You are English?' she asked, her voice was warm with a touch of soft huskiness and there was no hint of mockery in her smile. Now Jake didn't know whether to respond in English or German. The girl took his hesitation to mean that he had not understood and so she spoke again. 'I am sorry, my English is very bad.'

'No!' Jake said quickly and just a little too loudly. 'No,' he said again, 'your English is very good.'

'Very sorry, there is no… err… Touristinformation in this town. Is there something you want to know?' The girl's friends erupted in gales of laughter at her hesitant English and she turned and shushed them with a stern look and some rapid German that prompted even more laughter.

She turned again to Jake, inclining her head and rolling her eyes as if to apologise for her friends. Jake smiled.

'My granddad and I are looking for… err… a bed and breakfast.' Jake searched his brain for the German word, '…Ein Gästehaus.'

'Ein… Gästehaus.' The girl nodded looking thoughtful and then spoke rapidly to her friends before waving them goodbye. She turned to Jake and granddad and said, in a decisive voice, 'I show you,' indicating that they should follow. Her friends waved and called out 'Goodbye!' in what Jake assumed was their attempt at an English accent. The girl smiled and led the way down a road leading off the square.

They passed a very elegant looking hotel which the girl pointed at and said, 'Is much money, this way is better.'

Further on, she turned left into a narrower street which was lined with houses. Ahead of them, down the hill, they could see that there was an old, medieval gatehouse which must have been part of the town's defences. Halfway down, she stopped and indicated a pink house which had two neatly clipped, almost perfectly round privet bushes in tubs either side of the doorstep. There was a discreet copper sign by the big, heavy oak door that read *Pension Herscher.* 'Is the only Gästehaus here.' She indicated the town around her and Jake nodded solemnly.

'Looks alright Jakey Boy,' granddad said, using his hand as a shade and peering in through the window. He turned to the girl. 'Thank you very much young lady. What's your name by the way sweetheart?'

Jake could have laughed out loud at granddad, as he was talking extra slow and louder than normal, as if that would make himself understood. Unfortunately, the girl didn't seem to comprehend, however she caught Jake's look and seemed to be on the point of laughing along with him.

'Was Ihr Name ist?' Jake stepped in to help and the girl turned back to granddad.

'Mein name ist Kirsten.' As Jake was introducing himself and granddad, the handle of the oak door behind them turned with a clunk and the door opened to reveal a large cheerful-looking lady who had come out to see who was speaking.

Kirsten spoke rapidly to the lady explaining why they were there. The lady, who was introduced as Frau Herscher, shook hands with them and beckoned them inside. Jake thanked Kirsten and she smiled, 'Is OK, I think?' gesturing at the guesthouse.

'Yeah, it's great thanks…' There were times, Jake thought, times when it would be really good to be able to think of exactly the right thing to say. Right at this moment, it would be great if he could say something cool and witty, without appearing to be too smart or clever. Unfortunately, looking into Kirsten's blue eyes framed by her pretty face and glossy hair, Jake found that this wasn't one of those times. 'Well, see you then.' Jake cringed inwardly. Why didn't he have Howard's gift of easy charm? Why was it always so awkward to talk to girls, especially attractive ones like Kirsten? With horror, Jake felt a flush of embarrassment start to creep across his face and he prayed that Kirsten didn't notice.

'Is a small town, Rheinhagen. I will see you.' She made a small, circular hand movement and Jake understood.

'Yeah see you around.' She waved and walked back towards the square, tossing her hair across her shoulders as she turned once to wave again.

'Come on Jake! I need you to translate.' Granddad had re-emerged from the doorway. Jake followed him into the hallway of the guesthouse. It had white walls and reddish-brown tiles on the floor. 'Well, you're a fast worker Jake!' granddad said with a mischievous smile. 'You've only been here two seconds and you've got a fan club already!'

Jake gave granddad an uncomprehending look. 'What do you mean?' he said innocently, yet anticipating his reply with a suddenly thudding heart.

'You mean you couldn't see that she was very taken with you?' Granddad's tone was gently mocking. 'Yes, you've definitely made a conquest there.' Granddad turned down the hallway, still smiling, following Frau Herscher. After a moment, Jake followed, a broad grin spreading over his face.

Chapter 13

An Appointment with the Bürgermeister

Jake woke from a deep sleep and, for a few seconds, he wondered where he was. He lay in a single bed made of wood under a thick, white, puffy quilt which was deliciously warm and cosy. He closed his eyes again and let the drowsy, sleepy feeling take hold once more. However, the details of the previous day gradually emerged from the sleepy fogginess, until the memory of a pair of blue eyes and shiny, dark hair banished it and he was fully awake. He fumbled on the pine bedside table for his watch. It was nearly ten o'clock, he'd slept in.

Jake's bedroom was a small attic room with a ceiling that sloped steeply up at either side of the bed. He had bumped his head a couple of times already, but he didn't mind, as the sloped ceiling gave the room a cosy feel.

A window set into the roof provided the only source of light and a view across the patchwork of Rheinhagen's tiled roofs. The bright morning sunshine was flooding either side of the roller blind which was set into the window frame. He loosened the string holding the blind down and let it roll up gradually, wincing as the sunlight spilled into the room.

Jake dressed slowly, the memory of Kirsten's smile making him take more care than usual to pick out the fresher, less creased items from his holdall. Wondering if granddad was up and about yet, he descended the steep stairs. Passing granddad's room, he noticed that the door had been left open.

Jake glanced in to see that he'd made his bed and his suitcase was propped neatly under the rather ugly dressing table.

When Jake reached the dining room, he found it deserted. It was a pleasant room with two small tables, a dresser with bowls of fruit, portions of butter and jam and a basket of bread rolls on it and what looked like a large stone oven in the corner. All was quiet apart from the cuckoo clock which ticked loudly and the occasional car which swished past outside. It felt like Jake had woken to find that he was the last person left in the world.

Frau Herscher came in wiping her hands on her floral apron. She didn't know much English, but she was very friendly and bobbed and nodded encouragingly at Jake's hesitant German. She had an open, expressive face and seemed to reinforce what she was trying to say with wide-eyed theatrical nodding. She gestured that Jake should help himself to the breakfast buffet and took his order for orange juice. Jake asked her where granddad had gone and she replied with a babble of rapid German and much pointing. He took this to mean that granddad had gone out for a walk around town.

Wondering what granddad was getting up to, Jake breakfasted on fresh, round rolls which he tore apart and smothered with butter and home made strawberry jam. The rolls had a crispy crust and yet were deliciously soft inside.

It was getting close to quarter to eleven when footsteps could be heard approaching down the street. Jake had finished his breakfast some time before and was debating whether to wait for granddad in his room, or go out and try to find him. The door opened and granddad walked in, a broad smile across his face. He pulled up a chair opposite Jake and called out 'coffee please!' in answer to Frau Herscher's enquiring face which had appeared around the kitchen doorway.

Granddad was looking tired after the days of travelling, but behind the dark rings around his eyes there was a mischievous twinkle which told Jake that he was clearly very pleased with himself. He ignored Jake's questions until Frau Herscher brought in his coffee, all the time looking like he was going to burst into giggles. 'So, come on, where have you been?' Jake demanded after granddad had taken a sip from his cup.

Granddad placed his cup carefully back on to the saucer and seemed to take a moment to choose his words. 'I've been up at the town hall Jake, hot on the trail of our Herr Meyer.'

'Did you see him? Is it the same bloke?' Jake jumped in excitedly, surely it couldn't be that easy? They'd only been in Rheinhagen a day!

'No Jake!' Granddad shook his head. 'No, I've not seen him.' He paused, a smile curling the corner of his mouth irresistibly upward. 'But you'd better spruce yourself up, 'cos we've got an appointment to see him in his office later today at twelve o'clock!'

Jake gave a short bark of incredulous laughter. 'So this was your big plan? You just wander into the town hall and make an appointment?'

Granddad's smile grew even wider. 'Yep. I walked up to reception and asked to see the Bürgermeister himself. There were a few questions about what I wanted with him and the girl on the front desk toddled off into the back office, before she returned to say he'd see us at twelve.'

Granddad's smile couldn't get any broader and he spoke again. 'So Jakey boy, we'll pop in there at twelve, take a good look and, once I have made myself sure that it's him, we can get off home and call the authorities! It'll be a piece of cake!' Despite this assurance, Jake couldn't shake the uneasy feeling that it wouldn't necessarily be quite that straightforward.

'So, hold on, what did you say to the receptionist? Enkmann must be a busy guy, how come he's agreed to meet with us?'

Granddad didn't answer straight away, but he sat up straight in his chair, looked down his nose at Jake and put on an upper class accent. 'You are looking at the chairman of the Churnthorpe Town Council Twinning Committee!' Jake laughed so hard that he nearly fell off his chair.

They spent the next hour, strolling around the cobbled streets and squares of the old town. They were both buoyed up by the success of granddad's scheme. However, despite granddad's "piece of cake" assurances, Jake couldn't quite bring himself to believe that it would be so simple and he worried about what they would say when they were ushered into the presence of the man himself.

They stopped for an early lunch at a café on the square. Granddad muttered to himself about the cost after the waiter had disappeared inside with their order and he peered over the top of his glasses at the foreign coins in his change as he counted out how much cash he had left.

The hot, midday sun hammered down on the café's striped awning above their heads and the slight breeze that would occasionally lift and ripple the fabric, was very welcome. A cheerful couple who were out shopping and were laden down with bags, flopped into the chairs of the next table along, fanning themselves with the menus and chatting in a friendly manner with the waiter. In the square, a slim, tanned lady, who Jake estimated to be around forty-ish stood in the sunshine and smoked a cigarette, her mobile phone pressed to her ear. She wore an expensive-looking sundress that accentuated her honey-coloured skin. Her eyes were shaded with sunglasses, the designer's logo displayed prominently on their sides and she teetered on the cobbles in the highest heels that Jake had ever seen. Her friend arrived, who was also slim, tanned and expensively dressed and Jake noted that she too was talking on her mobile. They greeted each other with air-kisses and walked off together, both of them still talking to other people as they went. An old lady in a dark dress and a cardigan shuffled across the square in what looked like carpet slippers. She was holding a plastic bag containing three oranges. Jake sensed that he was witnessing a typical Saturday in Rheinhagen. He felt somehow connected momentarily to this hustle and bustle which must have been going on in a similar way for centuries, people out meeting friends, buying food, having lunch. No doubt, long after he and granddad had gone back home, it would still be going on, week in, week out.

The thought of home brought back memories of the phone call of the previous evening. The sense of apprehension had built over dinner as they ate large spicy sausages and sauerkraut in a small bar down the road from the guesthouse. Jake had been feeling increasingly guilty about the worry his mum and dad must be going through. He knew from Chris's text message that they were already concerned and would probably be desperate to hear from them by now, but when he mentioned it to granddad, his response sounded irritable and noncommittal. 'Yes, I said that I'd call them tonight didn't I?' More and more, Jake found himself thinking that granddad was trying to delay making the call for as long as he could. Jake had become more and more irritated by this as the meal went on and there was still no sign of him making the call. Jake felt an indignant anger towards granddad. After all, this trip was all his idea and he had assured Jake that he'd take full responsibility and yet now he seemed reluctant to make the call to his parents which would at least tell them that everything was all right. Was he frightened of what they'd say? The meal seemed to drag and Jake felt an increasing impatience to get the call done and out of the way. Eventually granddad eased out of his chair, stretched and said, 'Well Jake, time to face the music I guess. Where's that mobile phone of yours?' He pulled a face which expressed dread at the prospect of telling his daughter-in-law that they were hundreds of miles away.

They walked back to the guesthouse, granddad sauntering along slowly behind Jake as if he was a reluctant schoolboy on his way to class. Jake retrieved his phone and switched it on. LOW BATTERY the large red words flashed across the screen as a warning note chimed out. Jake cursed himself again for forgetting his charger. 'It's low on juice and I'm not sure how much credit I've got left on it, so you'll have to get to the point quickly,' Jake instructed granddad. He nodded gravely, took the phone and stared at it uncomprehendingly.

'Here,' Jake said taking the phone and scrolling through the numbers until it read M&D@JUNES. 'Just press the green button to make the call.'

Jake passed the phone back to granddad who raised a stubby finger and pressed the button. There was a long pause as granddad looked serious. Eventually he looked up at Jake. 'It's just ringing and ringing, there's no one home.'

Jake took the phone back, listened to the insistent trilling of the dialling tone and cut the call off. 'We'll have to try my dad's phone,' he said. He was determined to get the message across tonight somehow.

He scrolled through his address book again until DAD MOBILE appeared and pressed the button to call it. This time there was no ringing tone, just his dad's talking in a curiously self-conscious voice. 'This is Jonathan Hargreaves, I'm not able to take your call at the moment, but please leave a message at the tone.'

Jake passed it to granddad and said in a whisper, 'It's voicemail, leave a message,' just as the tinny sound of the tone beeped.

'Oh, errm... right.' Granddad was clearly flustered at being put on the spot and, like Jake's mum, probably wasn't used to using answering services. 'Hello son, it's me and Jake here... sorry we've missed you... errm hope everything's OK there at June's... sorry we haven't called before now, but we've gone away for a few days on a little trip.' Jake waited to hear how granddad was going to break the news. For some reason his heart was thudding. 'So don't worry about us. All being well, we'll be back the day after tomorrow, so, like I said, there's no need to be concerned...'

'Still no mention of them being in Germany!' Jake thought. 'Get to the point Granddad!'

'So like I said,' granddad continued in a voice that sounded as if it was trying too hard to be hearty and carefree. 'We're having lots of fun, so don't worry about us we'll be... Hello...? Hello?' Granddad looked puzzled, took the phone from his ear and peered at the screen. 'It's gone off Jake,' he said, raising his glasses to his forehead to try and see better.

Jake took the phone back and looked at the screen. INSUFFICIENT FUNDS. The words shouted from the small screen and Jake rolled his eyes in frustration. Now his mobile was out of credit and nearly out of juice. Just great! Granddad on the other hand seemed positively cheerful. 'Well at least they'll know we're OK and that'll be a load off their minds!'

'Oh yeah!' Jake responded in a voice heavy with sarcasm. 'Apart from the small fact that they don't know where the hell we are!'

A disapproving furrow appeared on granddad's brow. 'Look Jake, we may well be heading home by tomorrow, so let's not stir up a hornet's nest shall we?'

Jake didn't know what to say. Inside he was furious that granddad was practically admitting to keeping his mum and dad in the dark. This whole trip was sounding more and more like a dumb idea. Later, as he lay in his comfortable, cosy bed that night, Jake found he could not sleep for thinking about what his mum and dad might be going through hundreds of

147

miles away. Eventually, despite the gnawing guilt and worry about their reaction when they got back to England, the tiredness from the journey washed over him and he slept.

Sat in the café, having finished their lunch and sipping a coke, Jake found that all the time that they were people-watching, he was looking out for Kirsten. Half of him wanted to ask granddad if he was serious when he had said that Kirsten was "taken with" him, but he knew that if he showed any interest in the pretty girl, he would be teased mercilessly. Jake didn't cope too well with being teased, especially if it was anything to do with girls. Girls were a bit of a mystery to Jake. He never knew if they liked him or not. He once plucked up the courage to ask Jennifer Burridge to the school disco. He never would have thought for one moment that she liked him, but his friend, Will The Weasel, had said that she really fancied him and all he had to do was ask her. He still recalled the excruciating embarrassment when she looked over her shoulder at him with a glance of utter disgust and said, 'Eeew! I *SO* don't think so!' It was as if Jake was some kind of alien with three heads and the teasing from his classmates that followed seemed to last forever. He vowed never to listen to The Weasel's advice regarding girls again.

The following term The Weasel came to Jake to say that a girl called Caroline Mason who was in the year below had declared her undying love for Jake, whom she apparently thought was "well fit". She was a pretty girl who was lively and popular, qualities that made Jake sure that The Weasel was trying to get him into trouble again. Why would a girl like that fancy him? From time to time, he'd see Caroline in the corridors and at lunch, but she gave him no indication that she liked him at all. Jake stuck to his vow and ignored The Weasel's advice to 'Get in there'!

A few months later Caroline's family moved away from Churnthorpe and a week after that Jake received a letter from her telling him that she missed him lots and what a great shame it was that they'd never got together. 'Well why didn't she just say something?' Jake had complained to Howard, bemoaning the missed opportunity. 'Why don't they just say "I like you". It would make things so much clearer!' Howard had nodded sympathetically, but the truth was that his relaxed, chatty manner meant that he was popular with lots of the girls at school and he never seemed to have any embarrassment or difficulty talking with them.

The more Jake thought about it, the more he thought that Kirsten had seemed interested in him last night. After all, she didn't have to leave her friends and walk them round to the guesthouse did she? And she had made a point of saying that she'd see him again hadn't she? Jake felt that excited grin curl his mouth at the thought of her. 'What are you smiling at?' granddad said with a knowing look.

'Nothing,' Jake replied just a little too quickly, as if he'd been caught doing something he shouldn't and he felt a flush spreading across his cheeks.

Jake turned his face away, becoming suddenly very interested in the architecture of the building opposite. There was a pause and then granddad said, 'Don't worry Jake, I'm sure we'll see her around later.' Jake smirked mirthlessly at granddad in reply.

At twelve o'clock, they were sat on the comfy-looking, yet rather hard seats in the town hall reception. Jake twitched nervously every time the frosted-glass door at the side of the reception desk opened, but each time it was only one of the office cleaning team pulling vacuum cleaners behind them, or pushing trolleys laden with dusters and cans of polish. A disinterested receptionist, who clearly was not happy about working on Saturday, had nodded at them ten minutes previously when Jake had announced their arrival with a well-rehearsed line of German. She had spoken briefly to someone on the phone in a voice which made it difficult for him to follow what she was saying; was she talking to Enkmann?

Now they were so close to the object of their mission, they could almost feel his presence hovering around them. This was his territory and Jake felt like a traitor in the court of the King. Jake knew that granddad had the photograph of Meyer safely tucked away in his jacket pocket. In the next few minutes, they'd discover if it was dynamite, or if this whole trip had been a complete waste of time.

Part of Jake just wanted to go back home and spend the rest of the holiday doing "normal" things. Cricket, bike rides, getting up late and watching TV and yet here they were, hundreds of miles away and about to confront a war criminal. What type of person would Enkmann turn out to be? Granddad had hinted that he'd been responsible for some awful things. Would he be like a movie villain? All big eyebrows, wild stare and maniacal laugh?

The door opened again, but this time it was a young man of around twenty. He wore neatly pressed pinstripe trousers and a white shirt, but no tie. His round, open face expressed a nervy keenness to help. Jake and granddad were the only people in the reception, he came straight over to them.

'Hullo, you are...?' He checked the piece of paper on his clipboard, '...Hargreaves?'

'Yes, that's right, I'm Walter and this is Jake,' granddad chimed in heartily, with a broad smile on his face which Jake thought was like a mask, betraying a certain tension behind it.

'Of course.' The man nodded. 'You will come this way please?'

He led them through the glass doors and down an oak panelled corridor. Glancing through the open doors on either side as they passed, Jake saw office desks, deserted for the weekend and behind another, a large, highly polished boardroom table with black leather swivel chairs around it. The whine and rhythmical hiss of a vacuum cleaner being used somewhere on the floor above seemed to accentuate the feeling that the building slumbered, ticking over the minutes until Monday morning, when it would come to life again.

At the far end of the corridor was a broad wooden door and it seemed that this was where the man was taking them. Behind it would be Enkmann, this was it! Jake's heart was thumping so loudly now he thought everyone would be able to hear it. He glanced at granddad and saw that his chin was set in that grim, determined way which pulled his mouth downwards into a thin bow. But Jake assumed that he too was feeling the tension as his face had gone a greyish colour. Jake wondered just what granddad was thinking, now that he was going to come face to face with the man he'd grown to hate all those years ago.

The nervy man approached the door and knocked quietly on it, as if he was somehow scared of disturbing the person behind it. He opened it slightly and peered round. There was a brief exchange between the man and the person inside, but Jake couldn't make out the words. Then the man stood to one side and opened the door indicating that Jake and granddad should enter.

Jake's first impression of the room behind the door was that it was the office of someone important. It was a big room, oak panelled as in the corridor, with large windows at the far end which gave a view of the corner of the square. Oil paintings of previous town dignitaries in business suits lined the walls and they smiled down from their ornate, gold-leafed frames. The deep carpet, into which Jake's feet were sinking, muffled what little sound there was.

The modern offices they had passed in the corridor had contained lots of light-coloured desks pushed together with blue partitions between them, in an effort to squeeze as many into the room as possible. In here, however, despite the size of the room, there was just one desk, a large, chunky, rectangular block, with green leather set into the desktop. On top of it, a laptop fizzed away to itself and, behind that, was the figure of a man in a suit. He rose to greet them, leaning over the desk to shake hands, smiling a guarded welcome. Jake didn't need to glance at granddad to see if he could identify him, because one thing was clear, the man in the suit was not Enkmann.

'Mr Hargreaves, is it not?' the man enquired in a measured, almost cautious tone. Jake estimated his age as in his forties. He was clean shaven, tanned, his close-cropped hair was going grey at the temples and he had a sharp, shrewd-looking face. He was dressed very smartly in a charcoal grey suit, delicate pink shirt and an expensive-looking tie. He was slim and the shape of his suit accentuated his powerfully built arms and shoulders. There was a calm, purposeful air about him. Jake got the impression that here was someone who liked everyone to know that he was very much in charge of things.

Jake's brain seemed to be struggling to keep up. He couldn't understand why it wasn't Enkmann who was here to meet them. Who was this guy? Had granddad got confused and asked to see the wrong person?

Neither Jake nor granddad had responded to the man's question and a sharply analytical look crossed his face. For what seemed like an age, the only sound was the muffled wheezing of the vacuum cleaner upstairs and the tinny whirring of the laptop. The silence seemed to be interminable. A glance at granddad told Jake that he was struggling to adapt to this twist. Eventually, with a fair bit of err-ing and ahh-ing, granddad collected himself, shook the man by the hand and said, 'Walter Hargreaves, pleased to meet you.'

'I am Dieter Hauptmann.' There was a long pause and Dieter looked expectantly, seemingly waiting for granddad to say something. Eventually Dieter slid his eyes towards Jake and granddad caught on to the fact that Dieter was waiting for an introduction.

'Oh! Yes, this is Jake, my grandson.' Dieter's handshake was very firm and his gaze was steady as he ran an appraising eye over him. Jake had the strangest feeling that this Dieter guy already knew that they weren't what they claimed to be. Something about his manner gave Jake the impression that he was simply playing with them and the only reason they'd been allowed in was to provide him with some amusement.

Jake took a deep breath and tried to calm his thudding heartbeat, cursing himself for being stupid. How could he know anything about them? He was letting his nerves get the better of him! Jake had to admit, however, that they didn't really look like visiting dignitaries. He was dressed in a slightly creased hooped polo shirt and his least crumpled pair of shorts. At least granddad looked slightly more business-like with a pale blue shirt and beige trousers, but in comparison to the immaculate Dieter, they simply looked like tourists.

Granddad seemed to gather his thoughts together and spoke. 'Jake, can you thank him for taking the time to see us.'

Put on the spot, Jake struggled to bring the German words to mind. 'Errr... Danke...' Jake began.

'It is not necessary to speak Deutsch. It might be easier if we talk in English.' Dieter's smooth voice and half smile, together with the arrogant way he had cut across Jake, seemed to suggest that he regarded Jake's German as just not good enough, indeed, he was now solely directing his conversation and attention at granddad. Jake fumed at being ignored like a little child. He scowled at Dieter, wishing he had the power to burn holes with his stare through his perfect suit.

Dieter spoke. 'I was interested to hear of the unannounced arrival of a delegation from...' he checked a memo that lay on his desk, 'how you say...? Shurn-torp?' His condescending smile appeared to be fixed in place and had no humour behind it. 'I was curious. Whenever we have gone through the twinning process before now, we have done it through official channels.'

Granddad nodded gravely, clearly struggling to think fast enough. 'Ah, well you see, we thought that we'd scout the land out first like.' Granddad stammered, 'You know, have a little look first, before we do anything official.' Jake cringed inwardly at the way granddad sounded. Jake thought that, if Dieter had any doubts before about the reason they were there, he certainly would now.

'So you wanted to see if you liked us first?' Dieter's deadpan accusation made granddad face flush with colour.

'No... well... yes. In a way,' he flapped, trying desperately to gain some control of the conversation.

Suddenly Dieter's tone changed. It was as if this meeting had been an amusing distraction, but now it was over and time was being wasted. The half-smile faded altogether. 'Well I am sure that you will find much in Rheinhagen to interest you and, if you decide that you like us enough, maybe we will talk again in the future.' He rose out of his chair and extended his hand once more. The meeting was over.

Glad to be given the chance to get out of the spotlight of Dieter's examination, granddad stood and shook hands, then said, 'Sorry for the confusion before, but we thought that we'd be meeting Josef Enkmann. Is he not available?'

A frown momentarily creased Dieter's brow, but he regained his composure in a second. 'Josef Enkmann is Rheinhagen's longest serving Bürgermeister and is about to celebrate fifty years of service on Monday. He has been stepping back from his duties for some time now and will be officially retiring on Monday also.'

'Ah, so you're his second in command then?' Jake was taken back with the way granddad had said "second in command" like it was an insult. Dieter had clearly taken it the same way and an angry look flashed across his face. It was just for a second, less than a second, but Jake had seen behind the polite mask that he wore.

'Goodbye Mr Hargreaves.' The tone was flat and final. Jake noticed that Dieter didn't even glance at Jake, but he sat back down at his desk and began reading one of the sheaves of papers on his desk.

Chapter 14

Taking the Tour

Back outside on the town hall steps, eyes screwed up against the bright sunshine, granddad seethed with rage. 'That's just so typical of them! So arrogant and full of themselves!' Jake listened to the familiar, tired old prejudices which granddad had always held for the Germans and which had been awakened by their interview with Dieter. Jake agreed wholeheartedly with granddad that Dieter was arrogant and fully shared in his dislike of the smooth, patronising, condescending man, but he didn't agree that all Germans were the same. In Rheinhagen's sunlit square, granddad's rant sounded to Jake like the bile of a bitter and narrow-minded old man. Eventually he was interrupted by a fit of coughing. Jake found it hard not to smile at the furious, comical figure trying to make his point between coughs.

After the coughing subsided, granddad's anger seemed to fizzle out like a fire which had burnt with such heat, it had quickly used up all its fuel. There was a minute of silence whilst granddad calmed down, his face fading from angry red to a greyish colour. He breathed heavily, staring at the cobbles by his feet whilst the embers of his rage slowly cooled. When he spoke again however, it was a completely different tone. It was like he had changed suddenly from an angry old man, to a businesslike and determined soldier.

'Right then Jake, Plan B is now in force. How much money have you got?' Jake was taken aback. 'How much have you got?'

Jake blinked stupidly at the repeated question 'Why do you want to know that Granddad?'

Granddad rolled his eyes as if he were frustrated by Jake's lack of understanding. 'Because this operation is going to take longer than we initially expected and we need to conserve resources.'

Jake struggled to get up to speed with granddad's new plan. 'But can't you just get some more cash out with your card? Or maybe use a credit card?' It seemed like a dumb question to Jake, he couldn't see what the problem was, but granddad shook his head impatiently.

'I don't agree with credit cards. Never had one and I don't use a bank card, because I could never remember the code thingy to key into those machines. So this means that we've got what we've got and we'll just have to make the best of it. Don't worry though, I've got a plan that will let us lay eyes on Enkmann soon enough. Leave it with me!'

Jake was so shocked with the fact that they didn't have any access to more money, that, for a moment, he couldn't think of anything to say. Where were they going to stay tonight? What was granddad planning now? All Jake's enthusiasm for their mission to unmask Enkmann seemed to have evaporated. The idea of simply getting in the car and heading home seemed more and more appealing, especially after the humiliating experience they'd just had in the mayor's office. But this only seemed to have stung granddad into action and deepened his determination to see it through.

Jake took out the bundle of euros from his wallet and began counting them. Granddad took them out of Jake's hand, peeled off a 20 euro note from the bundle and handed it back to Jake, putting the rest of the notes into his own pocket.

He was clearly thinking hard about something and when he spoke, Jake didn't know if it was directed at him, or whether he was talking to himself, trying to organise his thoughts. 'Right, that'll be our petrol money to get back. Now we'll need to have a scout around and ask some questions...'

Jake could feel his anger rising at this silly old man who had dragged him across Europe to satisfy an ancient obsession. An obsession that looked increasingly like a complete waste of time. He felt his face start to go red with his rising resentment and was just about to tell granddad exactly what he thought about his plan B when: 'Hello there!' Kirsten's soft voice made Jake spin around on the cobbles and stumble slightly. There was that smile, the shiny hair framing the cute face. Jake became acutely conscious of his own rather red face and taut expression. He flinched inwardly as he tried to switch from being irritated and angry to friendly and succeeded only in pulling a procession of stupid expressions as he tried to adjust.

Kirsten laughed. 'Sorry, did I surprise you?'

Jake grinned, 'Err... yeah,' and they laughed together.

'It was OK last night at the guesthouse?' Jake noticed a certain cautiousness in her question, as if she was anxious that her recommendation had been well received.

'Oh...! Yes...! They were great thanks! They were nice rooms and I slept really well. Had a massive breakfast this morning, rolls and jam and everything.' Calm down! Jake told himself, you're talking too fast and saying too much and you sound like a right idiot! Just be cool! But he didn't feel very cool. Kirsten's presence alone was making his heart hammer away like an engine. He wanted to say something to fill the momentary silence that had fallen in the conversation. Ideally it should be something funny and witty, so he'd hear her beguiling laugh again. No. Ideally it should be something funny and witty and in faultless German so he'd hear her laugh and maybe see a flash of admiration in her deep blue eyes. Unfortunately, Jake's brain seemed to have chosen this moment to shut down completely. His mouth worked, but there were no words forthcoming in any language. Kirsten chuckled at their mutual awkwardness and Jake shrugged and shook his head self-consciously.

'Kirsten isn't it?' Granddad's bright and breezy voice broke into the conversation. 'Tell you what? Could you do me a favour?' Jake noticed that granddad was falling once again into the classic British trick of "If you can't talk the language, talk loudly in English". Kirsten nodded cautiously in reply as granddad continued. 'I need to do a few things this afternoon, so Jake here is at a bit of a loose end. Would you mind showing him around the sights of historical interest and that sort of thing? If you're not busy of course.'

Jake squirmed and prayed that Kirsten hadn't been able to translate. He could see that her brow was furrowed in concentration as she tried to make sense of granddad's English. On the other hand, he hoped that, if she did catch what granddad had said, Kirsten would agree and, if she agreed, it would mean that she wanted to spend some time with him and that might mean that she fancied him. He was in a dilemma; he wanted Kirsten to say yes, but didn't want the excruciating embarrassment of having granddad ask on his behalf. Part of him wanted granddad to shut up, but part of him was secretly grateful that granddad was asking Kirsten to spend a little time with Jake, something that he didn't think he'd ever be able to ask her if he was on his own.

'OK… yah… is no problem.' Kirsten was nodding and half-smiling at granddad, who beamed back his appreciation.

'That's wonderful! I'll meet you back at the car park at around four o'clock-ish then Jake. OK?' and granddad turned to go.

Jake felt a fluttery, panicky feeling. Four o'clock? That meant that he had to spend over three hours with Kirsten!

What if she decided she didn't like him, or they ran out of things to say, or what if...

A soft, warm hand had slipped into his, her smile was right there, it was genuine and was just for him. Jake stopped worrying. In fact, for that moment he stopped thinking altogether and smiled back. 'We go then?' Her voice was softly insistent and she led him away.

Jake needn't have worried. Being with Kirsten was simply great fun. Jake would try to talk in German as far as possible and Kirsten would reply in English. There were often moments where each couldn't find the word they wanted and this prompted a sort of game of charades where the word would be acted out or guessed at, misunderstandings ending up, on most occasions, in helpless laughter.

The first stop had been a music store where they browsed the CDs, showing each other the bands that they liked. There were one or two bands which they were both fans of, but some that Kirsten held up for Jake's inspection, were bands he'd never heard of. She wasn't keen on some of the rock bands which Jake enjoyed and she performed a mischievous imitation of a dumb headbanger, her glossy hair bouncing in a chestnut cascade around her shoulders. Jake pretended to be hurt, but took his opportunity to gently mock Kirsten's liking of a dance track which came over the speakers in the shop. He did a passable impression of a monotonous drumbeat in time with the music, pointedly glancing at his watch every few seconds as if to say "hasn't it finished yet?"

They wandered down the main shopping street talking about the fashions in the windows, or the different DVDs they had both seen. Everything seemed to spark a conversation or a joke or a funny story. Jake couldn't believe that he was finding it so easy to talk to this very pretty girl. It felt like he'd left the old, stammering, blushing, self-conscious Jake back in England and here, hundreds of miles from home, here he was the new, confident and funny Jake he always wanted to be.

Kirsten seemed very popular. She greeted many of the people they met, old and young, as friends. When Jake commented on this she just laughed and said, 'Like I say before. Is a small town.'

Kirsten had dropped Jake's hand when they had gone into the record store. Jake had enjoyed the electrical touch of Kirsten's slim, smooth hand in his. He wondered how he could engineer a way of taking hold of it again. 'Maybe,' he thought. 'Maybe I could pretend to trip into her, the cobbles on the street are uneven in places and then I could grab her hand.' He dismissed the idea quickly as being a stupid plan and resigned himself to waiting for Kirsten to make a move.

They strolled down the hill in the hazy sunshine, chatting and laughing. Jake was conscious that her hand was so close to his, that all he needed to do was reach out and take it, but at the last second, his nerve failed him and he carried on walking. Maybe before, she was just being friendly? Maybe taking hold of her hand now would imply an unwelcome romantic approach? Jake sighed to himself, why was this sort of thing always so complicated?

They stopped at a café which had a smell of coffee and greasy chips coming from it. A young man with spiky bleach-blonde hair, a pierced eyebrow and a nose ring served behind the bar. Pop music videos played on several TV screens. Jake sipped on his coke, conscious that most of his cash had now disappeared into granddad's pocket and he'd have to be careful with what little remained.

They made their drinks last for a while and then, as they emerged from the air-conditioned café and into the sticky humidity of the street, Jake heard a girl's voice calling Kirsten's name and two of her friends who had been on the town hall steps when Jake had first seen her, clattered over the cobbles to exchange hugs and a babble of German that

Jake couldn't follow. Suddenly, they dissolved into shrieks and giggles when they realised that Jake and she were together and Kirsten turned to introduce them, flashing Jake a quick, apologetic smile. 'This is Steffi and Inga. They are my friends from school.'

Jake found himself shaking hands with them, something that felt rather odd and a bit too formal, but it seemed to appeal to the two girls, as Steffi (or was it Inga?) didn't let go and chattered excitedly to Kirsten, looking Jake up and down appraisingly. Clearly they were discussing Jake right there in front of him and he felt the old, self-consciousness creeping back and his face began to flush red. Suddenly he felt Kirsten linking her arm in his and pulling him insistently away from her friends. 'Bye bye!' she called pointedly over her shoulder giving a finger wave to the two girls who whooped and giggled and called back 'Wiedersehen!' Jake felt Kirsten's arm slide down his until her hand found its way into his once more. He grinned at her and she smiled back coyly.

They made their way slowly down the hill until they came to another old fortified gateway. To either side of it, a path led up the grassy bank which was the remains of the old town defences. They walked up on to the top of the bank and stood for a while, staring over the flat farmland which lay beyond, a patchwork of gold and green fields, dotted with trees and barns. To their right, they could see the long, straight road which he and granddad had driven down the day before. In the hazy distance, Jake could see the rectangular blocks that were the hospital and hotel back at the motorway junction. To the side of the road wound the wide, steel-coloured river. Suddenly Jake felt a long way from home again, but this time it was a thrill that ran through him. It was as if, this time, this town and this girl who was holding his hand wasn't actually reality at all and a wonderful adventure. It felt like he was invincible.

Still holding hands, they wandered along the path on the top of the bank. Soon the drop to the right tumbled down to the greyish brown waters of the river. On their left, the back gardens of the houses ran up to the embankment. Jake was fascinated. From the top of the bank, they could see straight into each garden. It almost felt like they were spying. In one, a family were seated having a drink at a table in the shade of a large cream-coloured umbrella. The next was neat and tidy with regimented rows of flowers and shrubs and a perfectly smooth lawn on which a rather large lady sunbathed. The next was neglected and overgrown. There were three apple trees sticking up from the undergrowth, their branches bowed down with large, green cooking apples which no one would gather. Many of the high garden fences had gates set in them, allowing the owners to walk straight out.

They walked on until they came to a narrow alley between two gardens leading through a dark passage back into town. A winding cobbled street drew them slowly back up to the town square. At the far end of the square, two large white vans were parked and several workmen were unloading scaffolding and steel barrier fence panels on to the town hall steps. 'Was geschieht?' (What is happening?) Jake asked.

'There is to be a big... err... big party on Monday. There is music and bands are playing and the town is having a... a... vacation.'

'Nice,' Jake nodded his approval wondering if they would be on their way home by Monday.

'It is for our... err...' she shrugged apologetically 'You know...Bürgermeister?' Jake laughed out loud. Yes he did know what a Bürgermeister was! Kirsten looked puzzled at Jake's reaction for a second before continuing. 'Yah, so our Bürgermeister is here now for fifty years, so we have a big party for him.'

'Are you going to be there?' Jake asked, his heart leaping at the thought of spending another day with Kirsten.

'Yah, for sure! You see, the Bürgermeister is my grandfather.'

Chapter 15

Plan B

On a bench overlooking the car park, near the children's swings and slides, sat a lonely, dejected figure. Everything about him, from his bowed head, hunched shoulders and grim expression seemed to express confusion, misery and despair. As he stared at the ground in front of him, Jake's thoughts sprinted round and round inside his head until his brain seemed to turn to mush and any clear thought became impossible.

Once more, he tried to calm down and take in what had just happened. Kirsten had seen Jake's shocked reaction at the news that she was Enkmann's granddaughter. She had paused and asked him if he was OK. At the time Jake had passed off the moment casually, but his mind was racing. No wonder everyone knew her! She was Enkmann's granddaughter for crying out loud! What if he'd told her why they had travelled to Rheinhagen? His stomach lurched and he felt slightly sick at the thought.

Kirsten was talking, but he wasn't listening until he realised she had asked him a question. 'Oh... sorry... entschuldigung,' he blurted out a scrambled apology.

'You do not listen to me Jake.' Kirsten scolded him playfully and she punched his arm with mock aggression.

'Sorry, I'm really sorry!' Jake laughed and raised his hands in surrender. 'What was the question?'

Kirsten heaved a theatrical sigh and shook her head. 'I ask if you have Bürgermeisters in England?'

'Oh yeah, I think the closest thing we have are called Mayors.'

'May-yours?' Kirsten tried out the word.

'Yep, they kind of sit around and they wear these chain things around their neck and make speeches at summer fairs, that sort of thing.'

'It does not sound like the same thing at all!' Kirsten said, affronted. 'My grandfather works very hard for Rheinhagen for fifty years. He makes it a good place to be and a good place for working. He brings er...business here and makes our schools better and, you know the big hospital?' Jake nodded. 'That is new for us here. My grandfather gets the money to build it. Before this, the old hospital was... er... bad, it was... err... too... klein... too small.' Jake nodded his approval, but Kirsten wasn't finished. She seemed determined to make Jake understand that her grandfather wasn't just a figurehead who showed up at Civic receptions.

'My grandfather knows everyone in Rheinhagen. He helps everyone here. He is too old now to be Bürgermeister, but people don't want him to leave, so he is working for fifty years, but now he leaves, he... er...' Kirsten searched for the word.

'Retire?' Jake suggested.

'Yah, he retires now.'

There was a pause. For the first time that afternoon, Jake felt lost for what to say. He was still struggling to think about what the consequences of this new development would be. The pause lengthened and Jake felt awkward and self-conscious again. He checked his watch and immediately cursed himself for doing so, as it looked like he was searching for an excuse to leave. 'You have to go?' Kirsten had spotted the gesture.

Jake cursed himself again. 'No no! I've got nearly an hour still before I need to meet my granddad... just checking,' Jake finished weakly.

Kirsten nodded and appeared to be thinking about where they could go in the time they had. 'We could maybe go to my house for a little time?' Jake was about to say yes when he saw Kirsten's face drop as she saw something over his shoulder.

Across the square rolled a large, expensive looking, black BMW, its paintwork gleaming in the hazy sunlight. The slim, sporty tyres rumbled over the cobbles as it came lazily towards them. Jake turned back to Kirsten and saw that her normally animated face was now set into a cool, polite mask. Jake turned back as the car came to a gentle halt in front of them, its engine turning over with a quiet growl, giving the merest hint of its power. He couldn't see who was at the wheel as the side windows were tinted black. 'Hold on, it's my uncle, I'll see what he wants.' Her voice seemed flat, efficient and emotionless, Jake wondered what sort of person was in the car who could bring about such a change in Kirsten.

Jake stood still as Kirsten walked stiffly over to the driver's window. He felt somehow exposed and vulnerable without her by his side. As she approached the car, the window slid down without any noise at all. There was a brief conversation that Jake couldn't follow. Kirsten seemed to be having a difference of opinion with her uncle. She was shaking her head and half turned to indicate Jake. Kirsten blocked Jake's view, but he could see the driver was wearing a pale pink shirt and tie. Just then, the driver sat forward and Jake could see his face clearly. Dieter still looked as immaculately dressed as they had seen him earlier that day in his office and as relaxed in the leather seats of the BMW as in his swivel chair behind his desk.

Now he had finished work, Dieter had loosened his tie and unbuttoned his top shirt button. He had fixed his piercing gaze on Jake for a couple of seconds and that familiar feeling of being analysed and examined by Dieter's icy blue stare made Jake shudder. Dieter hadn't shown any sign of recognition, in fact he didn't acknowledge Jake at all and he turned back to Kirsten and spoke to her in a firm tone. She seemed to consider arguing for a second, but then her shoulders slumped a little in defeat and she turned and made her way back to Jake looking angry and upset. 'I have to go with him now, sorry. There is a… err… a party I have to get ready for.'

'That's OK, no problem.' Jake struggled to keep the disappointment out of his voice. 'Sounds like fun.'

Kirsten barked a mirthless laugh. 'I do not think that it will be fun. My uncle is having drinks for people who work with my grandfather. Everyone will be old and will ask about school, or say that they know me when I am…' She paused as the word came to her, her hand movements indicating something small. '…A baby.' Jake chuckled as he recalled several of his older relatives who would do exactly the same thing. It seemed that old people spoke to young people in the same way whichever country they came from.

Kirsten turned to go and walked slowly to the car. She looked genuinely sorry to go, something which made Jake's insides flutter with excitement. 'See you Jake.' And she turned away.

Jake had simply stood there watching her go, not knowing what to say or do. Would they see each other again? Was this how it ended? Would it just be a holiday memory of someone who, for a short while filled his world with carefree laughter and sparkling brown eyes? Kirsten had nearly got to the car when her whole body stiffened as if she had made a decision and was bracing herself to see it through. She turned back to Jake and ran, almost skipping back to him. She took his hands and giggled at the bemused expression on his face. 'Will you meet me tomorrow? Say around... drei uhr?'

Jake blinked foolishly. 'Errm... three o'clock?'

'Yah, at three o'clock. I see you then OK?'

'Errm... yeah. Cool.' Never mind granddad's Plan B, forget the stupid mission Jake had thought, a reckless smile curling his mouth at one side, I'm not turning Kirsten down for anyone! And then he had felt Kirsten's hand slide around the back of his neck drawing his head downward towards hers. Her lips were on his and her intoxicating perfume was all around him.

A second, an hour, a lifetime. The concept of time ceased to exist for Jake. Nothing else mattered, or existed outside of their embrace. All too soon she pulled away, Jake having to consciously force his arms to let her go as she backed away toward Dieter's car. Her smile was now shy and vulnerable as if she was uncertain that she'd done the right thing. As she opened the car door, a thought occurred to Jake and he managed to speak. 'Hey, where do you want to meet?'

Kirsten shrugged and laughed, 'Just around here,' and she indicated the square.

'But what if we miss each other?' Jake wanted to make sure nothing went wrong, he might not get another chance to see her again.

Kirsten raised a mocking eyebrow. 'It is a small town, remember?' Jake's grin simply beamed as she slid into the car seat and waved at him.

However, his smile and his mood of elation faded slightly as Dieter slid the car into gear and Jake caught a glimpse of his face. Dieter was facing pointedly straight ahead trying to give the impression that he hadn't seen what had just occurred. Jake could see that his jaw was rigidly clamped shut, teeth grinding and his brow was gathered in a tight furrow. He wore black leather driving gloves and his hands worked on the padded leather of the steering wheel like he was trying to strangle it. Jake knew that Dieter was now way more than being simply annoyed by this English boy who had been the cause of some amusement for a short while. No, Dieter was way past being annoyed and he was no longer amused, he was furious.

On the bench in the park, Jake heaved a sigh and sat back so the hazy sun was falling directly on to his face, absorbing the heat like a sponge. The day had become gradually stickier and more and more humid. Through gaps in the haze, Jake could see enormous cloud formations rising thousands of feet into the sky. He didn't know the proper name for these formations, but his mum always referred to them as Thunderheads. Jake watched as one of these vast clouds drifted past a few miles away, he listened hard, but he could hear no tell tale rumbling.

He could still feel the gentle, silky pressure of Kirsten's lips on his. The thought of the kiss they had shared made him smile, but then, all the complications that surrounded their situation twisted Jake's insides around. Kirsten was pretty and smart and feisty and if he were back home, his friends would be green with envy that a girl like her was going out with him. Jake smiled despite his mood at the thought of what The Weasel would say if he saw them out together. Unfortunately, Jake remembered with another twist of his insides, she may well be pretty and smart and feisty, but she's also the niece of Dieter, who thinks we're definitely dodgy and the granddaughter of the man we've come all this way to unmask as a war criminal. 'This situation is not a good foundation for a lasting relationship,' he said to himself with a heavily ironic laugh. Why was everything always so complicated?

His thoughts were interrupted by the sight of the familiar shape of the Rover turning into the car park. Jake waited until granddad had peered around and spotted him before raising his hand in a wave. Granddad wore a broad smile, but even at a distance, Jake could see that there were dark rings around his eyes and he looked weary. Granddad parked close to where Jake was sat, turned off the engine and got out. He walked over to Jake's bench and sat down. 'How did you get on with Kirsten then? Have a good time?'

Jake felt a sour looking smirk crawl across his face. 'Oh yeah, we had a great time,' he said, his voice dripping with sarcasm. 'Right up to the point where I found out she's Enkmann's granddaughter and her uncle is that Dieter bloke.'

It took granddad a few moments to process this news, so Jake told him what had happened. He looked thoughtful for a while and they sat in silence, the sticky heat wrapping them in a suffocating blanket. The only noise was the hum of bees buzzing in the flowerbeds and the mournful, rhythmic squeak of the recently abandoned roundabout in the park as it slowed gently to a standstill.

'Hmm. Well she's not going to want anything more to do with you when we tell the world who her grandpa really is.' Jake laughed mirthlessly.

'Yeah? You think?'

Granddad let the pause hang between them for a few seconds. 'Sounds like you're up a creek without a paddle Jake.' Silence fell again. Jake couldn't think what granddad might have said to make him feel better, but this response was hardly designed to encourage him. 'I'm just being straight with you Jake. You must have known that if Enkmann turns out to be who we think he is, people would get hurt.'

Jake said nothing. He knew granddad was telling the truth, but at this point he was sick of this whole business.

'But you never know,' granddad said brightly, 'when we finally see Enkmann tomorrow, we might find he's not our man after all and you can maybe see her one more time before we get off home.'

Jake was still feeling depressed and his enthusiasm for granddad's mission was at an all time low, but his curiosity had been tweaked. 'How are we going to get to see Enkmann tomorrow? It's Sunday, so he won't be at work.'

That familiar smile crept across granddad's face again. 'Come and have a look.'

Inside the car, it was stiflingly hot and when the air-conditioning came on, it initially blasted out warm air which had a pungent smell and steamed up the windscreen. Soon enough, the air jets cooled, the windscreen cleared and Jake sat back in his seat and relaxed whilst the cold air washed over him.

Granddad drove hesitantly through the narrow streets of the old town. They were quiet now as the shops were closing one by one and it was too early for the bars and restaurants to have become busy. Granddad sat forward as he drove, peering anxiously at the roads in front, concentrating hard, as if he were afraid he might lose his way.

Soon, they were out of the town and heading through a pleasant suburb, with large houses lining a wide avenue. After crossing a busy junction, Jake saw they were now passing through rolling fields and approaching a large pine forest. Suddenly, granddad turned off the main road and slowed the car as they approached a large house on their right. Jake shot a curious glance at granddad and he smiled back at him jubilantly. 'That's where he lives Jake. That's Enkmann's house.' They cruised past and Jake stared out with renewed interest as if he expected to see Enkmann pruning his roses in the pristine front garden, or searching in vain for a weed on the long, immaculate driveway.

'How do you know it's his house?' Jake asked.

Granddad chortled smugly at his cleverness. 'You've just got to know the right questions and the right people to ask.' He paused and Jake wondered if he was ever going to tell him. 'You know the chap who spoke English at the town hall?' Jake nodded. 'Well, I spotted him talking to the receptionist and so I popped back in and told him I'd left my glasses behind.'

'You went back in?' Jake was incredulous. Wild horses couldn't have dragged Jake back into that place. 'Did you speak to Dieter again?'

'Oh I didn't talk to *him!*' Granddad's face grimaced at the thought of it. 'I "found" my glasses in my jacket pocket before he went off to check Dieter's office. He was very understanding and we had a little laugh about it. Then we got talking and I said that we'd just heard about Enkmann's long service award and we'd like to send him a congratulatory letter and a gift when we get back home. He swallowed it completely and wrote his address down for me on town hall notepaper no less. After that, I dropped into a bookstore off the square and bought a map, found where he lived, drove out here and went up and down his road until I spotted his house number on the gatepost.'

They continued up the small country lane, past a farm and another small clutch of houses. Jake was lost for words at granddad's ingenuity and daring. Granddad was struggling to keep a broad, self-satisfied smile from turning into laughter.

The pine forest on their left deepened and thickened as the land rose. 'So how on earth did you find out where he lives?' Jake asked. 'And what's this plan of yours?'

'Ah well, you'll see,' granddad replied and he said nothing more for a minute or two before he suddenly turned left off the road and up a rough track that led into the trees. Jake experienced a sinking feeling. Surely there was nothing up here in the way of accommodation for the night? Not anything comfortable anyway.

The Rover bumped up the trail gamely, the grass in the middle of the track brushing noisily at the underside of the car. Granddad seemed to be enjoying himself. 'Found this place by accident really. I'd managed to find Enkmann's house and was looking for a spot to turn the car around. I drove up this track, but, as you see, it was too narrow and I couldn't reverse, so I ended up here.' As he said this, the trees on either side parted and they emerged into a small clearing in the forest.

All around was scrubby grass and the remains of tree stumps sticking out of the ground. They had pulled up in an area where the forest floor had been carved into large chevrons by tractor tyres at some time when it had been muddy and now the pattern had been baked into the rock-hard earth. At the side of the clearing a large pile of wood stuck out of the weeds like bleached bones.

Granddad switched off the engine and they got out. The humidity and baking heat hit them hard as they emerged from the air-conditioned comfort of the car. Jake could feel sweat beading on his forehead and upper lip almost immediately. The shelter offered by the trees all around them, seemed to intensify the humidity enormously. For a while neither of them spoke. The silence was complete. The heat was overwhelming. No birds sang. No crickets chirped.

It was a while before Jake summoned up the energy to move. The day's events had left him feeling drained and lethargic. He could hear granddad busy doing something at the back of the car, but his gaze had settled on a colourful butterfly which had alighted on a tall weed in front of him. Its wings opened and shut as it moved around the flower head, its long tongue probing busily for nectar. A wave of tiredness washed over him and he began to feel drowsy behind his eyes. Part of him felt that he should get up and help granddad

173

do whatever he was doing, but he found that he couldn't take his eyes off the butterfly, everything else was blurry and indistinct.

'Jake? Give us a hand here will you?' Granddad's voice seemed to come from a long way off. Still, Jake couldn't wrest his eyes away from the butterfly. 'Jake.' Granddad's voice was more insistent. 'Come on I need your muscles.' The butterfly flew away suddenly. Jake blinked and shook his head, trying to rid himself of the cotton wool feeling in his head. With an effort, he pushed himself off the car bonnet where he'd been sitting and trudged round the back of the car to see what granddad was up to.

The boot of the car had been emptied. Jake's holdall was in a pile on the floor, along with granddad's case, the camera, a foot pump, a first aid kit and an assortment of carrier bags containing various items. The only thing left in the boot was the large, green, lumpy canvas bag that Jake had asked about when they were packing the car, which seemed about one hundred years ago. Taking one end and with granddad on the other, they heaved it out of the car and dumped it on to the dusty ground.

Nearby, a small lizard, frightened by the noise, scampered away through the dry grass and twigs. Granddad knelt gingerly down and started to untie the knot at the top, his gnarled fingers picking away at the stubborn twine. Eventually, the knot relented and granddad opened the bag. He reached in and pulled out another, smaller canvas bag, but this one was a faded blue colour. He tossed it over to Jake who caught it. The bag rattled as he grabbed it and Jake groaned. 'Tents?' His grimace clearly showed his disapproval.

'Plan B, Jakey Boy!' granddad said cheerily. 'Can't afford a guesthouse now and it's ideal for getting near to Enkmann's when we take a recce at his place.'

174

'Recce?' Jake had heard the term in films about the army, but he didn't know what it meant.

'Reconnaissance Jake. Scouting it out. Enkmann's house is on the other side of this wood, all we have to do is to get into position early tomorrow, get well hidden and, when he pops out, we can take a good long look at him.' Another thought seemed to occur to granddad. 'We might even get a photo of him if we're lucky,' he continued, grabbing Jake's camera from the pile. 'Then we'll have something concrete to take to the authorities. What's the zoom like on this?'

Granddad seemed exuberant and energised, a sharp contrast to Jake's lethargy. He didn't like tents. Not after a disastrous camping holiday in Devon which was a complete wash out. He was only young, but he remembered the incessant noise of the rain pattering on the nylon overhead. That, and feeling cold and damp the whole time and just wanting to be back in his own dry house, sitting on his own comfortable sofa, sleeping in his own warm bed.

'Cheer up Jake!' granddad said brightly, spotting Jake's glum expression. 'You're on holiday you know!' and he chuckled, but his laughter turned into a coughing fit, a deep, chesty, wheezing sound. As it subsided, he smiled up at Jake with watery eyes.

With a sigh, Jake took his tent and found an area nearby which looked fairly flat. He undid the blue bag and tipped the contents on the floor. At least he should be dry this time, he thought. The ground was parched and thousands of little cracks in the dried mud made a dull mosaic. A small spider scuttled away and disappeared inside one. Granddad pulled out another tent just like Jake's, two green, old-fashioned looking sleeping bags and another canvas bag whose contents clashed and clattered. 'Cooking gear,' granddad explained. Jake was starting to feel hungry and very thirsty by now, but when he mentioned it, granddad said, 'Priorities Jake, shelter first, then we'll take care of provisions.'

'Provisions?' thought Jake. Did granddad think he was back in the army or something?

Jake started to try and make sense of the rather ancient looking tent that lay in front of him in a crumpled heap of faded orange nylon and heavy wooden poles. The heat and humidity were giving him a headache, making it hard to concentrate. He glanced over to where granddad had neatly laid out the tent and poles and was counting the thin metal pegs as he removed them from their bag. Jake did the same. He had never put up a tent on his own before and he tried to keep an eye on granddad who seemed to know what he was doing. After laying out the poles and pegs, Jake looked up to see that granddad had disappeared under the fabric of the tent which gradually took the familiar triangular shape. Granddad emerged, perspiring and looking dishevelled. He smiled encouragingly at Jake, grabbed some pegs and soon had the tent stable with its fabric taut.

Jake was not enjoying himself. In the orange light under his tent, it was stiflingly hot and sweat was pouring off his face and down his back. He had a raging thirst and he could feel his anger rising as he wrestled with a pole, trying to feed it down a loop in the fabric. He cursed under his breath. Exhaling heavily and willing himself to be patient, Jake twisted and poked the pole furiously until the tent seemed to surrender and the pole slid home. He sighed in relief and fought his way clear of the suffocating fabric. After a few breaths of the comparatively fresh air of the clearing, Jake dived back into the tent, fitted the remaining poles quickly, hastily drove the pegs into the ground and tightened the guy ropes. Jake had copied everything that granddad had done, so he couldn't understand why his tent looked wobbly and skewed with loose creases across it, whilst granddad's was straight and rigid.

Too tired to bother any more with it, Jake went to see what granddad was doing. He discovered him crouched over a small camping gas stove, its fierce, blue flame hissing as granddad held a billycan full of water precariously over it. He looked up and grinned at Jake. 'Nice cup of tea first, and then we'll get some grub on.' Jake's smile didn't have a great deal of enthusiasm behind it.

A few hours later, in the deep darkness of night time in the forest, Jake rolled over again, trying in vain to get comfortable. A rhythmic, rumbling, grumbled across from granddad's tent. 'At least his snores aren't as bad as his coughing,' Jake thought. The last coughing fit seemed like it was never going to end. For a while, Jake had panicked that granddad was struggling for breath and there was something wrong, but finally the chesty wheezing had subsided and granddad had waved away Jake's concerned enquiries.

Jake shifted in the hot, clinging fabric of his sleeping bag trying to get to sleep. It didn't help that he had heartburn from the meal granddad had cooked. He'd been handed a spoon and a billycan full of baked beans and told to tuck in. Granddad had fried some large, spicy frankfurter sausages which had to be cut in half before he could get them all into the pan. These had been served up between two slices of hard, chewy bread that Jake was told was the local speciality. The other problem he was experiencing, was the fact that the piece of ground he'd pitched his tent on was slightly sloped and he kept finding himself at one side of his tent where, as luck would have it, a tree root or a rock stuck upward into his ribs.

The air inside was hot and stuffy. He had tried sleeping with the doorway opened up, but a large moth had fluttered in, attracted by the weak glow from his torch bulb. The moth flapped around in chaotic circles until Jake's flailing hand made contact and it was batted back outside. He had hurriedly closed and zipped the doorway again, his body shuddering involuntarily at this close encounter with the forest's wildlife.

Back in the stifling darkness, Jake had tried to relax and he closed his eyes. Now he'd switched his torch off, the blackness was complete and there was no difference between when his eyes were open or shut. He lay back for a while, experiencing this utter blackness. Even in the darkest night in his room at home, the street lights in Clayfields Avenue would cast a yellow glow around the sides of his curtains. The thought of home sent a pang of remorse through his insides. If he was honest with himself, Jake knew that they hadn't made much of an effort to get in touch with his mum and dad and let them know they were OK.

Jake squirmed guiltily in his sleeping bag. The thought nagged at him until he became frustrated and angry at his inability to drop off. He heaved himself furiously over on to his other side, only to find another tree root that dug into his shoulder blades. Sighing, Jake tried to force himself to think of something else and straight away the memory of the kiss returned to him with renewed clarity. He didn't think of all the complications that would inevitably come if Enkmann was actually Günther Meyer. He didn't spare any thought for what the arrogant Dieter might think about him. Jake thought only of Kirsten. Her smile, her fragrance, her soft hair and her touch. The memories burned brightly and made Jake's heartbeat flutter as he thought about tomorrow and seeing her again. Jake sighed. It looked like it was going to be a long night.

After what seemed like a very long time, Jake's tired eyes began to close and he gradually drifted into sleep and absolute silence fell over the camp.

Had Jake been awake and able to look beyond the trees of the clearing, beyond the slumbering town of Rheinhagen and beyond the line of distant hills, he would have witnessed the occasional flash of white light making the humid haze flicker like a faulty fluorescent tube. The thunder was so distant that, at the clearing, the sound was soft and muted and did not disturb the sleeping campers.

Chapter 16

Stakeout

A large, unfriendly looking fly buzzed around Jake's ear. He flapped at it, but it refused to go away, prompting renewed and more vigorous thrashing. 'Jake!' hissed granddad in a cross whisper. 'Leave it alone! You'll be spotted for crying out loud!' Jake's scowl deepened as he flopped down on to the carpet of pine needles once more.

The day had started early, Jake being woken by the bright daylight coming through the orange fabric of his tent. He felt as if he'd had no rest whatsoever. A headache pounded at his temples and throbbed behind his eyes. Birds sang joyfully in the clearing, their mood in stark contrast to Jake's glumness. The inside of the tent was damp with condensation and smelled musty. He had been too hot in the night and his sweat made the sleeping bag cling to his legs. It felt like the tree root he'd been lying on had bored a hole in his shoulder blade and his back ached. He had emerged into the clearing which was already warm and humid, the night had brought no blessed coolness and the hazy sunshine beat down.

Jake had opened the car and laid across the back seat, but he couldn't get comfortable even here and ended up sitting upright waiting for granddad to wake up. Eventually there was the reedy bleeping of a travel alarm which was rapidly cut off. Then came the noise of a tent door being unzipped and granddad's thin grey hair, normally plastered neatly down, but now wildly stuck up into unruly wisps, popped out of the doorway of his tent. He blinked foolishly, found his glasses, put them on and looked over to where Jake was sitting. 'Morning!' he said, his voice deep and rumbling with sleep. This triggered another coughing fit that made further conversation impossible until it subsided.

For breakfast, granddad had produced a cup of tea and thin slices of spicy garlic sausage on the tough, dark, bread that had become even chewier overnight. Jake decided to forego the sausage as it smelled rather pungent and was thinking about his date with Kirsten in the afternoon and the heart-poundingly exciting possibility of more kissing. He'd accepted the fact that he was going to look rather dishevelled for their date, as his clothes, which had once been freshly laundered and fairly neatly folded, had somehow become a crumpled heap in his bag. He wouldn't be showered and fresh, so a liberal spraying of deodorant would be the best he could manage under the circumstances.

Jake realised that he'd not mentioned to granddad about heading off to see Kirsten in the afternoon. He hoped that they'd get an early look at Enkmann and he'd have the rest of the day free. 'Let's hope he's a keen gardener and he's out trimming his roses,' Jake thought to himself as he forced down the last of the dry bread with a swig of tepid tea.

It was a little before six thirty when granddad got together a bag with the camera, binoculars and some bottles of water and looked over to Jake expectantly. 'Come on then, we've got to get into position before they're awake, we don't want to be spotted. We should have been awake at four really and gone in undercover of darkness.' Jake snorted at the absurdity of them stumbling around in the darkness of the forest in the early hours. Was granddad losing it?

They trudged through the forest, Jake following dolefully in granddad's wake, their footsteps making no sound on the pine needles underfoot. Granddad was navigating through the forest using a compass and following a bearing calculated over the map back at the campsite. Jake had scoffed inwardly at the sight of granddad stumbling through the twigs whilst staring at the compass and pointing rigidly ahead.

The trees thickened around them until they were walking in a sort of half-light and Jake had no idea what direction they were heading in. 'Good job you brought your compass along.' he said. 'We'd be completely lost here without it.'

Granddad paused and smiled. 'Oh, I'd never get lost Jake, there's got to be nearly a dozen ways of finding north if you didn't have one of these things.' Jake was intrigued. 'See up there on that tree trunk?' Granddad pointed a gnarly finger up a nearby pine tree. Jake nodded, not knowing what he should be looking at. 'See that greyish moss up there that's only growing on one side of the trunk?' Jake could see the thick, velvety tendrils of the moss covered one side of the trunk, but the other side was clear. 'Moss tends to grow on the north side of trees. It's not foolproof, but most of the time it'll see you right. This time it's right see? We're heading roughly north-by-north-east and it's on the side where we're heading.'

If Jake had been surprised at granddad's knowledge, he was amazed when the trees in front of them thinned, the ground dropped away towards a road and there, straight ahead of them through the trees was Enkmann's house. Granddad turned to look at Jake over the top of his glasses with a raised eyebrow and smug smile. 'Alright Granddad,' Jake admitted smiling wryly back. 'I'm officially impressed.'

Granddad moved forward cautiously and peered down the steep slope in front of them. He was moving from tree to tree in a stoop, making the most of the cover. Jake realised that, by the way he moved, the training and experience from all those years ago was now flooding back and, although his body was slower now and he moved gingerly, he was a soldier once more.

Eventually, granddad made his way back to where Jake had been standing. 'It looks like they're all still asleep over there.'

'Lucky for some,' Jake said sarcastically as he stifled a yawn.

Granddad frowned and he held Jake's arms, looking earnestly into his eyes. 'This is important Jake. We can't afford to be seen by anyone in the house, or by anybody passing on the road. We need to climb down the bank quickly and quietly and, about halfway down, we take up position behind a pile of wood and weeds. Now Jake, it's important that from now on we don't talk unless it's urgent, we don't move unless it's critical and you don't get caught short after twenty minutes. So find yourself a tree now before we get down there.'

They had started to creep down the bank, wincing at the sound of small twigs snapping beneath their feet. Suddenly granddad froze and held one hand up, flat, an unmistakeable signal to stand still. Following him down, Jake could not see why he had stopped and was about to ask granddad what the problem was, when he heard a steady squeaking and an old man wearing heavily stained overalls pedalled slowly past on a bicycle. The cyclist squeaked down the road ahead of them unhurriedly, staring straight ahead. Once he had disappeared around the bend, they continued down the steep bank. Jake nearly slid on the dry dusty earth which had crumbled under his tread, but he caught himself in time to see granddad looking over his shoulder at him and making a shushing gesture. Jake bridled, it wasn't like he'd done it on purpose.

They descended the bank and Jake flopped on to the forest floor next to granddad behind a pile of branches which had tall weeds growing up through them. Raising himself on his elbows, Jake found that he could see Enkmann's house through fluffy seed heads of the weeds. It was as granddad had said, the curtains behind the windows were all drawn and the household slept. Jake remembered that Enkmann would have been at Dieter's party the night before and would probably be sleeping in. He had pictured Enkmann surrounded by well-wishers, being congratulated for all the good he had done for the town, laughing and shaking hands with friends. Could the genial, respected and well-liked figure of Enkmann that Kirsten had described, really have evolved from the cold, vicious and heartless Meyer? Not for the first time, doubts about whether this trip was going to be a complete waste of time and Enkmann would turn out to be entirely innocent, gnawed quietly at the back of Jake's mind. He sighed to himself, trying to push them aside and then settled down behind the woodpile trying to get comfortable.

Despite his headache, lack of sleep and increasing cynicism about granddad's mission, Jake found that he couldn't help feeling a little excited now that he was spying on Enkmann. It felt dangerous and risky. Lying in the crackling undergrowth of the forest, it was easy to imagine what it would have been like all those years ago, looking out on the grim, forbidding gates and watchtowers of St Gille camp instead of Enkmann's lush, green garden and large, luxurious house. However, Jake struggled to imagine how it would have felt to be putting their lives in jeopardy, rather than merely risking some embarrassing and awkward questions.

Granddad kept his archaic binoculars trained on the house, but nothing moved, its occupants slept on. The first two hours crept by so slowly that Jake had forced himself not to look at his watch because it seemed that every time he did, its hands had hardly moved at all from when he'd last checked. The day had become warmer and more humid. There was no breath of wind to stir the branches of the trees. Once more, the sun was indistinct behind the hazy cloud. From time to time, gaps in the cloud would appear to reveal glimpses of massive thunderheads like vast, moving, snowy mountains.

Flies buzzed around them in randomly geometric patterns, crickets fizzed their chirping song in the long grass and Jake sweated. It was now half past ten in the morning and the most exciting thing to happen so far was around half an hour ago when a door at the side of the building had been opened to admit a grey and white cat. From where they were concealed, they were unable to see who had opened the door and had to be content with watching the cat trot happily indoors after a night hunting in the fields.

A white-haired old lady appeared at the bedroom window and pulled the curtains, gathering them carefully so they hung straight, before disappearing back into the darkness of the room beyond. Her appearance turned out to be the only sign of life and time slowed back down to its previous grindingly sluggish pace.

As the day toiled by, nothing else happened and Jake had become fidgety and restless. He was deeply bored and he kept checking his watch, not to see how long they'd been in the forest, but calculating how long it would take him to get back to camp, freshen up as best he could and walk into Rheinhagen in time to meet Kirsten at three. He was not looking forward to breaking the news to granddad that he was leaving him alone in the forest while he went on a date. A date? Yes, he supposed it was a proper date. Here he was hundreds of miles from home and going on his first proper date.

Jake smiled to himself. The hands on his watch had crept to one o'clock when Granddad put down the binoculars and rummaged in the carrier bag he'd brought with him. He retrieved two small bottles of water which Jake thought would be nice and warm by now, some more slices of the tough, dry bread that now looked stale and practically inedible. Along with this, he pulled out a smaller bag and an overpowering, spicy smell hit Jake's nostrils like a tidal wave. The remainder of the sausage hadn't improved its appeal after spending a warm night in the back of the car and half the next day in a stifling forest. 'No thanks,' Jake whispered, pulling a face.

'But you need to eat Jake. It'll help you stay alert,' granddad insisted.

Jake took a breath and exhaled steadily. It was now or never. 'I'll get something in town later when I meet up with Kirsten.'

Granddad stopped trying to arrange the slices of sausage on to his bread and froze for second or two as he took in what Jake had just said. He glanced over at him. 'Oh...! right. So what time are you meeting her?' Granddad's voice had changed somehow. It still sounded like a friendly enquiry, but there was no mistaking the dangerously flat tone to it.

Jake could see that granddad's face was suddenly blank and expressionless, all except for the telltale jutting of his jaw that suggested his teeth were grinding. 'Three o'clock in the square.' Jake tried to make his voice sound firm and assertive, but it was difficult when he had to whisper.

Granddad nodded slowly to himself, no longer looking at Jake. He looked at his watch. 'Well, you'd best be getting off then Jake. Get yourself spruced up for her.'

'OK,' Jake said. He didn't know what else to say. He didn't really want just to go and leave him there, but he wasn't about to stand up Kirsten for the chance of lying in a forest for hours. 'Well then...' Jake whispered to the back of granddad's head. 'I'll see you back at camp this evening.'

There was no reply. Granddad's wispy grey hair remained impassive and cool. This was awful Jake thought, he just wanted a response from granddad. Anything rather than this horrible silence. The truth was, that before this trip, granddad had always been the cheerful grandparent, always smiling, always with time and a toffee for Jake and now... now Jake realised that this adventure had revealed granddad as just human after all, with all the usual human emotions and failings.

A sudden wave of anger blazed within Jake. How dare he try and make Jake feel guilty, when it had been granddad who had practically forced him to come on this trip. Even as he was thinking this, Jake admitted that he had been just as excited about going on an adventure in the beginning, but he wouldn't have come along if he knew he'd be expected to live in the forest like nomads. He raised himself up on to his knees to go. 'Don't make a racket when you leave,' granddad whispered without turning around, or removing the binoculars from his eyes. The sulky tone in granddad's voice stung Jake and his temper flared.

'Oh that's right,' Jake hissed sarcastically. 'We wouldn't want to show ourselves would we? After all, it's been SO busy with people coming and going all morning hasn't it?' Granddad had turned to look at Jake, his face indignant and angry, but Jake gave him no chance to interrupt him. He'd had enough of this creeping around and sneaking about. He wished he'd never found the photo all that time ago.

'I mean, what a complete waste of time! All we've seen is an old lady pulling the curtains! Big wow!' Jake felt strangely exhilarated now he was venting all the frustration and anger which had been building up for the last few days, but granddad cut across him with a furious whisper.

'Go on then! Don't wait here on my account. Go and have a nice time Jake, I don't expect someone like you to understand what this is really all about.'

' "Someone like me?" What do you mean "someone like me"?' Jake was struggling hard not to scream at this stupid old man.

Granddad turned away a little so he was not meeting Jake's eyes. 'A typical teenager! Only interested in getting what *you* want. It's all about you, isn't it? When I was not much older than you, I was risking everything for my country, *your* country. We sacrificed so much. Many of us gave their lives just so we could keep our country free. But does anyone thank us? No! All the thanks we get is having to put up with a generation of whingeing kids who don't even know what sacrifice is and think that the world owes them and that they're hard done by! Sometimes I think...' He seemed to have stopped himself from going too far.

'Sometimes you think? I haven't seen much evidence of that lately! Sometimes you think what?' Jake goaded, blood thundering through his veins eager for a fight.

Granddad's gaze flicked firmly back on to Jake's and when he spoke, his words were softer and slower. 'Sometimes I don't think you deserve the freedom we won for you.'

There was a heavy silence for a moment and then Jake snorted derisively. 'You know what? I think my mum was right. You do belong in a home. You're losing it Granddad!' Jake tapped his temple with a finger. 'You're hiding in a wood like it's 1943, spying on an old man whose only crime is to do good things for the people of the town where he lives! Improving schools, building hospitals, helping people!'

A sour expression crossed granddad's face. 'Your new girlfriend tell you that did she?'

Jake didn't know what granddad was hinting at. 'Yeah. So?'

'Well it's all very tidy isn't it? We arrive in town and start asking a few questions and all of a sudden you've got a new girlfriend who just happens to be Enkmann's granddaughter and Dieter's niece! How very... convenient.' Jake stared hard into granddad's cold, impassive eyes for a few seconds and then he stood, turned and walked away.

Chapter 17

Saving Private Hargreaves

Jake scrambled quickly up the bank, his fury and burning desire to get away from granddad spurring him on. Angry tears welled up as he ran through the forest and he brushed them away with his sleeve, his anger now directed at himself for letting granddad get to him. He crashed recklessly through the branches which snatched at his clothing and skin, but the scratches and stinging just inflamed his fury more and he ran on, twigs popping and snapping beneath his feet.

Eventually his fury and energy abated and he could run no more. He pulled up and looked around to get his bearings. All he could see was the rough bark of pine trees, their thick branches turning the daylight into a kind of dusk. There were no landmarks, just trees as far as he could see in the half-light. On the edge of his vision, he saw a sort of silvery smudge and he moved closer, the carpet of twigs crackling sharply under his feet. The silver thing turned out to be a stump of a dead tree which had been split by a bolt of lightning years ago and bleached by time. Jake sighed with relief. He recalled seeing it on their way through the forest this morning. He was back on the right track. He looked down on the forest floor to see if he could see evidence of their passing, but the carpet of pine needles seemed to have been undisturbed. However, a little further on, where the ground was muddy, Jake saw a footprint; his footprint, the blocky pattern of the sole of his trainers was clearly shown.

Jake jogged along, more careful of the branches now, as the scratches on his arms and legs were starting to smart. From time to time, Jake would see a familiar landmark they had passed that morning: a fallen tree, a boulder, a small clearing with sunlight streaming into it. And here and there, he saw more footprints in the black mud. Before long, a mosaic of red and orange which Jake could see through the trees ahead, gradually transformed into the familiar shape of the Rover and the tents.

Jake reached into his tent to retrieve his holdall and he looked in vain for fresh clothes. He eventually selected the least smelly T-shirt and a pair of shorts which were crumpled, but not too badly stained. He sprayed deodorant liberally and gelled his hair in the reflection of the car's wing mirror. He considered putting on some of granddad's aftershave and he looked through the doorway of granddad's tent for his toilet bag. The inside of granddad's tent was completely different from Jake's. Jake had left his sleeping bag in a heap in the far end of his tent, and clothes were strewn around, on top of, but not inside his holdall. In sharp contrast, granddad's sleeping bag lay in a tidy rectangle down one side and his travel bag contained all his clothes, all of them neatly folded. Thinking about granddad brought back Jake's anger anew in a hot wave and Jake changed his mind. He didn't want granddad's aftershave, he didn't want anything to do with him again and he hurried out of the tent.

Jake checked the money in his wallet and cursed granddad for again taking most of his cash. He hoped that Kirsten didn't have any plans that involved spending more than twelve euros. He didn't want the embarrassment of telling her he was broke.

He checked his reflection once more and decided that he couldn't do anything else to make himself more presentable and he set off down the track towards the road. Once there, he realised that he couldn't take the right turn and walk back the way they'd come the previous night as that would take him past Enkmann's house with granddad, still hidden in the forest opposite. With a renewed jolt of anger at the thought of him, Jake turned left abruptly and strode out.

The road followed the line of the forest, but, cresting a small rise, Jake could see a junction half a mile ahead with a road leading off towards the grey-blue hazy shape that was Rheinhagen. The day had become more and more humid and the sunshine was indistinct as it fought through the haze. Jake kept checking his watch, trying to estimate if he would be on time. The small road wound through the countryside past fields and farms. Apart from a noisy, old tractor which kicked out a cloud of smelly diesel fumes as it clattered by, its driver impassive in filthy green overalls, there was no traffic at all.

Gradually the grey-blue outline of the town became clearer and Jake could make out the details of the individual buildings. He checked his watch again and quickened his pace. He didn't want to be late and the town still looked a fair way off. After another ten minutes, the farms gave way to large houses, set back from the road with big, luxury cars parked on their drives and at ten to three, Jake arrived at a junction on the busy bypass. He waited impatiently for the lights to change and sprinted across at the signal.

He walked quickly up the now-familiar, narrow streets. He felt rivulets of sweat run down the hollow of his back and his T-shirt had started to stick to him. He didn't think he'd make too good an impression on Kirsten if he turned up like this, but it would be an improvement on not turning up at all.

By Jake's watch, it was five minutes past three when he emerged from a narrow alleyway into the square. He glanced around hurriedly, looking for the figure of Kirsten. It looked liked the stage on the town hall steps was nearly complete. Workmen were hauling a tarpaulin over the top of the scaffolding and tying it in place forming a roof which would protect the lights that were slung underneath a steel gantry.

The dark blue cloth hung at the back of the stage sagged and bulged limply in the hot, damp air.

Jake was just beginning to think that Kirsten had given up waiting for him, when, with a flooding feeling of relief, he caught sight of her looking in a shop window chatting on her mobile. Jake walked over to her slowly, when inside he wanted to run. She looked stunning in figure-hugging jeans, a sparkly white T-shirt and, despite the mugginess of the day, a pink silky scarf which had tassels hanging down draped casually around her shoulders. Jake's self-confidence suddenly lurched. How was it that this lovely creature wanted to spend time with him? He felt clumsy and awkward and suddenly very aware of his damp hands and flushed shiny face. He had to fight the urge to kiss her again right now and to crush her to him. 'Be cool!' he told himself firmly. Kirsten looked up, saw Jake and smiled warmly. She waved and reached out to take his hand, inclining her head to indicate they should go.

The touch of her hand conveyed its familiar electricity and Jake found himself grinning broadly. Still talking into her mobile, Kirsten glanced at Jake quizzically, wondering what he was smiling at. Jake simply laughed and shook his head. He was unable to express how he felt about her in English, let alone in German.

Kirsten hurried him down a side street, heading down the hill on the other side of the town. They passed through another of the old gatehouses, marking the limit of the old town. Abruptly, Kirsten turned right up a wide access road between a furniture store and a car dealership.

She chattered away in rapid German down her phone for a while longer before hanging up and turning to Jake with an exaggerated sigh and a shrug of her shoulders.

'Sorry, it was my friend. She likes to talk.' There was a tiny pause. She had stopped walking and had moved ever so slightly closer.

'Kiss her you idiot!' the voice thundered through Jake's head. 'Do it now!' and Jake found himself moving closer to her as if drawn by an irresistible force. Kirsten's head tilted back and up ever so slightly. They were very close now. Just then, a loud greeting intruded on them, the moment was lost and Kirsten broke away to see who had spoken.

They had reached a concreted yard in front of an ugly, red brick industrial unit. At one side of the building, there was what had been a loading bay for trucks, sheltered from the elements by a zigzag corrugated iron roof, but where there used to be wagons and fork lift trucks, the floor was now covered in a series of plywood ramps and jumps. A steady whooshing and rumbling noise echoed around the roof as a young skater raced over the ramps from side to side like a bizarre pendulum.

A tall, thickset man with curly black hair and beard was walking across the yard towards them. Jake estimated that he was in his mid-twenties. He wore a black T-shirt with the emblem of a popular American rock band on the front, faded blue jeans and tattered converse trainers. He smiled at Kirsten, his teeth looking dazzlingly white against the backdrop of his black beard and repeated his greeting. Kirsten turned to Jake. 'This is Ernst, he err... he runs this place.' And then she turned to Ernst to introduce Jake.

His bushy eyebrows rose in surprise, 'Ah Englisch! Entschuldigung, spreche ich nicht Englisch. Err...' His forehead knitted in a frown of concentration, 'Welcome to Die Fabrik.' The young man's handshake was crushingly firm to the point of being almost painful. Ernst turned back to Kirsten and rattled off a stream of German which was too quick for Jake to follow. He finished by indicating that they were both welcome to enter the building.

Kirsten nodded enthusiastically and linked her arm through Jake's. 'This is a place for... errr... teenager? Yes?

Teenagers to come and err... play,' she laughed at the word. 'It is an old err... fabrik... err...'

The word niggled a memory in the back of Jake's recollection of his German classes. 'Do you mean it was an old factory?' Kirsten looked bemused at the English word. 'Where people make things?' Jake tried again, this time Kirsten nodded.

'Jah. It was empty and we had nowhere to go after school, so my grandfather got the town to buy it and so we now have a place to go.' Her hand swept around the yard and Jake now saw that the yard had markings for a five-a-side football pitch and a basketball court painted on the concrete. There were basketball hoops mounted on the walls at either end and the five-a-side goals had been folded and propped in the corner.

Kirsten led him to the entrance. Behind the glass double doors there had once been the factory's reception desk, but now was Ernst's office with papers and letters and diaries scattered over the desk. Corkboards on the wall behind the desk were littered with notes which had been pinned up. It seemed that Ernst also ran the small tuck shop which sold cans of cola and various brightly wrapped sweets.

Jake was led on through the building. They passed into what had clearly been some kind of workshop. Bright white paint covered the walls including the heavy brackets bolted there which must have once held some kind of machinery in place. On the floor where the machines would have whined and rumbled, stood two table tennis tables and three pool tables. A small group of boys were watching a match at the far side of the room shouting encouragement and arguing noisily. The next room was smaller, and contained an internet café. Three rows of desks contained monitors, mice and keyboards. Several young girls were laughing at a video one of them had found on YouTube. Pop music was playing over the speakers set into the ceiling, but Jake could hear a rhythmic thumping and humming that seemed to be coming up from under his feet vibrating the whole floor.

Kirsten turned to Jake as she went through another door and the thumping noise became louder. 'My friend's brother has a rock band and he is playing at the party in the town tomorrow.' Jake nodded 'They are... playing now so they can be good tomorrow.'

'Oh, like a rehearsal, they're practising?' Jake suggested and Kirsten nodded.

'Jah, they practise,' and she led him downstairs.

The glass door at the bottom must have been soundproofed, because the noise from the band increased dramatically when they opened it and walked through. The low-ceilinged room beyond had been divided by a glass partition. In the larger section, three young men in T-shirts and jeans tweaked and tuned guitars and a fourth was sat on a stool behind a large drum kit, tightening a wing nut on his cymbals and occasionally testing the pedal of his bass drum which accounted for the thumping noise Jake had heard earlier.

In the other section of the room, there was a large mixing desk with hundreds of knobs, dials and sliders, the kind of recording studio equipment which Jake had only ever seen pictures of on TV. Behind the desk, a scary looking man sat in a swivel chair. He had long black hair, his arms were heavily tattooed and he had about half a dozen silver rings in each ear as well as a small silver spike protruding from the black stubble of his chin below his lip. Set back behind the mixing desk there stood a squashy leather sofa and a number of bean bags, across which were draped, Kirsten's friends, Steffi and Inga, along with another girl and two boys about Jake's age. Jake began to feel awkward and self-conscious again. The girls came over to them, giggling and chattering with Kirsten, clearly talking about Jake right in front of him. Jake wished he was fluent in German and he might be able to join in the conversation. He was able to pick out about one word in four. The two boys had remained seated and nodded unenthusiastically at Jake when he was introduced, Jake couldn't tell if they were being rude or simply trying to be cool. Just then, the band struck up the opening riff and launched into their first number.

An hour later, Jake was finding it hard to fake enthusiasm for the music which continued to shake the room and pound his eardrums mercilessly. It wasn't that the band were no good, they played well together, but the music was so loud in the cramped, stuffy room that conversation was impossible and his ears sang in the relative quiet between songs. The basement room had no outside windows and its harsh fluorescent light, combined with his lack of sleep and hunger was giving him a headache. On top of this, Jake had noticed that when the band was not playing, Kirsten chatted to her friends more often than she did with him. He couldn't help thinking that he preferred having Kirsten all to himself. He certainly felt more self-confident when it had just been them alone together.

He found himself thinking about what granddad had said and a tiny, nagging thought at the back of his mind wouldn't go away. What if granddad was right? What if Kirsten was only letting him hang around so she could find out what they were doing in Rheinhagen? As soon as the thought took hold, he dismissed it angrily. He scolded himself for being as paranoid as granddad clearly was. Kirsten seemed to like him, so what if she talked to her friends? Maybe the rehearsal would finish soon and they could have some time together.

Jake resolved to make more of an effort. He told himself not to be so anti-social. These people were not out to get them as granddad clearly thought, no, they were just normal kids. It was true that neither of the boys on the sofa had spoken to him at all, but maybe they were simply shy of talking to a foreigner.

Spurred on by a fortuitous break in the music, Jake tried out his German on the closest of the two boys, asking him what sort of music he liked. The boy stared blankly at Jake and shook his head before turning to his friend in a brief exchange that ended in laughter. Jake felt a sudden anger stirring. Of course he'd understood Jake's question! He was just being awkward, trying to make Jake look stupid. Kirsten had spotted Jake's discomfort and embarrassingly volunteered to translate the question, but by the time the question was asked again and the boy had shrugged and had given a noncommittal response, Jake wished he hadn't bothered and vowed not to go to the trouble of being sociable again.

As a drumbeat began yet another song, Jake's mind wandered back to what had happened in the forest. What was granddad doing now? Was he still spying on Enkmann? Had he seen him by now? Had he realised that he was mistaken about him? With a start, Jake realised that he no longer believed that Enkmann was Gunter Meyer. How could the man so respected and loved by the people of Rheinhagen be the same as the monster of St Gille? It was ridiculous. This whole trip was ridiculous! Granddad was obsessed. He seemed to think that it was still 1943 and these people were the enemy. He glanced at Kirsten's profile as she nodded her head in time with the music, her hair bouncing around her shoulders. She seemed to feel Jake's gaze and glanced over, meeting his stare, a warm, private smile lighting her face up. No, Jake thought, these people were not the enemy!

Jake made a decision. As soon as he got back to the campsite this evening, he would apologise for losing his temper, but he would insist that granddad get in touch with his mum and dad. He couldn't ignore the gnawing, guilty feeling any longer. He would insist granddad tell them everything and let them know they were OK. He'd get granddad to do it, or he'd do it himself. His mum and dad could send over some money somehow and at least they would be able to sleep indoors on their way home and have decent meals, Jake was starving. His decision made, Jake felt much better and even started to relax and enjoy the song, a cover version of one of his favourites which had a catchy chorus. Before long they were all singing along, Jake singing as loudly as any of the others when suddenly, there was an enormous bang and all the lights went out.

The girls screamed as the noise of the explosion rolled on, echoing around. Without an inside window, the only light that Jake could see was coming down the stairs beyond the soundproof door and leaking dimly through the glass. Inside the room, everyone was talking at the top of their voices. Jake opened the door and a little more light came into the studio. The light in the stairway came from two small windows high in the wall. It was somehow different from before, the brightness had gone from the day and a pale, sickly, yellowish glow made Jake wonder what he would see when they got outside.

There was no power in the building at all now and all the monitors in the Internet café were grey and blank. Another massive crash made them all jump. Steffi and Inga screamed again and hugged each other. As if this were a signal, they all began to run toward the exit and they sprinted out of the entrance and into the yard.

Ernst was standing there, his back to them, looking up at the town and the sky behind it. Jake swore loudly. He had seen storms before of course and he'd heard his mum describe the sky as turning black, but Jake had always thought that this phrase was an exaggeration, dark blue, or grey maybe, but not black. However, the sky which hung above the town now was completely and absolutely black from the eerily sunlit roofs of the old town, to a point high above his head.

It seemed that the last few days of increasing humidity and heat had been building up to something big and this storm looked like nothing Jake had ever seen before.

Lightning flashed and forked against the black, velvety backdrop of the sky, followed almost immediately by another shuddering, rumbling crash that seemed to vibrate the very air in his lungs. Now they were out of the claustrophobic rooms in the basement, the sights and sounds of the storm were no longer scary, but thrilling and exciting, the storm's raw, elemental force at once humbling and exhilarating.

The sickly light faded from the rooftops of the town as, somewhere behind them, the angry cloud consumed the sun.

A large raindrop plopped wetly onto the concrete in front of Jake. For a while, it made a lonely circle in the dusty yard and for a few seconds nothing else happened, Jake almost laughed. Was that was all the storm was going to do? He was answered when the raindrop was followed quickly by another and then another, dropping heavily with increasing rapidity. They all took shelter under the roof of the skate park, the rain pinging noisily on the corrugated iron.

The rain became heavier and heavier until soon the noise from the roof made conversation possible only if they shouted. The rain was so torrential that it made a layer of fine spray which was kicked up as each drop hit the ground. Thunder crashed and rumbled almost constantly as lightning flashed in crazy, jagged shapes.

Jake felt an arm slide around his. Kirsten's eyes shone with the same excitement that he was feeling and they smiled at each other. A flash of lightning, brighter than before made her hug his arm tighter and the thunder shook the ground beneath them.

One by one, the others made their way indoors, but they stood for a long time staring at the storm, feeling the air around them cool as the rain fell steadily. With a guilty rush for not thinking of him before, Jake thought about granddad. The storm would have reached the forest first. Had he been able to get to shelter before it hit? Would the tents stand up to the rain? The thought of spending another night in the forest was bad enough, but what if they had leaked and everything inside was soaking wet? Jake shuddered. Kirsten felt the movement and looked up at him questioningly.

'My granddad might be out in this,' Jake explained. 'We're camping in the forest.'

Kirsten's face fell and she looked concerned. 'You should go and see if he is OK,' she said. Jake felt rejected. Was she trying to get rid of him? She seemed to spot his disappointment and smiled wryly. 'I will see you tomorrow at the party yes? You should go now. Go and look after him.' She playfully pushed him away laughing at his crestfallen face. 'Awww,' she said looking at Jake with that mischievous glint, her head tilted on one side. 'Don't be so sad Jake,' and suddenly they were kissing.

Jake didn't ever want the kiss to end. He didn't ever want to let her out of his arms, but Kirsten broke away laughing playfully. 'Go on now!' she chided him with a stern voice which didn't match her beaming smile. 'Go on!' and she pushed him out from the shelter of the roof where he felt the warm rain pattering down on his head and shoulders.

He sighed. 'See you tomorrow,' he called and reluctantly he turned and set off back to the forest, his heart hammering a joyous rhythm loudly within him.

The rain was the heaviest Jake had ever seen. By the time he'd passed through the old gatehouse, he was soaked to the skin and his trainers were squelching when he walked. He blinked the rain from his eyes. It was like taking a shower fully clothed. He jogged steadily through the deserted gutters of the town, rivers of dirty water gushing down the streets, inundating the drains which couldn't cope with the sheer quantity of water. Jake splashed across the town square marvelling at the amount of water running off the tarpaulin roof of the stage which was chattering down on to the cobbles like a waterfall.

The daylight had faded into a kind of early dusk as Jake doggedly jogged back the way he'd come earlier, but where there had been dusty tarmac and parched earth, now the road swam with water. The rain had changed from being a violent downpour to steady, heavy rain which looked like it was going to be around for some time. He felt curiously elated, being out here on his own whilst the thunder rumbled around. It seemed such an eccentric thing to be doing and he laughed at the growling sky.

He found the track to the campsite branching up from the road into the darkness of the forest. By this time, he was feeling a little chilly, the storm had certainly cooled things down. He slowed to a walk, he had a painful stitch which had been forming in his side for the last half a mile. He trudged up the track, his eyes gradually getting used to the light. His plan was clear in his mind and he was determined to carry it out. He would apologise first and then they'd head into town to use a payphone to call his parents, after which, they'd book back into the guesthouse where Jake would wallow in a hot bath and sleep in a cosy bed. As he walked into the campsite, visions of the massive breakfast he'd eat tomorrow morning flashed around his head, making his stomach rumble and his mouth water.

He didn't have to check the tents to realise that the camp was deserted. There was an unmistakeable air about the cold, sodden, sag of the orange nylon fabric and the cool, impregnability of the locked Rover. Granddad wasn't here.

Jake looked briefly inside the tents, but a glance confirmed his first instinct. Surely he wasn't still out there in the forest spying on Enkmann? He felt anger boiling up again at the thought of just how stubborn this old man was. Why couldn't he accept that he wasn't sixteen years old anymore? 'Oh this is just wonderful! He'll make himself sick sitting in the woods soaking wet. It'll be just my luck if he catches a chill and we'll be stuck here 'til he gets better!' Jake raged vehemently to the empty, impassive forest.

Jake's anger cooled gradually in the silence of the clearing, broken only by soft pattering noises of the raindrops falling on the tents. He blinked the water out of his eyes and shuddered involuntarily. Beneath the trees, in the dim light, the air had cooled and, in his soaking wet clothes Jake had chilled and was starting to shiver. He dived into his tent and found a tracksuit top under the pile of clothes. It felt rather damp, but at least it offered some extra warmth. The tent had leaked under the onslaught of the downpour. There were puddles on the groundsheet and his sleeping bag looked rather soggy in places. Jake shuddered again at the prospect of spending another night under the sodden orange nylon.

Jake realised that he didn't know what to do. Should he wait for granddad to come back? Should he go and fetch him? What if he set off to find him and they missed each other? The anger he felt towards granddad and his tiredness from a lack of sleep was confusing him. He needed to think! He took a deep breath and exhaled, blowing his cheeks out. Where the heck was granddad?

He realised that the light was fading even more now and that made up his mind. If he didn't set off to find granddad soon, it would be getting really dark. He struck out into the forest.

Ten minutes later he realised that he was in part of the forest that he'd never passed through before. How on earth had he gone wrong? As he looked around, he could see that no footprints had disturbed the thick layer of pine needles on the floor of the forest and he'd passed none of the landmarks he'd seen previously.

Jake swore through his gritted teeth. Brilliant! Surely he couldn't be lost? On the edge of his vision, he could see a slight brightness through the tree trunks, way off to his right hand side. Was that the edge of the forest? Had he got there already? He made his way as quickly as he could through the branches towards the patch of brightness. Jake realised that the trees around him were thinning, but instead of emerging near the road overlooking Enkmann's house, he found he was looking out over a ploughed field with more woodland beyond it. The sky was still dark and brooding and lightning illuminated the clouds beyond with a flickering light. Jake couldn't see any clues as to where he was and which direction he should be heading.

Jake was aware of a fluttering, panicky feeling that he got when he knew he was lost. He span around and with renewed care, he retraced his steps back until he could see the campsite dimly through the branches. Back on more familiar territory, he cast around, looking for the trail which led to their lookout point. However, the ground had been churned up in places and seemed untouched in others, making it very confusing and impossible to follow. He realised that whilst he'd been looking around, he'd made a whole bunch of new footprints which was only making things more confusing.

He needed to figure out which direction he should go in. He knew the road lay somewhere to the north, but without granddad's compass, the likelihood was that he'd just end up going round in circles again and again until it got dark, after which, he'd have no chance at all of finding granddad and he may not even be able to find his way back to the camp. So which way should he go?

With a recollection so sudden and so forceful, Jake laughed loudly and whooped to himself, the sound deadened by the forest almost immediately. He looked eagerly at the closest tree trunk. High up in the branches, he could see the layer of fuzzy moss which was growing on its northern side. Now Jake had his direction he scampered off with reckless speed through the trees.

He seemed to have been running for ages and still hadn't seen any evidence that he'd been that way before. He kept stopping and checking that he was heading in the right direction, but he'd like to have seen some clue that he was on the right track. Thunder continued to rumble and rain fell unceasingly. Under the trees, Jake could not tell if it was raindrops falling on him or the water falling off the trees, all he knew was that he was soaking wet and starting to get cold. He wondered how granddad was coping, a thought that made a number of disturbing images flash through his imagination. 'Please God, let him be OK,' Jake prayed silently and he quickened his pace.

With huge relief, Jake saw the silvery lightning-struck tree stump swim out of the deepening gloom ahead of him. He was going the right way after all! He ran on, pale tree trunks flashing past his vision and twigs snapping smartly as he sprinted onward. Suddenly, he found himself at the top of the bank and he slithered to a rapid halt narrowly avoiding crashing straight down the steep slope. There was Enkmann's house, its windows dark, dead smudges in the murk. Jake looked down to the bottom of the bank and with enormous relief he saw the figure of granddad sitting huddled where Jake had left him. The gathering tension that Jake had been feeling, slid from his shoulders as he bent forward, hands on his knees panting for breath after his run through the forest.

He'd not realised how much he depended on this stubborn old man and how much he loved him and how much better he felt now that they were together again. Oh yes, he could be obstinate and thoughtless and selfish and narrow-minded and intolerant, but he was his granddad after all and he could be kind and warm and funny and caring and mischievous and recklessly impulsive. The rush of warm feelings towards his granddad prickled at the back of Jake's eyes. He needed to get down there, apologise and make things right between them.

As he started down the bank, Jake looked again at the figure of his grandfather. There was something not quite right with the way he was sitting. His legs were drawn up and he was hunched against the cold and rain. 'Granddad?' Jake seemed to hear his own voice as if it were someone else talking and it was heavy with concern. 'Granddad? Are you OK?' and he took another step down the slope. As he did, his footing slipped on the wet earth of the bank and his legs shot out from underneath him, sending him crashing noisily down the bank to land with a clatter near to the pale, grey-haired figure.

Jake picked himself up from the forest floor. He'd been scratched down his arms and hands as he'd snatched at tree roots trying to save himself. Down the side of his left knee there was a wide, red graze where he'd slid on it. However, despite his injuries, Jake felt no pain. He had no room in his consciousness for pain. He'd just realised what was wrong with granddad. Granddad hadn't reacted to Jake's voice and he hadn't looked up when Jake crashed down next to him. With an icy dread Jake realised that granddad wasn't moving at all.

Chapter 18

Rescue Mission

'Granddad?' No response. 'Granddad!' Jake's voice rose in panic as the hunched figure remained motionless. Jake scrambled over to him, took hold of his shoulders and shook him, heart thudding as the dreadful fear took hold. 'GRANDDAD!' There was the slightest movement of the eyelids and granddad jerked awake with a noisy inhalation. 'Oh thank you God!' Jake muttered fervently to himself as the sense of relief loosened the tension within him. He was alive! He shook granddad again, his shoulders seemed bony and the muscles on his arms were slack and flabby beneath the cold, wet fabric of his shirt. His eyes flickered open and shut a few times before closing again, his head drooping forward onto his chest. Not good! 'Granddad! GRANDDAD! You need to get up now! Come on! Wake up! WAKE UP!' Jake shouted. He didn't know what to do, but he knew that he had to wake him up and get him somewhere warm. 'Wake up Granddad please, PLEASE!' Jake could hear the panicky sob in his voice.

Granddad jerked awake again, a gnarled, liver-spotted hand rubbed his eyes and he looked around groggily. 'Hello Jake,' he said weakly. 'When did you get back?'

Jake was so grateful to hear his voice again, he laughed in a near-hysterical barking sound. 'Come on now, you need to get up, you're freezing cold and we need to get you warm.' With a sinking feeling, Jake realised that granddad was a long way from standing upright, let alone tramping through the forest back to camp.

'There's no one home,' granddad croaked. Jake blinked stupidly, wondering what granddad could be talking about? 'There's no one home,' he repeated, waving a finger weakly at the dark, empty house across the road. 'A big car came to pick them up just as the rain started. They all got into the car, under the driver's big umbrella so I never got a good look at him. It was really coming down by then, so I tried to get up the bank and head back to camp, but I kept slipping down before I even got halfway.' Granddad's voice tailed off as if the effort of talking had exhausted him. Jake noticed for the first time that there were broad muddy streaks down the side of granddad's trousers where he had fallen and slid down.

He nodded absently as he tried to think how they were going to get back to camp. It was nearly dark now. Jake was in no hurry to get lost in the forest again and his heart sank at the thought of getting granddad back through the maze of fallen branches and slippery tree roots, even if he could get him up the steep bank.

Jake stood up and surveyed the edge of the forest which ran down to the road. It was another steep slope to the wet tarmac below, but there was a shallow gulley at one side that led downwards at an angle. It was a little overgrown in places, but it looked like their best option. Once they were on the road, it would be a longer walk back to the campsite, but it would be easier going and at least they wouldn't get lost.

Turning back to granddad, he saw that his eyes had glazed over again and seemed to be fixed on to a point somewhere on the ground in front of him. An instinct told him that it was very important that he didn't let him fall asleep again. 'On your feet soldier!' Jake shouted. 'We're heading back to camp right now! That's an order! Move it!'

Jake's shouted commands sounded flat and feeble in the deadening air of the dripping forest, but granddad's eyes snapped away from where he'd been staring and, with trembling hands, he started to manoeuvre himself into a kneeling position. He gestured to Jake that he needed help to get to his feet. Jake took hold of granddad's hand. His skin was clammy and cold. Then, with a groan, granddad heaved himself upright. The effort provoked a deep, chesty coughing fit and he pulled his sodden handkerchief from his pocket to place over his mouth, his eyes red and watering.

After a while, the coughing seem to settle down and he stood, swaying a little and holding on to Jake, puffing his cheeks out as he tried to get his breath back.

'Are you OK now?' Jake asked, his eyes wide with concern. He'd always thought his granddad to be a healthy, active person. When he walked, it was with the confident stride of a much younger man, he never seemed to get ill and sometimes he could even be persuaded to bowl a few balls to Jake in the cricket nets. However, the old man in front of him now trembled with cold and fatigue, his hair was a tangled silver mess, pine needles clung to the mud-stained fabric of his shirt and trousers, his face was a shocking ashen grey and his breath wheezed in and out with a sickening bubbling sound. Jake took off his tracksuit top and helped granddad to put it on. It looked ridiculous on him, but at least it might keep him a little warmer.

'Right then... That's good Granddad... OK then, we need to get back to the camp now, alright? Just follow me.' Jake led the way to the top of the bank, granddad gripping tightly to Jake's hand and shuffling through the pine needles painfully slowly. 'Right then, we need to get down to the road, OK?' Jake stepped backwards into the gully, still holding granddad's hand. The road was only a few feet below them, but it now seemed like a long way and Jake couldn't see how he was going to be able to get this feeble, shambling old man down without him falling and hurting himself. He shook himself. No, he would not let that happen!

He looked up at granddad and saw the fear there. 'OK Granddad, just take little steps yeah? Come on now let's get you out of here.' Jake made his voice sound as firm and purposeful as he could and granddad nodded in response. He gingerly stepped downward, paused, as if testing his footing, before bringing the other foot down hurriedly. The loose stones at the bottom of the gully shifted and granddad slid a few inches until they jammed painfully against the side of Jake's foot, stones skittering down the slope and across the tarmac of the road.

'I'm going to fall! I'm going to fall! For God's sake don't let go!' Granddad's voice was high and panic-stricken, almost child-like, his body stiffening with terror. Jake had never heard him make a noise like it. Its shrill whine disturbed Jake deeply and he needed it to stop. Granddad's eyes were wide, his body frozen and he was emitting a weird whimpering noise like a scared child. Jake couldn't bear it. His temper ignited. 'SHUT UP! Just shut up NOW!' he screamed. The whimpering stopped and granddad blinked in surprise. 'We are getting down here NOW! There is absolutely NOTHING to be scared of, because I'm right here and I will NOT let you fall! Do you understand? I will NEVER let you fall!'

In the silence which followed, Jake held granddad's gaze and, as he looked, he could almost see the panic leaving him. Granddad's shoulders relaxed, his grip loosened and he nodded. 'Sorry Jake, I'm sorry,' he muttered. 'Right then, I'm ready.'

They descended the slope slowly, one tiny, shuffling step at a time. Once or twice Jake found his footing slipping from under him, but he managed to catch himself before he slid too far. Eventually, after what seemed like ages, they stepped on to the wet tarmac of the road.

The rain had eased slightly and was now a steady drizzle which had brought a low, foggy cloud that draped itself across the tops of the high pine trees. It was now properly dark and the silence was only broken by the soft drip, drip, drip of water falling from the trees and a quiet gurgling as it drained away down the gutter.

Standing in front of Enkmann's house gave Jake a strange feeling. He felt oddly exposed, as if they shouldn't be there. It was a kind of uneasiness, like there was someone watching them from the house, even though he knew it was deserted. 'Come on Granddad, let's get out of here.' Granddad was swaying slightly, still holding on to Jake for support. They walked off down the road together, the old man clinging on to the young man's shoulder.

The road seemed to go on forever. Jake recalled from when they had driven there, (was it just a day ago?) that it had curved this way and that for a mile or two as it skirted the edge of the forest. However, every time they went round a corner expecting to see the track leading off to the camp, they were met with yet another unbroken wall of pine trees and another bend to walk around.

Jake wondered what he would say if a car passed by. He was certain that a driver seeing an old man with his grandson walking in the rain in summer clothing after dark would be sure to stop. Jake almost started wishing someone would. They might know what to do about granddad. He hated the crushing responsibility which he now felt. This had been granddad's trip, his idea, his responsibility and yet now? Now it was Jake's job to look after granddad. He fought back the fluttering dread which nagged at the back of his mind. He would get granddad back to camp, he'd put him into the car where it was dry and he'd start the engine and get the heater going to warm him up. He reassured himself that all granddad needed was a dry, warm place to sleep and he'd be as good as new in the morning. He nodded as if he was agreeing with himself, but the flickering dread intruded again. What if he wasn't? What if he was really ill?

Their progress was painfully slow. Granddad couldn't seem to walk any faster than a sedate stroll. When Jake had tried to encourage him to pick up the pace, granddad had been convulsed with another coughing fit and they'd had to stop completely until it had settled down and he'd caught his breath.

The miles passed grindingly slowly. Jake found his mind wandering whilst they trudged along. At first, Jake had tried to keep an encouraging conversation going with granddad. He thought it important that granddad stayed alert, so he'd tried to talk about all sorts of things, but it had been a very one-sided chat as granddad seemed to be using nearly all his energy on simply putting one foot in front of another. Soon the conversation died altogether.

It was almost as if Jake was detached, an interested onlooker watching some kind of TV show where it was someone else plodding along a quiet country road in rural Germany as the drizzle pattered down on his already soaking clothes.

Finally, they rounded a bend and there, in front of them, was the track. Even then it seemed to take ages before they saw the red paint of the Rover gleam dully through the branches.

Jake took charge. 'Where are the car keys Granddad?' he asked. Granddad didn't seem to have enough energy left to talk, but he fished in his pocket and passed Jake the keys with a trembling hand. Jake unlocked the car and opened the passenger door. 'Come on then Granddad, you'll be dry in here and I'll get the heater on in a bit.'

Granddad didn't question Jake's order, but manoeuvred himself stiffly into the seat. As Jake closed the door with a clunk, granddad closed his eyes and laid his head back. Jake's body was crying out for rest. He'd hardly eaten anything today and this, combined with his fatigue, was making him feel dizzy and light-headed. He shook himself to try and wake up, but it just made his head ache.

Jake dived into granddad's tent and unzipped his sleeping bag until it was fully open. He could feel that it was wet in places where the rain had leaked through, but it would be better than nothing. He pulled it out of the tent, oblivious of the water which dripped down his neck from the wet nylon as he did so. Holding the sleeping bag in a big bundle in front of him, Jake made his way back to the car. Worryingly, granddad didn't make any response when his car door was opened and Jake wrapped the sleeping bag around him. Jake looked into his own tent, stripped off his sopping T-shirt and tossed it in a corner, where it landed with a soggy sound.

He grabbed another shirt which didn't appear to be too damp from the leaking rainwater and put it on. With a dismayed groan, Jake discovered that his sleeping bag was saturated. He wouldn't be using that tonight.

Jake dashed back to the car and sat in the driver's seat. After coming so many miles together in the Rover, it seemed strange now they had swapped seats. 'Alright Granddad?' Jake enquired of the grey face above the mound of blue sleeping bag. Without opening his eyes, granddad nodded. 'I'll get some heating on,' Jake said and, trying to remember the dozens of times he'd seen granddad do it, he fitted the key in the ignition and turned it.

The car gave a lurch forwards as the motor turned over and the noise died almost immediately. The jerk had shaken granddad awake long enough for him to look around him woozily. 'Still in gear,' he said shortly and his eyes closed once more.

Jake pressed down the left hand pedal which he knew to be the clutch and eased the gear stick backwards, until it popped out of its slot. Although he knew that it should be in neutral now, his face was still screwed up with anticipation when he turned the key once more. This time the engine spluttered into life easily and settled down into its familiar ticking-over noise. Jake realised that the air-conditioning was still switched on so he turned it off immediately, he didn't want to make things cooler! After a short while, lukewarm air started to dribble through the air vents and Jake felt his muscles start to relax as the car warmed up.

Time crept by. It felt weird sitting in the blackness of the forest; the engine ticking over and the steady ping of raindrops falling on the roof the only sounds. Despite the fatigue which made his whole body ache, he found that sleep would not come easily and he shuffled around in his seat trying to get comfortable. It was odd that, now he had gone so long without food, he wasn't actually hungry at all. In fact he had a rather sick feeling in his stomach and a throbbing ache behind his eyes.

If he was honest with himself, Jake knew that the main reason he couldn't sleep was his deep concern about granddad's condition. He looked more comfortable now the interior of the car was warm to the point of being stuffy and he had dozed fitfully beneath the sleeping bag. However, he still looked unwell, his face a pale blur in the darkness. His coughing caused him to wake up every ten minutes or so. Jake would watch granddad's trembling hand hold a handkerchief to his mouth until the coughing subsided, after which, he would lie back as if exhausted.

The truth was, Jake was uncertain what he should do. He'd never had to look after anyone before. He'd always been reliant on others to know what the best course of action was, but now he felt very much alone. A rumbling wheeze from granddad announced the beginning of another coughing fit. Jake checked the luminous dial of his watch, it was nearly eleven thirty. Was granddad going to be OK? He had hoped that a good night's sleep would make him good as new, but how was he going to get any rest if he was coughing all night? Finally, Jake admitted to himself that granddad needed medical help and the realisation made his insides turn over. If they had been back in Britain, he would simply call 999 and get an ambulance to come out, but here he was, in a forest in Rheinhagen, his phone a useless, dead lump of plastic and wires in the glove compartment. He had no way of getting help, no one to ask for advice, what was he going to do?

Suddenly he wished that his mum were there. She would know what to do. She would take charge and sort things out. Right now Jake would cheerfully have put up with all of the things about her that annoyed him so much, just to be able to push all the worry and responsibility on to someone else. For a second or two, Jake imagined his mum whooshing into the clearing like Superman with a fleet of ambulances racing up the track, lights flashing and sirens blasting. The image faded and a sense of loneliness crept out of the sodden darkness all around him, increasing his feelings of isolation. Nobody would come to their rescue. Nobody knew they were here. It was all up to Jake.

Panicky, confusing thoughts flashed through his mind and he had to force them away so he could think clearly. 'OK,' he said to himself, his tone firm and decisive, even if he didn't feel decisive at all. 'OK, we need to think about priorities. What's the most important thing we need right now?' Somehow, talking to himself was helping him think straight. 'Granddad needs a doctor,' he muttered, 'that's it.'

There it was. He had to get medical help. That was his priority. But how was he going to get help out here? It was late on a Sunday night and they were miles from anywhere. He really didn't want to get out of the warm car to walk back into town to fetch help. He didn't even know where he could find a doctor anyway. Think! He slammed his hands on to the leather steering wheel in frustration. And then the thought struck him. 'The hospital! Of course!' he exclaimed, wondering why he had not thought of it before. And now he knew where they needed to go, in the same moment, Jake knew how they would get there.

'Buckle up Granddad,' Jake said brightly, leaning round him to pull the passenger's seat belt down and clicking it into place. Granddad was now so drowsy that he scarcely responded; his heavily lidded eyes flickering open for just a moment. Jake sat back and fitted his own seat belt in place. It felt very strange to be sat in the driver's seat, but there was no other way. Trying to relax and breathe steadily, he switched the car's lights on, the beam reflecting back off the silver-grey tree trunks, making him screw up his dark-accustomed eyes.

'Come on now!' Jake told himself. 'You've watched mum and dad drive often enough and you were thinking you could drive better than granddad on the way here.' His foot eased down on the accelerator just slightly and the engine revved loudly. 'Whoa! That's a little sensitive! Nice and easy now,' he laughed at himself with high-pitched chuckle. This was insane! 'Right then… here we go… clutch in… into first gear… and let the… clutch… out… slowly.'

The car lurched forward suddenly and the engine coughed and died. It seemed very quiet without the engine running. Jake could almost hear the thudding of his heart. He breathed out slowly, glanced at granddad who, rather worryingly, hadn't woken with the sudden movement. 'OK. Try again.' This time, he tried to keep the revs up as he let the clutch out, but it wasn't enough and the engine died again. This was proving to be more difficult than it seemed. 'Third time lucky!' Jake muttered. This time, he took it really slowly, concentrating on the engine noise as his left foot gradually lifted off the clutch.

He was rewarded when the car started to move forward slowly, its engine spluttering a little with the effort. Now Jake had to focus on steering as well. The car bumped over the ruts as he peered out of the window at the point in the clearing where the track led down to the road. The car seemed happy to trundle along slowly in first gear and Jake certainly didn't want to go any quicker, as he tried to get a feel for steering.

Once Jake had managed to nose the car into the track successfully, he found he had two new problems. Firstly, as they were now going down a slight slope, the car was picking up speed. It wasn't exactly going fast, but it was faster than Jake wanted to go. The other problem was that the track looked extremely narrow and he wasn't used to judging the width of the car. Tree branches scraped and clattered up his door, so he steered left a tiny bit and they started to do the same on the other side. Jake decided that this was one too many things to think about right now and simply ignored the noise and concentrated on getting to the road.

With a bump, the tyres rode up on to the tarmac and Jake allowed himself to relax a little. Here on the road at least, there was more space and, although he prayed that he wouldn't meet any other cars, he could simply drive the car along and just concentrate on steering.

The realisation that he was now breaking the law by driving on public roads, under age and with no insurance, nagged at the back of his mind. However, Jake found it surprisingly easy to ignore. He knew that this was the only course of action he could take right now. He had no choice. He had to get granddad to the modern, white hospital which they'd passed on the way here. The hospital he'd last seen in the distance when he was walking on the town walls with Kirsten. Kirsten. Now was not the time to be thinking about her and Jake focussed on how he was going to get to the hospital. He would go back the way they'd come until he reached the main road. Once there, he would simply follow it as it looped around Rheinhagen and went out towards the motorway, when he would turn off into the hospital car park. Simple.

The Rover sloshed along through the rain. There was no traffic at all, and Jake began to feel that he had the road all to himself. Still trundling along in first gear and a long straight stretch of road in front of him, Jake began to feel more confident and decided to try and change into second gear, which he managed after a good deal of crunching gears and swearing. They seemed to be travelling much faster now and Jake's heart thumped with the sensation of speed, although the illuminated dial on the dashboard indicated a speed of something less than twenty miles an hour.

A few minutes later, the dark shape of Enkmann's house could be seen on their left hand side, Jake spared it a quick glance as they rolled past. The house was still in darkness, but the upstairs curtains had been drawn. He didn't spare any further thought to the old man asleep behind those curtains. The whole question of Enkmann's real identity now seemed completely trivial and frankly a little ridiculous. What was important to Jake right now was getting help for the hunched, silent figure sitting next to him. Jake drove on.

As they reached the first junction, Jake slowed the car too eagerly and came to a stop several metres from the end of the road. Breathing hard with concentration, he changed back down to first gear and crept forward again, engine revving wildly. A glance told him that the road was deserted and, with great care, the Rover rolled slowly out into the main road, a triumphant grin spreading across Jake's face. He was feeling curiously exhilarated and had to stop himself from giggling excitedly. He felt somewhat guilty about feeling this way. He should be serious and concerned about granddad's health, but he couldn't help it. Driving a car illegally through the rain, late at night in a foreign country was undeniably thrilling.

Jake could see the junction with the ring road up some way up ahead. The red traffic lights creating crazy, ruby coloured patterns as they refracted through the rain falling on his windscreen, only to be swept away as the wipers cleared the glass with a rhythmic flopping noise. As he approached the junction, Jake's eyes swept the signs and arrows which glowed in the beam of the car's headlights until he found the one he was looking for. Pointing to the left, it had a red cross under a triangular symbol that could only represent a roof or building and underneath, the word Krankenhaus. Jake recalled chuckling at the funny-sounding word back in the languages schoolroom at Churnthorpe Secondary School. He even remembered Mr Brown's disapproving frown sweeping the class to see who dared to have fun in one of his classes.

As they approached the lights, Jake slowed the car down and changed back into first gear. The car nearly stopped dead before suddenly heaving itself forward as Jake tried to keep it going, cursing softly under his breath. Up ahead, the red lights changed to green. Time to go! He crunched back into second, but there wasn't enough power and, just as he moved across the junction the car lurched and its engine died. 'Dammit!' The lights were still on green, but would change soon. Jake turned the key and the car jumped forward. 'It's still in gear you idiot!' Jake hissed furiously between gritted teeth. He was aware of the headlights of the three or four cars waiting for their green light to cross the junction. They shone brightly across Jake's face, the Rover completely blocked their way.

Just then Jake's green light winked out and turned red. He yanked the car out of gear and twisted the key frantically and the engine roared into life again. The cars to his left were moving slowly across the junction towards them as he found first gear with the usual crunching sound and the car leaped forward to the other side of the junction. A car horn sounded very loud and very close, making him jump and nearly stall again. A car coming down the carriageway into which he was turning had swerved to avoid him, the driver was a young man wearing a baseball cap, his furious face mouthed angry words behind the glass, his hand gestures starkly illuminated by Jake's headlights. The car passed by, before accelerating away, its engine roaring aggressively. Heart thumping like a drummer in a rock band, Jake checked carefully to see if there were any more cars coming. It was clear now, so, pulse hammering with the delayed shock of the near miss, he let out the clutch and slowly moved off towards the hospital.

Chapter 19

In the Waiting Room

Jake shifted on the plastic chair and tried to get comfortable. The stark, fluorescent lighting in the waiting area of the emergency room made him want to rub his eyes.

A doctor in a white coat strolled in through the double doors, walked behind the reception desk and, after a very brief exchange with the bored-looking girl who was sat there, picked up a stack of folders and walked out again.

Jake didn't like hospitals. There was a kind of antiseptic air about them which, rather ironically, made him feel sick. Posters advertising healthy living and the dangers of smoking were stuck on every wall.

The only other person in the room was a man on the row of chairs behind Jake, who had fallen asleep and was snoring loudly. He had a gash across his forehead which had been cleaned up and stitched together with small strips of tape, but his T-shirt was still caked with dried blood and looked most alarming.

Jake couldn't keep his eyes off the curtains which had been drawn across the cubicle where granddad had been taken and where he was now being examined. Occasionally the sound of his wheezy coughing and the low murmur of conversation between the doctor and nurse drifted to where Jake sat, but he couldn't make out the words. He shuddered involuntarily, although the air inside the hospital was warm, his clothes were still damp and the lack of any fresh, dry clothing made him feel thoroughly miserable. This whole trip was a complete mess.

The curtains parted and the young lady doctor came out making notes on a clipboard. She looked up at Jake and walked over. 'Please, please God, please let him be alright PLEASE!' Jake muttered under his breath as he realised that he was going to be told how serious things were.

When Jake had steered carefully off the main road and into the hospital entrance, he had come to a small roundabout with three exits. He realised that granddad required medical help quickly, so Jake really needed to park outside the door of the casualty department. But where was it? By all three exits there were what seemed like dozens of signs for the different departments or wards, along with maps of where to go. He had stopped the car and scanned the signs, but the panicky feeling he was fighting down, meant he couldn't take in the words, let alone make any sense of them.

However, on the third exit, there was a sign which was different from the others as it was bright red. Crunching into first, Jake had followed it and driven along a short road which led around the side of the hospital. Before him, Jake saw a row of ambulances parked neatly beside wide glass doors and he exhaled with relief. This must be the place. Covering the area in front of the glass doors was a wide, flat roof which jutted out of the main building and would keep the rain off when the ambulances were bringing in patients. There were parking spaces for cars, but they were too far away for granddad to walk, so Jake steered the Rover in a wide circle and brought it to a halt beneath the canopy.

Getting help had been, thankfully, very easy. An ambulance crew were just walking in from their vehicle as Jake got out of the car. They had come over to find out what the problem was, saw the grey-faced, hunched figure in the passenger seat and immediately moved into action. One of the crew disappeared inside to get help, as the other started to examine granddad, who seemed barely conscious. The ambulance driver had fired questions at Jake and with some faltering German, Jake managed to tell them that they were English, what granddad's name was and a few details about how he came to be in such a state. With reassuring efficiency, a number of nurses had arrived and they got granddad out of the car and on to a stretcher. Once inside the hospital, granddad had been whisked off into a cubicle and Jake had been told to sit in the waiting area. The receptionist had tried half-heartedly to take Jake's name and address so they could find granddad's records, but gave up when she realised he was English. Fortunately the lady doctor, who arrived soon after, spoke enough English for Jake to answer her questions and she had disappeared into granddad's cubicle

'Your grandfather is very... errr... cold. He is... tired now and needs to rest.' An optimistic fluttering coursed through Jake's insides. Was granddad going to be OK then? The doctor continued. 'We wait now for tests to come back... and then we will know...' The fluttering stopped suddenly like a swatted butterfly. "Then they will know?" Know what? What was wrong with him?

The doctor seemed to take Jake's silence for a sign that he'd understood. She smiled tenderly, her tired eyes crinkling up at the corners. 'Do you need to call someone? Your parents maybe?' Jake nodded. Yes he did need to call someone. The thought of how he was going to tell his mum made him feel sick, but it had to be done. 'You can use the phone in my office if you like?' Jake smiled back weakly and for a second he felt like crying. 'Would you like to see him now?' Jake nodded dumbly and followed the doctor to granddad's cubicle. He hesitated, before entering, afraid of what granddad would look like. Jake took a deep breath and went in.

The first thing that Jake noticed was that granddad had had his wet clothes taken off him and was now wearing a pale blue gown. The next was the shock of seeing the large number of pipes and wires which were connected up to him. With a squirming, queasy feeling, Jake saw that there was a drip stuck into the back of his hand and one of his fingers had a kind of clamp on it which was attached to a machine which beeped quietly to itself. Most alarming, was the clear plastic oxygen mask held in place over granddad's nose and mouth which was making a gentle hissing noise. Jake swallowed hard. 'Granddad?' Granddad's eyes flickered open in response to Jake's quavering voice, but closed sleepily almost immediately afterwards.

Jake sat on the chair next to the bed. Confused thoughts and feelings nattered away on the edge of his consciousness, but Jake was numb to them all. All he wanted to do now was to talk to granddad, to say he was sorry for that stupid, stupid argument. He wanted to tell him everything was going to be alright, he wanted… he didn't have the words. He didn't want to speak, right now he didn't even want to think, so, ever so gently, Jake slid his hand under granddad's. The patient lay still, breathing quietly whilst the sounds of the machines beeped and hissed softly. Jake listened to their diligent sound until it faded into background noise which he didn't hear anymore.

When the doctor returned after nearly an hour, her greeting, though hushed, seemed loud and grating. She checked the machines, made a note on the clipboard hung on the bottom of the bed, and disappeared. After she had gone Jake settled back, only to find that granddad had opened his eyes. 'Jake… where did they put… clothes… where did they put my clothes…'

His voice was frighteningly weak and breathless. Jake started to tell him to rest and be quiet. He didn't want him to start that awful coughing again. However, although his face looked weak and pale, granddad's eyes had taken on that familiar stubborn look. 'Where… are… they… Jake?' Seeing that it would be useless to argue, Jake glanced around and discovered them, in a soggy lump under the bed, contained in a plastic bin liner.

Jake looked at the damp mass unenthusiastically. But granddad was trying to tell him something. 'In… the pocket… shirt… pocket.' With thumb and forefinger Jake plucked the mud-stained, sodden shirt from the bag. It slithered damply out of the bag and a part of it flopped on to Jake's leg. He shook it off. It was cold and wet and smelled of the forest and made him shudder with the memories it brought back. The shirt had something flat and rectangular within the breast pocket. Still holding the shirt like it was something contagious, Jake pulled it out of the pocket carefully. It was some kind of card held within a plastic wallet. The damp had got into it and the corners and edges were starting to go mushy.

Granddad nodded to Jake to open it. Carefully Jake slid it out and opened it up. The arrogant, smiling salute of Günther Meyer stared up at Jake as if mocking their feebleness. Jake's heart dropped. Didn't granddad know when to quit? 'Listen,' granddad spoke again, the voice low and earnest. 'He'll be there… he'll be there tomorrow… in the square… go and see if it's him.'

Jake's shoulders dropped. 'Granddad I need to stay here to look after you.'

'PROMISE ME!' Granddad shouted suddenly, tearing the mask off his face, eyes pleading. He had sat up in bed and had grabbed hold of Jake's arm. 'I know you think I'm an old fool Jake… but you've got to… got to promise me that you'll go… for those poor souls back at St Gille,' and he was seized with another fit of coughing.

'Yeah Granddad, of course I'll go. Now sit down and take it easy,' Jake said anxiously, trying to get granddad to calm down. It was an empty promise. Jake didn't want to go anywhere, and even as he made the promise, he was wondering what excuse he would give granddad. Maybe he could just tell him that he'd been to town and seen Enkmann and it wasn't the man they were looking for? Maybe.

He was helping him back on to his pillows when the nurse appeared around the corner. She was a rather large lady with a sour-looking face and her expression was one of disapproval. She didn't allow shouting in her ward and clearly thought Jake was to blame. Jake folded the photo quickly, replaced it in the wallet and slid it into the back pocket of his jeans.

He was ushered away from granddad's bedside and was directed back to the plastic seats once more. The injured man had gone now and Jake was entirely alone. Soon after, the doctor came back in with yet more files. She spotted Jake, smiled the same tired smile and came over. 'You can make your phone call now if you like. My office is just there.' She indicated a small glass-walled room with a desk in it. 'Oh, and please can you move your car from where it is?' Her enquiring look when she said this made Jake wonder if she was thinking about how young he was to be driving, but the moment passed and she decided not to ask.

Jake realised that he had abandoned the car where ambulances may need to park. He thought about the phone call he was going to have to make. He was not looking forward to it at all. Not only would it wake his parents up at two thirty in the morning, but also he had no idea how he was going to explain the fact that they were hundreds of miles away and granddad was ill, possibly seriously ill, in hospital. Getting to his feet and stretching, Jake pulled the car keys from his pocket. He might as well move it now and delay making the call for as long as possible.

Wearily, he walked back down the corridor. The wide glass doors swished open automatically as he got near them. The cool, damp, night air swirled around him and he shuddered, wanting to be back in the warm as soon as possible. As his eyes became used to the comparative darkness outside, he noticed that there were the figures of two men looking into the Rover. His first instinct was that they were trying to steal the car, but as his vision adapted to the yellowish lighting in the car park, he saw that the figures were policemen who had opened the car door and were looking inside. An icy fear clutched at his heart, they'd seen him driving here! He'd broken the law and they must have seen him do it and followed the car here! He was in real trouble now. Jake wondered what the penalty was for driving underage and with no insurance in Germany.

Jake was frozen to the spot. The police were busy with the car and hadn't seen him yet. Maybe he could sneak away somehow? But where would he go? Just then a voice to his right made him spin around. 'Jake isn't it? I am happy to see you again.' Dieter walked unhurriedly towards Jake from where he'd parked his BMW. At the sound of Dieter's voice, the policemen looked up from the Rover and spotted Jake. 'The thing you need to know about Rheinhagen Jake, is that it is only a small town. We all get to know everybody's business in the end. We hear things,' Dieter continued, getting closer all the time.

The policemen had stood up now and were looking intently at Jake. One of them was talking into his radio. 'For example, I heard from my assistant that your grandfather was asking questions after your little "official visit" and that made me curious.' He was getting closer all the time. Jake wanted to run and yet his feet remained immobile. Dieter's voice was nonchalant and oozed with politeness, yet had an unmistakeable hint of steel behind it. 'I asked myself, why so interested in an old man like Josef? And then I find that you have become friends with my niece, coincidence maybe? But when I hear that the police are looking for two English people, I stop believing in coincidence. So when I get a call from a friend of mine telling me that your car was seen on our traffic cameras late at night driving here, I get dressed and come over to see you.'

Dieter wore a polo shirt with a v-neck pullover and smartly creased slacks. Jake didn't think he looked like he'd just got dressed; he looked like he was at the country club to play golf. 'I come to see you because I have some questions. I would very much like to know why you are here and why are so many people trying to find you.'

Jake wanted to know the answer to that question as well, but right now his pulse was racing, thudding through his whole body his instincts, shouting in his head 'RUN'! The policemen were walking over now. One of them asked Dieter a question, and he turned to answer, talking to the policeman in a superior tone as if he was giving orders to one of his staff. The voice in his head shouted at Jake, 'RUN NOW!'

Jake sprang away to his right, away from the policemen and away from where Dieter was looking. However, Jake's sudden movement must have caught Dieter's eye and he twisted back with frightening speed, shouting something and grabbing at Jake's T-shirt. At his touch, fear that he had been caught released an almost instantaneous surge of adrenaline. Jake twisted with ferocious speed and felt Dieter's grasp slip. He was free. As he sprinted away, there was more shouting behind him. Jake felt the energy of the hunted animal course through him and increased his pace, the wet tarmac of the car park flying beneath his feet.

Chapter 20

On the Run

The river south of Rheinhagen, muddy and swollen with the rain, roiled and slithered between its steep banks like an immense beast.

The heavy rain had faded into a light drizzle now and the clouds had come down to trail their misty fingers through the branches of the tallest trees. The only sounds were the occasional, muted swish of vehicles passing on the main road behind the wood and from time to time the wrestling currents of the river would make a clopping noise. A dull, dead sound.

By the dim radiance of the distant streetlights, a figure could be seen emerging from the trees and on to the gravel footpath which traced a pale streak along the side of the river.

Jake paused, his hands on his knees gasping for breath, lungs burning. He tried to control his breathing so he could listen for signs of pursuit, but he heard nothing.

He stood upright, his pulse still thumping, hands and knees trembling and he tried to figure out where he was. After he had twisted out of Dieter's grasp and sprinted across the casualty car park, he had hurdled a small privet hedge, slithered down a grassy bank and staggered to his feet in the large main car park. There had been angry shouting from behind him and the sound made him run even faster. He'd dodged his way through the cars with an agility which surprised him. He was running blindly, focussed only on trying to get away. Instinct drove him away from the hospital towards the junction with the main road. He'd hurdled another hedge and found his speed had carried him halfway across the first two lanes of the dual carriageway, just as the lights were changing to green. A startled, half-asleep motorist jammed on his brakes, tyres making a harsh noise as they slid across the wet road, but Jake had already passed by, jumping the central barrier and crossing the other carriageway in four strides. His momentum pushing him forward, he had crashed recklessly through the small copse of trees on the other side of the road, desperate to get out of sight of his pursuers.

A noise in the trees set Jake's heart pounding again. Was it Dieter, or the police coming after him? His body was running on pure adrenaline now, primal instincts screaming 'RUN'! Fear spurred his body into action once more. He turned and raced off down the path which led back to Rheinhagen, his sodden trainers splashing carelessly through the puddles.

Half an hour later, Jake trudged slowly along path on the riverbank. The burst of adrenaline-fuelled energy which had helped him to escape had now evaporated, leaving him feeling drained, feeble and weak. He was certain he wasn't being followed, but now he simply didn't care anymore. He was feeling numb, like he was a robot on autopilot, placing one weary foot in front of another over and over again to some unknown destination.

In front of him loomed the overpass where the ring road crossed the river, just outside of the old town's fortifications. Another shower of light rain was starting, the telltale rings appearing on the surface of the river as crescent-shaped reflections of the lights from the road above. Jake grimaced, he was so sick of being cold and wet. He couldn't remember the last time he'd worn dry, warm clothes. The T-shirt and shorts he was wearing clung damply to him and he really needed a shower. A shower! The thought of a hot shower, or, even better, a deep, steaming bath in which to wallow. The thought tortured him.

The low, misty cloud meant that Jake couldn't be sure, but he thought that the sky in the east had started to lighten ever so slightly. The spitting rain became a little heavier and Jake took shelter under the road bridge. It was very dark, but at least the gravel of the path was dry and Jake sat against the concrete wall and hugged his knees, trying to keep warm. His head sagged forward.

Utter misery took hold of Jake. He felt numb, like a zombie, like this wasn't real life at all, but some sort of reality TV show which Jake was watching through the eyes of somebody else.

He tried to come up with a plan of action. What was he going to do?

He tried to examine his situation logically. It was no good, he was too tired to think, he was too tired to do anything and a desperate feeling of loneliness engulfed him.

The worry, hurt and anxiety was an almost physical pain and his insides twisted as the reality of his situation hit home. He was in a foreign country, somehow he was now on the run from the police, he had nowhere to go, he was hungry, thirsty, cold and hugely tired, he had very little money and the person who was supposed to be looking after him was seriously ill in hospital. He had no phone and his parents must be going crazy with worry about them. The thought of home and family hit Jake with a powerful jolt of mixed emotions. Jake felt like crying. Maybe that would make him feel better and ease the tight, tense ball of emotions inside him, but the tears wouldn't come.

After a few minutes, Jake stumbled to his feet and began to plod slowly along once more. He emerged from beneath the ring road bridge to find that it was noticeably lighter and the rain had stopped. He hauled himself step, by weary step up the embankment and looked once more into the gardens of the houses of Rheinhagen. The last time he'd been here, he had been hand in hand with Kirsten. He realised that it had

229

been a long time since he'd thought of her and the image of her waving him off as the thunderstorm had broken, flickered fleetingly through his mind. 'Not now,' he thought. He was so very tired and so very depressed right now, that bringing thoughts of Kirsten into this situation would only spoil the memory and he pushed the image away.

In the steely, pre-dawn half-light, Jake could see the line of the river winding off like a green-grey snake, back the way he'd come. A cluster of bright lights in the distance was the hospital and somewhere in there was granddad. The tense ball in his stomach squirmed again and Jake turned his back and walked away down the path.

He trudged along the top of the bank, the river on his right and the gardens of houses on his left. There was nobody about, the town seemed deserted and Jake felt like he was in one of those science fiction films where there has been a great disaster and he is the only human left alive. It was as if, just for this moment, Jake was the King of Rheinhagen; its cobbled streets and medieval houses were his. It was too early even for the birds to start singing. Silence seemed to press on to his eardrums.

He checked his watch and groaned. It would be hours before the town would wake up. What would he do with himself between now and then? Somehow he had made a decision, almost without thinking about it. He would go back to the hospital. He needed to be there with granddad, he knew that now. He would call his parents and face the consequences and, if the police were going to put him in prison, well, let them do it. But before he walked all that way back, he was going to buy himself the biggest breakfast that he could with his last few euros. Of course now he had a few hours to kill before the cafés opened and the prospect of spending the time shivering in a doorway didn't delight him.

As he approached the turn into one of the alleyways which led between the houses and up into town, Jake heard a sharp hissing and crackling noise which ended with an electronic beep. He froze, straining to make out what the noise was and where it was coming from. Now he could hear the tread of footsteps and the low murmur of conversation and from his position on the top of the bank, he spotted some movement behind the high garden fence next to the alleyway. The realisation was instantaneous. What he could see were the caps of two policemen bobbing up and down as they walked down the alley towards him. The noise that alerted him crackled again and Jake realised that it was the sound of their two-way radio.

A few seconds before, Jake had been contemplating the walk back to the hospital and giving himself up, however, the abrupt appearance of the police, made Jake look round desperately for somewhere to hide. He knew that he'd have to turn himself in when he'd get to the hospital, but it wouldn't be before he'd had a chance to check on granddad and call home.

On his right, the bank dropped steeply, straight down to the swirling waters of the river. There was no cover that way and, if he lost his footing, he might easily get swept away. On the other side of the path, the garden fence nearest him was one of those he'd seen with a gate set in it. It would be his only chance; the policemen would be emerging from the alley in just a few seconds. Grimacing at every small sound he made, Jake dropped down the bank, grasped the rusting iron handle of the gate and twisted it as quickly as he dare.

With huge relief, he felt the catch give way and the door in the fence swung open. Swiftly, Jake slid through the gap and into the garden beyond, holding the gate closed behind him and praying that the policemen hadn't spotted the movement.

He fought to keep his breathing under control as the two men walked slowly to the top of the bank just a few yards from where Jake had been standing only seconds before.

They chatted in low voices before there was a short snapping noise and Jake became aware of the smell of cigarette smoke. He smiled to himself despite his predicament. He wondered for a second what their reaction would be if he jumped out and caught them having a crafty fag-break. After around a minute, a fuzzy, crackly noise came over the radio which Jake assumed to be a voice from the police station. One of the policemen replied, there was a crunch as the cigarette was stamped out on the gravel and they walked off down the path.

Still standing by the gate, Jake exhaled the breath that he'd been holding and, for the first time, he looked around the garden. He was standing in an orchard. Five fruit trees, each of them heavy with green apples occupied the rear of the garden. There was a beech hedge with an arched gate through it which divided the garden in two and a shrub-lined path led to a patio by the back door of the house. On Jake's right, in the corner of the garden was a wooden shed with windows, glass doors and a veranda. Jake wondered thickly for a second or two, why anyone would have such a posh looking doors on a humble garden shed and then he realised that this was in fact a summerhouse, somewhere where the owner could sit in and enjoy the garden whatever the weather.

Jake spotted that the summerhouse contained a wide, cane sofa with thick, comfy-looking cushions on it. The door handle turned smoothly and he went inside. The air inside the summerhouse was still and smelt resinous. Once the door closed behind him, the silence descended like a quilt. There were two long seat-pads from outdoor reclining chairs which had been thrown haphazardly across the sofa. No doubt the owner had hurriedly cast them inside the summerhouse so they would keep dry when the storm hit. Jake lifted them off the sofa and sat down.

After the night Jake had just been through, it felt like the most comfortable sofa he'd ever sat on. He flopped backwards and closed his eyes. The nagging worries about granddad, the police and his parents chaffed briefly somewhere at the back of his consciousness, the image of Kirsten flickered once more behind his eyes, but Jake wasn't going to let anything spoil this feeling. For a few hours at least, he was in a safe, dry, sheltered and comfortable place and that was all that mattered right now.

His eyes opened again and he reached over to pull the seat covers over him as he lay down. They weren't as cosy as a quilt, but he had started to feel warmer already underneath them. He felt drowsy and his eyelids seemed to be dragging themselves closed. Jake shook himself to try to clear the downy cobwebs that were filling his head. 'I can only stay here for a while,' he thought. 'I'll have to get out of here before the owners of the house wake up and find me.' But that wouldn't be for a few hours yet. In the meantime he would just have to stay alert, stay focussed and stay awake.

He slept.

Chapter 21

The Mayor of Rheinhagen

A half-heard noise intruded into the sleep of the teenager curled up on the cane furniture and covered with the floral-printed seat cushions. However, Jake wasn't ready to give up on the sleep which he needed so badly and he slumbered on.

The mist had been dispersed by the strength of the sun and, washed clean by the storm, Rheinhagen looked renewed, fresh and dazzlingly bright under a blue sky dotted with fluffy white clouds. It was as if the weather was apologising for losing its temper.

The sunlight fell through the leaves of the apple trees and cast a dappled pattern over the sleeping boy. The glass of the summerhouse doors refracted the light in places, so that when the gentle wind stirred the trees, rainbows danced across the prone figure.

Very, very gradually, Jake became aware of the light which flickered across his eyelids. Even with his eyes shut, he thought that it looked like a kind of midday light, not an early morning light at all. Somewhere in his sleep befuddled brain, Jake had the feeling that the consequences of what this might mean was important, but he had no idea why. He tried to recapture the sleepy feeling and drop off once again, but it was too late, the unstoppable process of waking up had begun.

Jake opened his eyes very slightly and peered through the slits. The fuzzy image of sunlight through leaves and brown, wooden window frames confused him. He didn't have the faintest idea where he was. He knew that this fact should bother him, but he was too sleepy to let it. There was that noise again, what was that...? He let his eyes close once more.

A few seconds later, his eyes popped open once again. This time they were opened fully. Jake sat up and immediately wished he hadn't as the movement had made the room spin with a sickening swoop and suddenly it felt like someone was trying to hammer their way out of the front of his head.

He waited for the feeling to fade a little and tried to force himself to think. He was still uncertain where he was and why he was there and why there was a horrible feeling that he was in trouble for some reason, looming in the back of his mind.

'First things first,' he thought. 'Where am I?' Being curled on the cane sofa all night had made his spine feel like it was permanently twisted out of shape. There was a crick in his neck which was making it painful to turn his head to the right, the red scratches on his arms and legs throbbed and stung and his muscles ached like he'd run a marathon the previous day. Running? He remembered something about running, running away from someone... Then the memories of the previous day poured into his consciousness with complete and horrible clarity. The storm, dragging granddad to the camp, driving the car and Dieter's grasping hands and angry shouts.

Jake let his head sink forward into his hands and let the fresh wave of misery wash over him. 'What a mess,' he said to himself. He raised his head once more and it suddenly occurred to him that he had planned to be out of the summerhouse before the owner woke up. He checked his watch. It was nearly twelve o'clock! He'd been asleep for hours! He peered through the glass doors to see if there was anyone in the garden, half expecting to see some irate German gardener ready to chase him away with a spade held aloft. His heart thumping again, he recalled that, a long time ago, he had thought that being on the run might be a romantic, exciting life, full of daring plans and clever escapes, but Jake had changed his mind. 'Being on the run officially stinks!' he thought. He had a raging thirst, his clothes were still damp with rain and sweat, his head and body ached like he'd gone ten rounds with the heavyweight champion and more than anything else in the world, he wanted to go home.

With another glance around to make sure the coast was clear, Jake opened the summerhouse door. It stuck slightly before it gave way with a shuddering noise which rattled the glass in its frame and made him wince. He quickly tidied the seat cushions and the cane sofa and slipped quietly out of the door and to the gate in the back fence. A twist of the handle and he was through and out and back on the grassy bank of the fortifications.

The sunlight was making him screw his eyes up. The noise that he'd been hearing in the background since he'd woken up, filtered into his foggy brain once again. It was music, some kind of brass band maybe. He rubbed his eyes again and listened hard. It was coming from somewhere up the hill at the top of the town and then he realised what it was. Of course! By this time the celebrations for the mayor's award ceremony would be in full swing. Maybe Enkmann was on the stage even now, clapping along with the oompah music, but the thought failed to arouse Jake's excitement or spur on his determination to carry out the promise he made to granddad. Right now, he needed a drink and something to eat and then he'd walk back to the hospital to face the music there.

Many of the cafés and shops on the street which led up the hill were closed, displaying handwritten signs apologising for the inconvenience. Obviously the owners were themselves in the square enjoying the celebrations. Jake was so thirsty and the sight of glass-fronted displays of ice-cold coke and bottles of water behind the locked doors was torture. Eventually, he came across a mini supermarket which was open. The aisles were deserted as Jake selected a large bottle of water, a pre-packed chicken sandwich and a packet of chocolate biscuits. He carefully kept count of the cost of the items to make sure that he had enough money. He paid the large, bored-looking lady. She looked almost annoyed at having to serve a customer and she put down the garish celebrity magazine she had been reading to take Jake's money.

As soon as he'd got out of the shop, Jake unscrewed the top of the bottled water and drank deeply. It was so cold it made his teeth ache and gave him a sharp pain across his forehead, but he was so thirsty he couldn't stop. He drank most of the bottle before coming up for air. The water tasted so refreshing, it felt like his dehydrated body was soaking it up like a sponge. Jake tilted his head back and felt the warm sun on his face. He was feeling more human already.

Looking for a place to eat his food, he wandered further up the hill. The music, interspersed by the applause of what sounded like a sizeable crowd, was getting louder as he went. Not too far from the back of the large church was a small cobbled square with a fountain surrounded by colourful tubs of flowers. There was no one around and the tree-shaded benches were deserted. He sat down. Now his thirst had been satisfied, his hunger was now raging for food. He tore open the sandwiches and took a huge bite out of it. Chewing and swallowing the rather dry bread and chicken so quickly, he got hiccups and had to have another drink.

Soon the sandwiches had been consumed and Jake was munching his way contentedly through his third biscuit. He was feeling much better now. He still had that slightly woolly feeling, like he wasn't really there, but at least he felt full.

Whilst he had been eating, the brass band had played on. The music was unfamiliar, but the simple tunes and rhythms were really catchy and Jake found his feet were tapping along in time.

The band finished their last tune with a flourish and the slightly muffled voice of the announcer could be heard. He was talking rapidly and Jake found that he could only pick out the occasional word or phrase. There was another rush of applause, whistling and whooping for the band and then the announcer's voice changed slightly, became lower and somehow sounded more serious.

Sat on his bench behind the church, Jake finished his biscuit and started to think about heading back to the hospital. His legs still ached and he didn't relish the long walk, but the day was sunny and warm, so it wouldn't be too unpleasant. In fact, he was feeling OK about things. It was still a mess, but at least he had a plan to start sorting it out. He wasn't going to run anymore.

There was some more applause, but this time it seemed more polite, restrained somehow and there was no whooping. A new voice began to speak. From where Jake was sitting, it was just a noise and the words were indistinguishable, but the voice sounded oddly familiar. Shoving the wrappers in the bin nearby and pocketing the last biscuit, he felt his curiosity get the better of him and walked towards the square.

As he got closer, he passed through the small alley between the church and the town hall which he and granddad had walked through when they first arrived in Rheinhagen. It seemed like a million years ago now. Beyond the corner of the church, Jake could see crowds of people. Many of them were leaning over the barriers at front of the stage, or standing in the square behind. Rows of chairs had been set out at the sides of the square where some of the older townspeople sat. Several dads had hoisted their small children on to their shoulders, so they would be able to see, but all of them were looking attentively at the person who was talking. The alleyway emerged into the square by the side of the stage. The crowds were thin here, because the lighting rigs, amplifiers and scaffolding restricted the view. This suited Jake fine, he didn't want the speaker to see him. He thought he had recognised Dieter's voice and through a gap in the scaffolding, Jake watched the man, clad in another immaculate suit, address the crowd.

At the back of the stage, Jake could just catch glimpses of some smartly dressed people sitting in two lines of comfy-looking chairs. No doubt these were local VIPs, special guests and civic dignitaries come to honour Enkmann. He scanned the seated figures, straining to try and see if one of them was the guest of honour, but his line of sight was blocked. Enkmann must be at the side of the stage near where Jake was standing.

He found that his pulse had quickened and he felt curiously nervous, his hands shaking. He moved up to the steel barrier and gripped the cold metal. He was finally going to lay eyes on Enkmann, the man they'd come hundreds of miles just to see.

Lots of different emotions had started to natter at Jake, fighting each other for his attention. Images and feelings flickered momentarily through his mind to be replaced by another and another. His sunlit bedroom back home, a lizard scampering through the dry grass at St Gille, the smell of damp tent fabric, the lights of England retreating from the figure of himself standing at the rail of the ferry, his finger tracing the line of the autobahn on the map, the photo of a smiling, kindly old man shaking hands, the beeping machine by granddad's bedside.

Dieter was coming to the end of his speech and from the way that the tone of his voice was rising, Jake could tell that he was building up to big finish. Was this going to be the moment? 'Damen und Herren, willkommen JOSEF

ENKMANN!' Deiter turned to his right, clapping enthusiastically as a grey-suited, grey haired figure emerged into Jake's vision, his back to him.

Wet, cold feet splashing through puddles in the dark, his mum waving from the car as his parents drove away, the taste of Veronique's rich beef casserole, the tyres of the Rover humming over mile after mile of tarmac, the feeling of Kirsten's soft lips on his, the resinous smell of the trees in the forest, granddad's grasping fingers on his arm and the sound of him shouting, 'PROMISE ME!'

The roar of the crowd hammered on to Jake's ears and made him shudder. Gone was the polite reservation that they had shown Dieter as wild applause and shouts echoed around the square's old buildings. The sound rolling around like the thunder had the night before. Everyone was on their feet, cheering and clapping and whooping as Enkmann reached the middle of the stage, shook hands with Dieter and turned to wave at the crowd. Jake realised that he was the only person not applauding as his hands were gripping the top of the barricade tightly.

The tension Jake had been feeling suddenly let go in one huge release. Enkmann was not Meyer. He was sure. The man on the stage didn't even look much like the one in the photo which he'd found on the Internet. Yes, his right hand was maimed, Jake could see the reddish scar tissue where his index finger had been and the middle finger was just a stump, but the smiling, wrinkled, suntanned face of this cheerful old man was...well it was different enough from the image Jake remembered to make him absolutely sure. Enkmann was not their man.

The crowd had been cheering for a good three or four minutes before Enkmann could get them to quieten down and even then there were one or two good-natured cat-calls from the gathered townspeople that caused laughter to ripple across the square. Enkmann laughed along with them, beaming broadly like he was the proud parent and the hundreds gathered in the square were his family. Indeed he talked back to the hecklers, using their names, his comebacks prompting more laughter and applause.

When he spoke, it was in a gentle, measured tone. He didn't have to raise his voice to make himself heard, because the crowd were hushed, wanting to catch every word he said. From time to time Enkmann would make a joke, or funny comment and the audience laughed and applauded but settled down quickly, so as not to miss whatever he was going to say next. They laughed at every one of his jokes, even when Enkmann's delivery was sometimes slow and awkward and Jake realised that, although at first he had thought Enkmann looked proudly on the people of Rheinhagen, it was the people of Rheinhagen who were immensely proud of Enkmann. There was such a mutual respect and fondness and familiarity in the square that, if it wasn't love, then it was something very close to it.

So, that was that. The words of Enkmann rolled on over Jake unheard. That was that. He had promised granddad he'd come here and look at Enkmann and, despite his plans not to bother, he'd done it anyway.

A strange kind of euphoria washed over him and he grinned foolishly to himself. How ridiculous! How stupid they'd been! All that misplaced excitement, all the planning, all the anxiety and worry and pressure, all the fear and fatigue, all for nothing! How ridiculous! He chuckled quietly to himself shaking his head. He wanted to whoop and go crazy. It was over. Their adventure finished, extinguished to the soundtrack of the soft voice of an old man on stage in a small German town.

'Well, best be getting back to granddad,' he muttered to himself, the strange euphoric feeling still bubbling away inside and he allowed himself one more glance around the square.

As his eyes scanned slowly across the crowd, a wave of warm affection for the town, the people, for the whole world washed over him. He felt like he was an outsider, an observer, but that was OK, because he was going home. Job done.

At the microphone, Enkmann finished his speech his voice husky with emotion and the scattered applause swelled, multiplied, erupted and burst upon the square with a thunderous roar.

Jake clapped along with them, as the figure on the stage acknowledged the crowd with a wave. Everyone was on their feet, cheering lustily, the rolling roar heightening the exhilaration which Jake felt. He whooped and screamed at the top of his voice, now part of the people, part of the crowd, yet the sound in the square was so great, he could hardly hear himself.

It was then Jake saw it. Enkmann had moved to the far side of the stage, to wave to the crowds there. It was when he moved back to Jake's side, still waving, occasionally pointing and shouting a greeting to a friend in the crowd. He waved again at the applauding, cheering masses, his arms held aloft, the deafening ovation showing no sign of stopping. It was when he let his left arm come down to his side, his mutilated right hand still held high. A dazzling flashbulb of recognition popped inside Jake's head, leaving him breathless and momentarily stunned. He scrabbled feverishly for the photo in his back pocket. He unfolded it as carefully and as quickly as he could, there were mushy creases across it where the photo had been folded, but between the lines of the folds was Meyer's face, his mutilated hand held aloft on a ramrod straight arm. Jake's eyes flashed from the photo to the stage where Enkman stood smiling, his right arm held up and forward, his hand still waving. The euphoria was gone, the job was not finished after all, how could he have not seen it before?

Enkmann went back to the lectern in the centre of the stage to speak once more to the people who wouldn't let him go. Jake examined his thoughts for any scrap or shadow of doubt, but there was none. It seemed so obvious now, so unmistakable that this man, *this man,* was one and the same as the man in granddad's photo. The smile was no longer arrogant, but warm and genuine, yet, the mouth curled in the same way. The cheeks, though no longer full and youthful, lifted and arched in the same way. The eyes, now wet and glittering with pride and warmth, they were no longer cruel and dead-looking, but they were the same eyes!

In the end it wasn't a sense of justice for a terrible crime which made Jake hop over the barrier. It wasn't a burning revenge for the people in the camp at St Gille which drove him up the steps at the side of the stage past a startled sound technician. It was his promise to an old man who lay sick in a hospital bed not far away. The blood sang in his ears, so that the applause became a hissing, echoing white noise. His vision was fixed on the man at the lectern and his feet were moving, however, the distance across the stage seemed to bend and warp and stretch, until Enkmann appeared miles away.

Jake clung on to the detached feeling of unreality, he didn't want to think about what he was doing. He could feel the gaze of the hundreds of people in the square locked upon him, yet it didn't bother him, because Jake wasn't actually doing this, he wasn't actually here at all. Time seemed to slow down, his legs felt like they were constructed out of cooked spaghetti and he wondered if his knees would give way before he got to Enkmann. Out of the corner of his eye, Jake saw the dignitaries, still standing up applauding. One by one, they became aware of Jake as, step by step he got closer to where Enkmann was standing. And then he was at his shoulder. Enkmann was the only person who hadn't seen Jake yet.

As if he were looking through someone else's eyes, Jake saw a hand holding the creased, dog-eared photograph stretch forward to put it on the lectern in front of Enkmann. The realisation that Jake was there, made Enkmann start and take a step back, still smiling that warm, genial smile as if he thought Jake was a well-wisher with a surprise gift. The applause died and was replaced with a polite hush as the crowd waited to see what was going to happen next.

Enkmann still looked at Jake with an enquiring half smile on his lips. The detached feeling was suddenly evaporating and Jake was waking up to what he was doing, panic fluttered dangerously inside. 'Es ist Sie.' ('It is you.') Jake's voice, amplified by the lectern microphone echoed around the square. 'Es ist Sie.' With a bewildered crease forming on his brow, Enkmann's eyes slid in slow motion away from Jake and towards the photo on the lectern. 'Es ist Sie.' Enkmann's eyes rested on the photo, the half smile fading. 'Es ist Sie.' Jake waited, aware of a restless murmuring coming from the crowd. Enkmann gazed blankly at the photo. Didn't he get it? Jake thought. Didn't he understand? 'Es ist Sie!' Jake's voice rose in anger and he snatched up the photo and held it up to Enkmann's face so there could be no misunderstanding. 'Es ist Sie! der Gott von St Gille!' ('It is you! The God of St Gille!') Why didn't he respond? He couldn't deny it, the proof was right here! Why didn't he do something?

Just then, hands closed firmly on to his arms and neck, he was spun around roughly and was dragged away.

Chapter 22

Pandora's Box

Jake couldn't see who was holding him and he didn't struggle. To be truthful, he was grateful to be taken off the stage and away from the stares of the crowd. He'd expected something from Enkmann, a denial, a confession, even an escape attempt maybe, but the blank, bewildered stare confused Jake and made him feel embarrassed and unsure of himself. Why did he do nothing? Suddenly Jake became aware that the person taking him away was Dieter. Bent over, his hand forced up his back, Jake could only see his shiny shoes and the sharply creased Italian suit trousers, enough to identify him. Righteous anger boiled abruptly within him. He'd done nothing wrong and he certainly wasn't going to let Dieter have the satisfaction of dragging him away without a fight!

He was almost at the edge of the stage when Jake twisted and spun around with vicious speed, the sudden resistance from the boy who had shown none, taking Dieter by surprise. Jake wheeled away and saw Dieter, off balance, arms windmilling, fall backwards on to the sound technician's desk. There was a huge clatter, as equipment, coffee mugs and papers were knocked across the desk, some falling on the floor. The sound technician was a tubby little man, dressed in blue work trousers and a polo-shirt with the company logo on it. Around his neck he wore large padded headphones which he used from time to time to check the sound.

He had been sitting on his swivel chair making slight adjustments to the collection of slides and knobs on the control panel in front of him when Dieter fell on him. His first instinct was to try and rescue his equipment. However, the swivel chair he was sat on had wheels on the base and the impact of Dieter's body sent the chair, with the technician still in it, skittering across the cobbles of the square until the coiled wire of his headphones reached its limit and the technician was brought to a sudden and uncomfortable halt which resulted in him being dumped on the cobbles with a sore neck.

Some of the crowd laughed, many tutted and murmured in disapproval, one of the loudspeakers howled, its whistling making people wince as the piercing noise wailed around the square. The technician got to his feet, hastily adjusting some controls to kill the feedback. Dieter leaped back onstage with a black, murderous glare in his eyes. Oh boy! Jake suddenly feared that he'd gone too far. Dieter crossed the stage to where Jake was, in two angry paces and seized the front of Jake's T-shirt, his other hand bunched into a fist at his side. Jake flinched, anticipating the blow when a sharp, warning voice interjected. 'Dieter!'

The warning had come from Enkmann. He still stood at the lectern, his damaged, liver-spotted hand holding on to it. He was looking at Dieter furiously. Dieter's grasp loosened and he let go of Jake's T-shirt. Enkmann stood still for a moment before glancing at Jake, his eyes drawn to the photo Jake still held. Then he sighed, a deep, melancholy, resigned sound. His shoulders drooped, making it look like he was shrinking, becoming frail and old in front of their eyes.

With a slight shuffling limp, Enkmann walked over to them. He spoke rapidly to Dieter in an undertone that hissed ferociously whenever Dieter tried to interrupt. Clearly he was in charge, handing out his orders. Finally, with a last nod at Dieter as if to indicate that they were agreed, Enkmann turned to Jake. 'English yes?' Jake nodded dumbly. 'I would very much like to talk with you. Can I ask that you go to my office and wait for me please?' The tone was so courteous and respectful and not what Jake was expecting that he could only nod again, saying nothing.

At a word from Enkmann, there appeared the nervous man they had seen when they had visited the town hall. Enkmann spoke to him briefly and the man nodded his understanding before turning his gaze to Jake and saying, 'This way please Mr Hargreaves.' As they walked off the back of the stage, Jake could see the VIPs straining to make out what was on the photograph. Those who did, immediately turned to their neighbours, muttering excitedly over what they had seen.

Behind the backcloth of the stage, Jake followed the nervous man through the now familiar doors of the town hall, down the corridor and into the same office where they had had their disastrous meeting with Dieter. The feeling of unreality was back and Jake walked as if in a dream. 'If you would be so kind as to wait here for a short time?' The man's face shone with perspiration and he smiled uncertainly at Jake as if he thought he was about to explode.

Jake sank into the leather chair as the heavy door closed with a whisper. The sudden quiet of the office making him feel like his ears had ceased to work. Outside, the low murmuring of the crowd could just about be heard until it was stilled by Enkmann's amplified voice once more. The soundproofing of the office windows made it impossible to make out what he was saying and Jake was suddenly enormously tired and didn't care anymore.

He didn't know how long he'd sat there; Enkmann's voice droned on outside, but suddenly a new sound made Jake sit up. Someone down the corridor was talking in English! Not only that, but the voice was raised angrily with the occasional word or phrase drifting through. '...court of human rights... outrageous...! heard of anything so scandalous in my whole life!' There was something oddly familiar about the voice and it seemed to be getting closer. Jake leaped out of the chair, crossed to the heavy office door and opened it.

Down the corridor, the nervous man scurried along behind a tall figure who walked swiftly and purposefully, his shiny, black walking stick flashing under the office lights. He was walking so fast, that the nervous man was quite breathless as he struggled to keep up. 'But I can assure you sir…'

'Poppycock!' Lawrence's commanding voice blared, making the nervous man start. 'Ah! There you are!' Jake stood rooted to the spot, stunned at the sudden appearance of someone he'd never expected. Questions crowded into Jake's brain, so many that his brain seemed to shut down to stop overloading and he simply stood, mouth agape.

The nervous man had another attempt to placate Lawrence who seemed furious, but at that moment the doors down the corridor opened and Dieter swept towards them, his face set and grim. The nervous man started to explain to Dieter what was happening when Lawrence cut across him sharply. 'Are you in charge around here then? Well?'

Dieter blinked in surprise at this old man's hostility. 'Who are you?' Dieter managed to keep his voice calm, however there was an unmistakeable angry edge to his question. Lawrence heard it and bristled. His craggy face flushing with rage, he moved towards Dieter until he was inches away from him and stared him full in the face.

'Never mind who I am young man, I want to know why you have arrested this boy and why you are holding him against his will and I want to know what crime you are charging him with and I want to know it now!'

Confronted with this onslaught, Dieter quailed and took a step backwards. 'No no! You do not understand. He is not arrested, he has been asked to wait here until...'

'So he's free to go?' Lawrence was relentless and showed no mercy. 'Right then! Well, thank you for your kind invitation, but I fear we must decline and get on our way. Cheerio!' Lawrence turned his back on Dieter.

The conversation was over. Jake however, was still fixed to the spot, his mind whirling. He watched as Lawrence walked off. Halfway down the corridor, he must have sensed that Jake wasn't following and he turned round to see where he was. 'Well come on then!' His voice was commanding and galvanised Jake into action, but he'd also seen the telltale raising of his eyebrows, the slight widening of his eyes and the small inclination of Lawrence's head. Lawrence was trying to tell him that they needed to go and go now. Maybe, Jake thought, as he scurried after the retreating figure of the old man, maybe he wasn't actually as confident as he sounded.

Jake caught up with him back in the reception area where Lawrence had paused, thinking. He muttered softly to Jake, 'Can't go back out there, we need a back door Jake,' and he wheeled around and pushed through the double doors opposite the main entrance. Lawrence walked confidently through the offices as if it was perfectly natural for him to be there; as if it was something he did every day. With a surge of relief, Jake saw some glass doors ahead that led out to the car park behind the town hall.

The warm summer air outside seemed to taste sweet as they emerged near the kiddies playground. Lawrence didn't slow down. 'Keep walking Jake, don't run,' he said without turning his head. 'We need to be gone before he finishes his speech, not a good idea to get caught in the crowd.'

Jake was suddenly aware that Enkmann was still talking to the people in the square. For a second or two, he wondered what he was saying, but, just then, Lawrence uttered a cry of triumph and pointed with his cane. A lonely taxi stood in the rank at the side of the car park, its driver leaning on the bonnet, smoking and reading a paper. 'Get him to take us to the hospital Jake,' Lawrence said breezily as the man, noticing them for the first time, flicked away his cigarette and folded his paper. Jake did so and the driver nodded his agreement without speaking, got into the car, and started the engine.

As the car pulled away, Jake turned to Lawrence. 'The hospital? So have you seen granddad? Is he OK?' Lawrence sat back in his seat and smiled broadly at Jake.

'It'll take more than a bit of a cough and a wet night in a forest to see off that stubborn old goat!' He chuckled and for a second or two, Jake thought that that was all Lawrence was going to say. He opened his mouth to press him for the details, but, seeing that Jake was clearly desperate to know, Lawrence held up his hand to stop him.

'Walter is going to be fine. It seems that he'd managed to get a bit of a chest infection and he was suffering from mild exposure and exhaustion. He just needs a spot of rest, and he'll be right as rain. I told him he was too old to be doing these sorts of fun and games, but that's Walter for you.' Jake felt the warm wave of relief engulf him and lift the tense, tight feeling from his shoulders. Granddad was going to be alright! 'He told me what you did Jake,' Lawrence continued. 'How you got him out of the forest and into hospital, probably saved the grumpy old geezer's skin! Well done Jake. Well done.'

For a while, Jake couldn't speak and simply stared, unseeing out of the window as they drove through the streets of the old town. After a minute or two, they emerged through the familiar gatehouse and there was the river, glittering in the sunshine and there was the hospital beyond.

'So how come you're here then?' Jake's second question swam up through the confusing mush that was his brain at the moment. To Jake's surprise, Lawrence looked a little sheepish.

'Well, I don't mind admitting that your visit made me feel a little shame-faced. Something Walter said about being pampered and too soft for an adventure really made me think and it wasn't long after you'd gone before I was wishing I'd tagged along. The days went by and I was just itching to know if you'd got here safely and if Enkmann was our man. I tried your number a few times, but there was no response. I didn't like the sound of that, so I called your parents, introduced myself and asked if you'd got to Germany OK. It seemed that they'd been rather worried, they'd had no reply from when they called you at home and news of this little European tour of yours came as quite a little surprise. Needless to say, the phone call was... how should I put it? intense, but once I'd told them what your plans had been, your dear mother swung into action. Remarkable woman your mother Jake. She was on the phone to the British Consulate, she had the Rheinhagen police out looking for you two and she booked us all flights to come out here and lead the search.

'We met up at the airport on Saturday evening and spent much of yesterday walking the streets looking for some sign of you two. Up until that awful storm hit. We discovered that you'd spent the night in a guesthouse and then disappeared. Then, back at the hotel, your parents got a phone call from the police at some awfully early hour, to say that Walter was in hospital and you'd run off. They stayed with Walter, but I'd heard that Enkmann's little party was scheduled for today and I thought you might pop along to have a little peek at him, so I caught a cab into town and lo and behold, there you were. I dare say they'll be very pleased to see you.'

His mum and dad were here! The sinking sensation returned. What would they say to him? After all the trouble and worry he and granddad had caused them?

Contrasting emotions flashed through Jake's head as if they were competing for attention. In the end it became too hard to deal with and he shut out all feelings and went back to looking out of the window.

The taxi driver pulled up to the main hospital entrance, Lawrence paid him and manoeuvred himself stiffly out of the back seat. Jake glanced across to the accident and emergency department, half expecting to see the Rover, still standing there. Someone had moved it somehow, the car keys still jangled in Jake's pocket. Lawrence led the way into the main entrance. It was busy with porters pushing trolleys and wheelchairs here and there. Visiting families enquired after their sick relatives at the reception desk. Nurses strode through, holding sheaves of papers and files.

Jake followed Lawrence's confident stride, his walking stick clicking rhythmically on the shiny, tiled floor as they went. They passed some double doors, through which, delicious savoury smells wafted, making Jake's stomach grumble with hunger.

To his right was a glass wall, through which Jake could see a large, courtyard garden landscaped with shady trees, paths and benches. Several patients were sat out in the sunshine. On their left, they were passing the entrances to the different wards. Lawrence turned abruptly and went through the doors into Ward nine. After passing a desk where a nurse was sitting writing a report, a corridor led straight ahead with cubicles leading off each side.

Still following Lawrence, they walked down towards the end of the ward. Ahead, Jake could see a bed on the left at the end had a familiar shape in front of it. Someone was standing by the bed, his back turned to him. His dad was wearing the polo shirt he usually wore for playing golf and, as Jake walked closer, he could see that there was someone else in a chair next to the bed. Emotions lurched and cartwheeled within him as he recognised his mum's upright posture. There was another man at the far side of the bed. He was tall, tanned with sun-bleached hair and wearing a cool T-shirt and stylishly frayed jeans. Chris? Jake's already overworked consciousness reeled at the sudden appearance of his brother.

As they approached, Jake saw his mum look up, her face lighting up with recognition. 'Jake!' She rushed from her seat, swept towards him and hugged him tightly. A deep surge of emotion was welling up within Jake as she squeezed him, the scent of his mum's perfume seeming strangely familiar and at the same time out of place. She was talking to him, asking question after question, but Jake wasn't listening. He pulled clear of her embrace gently, feeling his dad's hand on his shoulder as he moved around the curtain of granddad's cubicle. Right now, all that mattered to Jake was to speak to granddad, to say that he was sorry for what he had said back in the forest and say he was sorry he had left him there on his own.

Granddad was sitting up in bed. The tubes and wires had gone, the dull greyness had disappeared from his face and, although still pale with dark circles under his eyes, he looked more like the granddad he knew. Jake tried to speak, but the surge of emotion was threatening to engulf him. 'I'm… I'm sorry…' was the only thing he could stammer before the dam inside him which had been holding back all the conflicting emotions of the last few days cracked, broke entirely and Jake was engulfed.

Holding on to granddad's hand Jake sobbed. He didn't care who saw him, and even if he had, he couldn't deny the unstoppable outpouring. Jake heard granddad saying, 'Don't be sorry Jake, it's all my fault, it's all my fault.'

When Jake managed to sit up, his breath still catching with half-sobs, he saw that there were tears in granddad's eyes and for a while nobody spoke. Jake sat in the chair which someone had found for him and rubbed his eyes; they felt puffy and sore. He felt exhausted now the tension inside him had been let go, he felt drained. Granddad was going to be all right and he had his family round him now, everything was going to be OK. Jake looked around at his mum stood at the end of the bed looking concerned. His dad seated, with his hand resting heavily on Jake's shoulder, smiling gently at him. Chris leaning casually against the wall, grinning and shaking his head in that gently mocking way that his big brother always did. Lawrence, a few paces away from the bed, clearly letting the family have their time together. Suddenly Jake was laughing, he didn't really know why, maybe it just seemed so bizarre that here they were, all together in a German hospital. The suddenness of it nearly started him crying again, but soon everyone was chuckling along, nobody knowing what was so funny, which made them laugh all the more.

Once the laughter died down, Jake's mum fussed over him, asking him where he'd been all night and clucking how pale and tired he was looking as well as being horrified at the state of his clothes. Jake found he hadn't got the energy to answer her, but her anxious voice was enormously comforting. Then granddad spoke. 'Did you see him Jake? Was it him?' His voice was still husky, but it was reassuringly stronger now.

Jake nodded. 'Yeah, you were right Granddad, it was him.' Granddad said nothing, but he sank back on to his pillows nodding almost imperceptibly to himself as he took the news in.

'You should have seen it Walter!' Lawrence's voice was tense with enthusiasm. 'There was Enkmann, large as life on the podium, chatting away to the assembled crowd and suddenly up pops Jake entering stage right.'

Granddad switched an incredulous look back on to Jake, 'You spoke to him? You spoke to Enkmann? What did you say?'

Jake shrugged, 'Not much, I just showed him the photo.' He pulled out the tattered image from his pocket and handed it back to granddad who stared at it like he'd never seen it before.

After a second or two, granddad snapped his stare back on to Jake. 'So what did he say? How did he react?'

Jake thought about it. 'I dunno, it wasn't what I expected. He just sort of looked at it for a while and then he asked to speak to me in his office and then Lawrence showed up and we came here. So I don't think I've managed to do anything really,' and he glanced up at granddad's face, looking for any signs of disappointment.

'That's poppycock Jake!' Lawrence looked like he was going to burst with excitement. 'Don't you understand? You've let the cat out of the bag! It's Pandora's Box dear boy! You've opened Pandora's Box!' When Jake looked blank, Lawrence made an impatient tutting noise. 'Pandora's Box! You've let out his secret and he can't hide it away again! All those bigwigs sat on the stage got a good look at that photo of yours and the audience heard enough to make them ask some very awkward questions of Mr Enkmann, oh, I'm sorry, Mr Meyer as we should now call him.'

Then everyone was talking at once and wanting to hear more details. It was an effort to get the events of the past twenty-four hours into the right order, but Jake tried his best to explain what had happened after he'd run away from Dieter and the police.

'They weren't there to arrest you! We'd asked them to look out for you, you numpty!' Chris had jeered good-naturedly.

Jake's mum took this as her cue to assert her authority. 'That's enough now! Chris, you need to get Jake back to the hotel straight away. You need a bath Jake and go to bed, you look shattered! No! No arguments. You can tell us all about it tonight. Off you go!'

Chris grinned ruefully. 'Come on bruv, let's go, mum's right, you stink!' Jake was feeling very tired now and was glad to go, but he did playfully punch Chris as they left.

To Jake's surprise and delight, Chris had managed to secure a suite in the Forbes hotel. The hotel was right next to the hospital, so the walk wasn't far, but Jake's legs felt incredibly heavy and it seemed to take ages. Finally, he wearily climbed the front steps and clattered across the wide, marble floor of the lobby. The wait for a lift seemed to take a lifetime, but eventually, with a pinging noise, the doors slid open and they rode up to the top floor. The suite was comprised of a modern, stylishly furnished sitting room with a leather sofa, desk, a large TV and some funky modern art pictures on the wall. Tall windows gave a view across the car park, the road and the river beyond. At either side of the sitting room, doors led into two bedrooms.

Chris pointed out the room on the left. 'We're bunking in here, I'll run your bath.' Jake flopped on to the bed which didn't have Chris's clothes scattered over it and closed his eyes. Apart from the rushing noise of the bath filling up, it was still and quiet, it was a peaceful cocoon and the bed was so soft.

'Oy! Jake! Your bath's ready, there's a robe on the back of the door you can use afterwards.' Jake blinked away the sleep which had been taking hold of him and struggled reluctantly off the soft bed and into the bathroom. The water was hot to the point of being just bearable and he eased himself into the bath gingerly, gasping at the heat and sighing with contentment alternatively.

Later, feeling relaxed, clean and toasty warm, Jake dried himself and pulled on the soft, white bathrobe with the Forbes logo embroidered on the front breast pocket. He wandered back into the bedroom. The only sound was the TV in the sitting room and Chris speaking softly to someone on the phone. Jake pulled back the quilt and eased himself into the bed, his eyes already closing. A few minutes later, Chris popped his head round the door. 'You out of the bath yet bruv?' He saw the sleeping form, smiled to himself and quietly entered the room to pull the curtains, before retreating back into the sitting room, closing the door softly behind him.

Chapter 23

Josef's Story

When Jake awoke, the first thing he noticed was that the room was bathed in an eerie red light. The bed was gloriously warm and comfortable, but Jake's curiosity was stirred. Where was the light coming from? He pulled back the quilt and crossed to the window. The curtains were glowing like hot coals and when Jake pulled them back, the light from the setting sun flooded into the room. The sun itself was a gleaming, red ball of light on the horizon and the trees and hedges of the farmland beyond the river cast long shadows.

The sound of murmured conversation in the sitting room drew Jake to the door. His mum and Chris were sitting on the sofa, sipping mugs of hot chocolate and watching a film on the TV.

At the sound of the door opening, his mum stood up, crossed the room and enveloped him in a hug. 'Hello sleepyhead, you could have stayed in bed you know, you look like you could use some more sleep.' Jake didn't squirm away awkwardly from his mum's embrace like he would normally do. He allowed himself to be comforted by her familiar touch and drifted contentedly as she fussed over him.

Jake sat on the sofa next to Chris, saying nothing, just enjoying being around his family once more. He nodded vaguely at Chris's, 'Alright bruv?'

'Your dad will be back soon, he's with Lawrence and granddad at the hospital, but visiting time is nearly over.

Granddad's much better now he's had some rest and the antibiotics are starting to clear up his chest. They say he'll be able to travel home by Thursday, so long as he doesn't overdo things...'

The sound of his mum's chattering voice washed over Jake like healing water and he allowed himself to drift again until he realised his mum had asked him a question. 'I said are you hungry Jake? We ordered room service, but it might be cold now.'

Jake became aware that there was a trolley parked near the door. It was cluttered with the empty plates from when his family had eaten, but there was one plate which held a pepperoni pizza, untouched. The pizza looked cold and limp, as did the bowl of French fries next to it, but Jake had suddenly realised that he was very hungry. He wolfed down the pizza, and cold, greasy fries as if he'd not eaten in a week.

A few minutes later, his dad came in and reported that the doctor had been round and was very happy with granddad's progress. He'd brought up a bottle of wine from the hotel bar and poured three glasses, Jake was handed a can of coke from the mini bar and they spent a happy evening together watching a film on the TV. Jake allowed his mum to pack him off to bed as soon as the film had finished. The woolly cobwebs of tiredness still filled his head and he was secretly glad to go.

They slept late the next day. The sun had climbed high into the clear, blue sky before they emerged from the hotel. Jake wore the new clothes that his mum had bought for him the previous day. He had noticed that the T-shirt and shorts must have been quite expensive. They were very cool and not at all the more "sensible" kind of thing that she usually bought for him. Jake wondered if he was being spoiled, but he decided not to ask his mum about it; he didn't want to jinx it.

Mum, dad and Chris were going into Rheinhagen to have a look around. 'It'd be a shame to come all this way and see nothing of the town,' his mum had said and she invited Jake to show them round. He winced, the jumble of medieval buildings held no charm for him now.

Instead, Jake and Lawrence walked to the hospital to see granddad. Lawrence was taking a cab to the airport that afternoon and catching a flight home, so he said his goodbyes to Jake's mum, dad and Chris, promising to keep in touch and to let them know that he'd got home safely. Jake and Lawrence walked in thoughtful silence to the hospital. It seemed that Lawrence's departure signalled the beginning of the end of their adventure, a fact that gave Jake a curiously melancholy feeling.

As they turned into Ward nine, they halted. Jake heard Lawrence exclaim softly, 'Well I'll be blowed!' Down at the end of the ward, sitting at granddad's bedside, was an old man. He was dressed smartly in a blue jacket and fawn trousers with highly polished brown shoes which gleamed expensively. Jake stood, rooted to the spot. What was Enkmann doing here? His first reaction was that he had come to wreak revenge and granddad was in some sort of danger, but just then, they saw Enkmann laugh at something granddad had said. They were acting like old friends, what was going on?

Jake knew that there was no way he was going to speak to Enkmann. He had to get away until the coast was clear. Muttering something incomprehensible to a bewildered looking Lawrence, Jake turned and walked away quickly down the main corridor, his mind racing. What was Enkmann doing here? Why were he and granddad laughing together? Had Jake got it wrong? Had it all been an horrendously embarrassing case of mistaken identity? No. Jake examined his inner feelings and there was no doubt there.

He shuddered at the near miss he'd just had. What if they'd not noticed Enkmann when they did? What on earth would he have said to him if they had met? 'Hello, sorry for ruining your life.' The thought of it making him giggle nervously to himself.

Jake accepted the truth. He didn't feel good at all about exposing Enkmann, not just because he knew it would have hurt Kirsten, but also because he'd come to see how much the town loved and respected him. He was an old man who had done such a lot of good for so many people. Enkmann may have been Meyer in a past life and, yes, he should be brought to account for his crimes, but Jake didn't feel that it was his fight. Whatever had happened all those years ago had nothing to do with him and he didn't want to be involved anymore.

He was walking quickly, eyes on the shiny floor in front of him, when he came to an open door in the glass wall on his right. Without thinking he passed through it into the courtyard garden. The bright sunshine made him screw up his eyes, but he kept walking, he just needed to get away.

In the middle of the garden, surrounded by shady trees and benches, was a fountain. Behind the low wall which encircled it, goldfish cruised lazily through the greenish water below. Jake stopped walking and leaned on the wall, staring at the fish and listening to the soft splashing. He was still spooked by his close call with Enkmann and he wondered how long he would have to hide here until the coast was clear. Some instinct told him that eyes were upon him. He turned around to see that someone was sitting on the bench behind him.

Thin, white wires of earphones could be seen disappearing beneath her glossy, dark hair. For a second, Jake wondered if Kirsten had been so absorbed in her music that she hadn't noticed him, but with a lurching feeling inside, he saw that the keen, bright brown eyes were fixed upon him.

For what seemed like a lifetime, they simply stared at each other. Then, slowly, Kirsten reached up and removed the earphones. Still nothing was said. What was there to say?

'Sorry.' The word seemed feeble, pathetic and completely inadequate. He wanted to say that he wished more than anything, that things hadn't worked out this way. He wanted her to know that he really, really liked her and he wanted her to know that he hadn't used her to get to her grandfather. He wanted her to know that if there had been any other way...

'Sorry?' Her head was tilted slightly, eyes ablaze with sudden fury. 'Sorry...? That's it? That is all you can say?' She stood up and took a pace forward. Jake wondered if she was going to hit him. He felt so bad that he almost wished she would. He tried to find the right thing to say, but his mouth worked soundlessly and no words came. Kirsten seemed to have the same trouble as she looked like she was about to shout at him, tears forming in the corners of her eyes. 'Forget it.' A look of revulsion twisted her face and she spun around and walked away towards the main entrance.

Jake stood dejectedly by the fountain. He felt awful. Why did it have to turn out like this? He watched as Kirsten walked away, her silky hair bouncing around her shoulders. Misery engulfed him, making him feel sick. He sank on to the bench where Kirsten had been a few seconds before, his head sagging forward into his hands. He tried to imagine what it had been like for her. She would have been in the crowd, with her friends, laughing and enjoying the day. She would have proudly watched her grandfather accept the plaudits of the townspeople and then...? And then her English friend appeared and unmasked her grandfather in front of everyone. No wonder she hated him. Right now, Jake didn't like himself very much either.

The quiet background noises of hospital life carried on all around him. Trolleys rumbled down corridors, the occasional voice drifted through the open doors, somewhere, a floor polishing machine thrummed busily. Jake became aware that someone had sat down on the other end of the bench. 'You will forgive my granddaughter please? She has had a hard time.' The voice was gentle and kindly yet it froze Jake's insides and he sat up stiffly. Enkmann was sitting neatly, knees together and hands in his lap. He was smiling at him. 'Your grandfather said that I might speak with you. I hope that is OK?' No it wasn't OK, it wasn't OK at all, but Jake found himself nodding guardedly.

There was a pause whilst Enkmann looked away as if trying to organise his thoughts. Then he turned his warm, disconcerting smile back on to Jake. 'I'm glad we have the chance to talk, you see, I wish to thank you Jake.' Jake thought he mustn't have heard him right, or Enkmann's English had let him down. Enkmann smiled. 'I know what you are thinking, crazy yes? But I do really wish to say thank you.'

Jake thought that he must have missed something, some detail. He couldn't think of one reason why Enkmann would want to thank him, alarm bells were sounding in his head. Maybe this is part of his plan for revenge? Maybe he was trying to trick him in some way, but as Jake met his stare, he could see no hint of deceit or malice behind Enkmann's heavily lidded eyes.

'Shall I explain?' Enkmann said, noticing Jake's bafflement. 'Where to begin... you are fourteen years old I believe?' Jake nodded again feeling slow and thick and completely unable to think of what he should say or do. Enkmann paused thoughtfully for a few seconds, looking down at his hands, as if he were organising his long-buried memories.

'When I was about your age, my mother and father had been dead for many years. They died within three weeks of each other. It was an illness. They had been without enough food for a long time and they were… err… weak. Things were very hard in Germany at that time, there was little food and what there was, we could barely afford.'

Jake had learned at school about a time of economic depression in Germany before the war. He was fuzzy on the details, but remembered that his teacher had mentioned that German money had become almost worthless and, if they were lucky enough to have a job, people had to use wheelbarrows to carry home the bundles of practically useless banknotes which was their wages.

'After they had died, I was moved to another town to be cared for by my aunt. She always seemed to be angry that I was eating their food and costing them money. My cousins were older and they grew to hate me. I spent more and more time out of the house and away from them.' He stopped for a second and looked back at Jake, his gaze earnest. 'You understand that I do not say this as an excuse. I have no excuse, I just want you to know how it all happened.' His voice was so serious and carried such conviction that Jake was unable even to nod, but Enkmann took his silence as understanding and carried on.

'One day, out in the streets I saw a number of older boys walking together. They were all wearing uniform and had… something about them… a kind of confidence that I found interesting. They were not much older than I was at the time and I followed them to see where they were going. They were part of the Hitler Youth Movement, you have heard of this?'

Jake nodded. He'd read about the Hitler Youth Movement, the organisation which trained young people in a military style and instilled loyalty and devotion to Adolph Hitler and the Third Reich. He'd seen grainy black and white propaganda films in his history lessons of hundreds teenagers lined up, doing exercises like star jumps.

'I went with these boys and soon joined them. It was almost like having a new family, one where, although it was sometimes hard and the older boys could be cruel, at least I was wanted. I started to spend most of my time with my new family and I grew up tall and became strong. Soon every young person had to join the Hitler Youth, by which time I had been given a rank and put in charge. My cousins had to join as well and I made their lives… very bad for a while.'

There was a pause and a sad frown crumpled Enkmann's face for a second or two as the memories returned. 'We were preparing for war and I was given more and more responsibility. Then, I was told that someone with my talent and loyalty should be rewarded and I was ordered to join the Shutzstaffel, the SS. It seems crazy now, But I was so happy, I trained hard and wished for war to begin, so I could demonstrate my loyalty and blow away the enemies of the Third Reich.' He shook his head sadly, an old man remembering the folly of his youth.

'Very soon it looked like I was going to have my wish. War began and I trained hard. I was taught English to prepare for when we invaded and then I had my accident. An explosive charge went off prematurely when we were training and part of my hand was blown away.' He flexed his damaged fingers.

'This was too much to bear for a young man. I could not hold a rifle, or pull a trigger, I could not fight, what use was I? After I got out of hospital, they gave me a job in an office for a while. It nearly drove me out of my mind. Everywhere war was happening and I was doing paperwork. Eventually they listened to my requests to do something more and they put me in charge at Saint Gille. I think I was very angry, very angry at not being able to fight. After all, what is a soldier who cannot fight? And at St. Gille, I had people there at which I could… direct my anger.'

Jake saw that Enkmann's eyes glistened with tears. He felt awkward and embarrassed. What if Enkmann broke down

265

and sobbed? He decided to pretend he hadn't noticed and stared straight ahead.

'And so the war went on and all over the world people were fighting and I was stuck in a quiet part of France looking after a camp full of people who I had learned to hate with a passion. After a while reports came in saying that we were suffering losses on the eastern front and the Allied invasion of France could happen any day. Gradually I realised that I was going to be on the losing side. The dream, the vision they had sold me was turning sour. Inside, I had become sick of seeing people suffer. I could no longer be angry, I was tired of war. I came to realise that I was here because of what they had given to me. I was only a boy and they had given me a cause to fight for, they had given me a new family, they had given me their own hatreds, fears and prejudices and, their biggest mistake of all, they had given me authority and the power to enforce it.' A single tear bulged, quivered on his thin eyelash and dropped, tracing a wet line which zigzagged down the deep creases of his face.

'The Allies landed in Normandy and started to move across France. I realised that it was just a matter of time before it would all be over and I knew that, when the Allies came, I would be a wanted man, so I made plans to get away. We had a room full of belongings which we had taken from the prisoners when they'd arrived. I secretly took a suitcase and found civilian clothes that fit me and hid them near the railway station. Then one day I told my officers that I'd had received orders to report to headquarters. I walked to the station, picked up the suitcase and caught a train heading to Germany.

'But now I had a problem. I had deserted, the penalty for which was death. I had no family to go to. They wouldn't want me and it would have been risky for me to go there anyway. Some instinct told me that I should head away from the big towns and into the country, so at the first station which looked quiet, I put on the suit and threw away my uniform. I bandaged my hand and made it look like it was a new injury and, as I walked away from the station, I looked like just another wounded soldier.

'You have to understand that things were starting to fall apart in Germany, so one man alone could easily disappear.

'I carried on for nearly a week, walking through the night, sleeping in barns, stealing food from people's houses and always staying away from the big roads. Everywhere soldiers were moving, travelling up to the front. After nearly a week, I was exhausted and had a fever. It had rained for two days and I was wet and cold and I took shelter in a barn about seven or eight kilometres from here. I remember lying, shivering on the hay and thinking that I would surely be dead by morning. The thought of it was comforting. I hated everything by now, the Jews, the British, the Americans, everyone! Everyone, including Adolph Hitler and the Nazis for losing the war. But above all, I hated myself. I hated myself for allowing them to turn me into something I was not. I remember, just before sleep came, just before I gave myself to what would be my death, alone, unloved, missed by no one, I cursed God. I cursed him with what I knew would be my dying breath for the cruelty and injustice that he had shown me.

'When I awoke, I was in a bed in the farmhouse. The farmer, a man called Karl Enkmann had found me, nearly dead, in his barn. He and his wife Anna had carried me inside. There was an old couple who lived on the farm, Otto and Irma. They stayed at my bedside day and night for nearly a week whilst the fever took hold. Eventually, the fever broke and I came around. Irma was there, smiling at me whilst she gently washed the sweat from my face. Karl and Anna never asked me what I was doing there, or where I had come from. They had taken the bandages off my hand and seen that the wound was not new. I was hiding something, but they did not ask what it was or make any judgment, they simply saw a fellow human being in need and cared for him.

267

'The fever had left me weak as a child. Otto and Irma took turns in feeding and cleaning me up. As the days went by, I gradually became stronger and managed to sit outside in the farmyard. I'll never forget the feeling of the sun on my face. A few days before, I would have welcomed death and now, it was like I was reborn. I began to work on the farm. It helped me to become strong again. Every day I expected to be found out. I expected questions about who I was and where I'd come from, but Karl and Anna never asked me anything. It was a good, wholesome, simple life and I hoped it wouldn't end too soon. Then, one day Karl handed me an envelope. As I took it from him he said, "If you wish, this can be the start of a new life for you, one where you can choose to learn from before, one where you can wipe away your mistakes. It is a chance few men get, choose wisely." I opened the envelope and there were identification papers for Josef Enkmann who was their nephew who had been injured in Normandy and sent home to recover. Whilst he was at home, a bomb had come down and killed the whole family, there was nothing left. Karl and Anna had figured out that I was a deserter, but instead of turning me in, they were giving me a chance to start a new life with their dead nephew's identity.

'Like I said, the country was in turmoil and one individual could slip through the system easily. I spent my days quietly working on the farm and people simply accepted Karl's story without suspicion. The war ended and we had British and American soldiers administrating the running of Rheinhagen.

'The community tried to return to normal, but there were some influential people in the town who were using their position with the Allied forces to take farmland which was not theirs. It was corruption. Nobody seemed able to speak out against this and I certainly did not want to get involved and risk discovery and losing my new life on the farm, so I stayed out of it.

'One day I was asked to take the cart into town to pick up some feed for the cattle. I had not got very far when the horse became lame and I had to return. When I got back, the farm seemed deserted, I went inside to find Karl and tell him what had happened. When I opened the door, there was a scream. I could see Otto and Irma at the table, with Karl and Anna standing nearby. They all looked terrified to see me. I was shocked and hurt that these people, who had become like my family and had shown me so much kindness, would suddenly recoil from me. I asked myself, why? Why were they frightened? And then I saw. Otto was wearing something around his shoulders. It was a tallit, a Jewish prayer shawl. It was the eve of Yom Kippur, a time when prayers for forgiveness are offered. I could not believe my eyes. Karl and Anna had been hiding Otto and Irma on the farm for the whole of the war. I was stunned, yet things began to make sense. The farm was remote, Otto and Irma stayed inside, or around the buildings for most of the time and they never went into town.

'But I still could not understand why they were sitting in silence, looking at me with fearful eyes. And then I thought back to what I had been before, when I was Günther Meyer. Günther had been a lost boy twisted and manipulated by hatred and fear into something less than human.

'It must have been a time of such fear for them and, even though the war was over now, they were unsure what my reaction would be. Maybe they knew what I had done. Maybe I had talked of St Gille whilst in the grip of the fever, I don't know. And now, now I was confronted with two of the people whom I had been taught to hate, two people who feared I would harm them, two people who had tended and gently cared for me and brought me back from near death. Me, the enemy of their people.' The emotion in Enkmann's voice caught and nearly broke. 'I fell on my knees before them. I begged for their forgiveness over and over again weeping helplessly. We prayed together, all of us, everyone crying, and Otto took my hands and offered me forgiveness.

'I had the chance of a new life, but I could not ignore what I had done before. The next day I went to Rheinhagen, I planned to turn myself over to the Allied authorities and face the consequences of what I had done. I walked into their offices. There was a young officer called Captain Herbert Wallingham. He was talking to one of the administrators. He was very angry with the people who were in charge of the town. He was struggling to make himself understood and he did not trust them. I told him in English that he was right not to trust these men and I told him how they were trying to cheat the farmers out of their land.

'He was very happy to find someone who could speak English and we got on very well. And then, he asked me what my name was and it was this moment that I have come to realise that the rest of my life has been built upon. I had come to him as Günther Meyer, to face the consequences of what I had done and yet, as Josef Enkmann I had an opportunity to help the farmers and the people of the town, a chance to pay back, in a small way, for the kindness that they had shown me. I told him that my name was Josef Enkmann.'

The noise from the floor polishing echoed around the courtyard as the machine passed the open door behind them and faded again as it progressed down the corridor. Enkmann stared at the ground in front of him, lost in thought.

'We talked for a long time and we found that we liked each other. After a while, he thanked me and asked if I would come back the next day and be his translator at a meeting with the town council. I agreed and together, over the next few months, we cut out all the corruption and things settled down. I became a trusted assistant and I found that people were coming to me for help with their problems. I had intended to confess to Captain Wallingham once we had helped the farmers, but now there were other people who needed me. I found that helping people made me feel good and I began to feel a little better about myself and so I decided to be Enkmann for a while longer. Time went by and there was always some new problem to sort out before I could tell people the truth. I was still helping Karl with the farm when I was given a position on the council where I found I could make a real difference to the townspeople. Looking back, I realise that I was making excuses for not facing up to my crimes.

'I was amazed that I had got this far without being discovered. Every day I expected to be exposed as Meyer, a finger pointing from a crowd, a phone call, a knock on the door. It never happened, but the thought that it could all come to an end any day, made me push for change with great urgency. This drive was rewarded when I was made Bürgermeister. I felt sure that my higher profile would be my downfall, but still I was not found out.

'And then I fell in love and married. I had become happy beyond measure with my life and Adelle completed me. Although she has been gone for three years now, I still thank God that he blessed me with such a precious, perfect gift. I never told her about what I had been before. I had begun to relax and believe that I would live out my life as Josef Enkmann, there was no need for her to know.'

Enkmann exhaled noisily, puffing out his cheeks as the emotions and recollections came.

'And this is why I want to thank you Jake. My wife is gone now and I know that I should have told her the truth. We shared everything else, but not the biggest secret of all. I cannot change this, but I can set things right with my family. I am an old man now and, if it wasn't for you and your grandfather coming over here and telling the world who I am, I think that I would have probably died as Josef Enkmann. I hate to think that, after I was gone, my children or grandchildren might find out who I really was and hate me for it. At least now I can be honest and do what is right.'

There was a silence between them that lengthened, but it wasn't an awkward silence; Jake felt no need to say anything, to console or accuse, it was just a pause whilst they both thought about Enkmann's story. Eventually, Jake said, 'So what will you do now?'

Enkmann sat up. 'Well, I have spoken to the authorities and they have told me that I am not to leave the country.' A small smile tweaked the corner of his mouth. 'They will be here tomorrow and I'll meet with them, after that…' He shrugged. 'The people of Rheinhagen have been very good to me, despite being deceived for all these years. My family stands by me, although it is hard for them, they find now that they are not who they thought they were, no longer Enkmann but Meyer.'

Jake thought again of what Kirsten was going through and his insides squirmed guiltily. 'Was Deiter OK? I didn't think he liked me before I knocked him over and I'm sure he doesn't like me now.'

Enkmann shared a smile with Jake and when he spoke, it was as if he was choosing his words with care. 'Dieter is very… ambitious. He likes to… know things about people. I think he may have found out something about my past. I don't know that, but, it is true that he gained his position partly through my influence and if my previous identity was discovered, then…' He shrugged again.

After a short pause, Enkmann grasped the arm of the bench and stood up. He shuffled his feet as he turned to Jake. He looked very old now, older than granddad. His eyes seemed sunken and there were dark rings under them. He held out a hand towards Jake. 'Thank you for listening to my story, I think I shall go and find my granddaughter now. Have a good journey home.' Jake stood stiffly, feeling suddenly self-conscious, awkward and clumsy now that the

272

conversation was at an end. On impulse, Jake reached out and took Enkmann's damaged, gnarled and twisted hand in his.

Jake simply didn't know what he should be feeling. He found that pity was the emotion that he felt most of all and he questioned why. Why should he feel sorry for this old man who had caused so much pain and suffering? Why, when he should be feeling triumph that they had exposed a monster, did Jake feel guilt for hurting an old man? As Enkmann gave him one last gentle smile and shuffled away, Jake's mind was in a whirl. When granddad had told his war stories, it had all been so black and white. The Allies were the goodies and the Nazis were the baddies. It was simple, and it was straightforward. But in reality it wasn't like that at all. Yes, Enkmann had been a monster, but he had spent the rest of his life trying to help others, a good, honourable caring man. How could someone be so bad and yet be good as well? His head ached. War. That was it. That was the answer. War damaged and maimed and twisted and warped and embittered and destroyed and, for a moment, Jake felt a vast, burning hatred of war roll over him like a wildfire, consuming him until there was nothing left but a sick, empty feeling inside.

Jake glanced over to the retreating form of Enkmann. He saw the old man ascend the sunlit ramp up to the door and disappear into the darkness beyond. Jake's head hurt. He didn't want to think about the war anymore. He closed his eyes and turned his face into the sunshine feeling numb, tired and a long way from home. Opening his eyes once again, he waited until the retinal images ceased flashing across his vision and made his way back to ward nine.

Chapter 24

Packing Up

The next day, Chris and Jake set out in the faithful old Rover which someone had rescued from the hospital car park with the spare keys granddad had kept in his money belt. It seemed very strange to be back in the familiar seat, navigating again, but this time for Chris, who drove swiftly and confidently around Rheinhagen's ring road. Jake kept his eyes straight ahead as they went past Enkmann's house and soon they were bumping up the familiar track to the campsite.

The tents were looking sad and neglected. Jake's tent sagged deeply in the middle, the guy ropes flopping loosely as if they just couldn't be bothered anymore.

Once they'd rescued the bags of soggy clothes from the stiflingly humid interior, they set about taking the tents down. It was so much quicker and easier than putting them up and Jake's mood lifted more and more. They stowed the clothes and tents in the back of the Rover. Somehow Jake's tent with its poles and pegs wouldn't fit back into the canvas bag. He couldn't remember how it had been packed, so he had tried simply stuffing it back. This didn't work and the boot of the Rover seemed to be piled high with damp, orange nylon.

Once they had managed to stuff everything into the boot, mainly through the use of brute force, they slammed the boot repeatedly until it closed with a clunk. Chris looked up at Jake. 'Let's go then.' Jake took one more glance around the clearing, hardly able to believe now what had happened that night. He hopped into the car and the Rover trundled down the track for the last time.

A thought occurred to Jake on the way back to the hotel. 'How come you got roped into this then?'

Chris grinned. 'Well, as soon as she'd heard where you and granddad had got to, mum wanted the invasion of Rheinhagen to go ahead without delay! She'd worked out that if I got the train from Cannes, I could be on the ground a full fourteen hours before they landed.' He chuckled. 'Sometimes she's really annoying when she's trying to control everything, but, you've got to hand it to her, she's a brilliant organiser. She told me to book the hotel rooms and I didn't even know we had a hotel anywhere near here. I think it impressed her when I wangled the suite though.'

For a while, they drove on in silence before Chris spoke again, his face was uncharacteristically serious now and his manner was sombre. 'When we got to the hospital, the police told us that you'd run off towards the river and when they'd got down to the riverbank, there was no sign of you. Well… we all started thinking the worst. Mum was in a right state and she was asking for the river to be dragged and helicopters and divers and stuff like that, sobbing her heart out she was.'

Jake's face fell, he'd no idea that he'd caused such trouble. 'So what did you do next?' Jake enquired hardly daring to ask the question.

'Well, I turned to mum and I looked her straight in the eye.' He paused.

'Yes?' Jake prompted.

'I looked her straight in the eye and said, 'Tell you what Mum, if he's dead, can I have his room?'

The huge guffaw of helpless laughter that followed left Chris blinking tears from his eyes. At first, Jake didn't think the joke was funny at all and he told Chris as much with some choice swearing whilst landing punches on Chris's arm. Soon though, the simple relief that a major search operation had not actually been launched to find his body and the comforting sound of Chris's laughter, curled an irresistible grin across Jake's face and soon he was laughing along.

As they turned off the main road and into the hotel car park, Jake noticed a small gathering of people by the front door. There were more cars than usual in the car park, but eventually they found a space at the back. They locked the car and set off towards the entrance. Jake could see that the group of people were mostly bored-looking men talking on their phones, almost all of them had cameras slung around their necks. As Jake and Chris approached the hotel, a large van pulled up with the logo of a television news channel splashed across it, a door on the side of the van slid open and a smartly dressed lady stepped out, along with a man who was holding a tripod and a large TV camera. Chris stopped in his tracks, suddenly tense and alert. They were still a fair way off and none of the reporters had seen them yet. Chris turned to Jake, 'This way!' he whispered through clenched teeth and he walked quickly around the side of the hotel, trying, as best he could, to keep out of sight of the reporters without looking suspicious.

At the side of the building was a door to the hotel's health club which opened with a swipe of Chris's room key card. They both tumbled inside giggling with excitement. 'You don't really think that they were here about the Enkmann thing do you?' Jake laughed as they made their way through the gym equipment and back to the hotel reception and the lifts.

'Don't be an idiot!' Chris said, playfully punching Jake. 'Of course they're here to see you! How many times does a high level politician get exposed as a Nazi war criminal? It's big news!'

They chuckled as the lift whooshed quietly upwards, but when they got back to the suite, they found that they had a visitor. Victor Kortig was the hotel manager. He had a badge on his lapel which told Jake as much. He wore a dark suit and corporate tie that bore the Forbes hotel logo. His black shoes gleamed and his long, thin, fingers were folded together as he sat stiffly on the sofa, talking to Jake's mum. They looked up as Jake and Chris entered. 'Oh, there you are, I wondered when you'd get back, how did you manage to get past those awful men at the front door?'

Chris told them how they'd outflanked the news people and then asked, 'How long have they been out there?'

Victor unfolded his hands and made an apologetic gesture. 'It seems that somebody informed the press of where you were staying. I can only apologise, I am sure that the informant was not a Forbes employee. We pride ourselves in our discretion and the privacy of guests is paramount.'

Victor's overly serious manner and fussy voice made Jake want to giggle again and he carefully avoided Chris's glance as he could tell that he wanted to laugh as well. They both caught the warning look from their mum which said very clearly, that she was not in the mood for silliness and they'd better behave.

'The phone started ringing not long after you left this morning and your dad was pestered and photographed when he set off to the hospital. He called me once he'd got there, but it took him ages to get through, as the switchboard was jammed with news reporters trying to speak to you. Mr Kortig here has kindly agreed to stop putting people through unless it's your dad calling.'

Mr Kortig nodded contemplatively and addressed Jake's mum, 'Also, I think it's best for you that, when you check out tomorrow, we can bring your car to the loading bay at the back of the hotel, where you can get away without them seeing you. I will also talk to the hospital and see what they can do for your father.'

They all thanked him and he shook hands with everyone before leaving. In the silence that followed his departure, Jake wondered what it would be like to go down to the front steps and speak to the TV crews and reporters. The image of him holding up the photograph of Meyer in front of a sea of flashing cameras flickered once more though his imagination. He shook his head as if to force the thought away, what if Kirsten saw him on TV, triumphant and gloating? No, he wouldn't ever let that happen. He'd caused her enough pain. At least he could spare her this final indignity.

They spent the remainder of the day inside the hotel. After a lunch of room service sandwiches, Jake borrowed some swim shorts from the leisure complex and he and Chris swam in the pool, whilst his mum was making calls, busily organising the details of their return home.

That evening, dad returned and they ate together in the suite. The news about granddad was good. He had been pronounced strong enough to fly home the next day, but, once back home, he would still require a period of recuperation until he was fully recovered.

Mum's mobile phone bleeped during the meal and, with an inexperienced eye and a frown of concentration, she gazed at the small screen. 'It's a text message!' she exclaimed excitedly. She hardly ever got text messages, mostly on account of the fact that she didn't know how to send them. Jake had tried to show her how, but she sent so few, that whenever she wanted to send one, he'd have to explain it all over again. After much pensive stabbing of the buttons with her index finger, she cried: 'It's from Lawrence!' She passed the handset to Chris and Jake read over his shoulder.

BACK HOME SAFE GOOD FLIGHT HOPE WALTER FIT AND WELL ALL OVER THE NEWS BACK HERE TELL JAKE DONT FORGET

Chris snorted. 'The old boy has done all right to send a text, but it looks like he's shouting, it's all in capitals, and where's the punctuation?'

Jake's mum rose to Lawrence's defence. 'Well, at least he let us know he'd got back safely like he promised.'

'Looks like you've caused quite a stir,' his dad said, peering through his glasses to read the message.

His mum took the phone back and reread it. 'What have you not to forget Jake?' she asked.

Jake really didn't want to talk about it, so he smiled blankly back at her and, just to wind her up, he said, 'I forget.'

Fortunately, nobody asked him again, but Jake knew exactly what Lawrence had meant. After he had got back to granddad's bedside, following his conversation with Enkmann, he had found the two old soldiers deep in conversation. Lawrence had looked up as Jake pulled up a chair. 'You've had a little chat with our Günter then?'

For a second, Jake didn't know whom Lawrence was referring to and with a jolt, he realised that he had begun to think of Günter Meyer as a name from the past, a name of someone who ceased to exist a long time ago. The old man who had spoken kindly to him just now, would always be Enkmann to Jake.

'Funny the way things turned out isn't it? If I hadn't known what sort of a chap he'd been all that time ago, we would have probably got on very well.' Lawrence smiled wistfully, seemingly lost in thought.

Granddad cleared his throat, his voice still sounded croaky and a little breathless as he spoke. 'So what did you reckon to him Jake?'

Jake had paused, trying to make sense of everything, a fierce, angry flame suddenly flickering inside him. He was furious that people allowed so many horrors to happen back then, the screams of which still echoed today. It all seemed so... so stupid!

Looking again at granddad and Lawrence, the anger had died. After all, it wasn't their fault. He'd smiled warmly at them. 'He seemed like a really nice old bloke.' And he'd shrugged as if to express his bewilderment that the twisted, hate-filled Meyer had become the loved and respected Enkmann.

'Ah, well young Jake, that's the thing, isn't it?' Lawrence's normally light-hearted tone was now serious and sombre. 'You didn't come here to find a monster. Meyer didn't have green scales and three heads, he was just a man, just a normal man and that, young Jake, that is the true horror.'

Later on, after Lawrence had said his goodbyes to Granddad, they had waited at the entrance to the hospital for Lawrence's taxi to show up. Lawrence seemed to have something on his mind, despite keeping a chatty conversation going as they sat in the sunshine, the town of Rheinhagen, a hazy jumble of shapes in the distance.

A large silver Mercedes had swept up to the entrance and the smiling driver hopped out to stow Lawrence's case in the boot. 'Well Jake I do hope you and Walter will come and visit very soon.' He stuck his hand out, his grip firm as he shook Jake's.

The driver had opened the door for Lawrence and waited for him to get in, but Lawrence had remained, still shaking Jake's hand, a troubled expression on his face. 'I think you've done a simply grand job Jake, simply first rate.' Lawrence had continued to hold Jake's hand, his expression thoughtful, as if choosing his words carefully. 'I really shouldn't put this on you Jake. Forgive me, but I've always admired Walter so much I really have to ask.'

Jake quailed inside. What was coming now? Wasn't this adventure over? What more could he ask?

'You see, Walter was right about me, I have gone a bit soft, being waited on hand and foot at Bluebell Woods. But that's just me, I've always been fortunate enough to have had a privileged existence and it comes naturally.' His watery smile was almost apologetic. 'But Walter isn't like me at all. He's fiercely, fiercely independent and I've seen people like him come into Bluebell Woods and simply fade away. They can't deal with having everything delivered on a plate you see? Life suddenly becomes too easy and they just...' He shrugged.

Jake had wondered just what Lawrence expected him to do? The taxi driver shuffled impatiently. 'From the conversations I've had with her, your mother, bless her, is going to have Walter out of his house and into a home once you get back to Churnthorpe. I don't know what we can do Jake, I really don't, but you need to try and think of a way to keep Walter's independence. He's not a gibbering old wreck just yet. I mean, just look at what you've achieved together these last few days.' He paused. 'I'm counting on you.' And with a final, earnest glance, Lawrence had got into the taxi.

He'd waved from the car, just once, his solemn eyes fixed upon Jake as the Mercedes slowly pulled away.

Chapter 25

Heading Home

The early morning sky over the small, achingly picturesque Cornish bay, was a sweep of unbroken blue. A tall, slim figure wearing a tight Billabong rash vest, baggy, Quiksilver board shorts and sandals emerged from the quaint cottage which overlooked the beach and walked slowly up the road to the local shop.

Howard made his way through the colourful racks of buckets, spades, beach towels, fishing nets, kites and sunglasses into the comparative darkness of the shop beyond. His face was newly tanned and dotted with freckles. His floppy hair was sun-bleached and dishevelled. This was due partly to the fact that he'd just got out of bed and partly because he'd spent most of his holiday in the sea and he hadn't washed the salt out after yesterday's surfing.

He walked up to the counter, pausing to pick up a large carton of milk from the glass-fronted fridge. The fat man behind the counter was sat on a rather squashed swivel chair, keeping half an eye on the picture of the small, portable TV which was tuned to breakfast television news. He looked up at Howard, seemingly debating internally as to whether he could gather the energy to stand up to serve this, the first customer of the day. He decided he couldn't. 'Lovely day out there,' he said to the tall young man. He recognised him as the lad from that family that always take the cottage down the road. 'That's 55p please.'

'Oh yes, and a paper please,' Howard's voice rumbled, still deep with sleep and he held up a *Daily Express* he'd picked up from the neat piles of papers which were displayed along the front of the counter.

'Oh... right,' the fat man said, attempting to do the sum in his head, whilst trying to persuade himself to make an effort for one of his regulars and get to his feet. In the end, he decided that he couldn't do two things at once, not so early in the day, so he gave up the idea of getting out of his chair and concentrated on getting the money right. 'That's one pound twenty-two then please.'

Howard looked at the pile of loose change his dad had given him when he'd shuffled into the kitchen in his dressing gown asking Howard to run to the shop. He counted out the correct number of coins and, when the fat man showed no sign of getting up to take them from him, he left them on the counter and turned to go.

'See you later,' the fat man called after Howard. He looked at the small pile of coins. He should really get up and check it was the right amount straight away and put the money in the till... but not just yet.

Howard trudged back down the hill towards Tregennan Cottage, his eyes taking in the size of the waves as they curled, crashed and creamed up the beach. Nothing really surf-able just yet, but by the time they'd had breakfast and made their way down to their favourite spot on the beach and then, maybe after he'd explored a few rockpools with his little sister for a while, the wind might have got up and conditions might have changed. Howard's dad was sat at the small kitchen table, still in his dressing gown, sipping a steaming cup of strong coffee. 'Oh cheers son.' He smiled at Howard and took the paper whilst Howard went in search of a bowl and cereal.

Howard munched sleepily on his cereal, staring blankly out of the window, whilst his dad read the sports pages at the back of the paper. 'Morning sweety!' Howard's mum came into the kitchen and kissed Howard on the back of his neck.

'Morning sugar plum,' his dad called out from behind his paper. Howard's mum rolled her eyes theatrically and prodded her husband in his ribs.

'Not you! I was talking to Howard!' This little joke took place almost daily at breakfast. It was almost a family tradition.

However, something had caught Howard's eye and he was suddenly oblivious to his parents' banter. The photo on the front page underneath a banner headline was of a boy who looked very much like… no, it couldn't be! And yet… just at that moment, his dad closed the paper and looked over at his son. 'I said how about having a wander up to St Ives today? Aren't you listening to me son?'

Howard wasn't.

'Hold on Dad, just give us the paper a sec.'

'You see Sandra?' his dad said with mock seriousness. 'You see how much respect my lovely children have for their dear old dad? Here I am trying to communicate and Hey!'

Howard had reached over and plucked the paper out of his dad's grasp, ignoring his dad's playful complaints. He looked at the front page again, well if it wasn't Jake in the photo, it must be his double. The headline read: "British Boy 14 Unmasks Nazi War Criminal". Howard tried to calm his suddenly thudding heart and concentrate on reading the story.

He read: "A British schoolboy and his grandfather have uncovered the secret identity of Günter Meyer, a former Nazi SS officer wanted for war crimes committed during the Second World War…" Howard found that he wasn't breathing. "Jake Hargreaves confronted Meyer at a special award ceremony celebrating fifty years of public service as the Mayor of a town called Rheinhagen in northern Germany

where he'd been living under the alias of Josef Enkmann."
The picture lower down the page was a grainy still from a
video recording showing Jake on a stage presenting a piece of
paper, or something, to an old man who was stood at a
podium".

'Flipping heck!" Howard reread the story to try and
make sense of it all.

'What's the matter Howie?' his mum asked.

'It's Jake,' Howard said, stunned.

'What's happened to him?' his mum said suddenly all
urgency and concern. Howard couldn't even put it into words
and simply handed his mum the paper.

The next ten minutes or so was spent rereading the story
and talking in stunned, incredulous tones about how it could
have happened. Howard startled the fat man at the shop by
reappearing and buying *The Times*, *The Independent* and *The
Daily Mail*, all of which had the same story as its lead, with
similar photos of Jake on the front page.

Whilst they were poring over the newspapers which
were strewn across the kitchen table, Howard's kid sister
Katie padded around the corner from the lounge in her pink
pyjamas which bore a glittery picture of the latest pop
princess. 'Mum!' Her small, strident voice cut through the
excited chatter at the table. 'Mum! Jake's on the TV!'

They all piled into the lounge in time to see fuzzy,
shaky, videoed footage of the small figure of Jake walking on
to and across a stage and talking to the old man at the
podium. The newsreader's voice was saying '...and his
grandfather uncovered the identity of Meyer and decided to
unmask him themselves after thinking no one would take
their claims seriously. Jake Hargreaves, who is fourteen years
old, was left to expose Meyer's true identity alone, after his
grandfather, Walter Hargreaves, became ill and was taken to
hospital. Jake Hargreaves confronted Meyer as he was

receiving a special award for fifty years of public service in the town of Rheinhagen. The International Criminal Court has instructed the German police to place Meyer under house arrest and have confirmed that he will face trial. Walter Hargreaves' condition is said to be improving and it is thought that he will return to the UK later today. In other news, government ministers warned that the recent hot, dry weather could become a drought if we are not more careful about the amount of water we all consume…'

The newsreader's voice seemed to fade into the background as they all stared around at each other completely at a loss for words. 'Well!' Howard's mum chimed in a stunned voice. 'I did say that he'd have fun with Walter.'

Jake's parents' hire car was a silver family saloon. Inside, it was immaculate and still had that distinctive new car smell. Following a leisurely breakfast in the hotel restaurant, they had all gone back to the suite to pack their bags. After several trips back and forth from their room to the underground loading bay, where their car had been moved to, and, after doing the usual checks and rechecks, they decided that everything was safely stowed away.

Chris set off for home at about 11 o'clock. He was taking granddad's Rover back to England, after which, he was going to spend the rest of his holiday at home. 'It's a no-brainer really!' he had told Jake, his smile, a dazzling white against the background of his tanned, friendly face. 'I mean, who wouldn't give up the South of France for the delights of Churnthorpe in high summer?' He bear-hugged Jake and said, 'Well done bruv, you did good. I'll see you in a couple of days.' Then, after hugs for his dad and mum and, cheerfully ignoring his mum's pleas to "drive really carefully", he set off, out of the loading bay.

Jake thought that the departure of Chris would leave him feeling down, but funnily enough he felt quietly content. After all, Chris would be home with them the day after tomorrow. Home. The thought of going home made Jake feel almost as excited as he'd been before he'd set off on this adventure.

They did one last sweep of the suite to make sure they hadn't left anything. Victor Kortig came by and escorted them to the car, where they all shook his pale, bony hands once again. An ambulance appeared around the corner and drove slowly into the loading bay, before parking in the space next to their car. The door at the back opened and a wheelchair was brought out. Then, down the steps, looking pale and tired under the fluorescent lights came granddad. He moved gingerly, holding on to the handles on the door of the ambulance, before easing himself into the chair. He grinned at them self-consciously. 'Don't know why they have to make such a fuss!' he said as he was wheeled the few feet to the back door of the hire car. Once there, he shuffled himself off the chair and into the back seat. There was a flurry of 'Thank you's' and 'Danke schön's', more handshaking and they got into the car and started the engine.

As they emerged down the service road at the side of the hotel, Jake looked over to the main entrance. The ruse had worked, all the reporters were still milling around, unaware that their quarry was making a getaway under their noses. Even as he looked over, Jake saw a movement by the door and Victor emerged leading two hotel workers who were carrying trays of coffee. Jake grinned at Victor's diversion, he was certainly going to a lot of trouble to see that they got away without interference. They waited at the junction for a minute until the lights changed and then they swept out on to the main road heading towards the autobahn and the airport.

From his rear seat, Jake could see the reflection in the wing mirror of the now familiar silhouette of Rheinhagen, slowly getting smaller and smaller. He knew with absolute certainty that he would never return. The finality of it didn't shock him like he thought it might, he knew that there were just too many emotions wound around the twisting cobbled streets to ever go back. As he took in the image of the roofs and towers and spires for a last time, the road curved in front of them and the town slid away across the mirror and out of Jake's vision. He didn't look back.

The journey passed by in a strangely subdued atmosphere. Granddad sat quietly occasionally responding to Jake's mum's questions about his medicine and the doctors who had looked after him and whether he thought the German health service was better than the NHS. She chattered brightly as if trying to lift the mood single-handedly. His dad drove on in silence, concentrating on the road and the occasional chirped instructions from the car's satellite navigation system.

Jake's mind wandered as the German countryside, dappled with the shadows of a few fluffy, white clouds, slid past the window. He allowed himself to doze a little, enjoying the drowsy feeling behind his eyes. He was brought back to wakefulness quite suddenly when he caught the end of something his mum was saying. '...very best in the area apparently. You remember? It was where Kenny Bradshaw was a while back, after his operation. It's a bit like a cross between a hospital and sheltered accommodation, they're called, what was it? Oh yes, they call it a monitored convalescence facility. They only have three rooms which offer this service, so we were very lucky to get you a place at all.

'Of course there are plenty of normal rooms at Orchard Court. They're really lovely I'm told and from what I've seen of the gardens when I drive past, well, it always looks wonderful! You may well want to stay there once you're better! In fact the manager I spoke with yesterday, has reserved a room for you if you do. Wasn't that nice of him? It would be much nicer than struggling with the steps at your place wouldn't it Walter?'

Jake froze. So this was how it was going to happen. Granddad would just be slid into a home and it would be dressed up as something they were doing for his own good! Surely granddad wouldn't stand for this? But granddad's voice seemed weak and submissive. 'Thank you for all your hard work Louise, you've been very kind.' Jake waited for the "but", but it didn't come, instead granddad finished weakly. 'I'm sure that Orchard Court will be delightful.'

Something in the way granddad spoke made him sound sad and apologetic and it dawned on Jake what the problem was. Granddad wasn't fighting for his independence because he was feeling sorry for all the trouble, worry and expense he'd caused. He was preparing to be a good boy and do what he was told as an act of repentance. Jake bristled. Yes, it had been granddad's discovery which had launched them on this adventure, but Jake took just as much responsibility for what had happened and he wasn't about to see his granddad shut away in a home because of him.

'No!' The words were out of his mouth before he'd had a chance to think about what he was going to say afterwards.

There was a silence in the car and then, 'No what dear?' his mum's assured and ever so slightly patronising voice enquired. Jake tried to think of a reasoned, watertight and flawless argument for keeping granddad out of a home, but as usual, he felt like a stumbling school-kid. Not this time though, Lawrence had said that he was counting on him. How could he ever look him in the eye again if he failed now?

'No, granddad's not going into a home,' Jake said, his mind still desperately looking for the solution. He cursed himself for sounding like a spoilt child.

'It's not a home Jake, it's a monitored convalescence facility and granddad's only going to be there until he's feeling better.'

Jake cursed his mum's calm, even, reasonable tone. It just wound him up all the more. 'But you were saying that you've got a room for him and everything!' Jake protested, panicking that his argument was sounding like it was over before he even got started.

'No, no!' his mum smiled in that condescending way that annoyed Jake so much. 'The manager simply is holding one as an option for granddad. It's only there as a choice for him if decides he likes Orchard Court.'

Jake felt like he was being outflanked, but he didn't know how to fight back. He soldiered on. 'But granddad's an independent person, he likes to look after himself, he'd hate being in a place like that.'

With a creaky rumbling sound, granddad spoke from the seat next to him. 'It's alright Jake, really, it's alright. Your mum's correct you know. I've found them steps hard work lately. Maybe it's time I thought about a new place. It sounds very nice and you can visit anytime you like.' Jake was thrown by what granddad had said, but the telltale lack of any real enthusiasm made Jake certain that granddad was going along with this as a way of making amends.

Jake flopped back into his seat, feeling betrayed and useless. There must be a solution, there must be another way! The car drove on down the long, straight autobahn. Two, maybe three miles went past the window and nothing more was said, the interior of the car quiet but for the metallic, nasal voice of the Sat Nav saying, 'Exit ahead.'

A few miles up ahead, Jake saw a plane rise above the trees which lined the road. It had just taken off from the airport. Grubby streaks of exhaust fumes trailed behind the engines as they laboured to heave the aircraft into the sky. Not long now before they would be at the airport to get on their own plane home. The thought of going on a plane for the first time, no longer filled Jake with excitement. He was awash with misery. He'd failed. Granddad would go to

Orchard Court and fade away. Just a memory of the bright, funny, complex, stubborn man he'd once been. Jake tried to imagine what home would be like without him. Home. The wave of images, memories and feelings that word evoked washed over him. The sofa in the front room, the sounds of Saturday mornings coming through his bedroom window, watching TV in the Den with Howard... The Den!

'Granddad's not going into a home. He's going to come and live with us.' Jake's voice was firm and resolute. At the same moment, his mum and granddad piped up to protest but Jake's voice rose to stop them. 'Listen to me! Please! You never listen to what I've got to say, so please, just listen.' There was a silence in the car. Jake used it to quickly run through his idea in his head to see if he could find any flaw or fault in it, but it was perfect. Now all he needed to do was to get them to agree.

'We all know that granddad would hate being in a home.' He raised his hand to stop the protests and carried straight on. 'Granddad is a very independent person and likes to look after himself, but yes, he'll need to move out of his old house soon. So here's what we're going to do.' Jake was astounded that his voice sounded so firm and assertive when his heart was thudding like crazy in his chest.

'When we get back, granddad goes to Orchard Court until he's strong again and in the meantime, we'll turn the Den into a little flat for him.' Jake's mum began to say something, but Jake cut across her mercilessly.

'It won't cost much. All the materials are there, even the carpets. You'd have a place of your own Granddad, but we'd be right next door if you needed us. You'll be able to come and go as you please and there's even a bus stop at the end of the street. We'd have to share the utility room, but apart from when you meet up over the washing machine, you'll hardly know he's there Mum. I've still got five weeks' holiday to work on getting it ready and Chris can help out as well whilst he's at home. Mum, you'll need to have a word with Uncle Bernie and get him to sort the kitchen out at long last. I'll have a word with Howard's dad to see if he can help us with the plasterboard and then all we need to do is to paint it.'

There it was. His idea. There was silence in the car. Somehow Jake knew that he mustn't be the first to speak, the pressure was on them. He would have to make them speak first, make them respond to his idea. The silence lengthened. He could see the side of his mum's face as she exchanged looks with his dad in a kind of silent discussion. Eventually dad shrugged his shoulders slightly and shook his head as if to say, 'Why not?' Finally, his mum broke the silence, she sounded uncertain, as if her son had somehow changed overnight. However, she gave it one more go.

'But it's your Den, Jake! What will you do without it?'

Jake grinned, he knew he'd won. He took a moment to calm himself. 'What sort of a grandson do you think I am Mum? Do you really think I'd watch my granddad be carted off somewhere, just so I could have my own room to slob around in?' That did it. His mum, unsure if he was being serious or not, had to come down on one side or another.

'No, Jake. I would never think you were not thoughtful, clearly you are, or you wouldn't have come up with the idea of a Granddad Flat... I don't know why we hadn't thought about it before.'

Jake turned triumphantly to granddad, but instead of a happy, grateful grin in return, granddad looked troubled and when he spoke, he seemed to be choosing his words with great care. 'It's a lovely idea Jake, but I'm not sure it's entirely what your mum had planned.'

Jake couldn't believe what granddad was saying. Didn't he want you come and live with them? Was he happy to be packed off into a home? His mum turned in her seat until she was looking straight at granddad. She reached over and took his hand. 'I'm sorry Walter, I never wanted you to feel like we've been railroading you into something.' She smiled warmly. 'We'd love you to come.'

Granddad said nothing, but nodded his agreement. They held on to each other for a while, then, with a small sniff, Jake's mum turned back into her seat and Jake heard the sound of a tissue being retrieved from her handbag.

The small voice of the Sat Nav chirped. 'In three hundred yards, take the exit.'

Jake could see the airport's tall control tower looming up ahead of them. 'I think we've got some curtain material that would do for your bedroom Walter. Of course you'll have to decide what furniture you'll be bringing. I wonder if Andrew Johnson's son still has that van for hire?'

Jake smiled. His mum was taking over again, but that was OK. It meant that things would get done. As Chris had said, she was a great organiser. He felt granddad's hand take his and squeeze. Jake looked up into granddad's eyes, they brimmed with tears, nothing needed to be said. Jake grinned and squeezed back.

Jake felt his body relaxing back into the seat; everything was going to work out. He glanced out of the window again. The plane he'd seen taking off was now a small speck against the blue sky, the sun caught on the airliner's wings as it tilted and turned for home.